01

OMNIBUS
BY
BARNEY HIGGINS

All rights reserved. Copyright 2025 by Bill Magill

Take the woke warning as read.
Hold on to your hats.

I'm Barney Higgins. I founded the Tinkertons Enquiry Agency. I crossed the line a lot and I don't have a lot to be proud about but that's alright with me. Pride as I understand the concept comes before a fall. This story could well be true, only the dames have been changed. But as the thieves in the Gulag used to say, if you don't believe it take it as a fairy tale.

PART ONE

Barney's office
There's a sign on the door: CAPTAIN MOONLIGHT WILL SEE THROUGH YOU NOW SO NO TIMEWASTERS.

I watch her walk in. I can't define what she has but she has plenty of it. She's carrying a book in a way no book has been carried before. It's my autobiography *Case histories of a soldier detective.* (one of these days I'll get round to reading it myself)

Two sweeps of her hand and my desk is cleared. She lies down on it. She hands me the book.

"You wrote this?"

"Looks like it."

"You spin good yarns and if they're half true you strike me as being greedy stupid and a boozy brawler." She taps me on the nose. "And you're just the man I'm looking for."

This sounds promising.

"In my donjon" she explains "I have twelve bodybags. I want you to fill them."

"That sounds expensive."

"Yes, you will have many purses."

QUEAN ANNE'S FOOTSTOOL

Wives are always causing trouble, going around confiscating and demanding money with menaces called housekeeping. O for yesterday's corkers of honest fame who called their husbands "master" and shut up when they were bid. Harriet is jealous too, that's why she called Mrs O'Harnessey "Mrs Suds". Talk about calumny. Those hands never knew a washtub. Men's cocks are a different matter"

"Sorry I'm late" I tell Mrs O'Harnessey, "Revenue men on the prowl."

"How stupid you once were" she says "to pay taxes that enrich the posh fellow travellers who betray this country."

"What makes you think I paid taxes? It gives me a warm patriotic feeling to know that I at least don't subsidise these traitors"

"I wasn't thinking. You don't even pay me."

"Yes there's money owed at these digs but I'll see you right one of these days"

But she can't talk about traitors. As a Leninist she's working with the unions and the parlour pinks to destroy British industry.

It's alright England we're only betraying you and you're paying us big money as we do it.

They crept out of the Garden of Eden with bells and brass necks; they promised each of the populace three aces and a crow with a chechin in every pot. The own the Hot Sheets Hotel down Gutter Lane. Secret rooms with en-suite tarts and hidden cameras, a cold room for stiffs, on-call hypnotists, dick doctors, escape tunnels to the catacombs, lessons on how to make the perfect conspiracy with guest speakers from the College of Cardinals. Welcome to the Russian Embassy.

BASEMENT OF THE EMBASSY
 "There's a potential Trotskyite if I ever saw one" says Miss Stark to Harriet. "A right deviationist if you ask me. He wouldn't have made a good husband if he'd tried. Not that he did" adds Harriet, glaring at the handsome middle aged man who is inside a statue of Richard Burton.
 Yes, this is me, defiant as ever, brazenly flaunting the fact that I'm not Richard Burton. "'Taint half bad in here" I say to myself. "Reminds me of the last time I was a prisoner"….

MISS WINK'S ACADEMY AND PRIVATE LUNATIC ASLYUM
Harriet is sitting on a bed, smoothing down her skirt over the ladder in her stocking.
 "This is the best place for you, Higgins. I was tired of you pawing over me. I've no men after me at all now, glory be to God"
 The door opens. A nurse is standing there. There's a curious notion that bald people wearing horn-rimmed glasses are intelligent. This palone is anything but. I knew she was bald when I pulled off her wig.
 "I'm sorry" says the nurse "I haven't been able to give him his injection"
 "Did you know" I ask them, "that in men the leading causes of heart attacks and high blood pressure is wives?"

Harriet shakes her head. "He needs to be restrained"

"I fully agree but he won't let me"

"You can see why he was excommunicated" says Harriet.

" I can indeed and I suspect he's still dabbling in those heresies. Is there any hope for him?"

"If only he'd *believe*" replies Harriet, smiling sadly "I wouldn't mind what he does."

You see! I'm a prisoner of conscience. I've always said I have one.

"The means don't justify the end" I tell them.

"There he goes again" remarks Harriet "taking hisself seriously"

"If only Dr Ragamuffin was here now" opines the nurse.

"If he's claiming to be a psychiatrist" I say "he should have learnt how to spell it"

Harriet touches nurse's cheek, puts on her demure Joan Fontaine smile.
" Just ignore him. Perhaps I'll see you upstairs later"

That's where she holds her soirees. She calls them Miss Winks Supper Rooms at the Academy.

"But really, Harriet," I tell her "it's not called the well of loneliness for nothing. You lot need men, even if it's just a mousey man to peck at"

BARNEY'S OFFICE
I better be straight with you. Slippery Sam and me pulled off this jewel robbery and he and Mrs O'Harnessey had me down as the fallguy, see.

But he who laughs last laughs last and I finished up with most of the loot. The coppers I had baffled too. They're usually hiding in their closed down stations and don't go out on account they might trip over.

I'm up to my wrists in brooches when this figure appears out of the wall. He has the head of a falcon and says "My name is RA and I'm not your da"

I expect he's fed up with being accused of creating the universe. Back into the wall he goes, Antichrist Atlas appears and says "I'm the one who controls you not him"

"No you don't" I tell her "Billy Graveyard who is a top magician tells me he can not manipulate my mind because it is too disgusting"

"He's been dead for years"

"Yes but nobody's told him."

I pick up a necklace. "This will look good around your scraggy neck"

"You have the unsure vocabulary of a moron but I know you mean well."

A rotund man in a red waistcoat enters. It is the Squire, a man of multiple personalities. He asks "Any room for dead tramps in here?"

He looks down at her bare ankles, falls to his knees, embraces them. He is now John Puddyfoot. The Antichrist quite likes this obeisance and stands smiling until Harriet bursts in. She is after the Squire's money. She tells him
"You have betrayed me"

She sets about poor John with her second best brollie. He wisely returns whence he came. The Squire is holding his head. The Antichrist says
"Don't be upset, think of Puddy's head as a balloon being kicked by playful girls"

"I shall not listen to your banalities. Of course if Lady Broomhilda was wearing tight wet clothing I might listen to hers"

Harriet looks relieved. "Only if we have an understanding."

"We shall, dear lady, and I will receive your admonitions and buffetings in terms of ambrosial delight"

It occurs to me that the wife has erotic attractions I'm not aware of.

EMMA'S FARM

I thought I'd done well pulling off that job for her but Mrs O'Harnessey comes to bully Higgins not to praise him. Deny him his corridor in the sun. Let him let him be spic but not span with less than half a smile on that slum of a face.

"I'd like a few more cobwebs in this dungeon" she says to me. "Adds atmosphere. See to it."

"You do know that slavery has been abolished."

"Oh don't be so old fashioned. Slippery Sam and the like are only simple men. They are mere dupes caught by my sweetened thighs"

it appeals to her purity of purpose to have these toilers steal for her then pull with their backs the ploughs that prepare the fields of Emma's farm. A glimpse of a bygone era and who dare say this modern complicated age is any better?

And who is Emma? What is she?

I have to say I never found that out

The farm foreman makes an agitated entrance. "The men be fainting for lack of grub."

"What's wrong with ships biscuit?" demands Mrs O'Harnessey.

"Aye, twas good enough for Nelson's sea dogs "I say.

"He didn't make them sit for it."

Some people don't know when they're well off. I like Emmas Farm, it is a wife free zone far enough away from Roachdale and the grim operating room of Quean Anne's Footstool.

Months after his castration the Waist remains unconstructional. Doctor Ragamuffin, who distinguished himself taking out kidneys and eyes from the homeless of Bombay, stands aside, as one does, as the Matron (Mrs O'Harnessey) barges into the ward.

"Grin and bear it, dear boy. It is about time the Footstool has its very own eunuch. So don't take it personal"

Don't feel sorry for the Waist. He was so fat he took to wearing a girdle and it didn't stop there. He was on a slippery slope. Nylons, mascara, powder puffs, all leading him across the Rubicon to Toni home perms.

What takes me to the fair is that when these people look in the mirror they don't see an absurdity looking back at them.

The same way politicians and civil service mandarins don't see self-serving liars.

Or maybe they do.

The Waist and me proceed down the stairs, avoiding flying high heels fired by Matron's cruel nurses. We reach this door. It is locked.

"Open up in there," I shout, "this is the detectives."

The Waist is fearful. "I'm going back."

I swipe him across the kisser. I use his head to batter down the door. I push him in. I say " bless this cellar and all who suffer here."

"Well done, Higgins" says the Blonde. "You're not such a damp squib after all"

"Who said I was" I will reply curtly.

I look at the Waist, the great slab of his cheeks still wobbling.

"I did" says Miss Stark appearing in front of me. "You know why you're here?"

"Nothing slips past me, sister."

"Matron has to be stopped" says the Blonde

"She's out of control."

"Why me?"

Miss Stark pokes may in the chest. "You want Matron to hear how you held back on those jewels?"

The Waist starts to sob. The Blonde pushes him backwards into the semi darkness. I hear a cry. I get a glimpse of razor sharp fingers tearing at his throat. It's the Ogre.

"Don't worry" Miss Stark assures me " we keep him chained"

" And keep him like that" I tell them

"That's for us to decide" say the Blonde and Miss Stark in eerie unison.

I hear a demonic voice burning through my head. "You will submit and obey, Higgins, you will submit and obey. You will release my Ogre"

Yes it's Harriet, who must have magnetised the steel plate in my head, making it into a receiver; fortunately I have over the years developed the ability to filter out her voice; the brain can do that to tortures too horrible to endure.

But it's not working this time. I enter into the gloom; the Ogre is delighted as I free him from his shackles, "Gad sir, bally fine chum you are. Absolutely wizard."

The two dames are livid.

"And what's this?" I say, seeing lipstick on his face. In 2 shades. I give these jades a searching look. They are about to say something. "Don't argue with me" I snap. I take his hand, careful with the fish hooks on his fingers. I lead him out of harm's way.

EDDIES MASSAGE PARLOUR

"You poor dear" she says, "of course you have". I am aware of the earthy aroma of her armpit as she places her hand on my forehead, "anyone can hear voices talking in their head. I have them too," she informs me as she puts a match to the used tissues in the fireplace, "from unknown people telling me I'm a tramp." I suspect she's hearing Frank Sinatra. The Ogre is sitting in the only arm chair, giving us winks and knowing smiles

Eddie asks "Does your friend ever take off that hood?"

"Don't pry" I tell her "there are forces beyond our ken"

"Like your voices, you mean"

"Only if you listen to them"

Eddie is almost impressed. "You say the most profound things"

"Don't I have as much right to be profound as anyone else?"

"Yes you do, and don't let Harriet say you ain't, and don't let her call you ducky"

"She's not the only one"

"Barney, can you honestly say you're enjoying yourself when you are rolling in the gutter with Luscious Louise and the only thing you're afraid of in your big soft brain is the truth? You stick with me and bear in mind that the truth is overrated and tends to spoil things."

  I like Eddie even though her brassiere is lined with sponge. The Ogre sits chinless at her semen fuelled fire, toasting bread held on his fish hooks. Eddie points at him, "I know him now. He used to sell postcards and pancakes on Brighton pier."

  "That's right" says the Ogre "I wasn't always like this, I am overcompensating because I can't get it up"

  I've heard enough. I leave to fence the jewels.

AT THE MANSE

  The local Anglican vicar has the perfect cover. No Levantine him, just an honest British fence who is on the best of terms with his Archbishop, slipping him his cut and sharing their catamites.

  I wouldn't fancy that but chacun a son gout. No Gimme girls or yelling kinchin for them and they can be their own bitches.

  Vic, pursing his plump lady like lips, shaking his head, tells me "Paste, I'll give you a fiver for the lot"

. No decent robber would fall for that. Not even me.

AT THE FAIR

Jack Pudding and his insolent sauce boxes of Caledonian nativity are offering hyperborean wanks known as 50 shilling shockers as a cure for insomnia and other manifold maladies. Nobody would fall for that. Not even me

Ester the chemist from Cologne has a stall too, Au Bonheure des Dames selling moody cosmetics. Alchemy is not dead, reads the sign. You can be 20 years younger for just £20.
. Nobody would believe that. Not even me.
"Ve haf our orders vrom Berlin" she tells me, pulling my ear.

AT THE DOCKS
"Links rechts, links rechts" Ester marches me and Widmerpool and a chap called Buckley down to the quay.
   (Widmerpool? If you really must know, just a poetical name I give to my penis)
   "And strike me barmy if it isn't Matron up ahead too" I say
   "No it ain't" Buckley informs me "it's Mrs Rouncival, her sister."
I've heard of her, no angel herself, hands never off the poison bottle or men's flies, she was sent to Miss Winks private asylum and nearly killed by doctor Ragamuffin who supposes blood to be not necessary for life
   "Let's get out of here" I say to Buckley. Ester stops and looks back. "Nein nein vor de submarine ve must vait, es ist fur das Reich"
   "Peppers the name, treasons the game" Major Peppar of M fifteen strolls over to Mrs Rouncival. "It becomes you well Madam to be one of the few to flee that asylum. And how fitting it is on this sunlit day that we bombard our enemies brains with the secret weapon. He points at me. "For our final Test we have the man with the thickest skull in England."

"Don't get me wrong" I tell Ester. "I'll do what I can for the master-race.
"But---"
"It must be you. Ve haf only 2 schweinhund left in stock. Sie und Buckley."
The sub arrives. She pushes me forward. Though I am more prurient than patriotic, I wasn't brought up to go into submarines with strange Germans, and I sigh with relief when a shore patrol arrives. And arrests me and Buckley.

THE SEVEN STARS PUBLIC HOUSE
Not that it worried me, being arrested, I mean. You can go abroad, take up arms against British troops then fly back into Heathrow and resume your life on benefits, plotting the next atrocity.
Chantal and Fabienne are two crackers. "Est il possible?" they cry.
"Mais oui" I reply.
"An you are ze famous Capitaine Moonlight?"
"Some call me that." I lean back, fire up a Camel, give it to them straight. "Why you strike my Buckley, eh?"
I didn't particularly like him but when your dogsbody is killed you're supposed to do something about it.
Poor Buckley. He was brought by horse and cart to A&E but it was too late. The bogies had a two day draughts and snap tournament so I decided to look into it myself. I'm a detective too, you know.
"Dis Buckley" says Chantal, placing my hand under her blouse, "he touches me here."
"Yes he was sneaky like that" I say. "I think he was spying for them Germans

too."

One thing I have learnt is not to judge people. Those girls may have had a perfectly good reason for battering Buckley with a hammer when he was in the bath. Yes, there was something odd about the way he took two baths in one week. That sounds like marinating to me.

The sea lords picked Ester up a week later. If only she'd taken off that U-boat captain's hat she might have remained at large. But that's German arrogance for you. You can't beat it out of them. They let her go after she agreed to let the Royal Navy have her submarine, doubling the size of our fleet.

QUEAN ANNE'S FOOTSTOOL

Mrs O'Harnessey is some pup. She's the last Leninist in Roachdale and stops at nothing to raise funds. Who else would hire out blindfolded wretches to ugly widows who never had their own way and now find satisfaction in ordering about those poor souls, prodding them, dropping used hankies on the floor and ordering them to find them, kicking them away as they come near.

"If only he could see me now" whispers the first ugly widow, strolling about her house in stockings and suspenders, her fat arse clad in tight black panties. "That would stir his stump."

"Come on, let's have it" commands the second ugy widow. "Hand over your pension book. You needn't think you're crawling about here for free."

Clothilda, the fattest woman to ever sail round the world, owns a pub called the Stranglers Arms.

For women the value of a secret is the pleasure of disclosing it to another woman. Notwithstanding solemn promises to the contrary, the secret makes the rounds; there is no power in the universe that can stop it.

"I wish you'd go instead of come" Mrs O'Harnessey says to me. "When are you going to pay me?"

"When Archie pays me."

Clothilda waddles into the room. I get up, stand outside, listen.

"Keep this to yourself" confides Mrs O'Harnessey, "but Barney's blackmailing the Archbishop."

"I didn't think he had it in him" Clothilda says "but don't worry, not a word."

She goes into the public bar. "Eddie, Eddie, come here. Barney knows top secrets. He knows the Archbishop is a spy. That's all I can say at this time. But remember, keep mum."

"I never betray a confidence" Eddie assures her, a finger to her lips. "Strike me dead."

She goes over to the wife. "O Harriet, you poor dear. You know how I hate gossip but...[sobs] I've heard at the very highest level." More sobs, shakes her head. "No, I can't tell you...."

"Eddie, Eddie, I must know..."

"Well if you insist, Barney's secrets are bringing down the Government. He's never out of the Russian Embassy."

Harriet catches sight of me as I'm downing a Double Diamond. She rushes over, grasps my legs as she falls to her knees.

"O Barney, don't go to Moscow. Not with your chest. Barney, please don't go. I can make all the cabbage soup you want."

I look over to see Ester eyeing me keenly.

A GREEN HILL NOT FAR AWAY
I have a yoke on my shoulders. It has two arms to which my hands are tied. It's my own fault, boasting about bringing down the Government. That's what comes of having Toad as a role model.

"Be von of us" Ester says fragrantly, her face inches from mine. "Here in Engeleland zie haf been out ov society cast."

"I was never in it."

When she realizes there are no secrets she pushes me, still tied to the yoke, down the hill. I finish up in a field near the harbour.

EARLY NEXT MORNING
I wake up as Clothilda is grasping my cheeks with one hand. "Sleeping on the job, eh?"

She'd employed me to check on the honesty of her smugglers.

"But you are very clever pretending to be a scarecrow."

There's a commotion as Harriet bursts through a hedge and runs into Clothilda. "Barney, get you down from that cross" she shouts. "You know very well you've been excommunicated."

IT has been said in surveys that seven out of ten royal valets prefer it up the bum but that is no reflection on Erix Napoleon who took a morning stroll with Mr Pierrepoint after information had been laid against him by two decayed beauties who haunted Fleet St taverns that he called the prince a prat.

Erix was groom of the stole whose duties ranged from tasting the prince's tea for the right amount of sugar to holding his dick when he had a slash. The prince prided himself on being ahead of his time, which was in evidence by the way he planned his adultery even before he married.

He may have been a crank but the prince was smart enough to bring balance to his life. Just as Napoleon waited on him, the prince was at the beck and call of Mrs Grantly-Hogg. His greatest concern was to know her pleasure. Her commands were sweet talk, his abasement a taste of honey, his halter more precious than the medals he wore for the combat he never saw. And money for the gifts he showered her with was easily found. It came from the rents paid by working people and hard-pressed businesses.

A FORGOTTEN MONASTERY

It's the day Quean Victoria comes to tea. She's giving a royal charter to Miss Wink's school of favouritism and privilege.

"How are all your stooges?" she asks of Lushous Louise.

"They are eaten away by time. The Keeper of the Saucepans in particular."

That's me, Barney Higgins. I'm not one to pass remarks but Miss Louise can't talk. Her slap doesn't hide the grooves that cover her face like a shunting yard. But there's nothing wrong with the rest of her.

"Excuse my pig" she says.

That's me too. She spies me looking at her buns. The monks are in a flurry. They scoured the pans and scattered. Silly buggers. After them making their beds perfect then sleeping on the floor. A waste of good ironing if you ask me. Not that you have. It's just a figure of speech. Lushous Louise isn't called that for nothing. Though I say it as shouldn't, there's too high a price put on cleavage. But in the trembling silence after she takes off that brassiere...

I'll have you know I was once a serious young man before I started to be eaten away. Then I was visited by sweat-soaked witches. They're the best kind. No half masts with them.

"I was waylaid by some Alleymen who fancied me," Quean Victoria informs us "and taken like my ancestor Eleanor of Acquitaine to Winchester Castle."

"You should have sent for me, Hardhearted Higgins, the toughest, most ferocious fallguy since King Lir drove the flakes out of that castle."

"So I knelt down on the stony floor and prayed and prayed."

"Waste of time" I tell her. "Never any of those holy ghosts around when you need them. Anyway, you must have got out otherwise you wouldn't be here today, would you?"

Step forward Sleepy Sid (only one leg, you know, and a humpy back). He says "I'm her personal gimp and I can tell you she's not all there. I'm inbred too so I know what I'm talking about."

The Quean Victoria starts moving up and down affecting a very fine Alexandran limp. I find this subnormally erotic so perhaps I'm not all there either.

She turns to Lushous Louise. "This here old crow is my Inspector of

Kitchens."

Well blow me down if it isn't the wife. On the run once more from the Home for Unwanted Wives. "Really, Harriet, is there no end to this spying on your poor husband?"

"Barney Higgins, I'm danged sure you're up to no good."

I expect she's wondering why I'm rubbing and shining this frying pan, which I hold up so she can see her ugly mug. She staggers into Miss Louise who clouts her and says to her majesty "These pans will soon be ready for those coarse feeders from Holland. Your cousins, I fancy."

"We have, Miss Louise, more hangers-on than we know what to do with."

"Blame it on William the Conk" I tell her.

"Where did you get that nut? Can't you send him back?"

"I've tried" sighs Lushous Louise. "They won't have him. He's a superannuated gigolo from Dame Looney's Dancing School for Stout and Strapping Spinsters."

Well I like that. I was a dancing instructor.

"And I don't blame them, for he is an idle bastard."

Actually I was an undercover dancing instructor. I was working for The Way of the Arch, the English Resistance movement and I still am. Which leads me down below the forgotten monastery.

I'm on my way to make my report to The Way of the Arch when I fall into a deep hole. A rope comes down.

"Watch out for the Critter" advises Uncle Cecil. Mean, mouldy and magnificent with a smile playing on his lips like a wizened Simon Templar.

"The Critter belongs to the Blonde. It's one of those humanoids."

Harriet has her head in a stove when I get back so I creep into a store room.

Uncle Cecil comes in. "Lady Broomhilda, I bring a bad tiding. Barney fell down a pit and was eaten by a varmint. This is all that remains of him" and he hands her my green bow-tie.

She stands there, pretending to be upset. She starts to cry. "He was a brute, he was dangerous but I worshipped him."

I pick up an empty beer bottle, blow into it to make a foghorn noise. Uncle Cecil throws up his arms. "Hear ye, hear ye, the ghost of Barney Higgins, come back to haunt those who were cruel til him."

Harriet falls to her knees. "O Barney, how can I live without a husband to torment."

Quean Victoria appears at the door. "Get up, you old bag. You've still got the Institute of Whole-Hoggers to inspect."

I shout out from the store room. "Leave her alone. That woman is bad enough with her nerves as it is without you telling her off."

Harriet collapses in a faint. Basher arrives in his mobile asylum and picks up Quean Victoria.

BARNEY'S OFFICE

Petticoat reasoning has its good points and who is to say that it is inferior to that, say, of Pythagoras.

That's the name of my ferret. He hears footsteps, takes up his position above the door. This nun opens it. He drops on her head. She screams. I dash over, lift him down. He's shaking.

"Look what you've done to Pythagoras" I tell her in no uncertain terms.

"You're so horrible, Barney Higgins. So many times I've asked the Big Boss to get rid of you."

"He won't do that. He knows how hindustrial I am."

By now I realize this is Lovely Miss Nightingale. She should have used this week's passwords – Things is weak in Chesapeake.

"Your mission is to go to Cardboard City and locate one of our agents called Hercules. Silence him before he talks. He's being held in a place owned by a Missus Megrim. But be careful. She is capable of cruelty unusual even in a woman."

"I laugh at that. Barney Higgins, Tinkerton, downtrod husband and experienced adulterer fears no Missus Megrim."

But just in case I take along Pythagoras and my homemade flamethrower.

CARDBOARD CITY

The door is opened by a spindly wee man.

"Welcome to the domain of the Dogess of Venom. We offer a range of oppressions including bloodletting, electric shocks and even lobotomies for those who wish to experience life as a zombie. Special rates for registered pain sluts."

I barge in. This dame appears and eyes me keenly as if looking for traces of obstinacy or intelligence.

"I am Missus Megrim. The name means nightmare."

She summons her creatures, half-naked with long hair and white faces. Miss Lovely told me these are called Subterraneans. They confiscate my flamethrower, push me down some concrete steps and when I come to I'm in a cage of little ease.

Missus Megrim looks down sternly. "The things I do to improve the manners of the lower orders."

"Don't think we're ungrateful" I assure her.

"Today a man, tomorrow a mouse" says this big blonde appearing behind her and blow me down if it isn't Lushous Louise herself, one of the local stacked trollops who want to be in pictures. (She caught me on the hop after I did that jewellery job and took great care to keep me hopping.)

She purses her plump shop-soiled lips, looks down at me through slitted eyes, she says

"What you get here, Missus, is Captain Moonlight who has tricked his way into your captivity and must be considered very dangerous..." I make a growl and rattle my cage. "... and is one of the craftiest customers in the country."

"Bless my soul, what a fearsome bully he is."

"If I was you I'd get your Subterraneans to put him out with the bins but be quick cos he'll be out of that cage before you can say Jack Robinson."

"Oh I don't know this Jack Robinson and my Subterraneans would perish in the fresh air,"

"Just as well then I brought my Awkward Squad with me."

She makes a long whistle and in they march, all five and a half of them. The Crusher is in front, pompous and important, being kicked in the arse by the goosestepping bloke behind him. His eyes light up as he sees me.

"Whatcher me old marrow"

Then, remembering himself, comes to attention.

"Awkward Squad reporting, Miss Louise."

"Take these prisoners to the harbour. Drown them like rats" says Missus Megrim dismissively.

The Crusher wants to know "How do you drown rats?"

"Still in their cages, you fool."

I remember I'm on a mission. I look around, see Hercules. He's in a cage too.

"Sorry, captain. I held out till she sat on my face."

What a no-hoper. Wild scorpions wouldn't have made me talk.

So there's me and Hercules being wheelbarrowed in our cages along the quay, being cheered by tarts and ruffians standing under dismal street-lamps. One of the brasses comes out of the shadows.

"Don't take the fall in Montreal" she whispers.

It's Lovely Miss Nightingale come to save me. "The Big Boss sent me, he said to look after you with extreme prejudice. Whatever that means."

I don't know neither but I have a fair idea as we approach the water.

HARRIET'S HOUSE

After Pythagoras and me recover from being drowned I go home to be greeted by a morning incubus of blazing eyes and bouncing breasts. Yes, Harriet is on the warpath. She gives me the back of her hand on account of me being the world's greatest liar.

BARNEY'S OFFICE
"She sapped him good, took the coins. He wants them back. She's in Newcastle somewhere."

Lawyer Longboat is instructing me. I don't believe a word but I let shyster lawyers think they can manipulate me.

"Say no more, Mr Longboat. You could go farther and fare worse."

I throw some things into the Jaguar and Crusher and me speed down the trunk road. I'm in high spirits. "And upon this charge cry Good for Barney, Geordieland and St Cuthbert's duck."

"I love it when you're classical, Mr H."

"Thank you, Crusher."

I take flattery wherever I can get it.

UP NORTH
We walk through the mist to a house on the canal.

"So you haf found me" says this dame despondently. "I should haf known I could not escape from Captain Moonlight."

She sits down, crosses her legs. Those shapely nyloned thighs with their fully fashioned stockings don't impress me one bit.

"But I am glad" she continues, "Fate has brought you here. Only you can stop the secrets leaving the country. You must go to Scotland. But hurry, it is a matter ov days, perhaps hours."

I haven't a clue who this broad is but I have a foreboding. Let her out of your sight and she'll be staggering about with a knife in her back. We push past her, go upstairs.

The subject is lying face down. The Crusher kneels beside him. "He's got blood all over the carpet."

"Messy bugger. Let's go."

We proceed down the stairs. The dame is lying on the carpet too. Crusher and me go back out into the mist.

THE SEVEN STARS PUBLIC HOUSE
It's remarkable how potent a cheap handbag can be when it's packed with cosmetic shrapnel bursting against the back of your head. I hear a voice:

"Have I got your attention?"

This turns out to be a rhetorical question as Uncle Cecil bursts in, confronts my assailant. He says

"We at M Fifteen have been on your trail for years, you Mata Hari. That's why we sent in Barney as an undercover lodger."

You see! I wasn't at Mrs O'Harnessey's digs just because Harriet threw me out and none of the daughters would take me in.

Poor Mrs O. She suddenly seems smaller as she cringes in despair.

"Deep down I knew I'd be found out. But I could not stop. I incorporated myself as a femme fatale into the very sinews of the British establishment but even I could not stomach the sneering double-dealing fellow-travellers I found there."

Uncle Cecil, his bald head illuminated by the gleam in his blue eyes, his frock coat flapping as she dances back into Mrs O's agitation. "I'll arrest you when I come back from the Coat over the Knees Festival at Great Yarmouth."

Mr's O'Harnessey, realization dawning: "He's not right, is he?"

Enter a tall thin man rattling his chains. "Who's the fop?" I ask Uncle Cecil.
"Duke of Wellington, non de guerre of the New Forest."
"No I'm not. I'm Rodney."
So we meet Sir Giles, who pops up now and again as a minor nuisance.

DOCKLAND
I expect you are wondering about Miss Merrylegs. But first I have to tell you what the Crusher did with my flamethrower. He only burned down half of Cardboard City, that's all. The Peelers let him off, saying it was an eyesore and needed done.

Still, it's been a hectic week and I'm back to talking to walls which I do when I'm uneasy.
This is the man who couldn't find the coins, the bank seems to say. Keep your dirty loans off me, I whisper through its keyhole.

There's married women in there, I say to the solicitor's office. Going across state lines.

I'm Barney Higgins, I say to the fishmonger's, and you can't cod me.

Here I am in a suitcase with a ribbon on top, I say to the police station where D.I. Merrylegs is wetting her knickers thinking she's snared Captain Moonlight. Come and carry me in.

Coppers setting up a sting are not known for their lovely and well-turned legs in seamed stockings. But Captain Moonlight knows better.

HARRIET'S HOUSE
I may not be a real hitman but I wouldn't have minded bumping off a few deserving cases. I don't particularly like people. That's why I rarely help them. I let them stew in their own gravity. Even those blondes I take for spins in my Jaguar are only using me as a chauffeur. Here comes Harriet, barging in as I'm reading the paper, her face a drink-blotched gob of insolence.

"Crusher's at the door."

So he is. Standing there in his pork-pie hat, his mug a mottled mask of simplemindedness. I hope he hasn't heard me talking to the walls.

"Put your cap on, Barney, the Alderman want to see you."

THE RUINS
Flaming Nora opens the door. Faintly attractive in a ripe overblown sort of way, she leads me into a courtyard. This palone in a suit appears.

"Come hither, you amusing rogue."

"You're not the Alderman" I say.

"And they said you weren't a real detective. How clever of you." (At one time I was so full of myself that irony passed me by) "But only a complete nutcase would go around with a radio antenna on his bonce."

She comes up to me, hand on my crotch, whispers, "Just joking. Only you have the brains to know how magnetic the future will be. You will have the admiration of the world which shall be your oyster."

Next thing I know, this other dame is towering above me, flapping a swastika. When she speaks her teeth have that upside down look.

"Sie vill mit me kum" says Ester, "to ze room ov many agonies."

"You'll catch it now, Higgins," sneers Miss O'Shea.

Yes, the palone in the suit, a high-quality faultfinder, known for her valleys and aspects and blue eyelids, She represents the Alderman who is a dwarf sporting much Brummagem jewellery and a billycock hat. He says

"What's your gimmick?"

I am standing in five feet of water, keeping out of the reach of a chained crocodile. "Saving your pardon, your worship, but could I go back to my cage now?"

"Look not for balm in Barbary. Only my discharged henchmen are allowed the comfort of the cages."

Well, I like that. I've been in far better cages than his.

"Enough of this chatter. I have foreskins to collect."

He leaves. A baldy head rises out of the water, coughing and gulping in air.

"What are you doing here, Uncle Cecil? I thought you and the Alderman were chums."

"So did I but he's now saying he's a direct descendent."

"I heard there are two of them."

"That's right. Another dwarf. He reckons he's a descendent too. They're at loggerheads---"

A giant shepherd's crook catches me under the chin, I'm pulled out, I'm dragged to this chamber where the Alderman is sitting on a highchair. He says: "I like to humiliate my Britishers even more that they degrade themselves.

He whistles and four uniformed police march in. The dwarf throws things about. I get glimpses of the union flag.

"Pick them up!" shouts the dwarf.

The coppers cry in unison. "I'm a gettin' of it, massa, I'm a getting' of it."

THE CATACOMBS

Sleepy Sid reckons he is in touch with the infinite and can take me to the underworld. I say I've been in and out of it for years, "Not that kind, this is more like the happy hunting grounds."

As we delve deeper the air gets colder. We go past dolly worshippers and ikons of St Sibyl, the angel who taught women to speak. There is a coffin with the inscription TO BE OPENED BY BISHOPS ONLY. I do it anyway. I see a woman in 18th century costume, she winks at me then starts to crumble. Like Schrödinger's cat she'd been alright till I opened the box.

Next up is a debtors prison for those souls with unpaid undertaker bills. I come across my old mentor who is trying to hide. "Is nowhere safe from you?"

"I hope you don't think I'm poking about where I have no business."

A voice from behind. It's the wife wanting housekeeping. "And you've lost Sleepy Sid too. Another good man perished because of you."

"That's not what you called him before, humpy wee bastard, I think it was."

Let's carry on. It was down here that the clients of Elsie the Suicide Blonde found final solutions and Herman the homunculus dreamed of nyloned feet which let to his eviction on account of Elsie not wanting to be dreamed about by the likes of him.

Of all the dragons teeth sown by the bien pensants the worst is not putting the welfare of the British people first. This is so undemocratic. When I was in the National Front we were very aware of this and that's why we took a dim view of students and cosmopolitans and we had suspicions too about the unemployed who watch daytime telly which rots the brain.

Ester is here in the house of many agonies feeding me schnapps to loosen my tongue about The Way of the Arch.

"All sauce vill be ours again."

"Excuse me ladies" I say to two nylon thighed bitches who are poking Uncle Cecil to see if he's still alive, "have you quite finished with me?"

The Crusher strides up. "As a qualified torturer I'm the one who does any poking that needs to be done."

"Crusher" I say, "have you any redeeming graces?"

"Not on me, Barney, try Ester. She might have some under the counter."

Ester is not amused. "Sie ist eine misanthrope if I ever saw vun."

I say to the Crusher, "I'm not so sure what she means but when a top blonde expresses views you have to sit up straight."

In their powder and paint they seem what they aint. If you give them a gift you might see their shift. That's big league blondes.
They'll suck out your blood, your toil and your tears, you're ardent and pressing and dumb for your years, you aint got a lifeline to stop you from sinking, they'll watch you go under without even blinking. That's big league blondes.

A talking head appears suspended in the the air. The bitches and Crusher start to chant. "Umpa, Umpa, stick it up your jumpa; Umpa, Umpa, stick it up your bum."

This is a ventriloquists dummy I bought in Brighton. I didn't mean to start a cult. I wonder what the cardinals would think; they might even make him a Christian ikon. At least they make an effort while the good old Church of England dithers and fades away.

Umpa speaks: "O you of mean rank, be discontented until you find your niche."

See what I mean. Sage advice, not mumbling platitudes called prayers. Even the bitches are impressed. But really, look at the cut of them. Decayed even below the level of nostalgie de la boue.

Look at the Crusher, strutting and bellowing. "Hey nonny no, hey nonny no."

Enter Basher and his Emergency Men looking for stray pensioners. It's a good job Uncle Cecil has a notice round his neck giving his address and whom he belongs to. Basher comes to the point.

"Mrs Grantly-Hogg regrets but she wants slaves for her new mine."

Miss O'Shea appears mysteriously from behind the bitches.

"What kind of a canteen does she have."

"Only the best for the slaves of Mrs Grantly-Hogg. Unlimited skilly and barbers and first aid too. A well groomed slave, she says, is a happy slave."

The Crusher is not happy. "If something sounds too good to be true then it probably is."

"Not if you apply rustic standards" says Basher.

"That's nothing" asserts Miss O'Shea, "if you only knew Jesuits; they'd have learned you."

"Pussy cats" chimes in one of the bitches, "compared to pirates I knew in the Chinese Sea."

"Wait till the New Gestapo get you" warns Ester.

"You don't know what captivity is" I tell them, not wanting to be left out, "till you've worked on Emma's Farm. I turn to the Basher. "And how commendable you are to have barged successfully into the den of the Alderman's many agonies."

"I had one of my Emergency Men clamber down the chimney and let us in."

Ah, his Emergency Men. They're excellent at frogmarching loonies but I can recall one time they were put to flight by a squad of Girl Guides. Though to be fair, they were Tawny Owls.

ALIMONIA

Two of the early husbands of Mrs Grantly-Hogg tried to obtain personal advantage by falling down the stairs but she soon caught on to that trick. After pursing her thin lips and adjusting her girdle she rings the bell for her new factotum Honest Harry, formerly an unemployed shoplifter. She says,

"Is it always a coincidence that when I pull on that sash you appear shortly after?"

"If you say so, mum."

"Well, now that you're here I want those malcontented husbands littering the stairs put in with the Scotch and Irish gits. That'll learn 'em."

"Certainly, mum. Will you be requiring your bromides tonight?"

Yes she does, dancing around in her agitation, her black heart racing as she flies down the great hall, past the stuffed footmen lining the walls, out into the night where the Boers are milling and roughing up the lawn with their heels.

EDDIE'S MASSAGE PARLOUR

Harriet has sent Herman to blackmail me.

"She wants her housekeeping."

"Such a reckless woman, she is. Come with me and we'll get some cash."

We go in my Zodiac. I drive around looking for a place to park. I think they should have special places for detectives like me. There's a notice on the door. MISS EDDIE GENTS TAILORING COLLARS AND CUFFS. I sock him on the jaw. I tie him to Eddie's cross. Herman comes round. "You're Harriet's creature" I tell him. "And what's more, you're wearing a tartan waistcoat. Now you'll suffer"

I find a pair of Eddie's knickers in a drawer. I shove them in his mouth as he cries for mercy. His brown eyes widen in fear and agony as I hammer a nail into each palm. I press a button. The cross starts to revolve. I stop when he's upside down.

"The blood from your legs" I tell him "will flood your brain like a carburettor."

A smile creases Eddie's face. "You have done well, Barney, but it's not enough. Have you ever wondered how your schemes have usually come undone, how you will never be rich until you do away with the spy in your camp, your secret enemy?"

"Harriet, you mean."

I take Herman down from the cross. He goes on to attract a following of women who are in awe of his bleeding stigmata and he was doing very well out of it, thank you, until he started to believe in it.

A HOUSE IN THE PANHANDLE
The newest members of Herman's cult are wearing low-cut dresses as they kneel before him.

"Get out if it, you whoremongers and lesbainians!" he shouts.

"O Hermanicus, we enquire of you as a Solomon. How can we be messengers of Umpa too?"

"You will know. He will appear before you floating in the air like a steam pudding."

The girls gasp in admiration. "You are a prophet or even a saint. God has great plans for you."

We see him next scrubbing his genitals with bleach. He is taken to hospital. Girls have been having fun with simple people for ages and I'm sure these ones meant no harm. It's just that certain notions don't sit easy on immature minds.

I wasn't surprised when the Blonde started her own religion. She called her followers Aztecs, robbed them blind with full tax relief. I can't talk. I ran a few scams, I mean religions myself, notably Umpa and the Old Believers. I kept them nice and hypothetical, and that was my mistake. They weren't fantastical enough.

MISS TWEEDIE'S DATING AGENCY
These short-time brassy dolls are alright if you like that sort of thing. I certainly do. After all, you only live once; if you are timid or fearful you might not even do that.

But let's get back to those sleepy-time dames. Brunettes who whisper in your mouth, redheads whose eyes ask you to visit them in heaven, blondes who settle your hash. Beauties all. Not lame, hunchbacked and one-eyed like that wretch Sleepy Sid. Here he comes now.

"Hello, Sleepy, good to see you."

"You still Miss Tweedie?"

"Depends on who wants to know."

"Still gulling people?"

"You have melodramatic leanings. You remind me of the miserly dwarf in the *Old Curiosity Shop.*"

He does a pirouette. "Daffadown Dilly is come to town in a yellow petticoat and a green gown---"

I have a procedure for clients who complain or otherwise annoy me. I pull a lever behind my desk, a net drops from the ceiling, trapping Sleepy; Uncle Cecil rushes in, bangs him on the bonce with a wooden mallet and we pull him down to the cellar.

BILLIE'S PLACE

Billie and me have been taking big loans on the Isle of Man and we're in a spot. "We got to give the rozzers somebody" I tell her... Then it comes to me. "We'll give them Portuguese Joe."

She's considering it. Joe is looking daggers. I just stare at him and smile. I get up and give him a shove. "We'll put him on ice for now."

But he doesn't want to be put on ice. He tries to elbow me. I lay him flat. "Tell him to get up."

"No, Barney," Billie cries, jumping on my back. "He's suffered enough."

The phone rings. Billie says "It's for you."

Uncle Cecil tells me Basher has picked up Lovely Miss Nightingale in his mobile asylum and I've got to get her out. Captain Moonlight is known for helping young ladies in difficulty down to their last pair of nylons or on the run from sugar daddies or wives. Captain Moonlight likes to bring civilization with him wherever he goes and it never disturbs his benevolent mind that the slatterns never repay the loans he makes them.

"Get off me Billie, I've got a rescue to make."

I step over Portuguese Joe who is lying lardaceously on the floor like he owns the place. He says "Barney, don't believe your own lies. You are without doubt a most corrupt and useless detective."

I kneel down, slap him hard on one ear. "If I do that to both ears at the same time it'll burst your eardrums."

I read that in a James Hadley Chase story. I know most tough tactics and dirty tricks but I'm always willing to learn new ones.

HARK hark the dogs do bark, the beggars are coming to town, some in rags, some in jags and one in a velvet gown. The last one is Boney the Bastard a seventh illegitimate son of a seventh illegitimate son. He rules the Barbary Coast where coppers fear to tread. His followers come from across the seas and the natives bow down to them.

I've come in my jag and I make do with Harriet's house coat, the black one with yellow sungods. I don't really think I'm the real Boney; I'll ask Eddie. She'll know if he exists or if I made him up.

The head of the Barbary secret police makes his report. I call him Fugleman X because I don't know who he is.
  Standing behind a screen he tells me
  "A fifth- columnist has been found."
  "Why didn't you tell me about the other four?...Bring him in."
  A secret policeman rolls in a hooded man. He's in a barrel with holes for his arms and legs.
  "This false knave" says Fugleman X "looks upon Eddie the quean in her chamber. He was catched bringing her breakfast in bed."
Does depravity know no bounds?
  A voice from inside the hood.
  "I came for you, Higgins"
  Fugleman X shakes his head.
 "Who is this Higgins? He is raving all the time about him."
  "He is a figment. This poor soul is deranged."
  "Ah, then we must hang him by the heels. That flushes the brain"

I have my doubts about this but it seems more humane than firing electric through the poor people's heads.

"Begin the treatment at once" I order, "and keep him in solitary."

It's possible Major Peppar doesn't know he needs to be put away for his own good. Not everyone does.

Fugleman X has one more report to make.

"Lovely Mis Nightingale is being held by Basher in his secret asylum and needs to be rescued."

Ah yes, I'd forgotten about her.

THE SWAMP

I have my flamethrower. Fugleman X and his spooks have the battering ram.

"We're in, Meredith, we're in" he shouts as the door swings open and we proceed into the underground depths to reveal a miasma of wretches with wooden stumps, hooks and patches. The results of the Blonde's failed experiments, who have regressed to a state of rolling on the floor, sucking thumbs. "Da-da, ma-ma" and there's Herman mumbling to himself in protoindoeuropean: "Fugh dis vor ein game ov soldats."

The secret police have fallen back. I always said Fugleman X was a paper tiger. I see a toad-like man with a big baldy head.

"You have done well, Higgins, to come through the Swamp. No honest man has ever done it. It drives people mad. But I knew you would do it."

You were mad to start with."

"What's the plan?" I say, cleverly leading him on.

"We must make amends to Madame Mao."

"Who's she?"

"I am here," this broad says, placing her fingers on my lips, "mais ne touchez pas lest I lay an evil wish upon you."

"Oh, do be patient" says Baldy. "Madame may yet train you in her mysteries."

"Yes" she smiles, "there will be treasures and troves as you've never seen before."

"But not before he's shown true Ammonite patience."

This sounds like the tune the old cow died of.

A biddy appears out of the atmosphere like a Lancashire witch.

"If it pleases your majesty, the prentice boys are turbulent again."

Madame Mao pulls my ear. "Follow me. Be brave and I will make you my Head Troglodyte."

I am glad I brought my flamethrower because it's not every day you're called upon to subdue prentice boys.

By the way, don't you hear echoes of Dante's *Inferno* in this saga of puzzlement and uncertain identity?

No, me neither. At least he had Virgil to guide him. I have nobody, not even a Beatrice.

Hold on, I hear a voice. "It's against the law in Arkansaw."

Yes, it's Lovely Miss Nightingale pulling on my sleeve. "There's not a moment to lose. Come with me."

"A Head Troglodyte doesn't leave his patrol" I tell her.

"How can you be a troglodyte? You've only been down here five minutes."

I'm a bit cross that my mission was to bring her out but now she thinks she's rescuing me.

"Don't feel bad, that malignant woman can be very duplicitous."

Madame Mao steps out of the gloom. "What did you call me?"

"An insult is only an insult" I tell her, "if you take it as one."

As I reel back from a shaft of lightning I catch a glimpse of Harriet as she slips away and is lost among the loonies.

BARNEY'S OFFICE
"The Blonde sent me" I am informed by Razor Ramsay the Second. "she wants Umpa."

"Oh she does, does she?" I reply wittily.

"Or you'll be the next varmint in the pit. Seen and not heard"

"I would have thought that if you have a critter you'd want to hear it roaring now and again, wouldn't you?"

This is too imponderable for him. He goes off and I'm left to figure out who has Umpa now. I reckon it's Billie aka Madam GeeGee. She has a dance hall called the Titanic. It's for old-timers who are generous to hostesses.

I soon have the Zodiac waltzing and foxtrotting through the evening traffic. I go in through the tradesmen's entrance (a coalhole at the back) Someday I hope I'll be allowed to use the seamen's entrance.

I'm in her dressing room looking for Umpa when I get clobbered from behind. Next thing I know I'm on my back looking at two enormous thighs towering up to a black triangle.

Billie says to the Basher, "Another one for your asylum."

"My asylum's too good for the likes of him. Put him in the furnace room shovelling coal"

"I should point out" I tell him "that I have served time in a better place than yours. Miss Wink's Private Asylum where you were given Cyprus sherry every Friday."

Basher is ripping it. "Damn Miss Wink, whoever she now is."

We look up as Antichrist Atlas comes in. Billie asks her to produce her bona fides for intruding at such an inopportune time.

"What the fugh do you want?"

This doesn't faze Auntie. She whistles in her bodysnatchers and here they come, crawling like curs. They're good dogs but dare not bite. Yes, they're expert snarlers but when I worked at Emma's Farm I could send them scampering with one swing of my machete and they never learnt to dig up bodies properly or even bones.

I don't think I've mentioned this before but you see those critters that live at the bottom of wells and pits they were once Scouse gits captured by Auntie and the Blonde as they staggered out of Yates Wine Lodges.

Billie's not happy. "Of all my nutters, Higgins, you have given me the most trouble...and now this."

Giddy up, Madam GeeGee, send these curs a-scattering, you've got what it takes, not just a-smattering.

It's the way she fills out her leggings that allows her to be rude to clergymen and rub tradesmen's groins in part payment. She was the model for Cynthia Candytuft star of my five-shilling shockers written and illustrated by yours truly, distributed to the discerning as a cure for accidie and an aid to masturbation.

I need to get out of here. As usual, I get my inspiration from Toad, he's so optimistic and daring. So up I rise, kick those curs out of the way and back out with dignity through the tradesmen's entrance.

EXECUTION DOCK

Uncle Cecil's codename in The Way of the Arch is Doormat, which is strangely relevant as we see him taken prisoner by Ester the teutonic trampler. I'm here as her undercover factotum.

"Sie may go now" she tells me "till I further notify you ov meine pleasure."

I make to go then hide behind the arras. I watch Uncle Cecil being forced on his back by her baldy eunuks.

"Dis allows me to interrogate visout laying meine pretty hands on scum like you."

A few minutes under high-heeled boots and Doormat is pleading. But Ester is enjoying it and soon his chest and thighs are spotted with heel marks and Doormat is now begging. But what for? His member is at full mast and there's a smile on his face.

"Meine Gott, Onkel Cecil, how kan sie be so stupid to ask vor more?" She is almost pleading. "Kom now, take it serious. Is zat too much to ask?"

But the damage is done. Her baldy eunuks look down at the floor and will not meet her eye.

EMMA'S FARM

Only a Grand Panjandrum could have an antichrist as a hand-maiden; she in turn has the disgraced and crestfallen Ester as her waiting woman; and the chemist from Cologne is tended by the Cranky Wee Brat on the basis that even big fleas have smaller fleas.

Because like phosphorus she glows at room temperature with tartan indignation she is kept under Ester's bed, blethering about the majority of Scotch who don't agree with her illiterate polices.

"Ye'll ken it's naie mair fault, it's thae sleekit Sassenachs tae blame. Nae greet the noo, ma jocks and luckies, aye ye'll gae doon the noo, the noo."

Ester still wants her chores done. Trying to coax her from under the bed she says: "Kom now, klein Kranky. I 'ave vor you eine cockyleek."

But the Scotch, once a talented hardworking race, have been subsidised by thae Inglish for so long they've grown lazy. That's the way of the world. When you help people they come to hate you for it and talk about it in pubs. Not that they have real pubs up there; just bars; and Janets in short skirts and big thighs on account of the cold.

HARRIET'S HOUSE

Harriet is sleepwalking in her petticoat.

"O, Father Finnegan how handsome you are in your shiny new bicycle clips. And your checked suit and trilby hat set at such a rakish angle. Makes my poor heart go pit a patter."

She doesn't mention his black shirt stained with snuff. Too much of that can rust the brain. Shame on you, Father.

EMMA'S FARM

And those baldy eunuks too need something to take their minds off women's bums.

"Fraulein, fraulein, there's a beadle at the door."

It's only one of those agricultural monks. "There's trouble in the bamboo fields. Send for Hardhearted Higgins."

"Why not send your Alleymen?" I say to Ester.

"Neine, Barney, they vill only burn ze plantation down."

"I'll go and get my detective badge."

The monk wants to know: "Can Hardhearted do it on his own?"

Ester shrugs. "He might. But iv not he is expendable."

"On second thoughts I may need help. Where's Portuguese Joe?"

"I'm here" he says, his head appearing as he lifts the lid of a long chest in which he is lying.

Ester strides over, beats his fingers with a ruler as she closes the lid. "Get back in your box!"

It is said in old times women were regarded as gentle creatures

I return to a grateful Ester. It's remarkable how potent the aroma of a palone's sweaty blouse can be when she's rubbing your beard with sandpaper.

"I vant a fat servant who knows my place" she says as she finishes my shave. "Wee Cranky kaput."

"I'm sorry to say Portuguese Joe is no longer available. Harriet put him in a coma by pretending he was me. There's always Sleepy Sid."

"So! Ich must have haf zis creature viv von leg, von eye und deave in von ear?"

"It is well known in aristocratic circles that deformed lackeys are more grateful; and I will tell him to always have his good ear turned towards you."

I track him down to Flaming Nora's Hotel. He's fresh out of a clinic for those who do what none should name but I can see he hasn't been cured. He's making do with a tramp when suddenly he's in the throes of apoplexy. The tramp skedaddles and I watch Sleepy bite his tongue. I wouldn't have liked electric shocks up my bum either but on the other hand 'tis better to have lisped and lusted than never to have lisped at all.

DOCKLAND
Harriet's become a renegade lately, putting on airs, giving me back-lip, staying out till the middle of the night. I follow her to this ramshackle villa. I hear a voice: "Come in, Master Barnacle. We've been expecting you."

This vision appears in breeches, tricorne, buckled shoes and an imperial on his chin.

"I am Sir Giles of Giles Hall. Excuse the dirt. I've been in prison with King Charles." A pause while he wipes away a tear. "Remember, remember, the blackbird's secret song," and with that, with a wink and flitting smile, he fades shyly like a tall thin fox.

HARRIET'S HOUSE

The priest has put up a notice condemning me.

"Put in a word for me, dearest Harriet, us being Catholics together and all that"

"Heathen, you are."

"Freethinker."

"Same thing."

"You're a nice old cup of tea, Harriet, but you know nothing. Religion is cultural more than belief."

Harriet, stockings at half mast, curlers sending out waves of vague thoughts, and a Kensitas bobbing in her gub, sits almost on top of the dying fire, poking it.

"I've known about it for some time" I tell her.

"What you mean?"

"As a freethinker, I don't begrudge your forbidden love."

"What you on about?"

"I think the Father has a wee notion about his Harriet," I say, smiling at the blush coming to her drink-bloomed cheeks. Ah, I can see it now. You sitting on his handlebars, giggling as he strides out of the parish house in his snazzy checked suit"

"God forgive you."

"And in Holy Week too," I remind her.

BARNEY'S OFFICE
Lord Spender of Grubstreet presents his compliments through the side of his mouth.
  "You're too spurious for me, Haggis---"
  Mrs O'Harnessey is sitting on my desk. "*Mister* Haggis to you."
  Lord Spender is looking down his nose at the Squire who has followed him in on all fours. "And that goes for your pal too."
  I don't fall for that penitent thief act either.
  "The game's up, Sir Giles" Mrs O'Harnessey informs him. "Mr Higgins is a Tinkerton and he knows all about you impersonating Lord Spender."
  Thie defeated impostor heads for the door. "Ach, let Haggis be Haggis, wol ye."
  "And don't come back" I tell him.

Later in my office
I've just lit up a Camel when I hear a clumping sound on the stairs. A heavy limps in. He looks like me, stocky, clean shaven, boxer's nose. An ugly customer if I ever saw one. He sits down, lays his walking stick on my desk, glares at me.
  "Bernard Holland's the name. I want you to find my Wilma."

THE SEVEN STARS
Both Eddie and me want Harriet out of the way. We lure her into a room above

the bar. It's a tarts' tavern bigger inside than out like the police box in Dr Who, a kind of place you enter for a drink, checking your watch in with the bartender and emerge days later with empty pockets.

"Dear Harriet, forty years this heart has beated, twenty years for you."

"You never know" she replies, "even rogues like you can change."

Eddie brings in the drinks. "There's hope for us all."

I watch the knockout drops take effect. I think she's seeing me and Eddie in about the same way I look at life without my glasses.

Eddie's still doubtful. "I'm not sure about this approach."

"What d'youse mean by this approach?" enquires Harriet.

I need a leak but when I stand up my face hits the carpet.

My head is like a rat shaken by a terrier, a sea of badwater as deep as we are human surges and eddies in the dark plugged mind of the city. I run for cover past twisted staggering houses and pubs of brown glass. The Stranglers Arms reach out as I pass. Open my doors, it calls, my warm tables are full of surprise. I am floating over Broad Street. I call down to the Footstool. Not on the drink tonight, Mrs O'Harnessey? Not on the barge, Mrs Batter? Not on the tear, Miss Adair? Now I'm walking along the quay. All is quiet and sunny.

BARNEY'S OFFICE

"What you mean I picked up the wrong glass?"

Eddie sits on my lap. "If you'd brains you'd be dangerous."

Bernard Holland barges in. "Wilma!"

Eddie hangs on my neck which allows him to crown me with his walking stick. He ties me up, pulls Eddie out the door. I hobble to the window.

There's a shapeless figure standing in the yard below, its back against the wall, its face hidden by a shadow, a hat pulled down over the eyes, the tip of a cigarette glimmers in a hand and as I watch, it comes slowly up to the lips, glow brightly for a second over a tough profile then is flung in an arc to the ground.

Yes, it's Harriet alright and I can only watch as her red Minnie Mouse shoes clump up the steps.

You see this blame business. So many people claim they are discriminated against. Women, old folk, fat folk, gays, ethnics, handicapped, Christians, gaol birds, trans, country folk, travellers...the list goes on.

It includes most of the people in the country, which means there must be a very small group that's doing all this discriminating. In fact, I can narrow it down to a single mastermind. Uncle Cecil.

It's a scandal those Christians are complaining. Them not turning the other cheek. Either you follow the New Testament or you don't. and what mad monk hallucinated the Revelation of St John. Why do we need to be told about star-crossed women and tarts with bowls of blood? There's never been a shortage of mad women if you ask me.

SUSIE'S MANSION
I ring the bell. A doll in a back blouse and white pinny lets me in. A butler asks if I'm expecting. I give him one, hang him over the banister. Clients like their detectives to be tough. Who wants to pay good money for a tec who

can be pushed around.

Susie looks up as I barge in. "Come in, Higgins. Suave as ever, I see."

"I don't like butlers."

"That was my husband."

"I suppose you need someone to hang up your mink coats."

"I need protection" she says, lighting up a Consulate, cool as a mountain stream. "Come, sit beside me. I need you, I need you...." Her red lips say. I know she's saying something because her hot smoky breath is steaming up my glasses. "I want a man who is fearless."

What did I tell you. When it comes to browbeating and other rough stuff I don't have much to learn. I'd watched Harriet often enough.

This is when I get a glimpse of danger. I hear the woman laugh. She's still laughing as she helps her husband hold me down as he presses a rag over my face,

NORFOLK ISLAND

Her name is Susie but you never knew her as I know her. Next to me, singing in his cage is Sleepy Sid. Susie strides in. "Do we have any sissy maids in here?"

"Yes miss, that one over there" says the buxom guard.

Thank heavens it's not me but Sleepy is upset. "All this make-up makes me look cheap."

"That's the point" Susie tells him, "you *are cheap.*"

"Even the fruits won't touch him" the guard informs us.

"The thought of him serving the tea makes me shudder."

Sleepy starts to whine. "But you promised me."

Susie is unmoved. "Tell WooWang to come and take him away."

"But miss, that means---"

"I don't wish to know."

"Quite right, miss" the guard assures her, "ladies should not be exposed to that sort of thing...whatever it is."

"It's a dirty job but somebody has to do it" I tell them.

"If Higgins doesn't shut up put him in the smother box and let Doreen deal with him."

"But miss, that's my job."

"She needs practice. I told her last time to let the prisoner breathe."

"She doesn't listen, miss, that's her trouble."

"Perhaps, but I think she just dozed off after eating Bobby Barlow's nose. At least Higgins is safe from that. Nobody would want to eat his horrible hooter."

Well, I like that. If my nose isn't good enough for her she can go to billio and find one that is.

"He's got dirty fingernails too" the guard advises.

Susie presses a button. A portly woman enters, rolling up her sleeves.

"Is this the subject here? Oh I hope not. There's twice the work with these black Welsh."

"Black Irish if you don't mind" I say, "All the way from the Black North."

"Is he always so cheeky, miss? It's hard enough being an honest washerwoman as it is, without back-lip the like of which I never thought to hear."

Later
Susie is inspecting my hands and face. The Chief Washerwoman tells her, "Such a fuss he made of getting his ears washed."
 "It's not in his nature to be clean" says a voice. Sounds like Harriet. "He's only gone and sold me front door."
  I am affronted. "The Council took it off 'cause she didn't pay the rent."
  Susie's fingers are playing up and down my knob.
 "I do like my underlings to be clean and" [gasp] "we certainly don't allow that."
 "O miss, I am aghast" says the guard. "How could he display such a thing in the presence of a young miss like you?"
  "Get the ice bucket."

THE MUSIC HALL
You might call it a storm in a puddle when tame cats exclaimed against Billie's new venture, The Titanic.
 I wouldn't. it deserves full-blown condemnation. It's unconscionable that mouldy old figs should have sex lives. Don't they have meals on wheels and home visits. What more could they want?
 Billie knew, the B-girls she hired knew. Here Billie stands statuesque on the stage in her ballgown, with her lorgnette, looking down and smiling at her cherished guests.
 "Get on with it, you old bastards, we haven't all day."
 "A little opprobrium never hurt anyone" surmises Uncle Cecil.

"Ester, take Uncle Cecil to the sponging room."

And Ester like a good German takes what does not belong to her, not to mention the legacy of Dr Dee but that's another story and only Pythagoras and me know the rights of it.

Billie says to me, "Why shouldn't frails make the most of their assets?"

"They'd be daft if they didn't," I reply. "While they can."

EDDIE'S MASSAGE PARLOUR

I expect you know her place down Gutter Lane. You're a sad case if you do.

"What's the news from Syracuse?"

"Look who it is. You've fooled me again. It's not easy being undercover when you don't know you are."

"Don't talk daft" says Lovely Miss Nightingale. "You're on rendezvous alert at all times."

Barney Higgins, this is your life.

"As it happens," I say, "Quean Victoria didn't jump out of that window. She was pushed. Crusher was there. He said this strange group of minders happened along, they had blue coats, domed hats and carried sticks."

"They're called *police*."

"She should have a ladder like the one in your stocking."

MRS O'HARNESSEY'S DIGS AT THE FOOTSTOOL

And now my fellow cutthroats I'll tell you about Little Lily Bullero whose ma was a nippy in Lyons and who da was a dance band at the Ally Pally. I was an undercover lodger at the digs where she used to lay the table. It put poor Alfred, Mrs O's hubby, right off his Coco Pops. He later went missing, presumed kidnapped.

"Barney, get him back, you're a detective aint you?"

Days pass and still no Alfred. "Upon this kidnapper much suffering will be laid...La reine le veult!" she cries, in remembrance of her time as a courtesan in the Parlour House in Paris.

Thing is, I was the kidnapper and when he refused to go back, my plot was found out and I'm made to stand on the roof for a day serving as a weather vane.

When I'm restored to a more detective-like position in the hall as a hat and coat stand, I'm able to fulfil my mission when I overhear the other lodgers talk about their plans.

BARNEY'S OFFICE

Little Lily Bullero and me go in for a cuddle. We're not alone.

"Who's the mug?" she asks.

It's Bernard Holland, the limping heavy, sitting in my chair, feet up on my desk, smoking a cigar.

"People usually knock" he remarks.

Ginger Jones is sitting on my filing cabinet. "But only if they've got manners like you, Captain Moonlight."

Little Lily looks confused. "I thought *you* were Captain Moonlight" she whispers.

"So did I."

Bernard Holland says to Lily, "Aint you one of the nocturnes on Mutton Walk?"

"This aint bon ton, Barney," she says. "Do something."

So I go over, pull out my mail-order piece, crack him on his grinning false teeth, tip him over. Ginger Jones makes a dash for the door, runs into Uncle Cecil's walking stick. Where'd he come from?

I reach for my mandolin-banjo, play the Marseillaise.

Ginger Jones wakes up. "What! Bastille Day already?"

Lily shuts him up by standing on his face. Uncle Cecil looks round as a tall thin man enters.

"Welcome to le chevalier sans peur et sans reproche"

It's no such thing. It's Sir Giles. "Sorry if I look a bit mouldy" he says, "After the Stuarts knighted me they buried me alive." He looks around him. "Well, if that don't beat the Dutch. Which of you villains be Captain Moonlight?"

"C'est moi" I reply.

"Be careful, Barney" says Little Lily. "I think he's French."

"Couldn't be," I say, "the Queen don't go round knighting frogs. All the other knights would be handing back their hoods."

Ginger Jones, still on the floor, remarks "He does have droopy wrists."

"Who's asking you?" says Lily, stepping on his face again.

"Come, Lord Spuddy" Sir Giles urges Uncle Cecil, "I'm here to fetch you.

We have our yearly bath at Vauxhall Gardens. I might even take off my wig. My protestant constituents are insisting on it."

Dirty old devils.

"That place has been closed for two hundred years" remarks Bernard Holland, standing in the corner, face to the wall.

Little Lily kicks the back of his knees. "Who's asking you?"

It seems to me she's taking over. I bang on my desk and shout, "I'm in charge here. That's right, me, Barney Higgins."

"I thought you said you were Captain Moonlight" mutters Sir Giles.

"Hand it over" commands Harriet, entering the office. She thinks she's due a cut of my earnings. I mean, if all wives were so grasping society would be full of friction. Maybe they are. Maybe it is.

"He's so mean" she disgraces me by telling the others, "Even to the kids, he was. He told them to save up for their holidays. I couldn't believe it when I saw them putting their shillings in the gas meter."

But I'm saved from further embarrassment when the door is flung open again.

Inspector Pompadour and three uniforms barge in. I point at my two prisoners.

"That's them. Captain Moonlight and the notorious Ginger Jones."

I take Harriet's arm. "Come, Lady Broomhilda, there is much social work still to be done among the poor and needy folk of the Panhandle."

The liver is choking old Pompey as the wife and me stroll out. It took some nerve on my part but if you can't get your own wife out of a tight spot you're not much of a husband, are you?

THE SEVEN STARS

Harriet's cordon noir is well-known and avoided and it is my mistake I supped that cabbage soup which contained a potion that dissolves brains and presents me with a vision of Ladie Adelaide, an eminent doxie with dragon-lady eyes.

"You want to make a deposit in my money box?"

"What's in it for me?" I ask.

"It's your dime, bub."

But the potion starts to wear off and I'm biting Harriet's ear.

"Men are such fools" says the wife.

I resolve to look t Harriet's face at least once every week so as to fix it in my memory and I go to the bar for a pint to wash out the taste.

ALIMONIA

There comes a terrific sense of freedom when one is finally free of all ungrateful relatives. Harriet is now in bondage under Mrs Granly-Hogg and I become even more liberated when I get word from Rome that I am officially disenfoliated. I am a freeman. I've finally realized that we make our own chains and that the chains themselves have holes in them.

I'm undercover as Amelia's maitre d'. I knock and enter. "It's happened again" she cries, "every time I pull this sash one of my underlings appears."

Uncle Cecil is lying on his back and I can tell he's as cross as a bear with a bald head. Mrs Grantly-Hogg starts to stroke his brow.

"Cross patch strike a match, place yourself under my rear, suck my plums, not your thumbs, give up and have no fear."

"I hope Harriet and Uncle Cecil are giving satisfaction, modom," I say.

Amelia pats his head. "Old geezers are there for the taking. I've already skinned him. Anymore like him?"

"'Fraid not, modom. Unless you're one of those necromantics I don't see the point."

"I don't wish to know any more, thank you. That's what you get when you let in the sweepings of the world. But tell me, why have you placed Harriet under my heel?"

"It wasn't easy. I had to threaten her with priests and when that didn't work I had to invoke Old Bloodybones. She had this creature, see, called Mr Tangle who lived under the sand on the Barbary Coast. Also, there was this monster who was minding its own business in the lake; but Mr Tangle ate it and it was Old Bloodybones' only crocodile. So when he came looking it back I had to tell him Harriet was to blame. He said he was going to eat her in revenge."

"Stop talking nonsense" Amelia interrupts, "and take your hand off my knee."

"Sorry, modom, but you see, I'd rather spend my money on you than in a burial parlour. I can't see the point of an oak coffin with brass knobs on if you're going to bury it."

"Why didn't you say so?" asks Amelia, pulling up her skirt to scratch her nyloned thigh. "I call that very sensible of you."

THE SEVEN STARS
Major Peppar is blackmailing me. Bump him off, you might say, now that I'm an old hand at it – according to Harriet, that is -and it made her proud to be married to a hitman.
But I *eschewed* that option. That's one of my favourite words. I expect you know what it means. I wouldn't have wasted it otherwise.
   "Too good for you, Portuguese Joe, stammer and stutter, soft as butter, it's you who has to do it, seeing as he's blackmailing you too."
   "Barney, don't tease me."
   "You're such a flower, floating on a tart's bathwater."
   "Oh that's the nicest thing anyone's ever said to me."
   "It's not meant to be nice. And remember this, always keep your little man under control when out in public."
   "I knew you'd understand."
   "Who was it said I was without doubt the most useless and corrupt private eye in Britain?"
   "Not me, Barney."
   "Yes it was you and I'll have to bash you for it."
   I hate to see a fat man cry.

THE BACK SEAT OF MY ZODIAC
"How's the avant-garde theatre doing? I ask Eddie.
   "The punters are getting blasé so Billie introduced the Can-Can."

"I saw Billie's fillies practising and it was all they could do to get those thighs up."

Mind you, I've been with worse.

"There's a mean-looking cow" says Eddie, "looking in at us."

It's like the shock David Balfour felt when he saw the trap his uncle had set.

"How many bimbos does this car hold?" enquires Harriet.

But I quickly recover. "'Tis a happy annoyance in the side of the great faultfinder that I run two cars instead of handing out cash to her."

Eddie agrees. "I know her alright, a very disagreeable and selfish woman."

"Don't look at her. They don't like it when you ignore them."

HARRIET'S HOUSE

I'm sitting there half-listening to the gossip according to Harriet. Eddie bursts in.

"The stiffs are mutinying. They say the soap contains pig fat."

"Them dirty stiffs don't know what soap is" I say.

"They don't like picking oakum neither" adds Eddie.

I agree. "Those old workhouse skills are dying out, more's the pity."

Eddie tells Harriet. "When you was Miss Wink all those stiffs got to eat was out of date grub."

Harriet is affronted. "The twose of you are very smart but we'll see what the professor has to say."

"And you had no straw for their beds" adds Eddie.

"We did in the pit. That's where the Untouchables were thrown. To stop them hurting themselves."

Eddie points that the former Miss Wink. "And they were seen climbing out."

"You mean those pariah dogs are running loose?" I put in.

Harriet shakes her head. "No, the professor put them in the cold room with the eskimaux."

"We better get down there" I say.

MISS WINK'S ACADEMY

"Look" I say, "there's a new sign up. *Top money paid to guinea pigs. No Irish need apply...*and what's this?"

"It's a pyramid" Eddie informs us.

"That wasn't there before" I say.

"Don't go near it" advises Eddie.

The wife pooh poohs this. "Barney's not afraid of a silly pyramid."

I go in. The door slams. The bloody machine starts humming. In the dancing darkness I hear Billy Graveyard. "You will have much rhino and French pastry too. But keep away from Ginger Jones."

I am travelling in cloudland in the direction of myself, spirits swirl about me like Scrooge and his ghosts.

IN THE STREET
"This here, ladies" I announce, "is called Plymouth which is the capital of Portsmouth."

"Oh poor Barney, I told you not to go in that pyramid."

"I blame them Untouchables" proclaims Harriet.

We find ourselves in Madame Mao's Round Table. The Crusher is sucking Madame's fingers.

"Stop that at once" orders Eddie, "you don't know where they've been."

"He knows exactly where they've been" responds Madame Mao who is sitting on the back of Uncle Cecil, a mere figment of the alternative world of human furniture.

There's stiffs in there. They start to shriek when they see Harriet.

"Be good boys and you can share a toffee apple..." She says to Eddie, "I brainwashed them to love me. Nobody else does."

The professor emerges from under the table where he's been a mat under Madame's heels.

"Then you were unethical and bizarre," he says.

"That's nothing" I tell him, "she's been trying to brainwash me for years."

A slim figure follows us out, shrilling like Chanticleer.

"Boil their heads! Boil their heads!"

Blow me down if it isn't Teasy Weasy. "I hope your stiffs don't have nits" I tell Harriet.

"I blame them Untouchables," she replies.

HARRIET soaked up every penny I made from boxing and when I said no more it was cold lips and hard shoulder or should that be hard lips and cold shoulder. Then came the pettifogging shyster lawyers trying to uppercut me in the clinch. It was a terrible time. I was tired. I was broke. I didn't know if I was a has-been or not. But I'll say this for her, she's still jealous after all these years. Take a look at this:

THE SEVEN STARS
Uncle Cecil of M Fifteen has come to arrest Mrs O'Harnessey for treason.

"It's a fair cop" she admits, "but before you take me in would you check if the seams of my stockings are straight?"

Uncle Cecil is agreeable. "For the privacy a lady is due we shall adjourn to the back room."

"What a gentleman" says the wife, who only yesterday had called him an alley cat.

"We can sleep sound in our beds now that he has stopped coming out of the sky" I say.

"Gosh this is like the Twilight Zone" exclaims Harriet.

"Not to mention my pyramid" I remind her.

Billie is not impressed. "I think this pyramid complex is a product of Barney's repressed libido."

"That's a psychological interpretation alright" agrees Harriet.

"You should have told me youse are Rhodes scholars and I'd have baked a cake."

Uncle Cecil and Mrs O enter hand in hand.

Harriet notes the lipstick moue on his bald head.

"You're an old fool. She'll eat you for breakfast."

"I can handle her" says Uncle Cecil.

The wife shakes her head. "That's what Profumo said."

At this point the old codger looks around as if there's a new presence in the room. I can feel it too. I've always said I'm a bit of a side kick.

"Barney Higgins," says an eerie voice. "I know your crimes. I was outside the pawn shop when you pulled that job."

"It was news to me Slippery Sam was robbing it" I reply. "I was just waiting in the car with the engine running to keep warm"

Harriet is disillusioned. "Oh Barney, I was so proud of you when I heard you was a big-time robber. Why'd you have to go and spoil it."

"You are never to blame" continues the voice. "That's your sort. But I know. And if you don't want the Peelers to know, you will do as Uncle Cecil tells you."

Billie whispers in my ear. "You shouldn't be talking to invisible men."

"Oh Barney" cries Mrs O, hugging and kissing me, "don't leave me."

"Enough of this" I tell her. "You know I'm a married man."

Harriet grabs her but Mrs O is not subdued from her passion until the invisible man mesmerizes her.

"All is serene, Mother Shipton, all is serene."

"Shut yer gob" shouts Harriet, punching the air where she thinks the invisible man is. Then she throws a haymaker at Mrs O'Harnessey.

MRS O is sitting at my desk, wearing a dunce's cap and writing 200 lines the invisible man has given her.

"This makes a change" she muses. "When I was at school it was me who disciplined the teachers."

HARRIET is a woman of principles. One being a resolve to annoy me as much as possible. She likes to wake me by running her foot over my face. This is a bit sore because it's inside a boot.

So I stir. I go out into the rainy outside, head into the seawind beating up the channel of houses.

Loathly lady is the name on the prison hulk. It does not hold POWs and convicts anymore. It's used to house dotards, narcoleptics and delusionists, an outpost on the NHS borderlands. One of the few cases ever to get out, Herman, looks back on it as an idyllic abode where he had been very happy roughriding with the Texas Rangers.

I'm thinking it's a good place to park Harriet. But the matron, Big Mary, says, "Sorry, Barney, there's a waiting list"

"You know, Mary, I do have some experience dealing with headcases and the more difficult unwanted wives."

Big Mary is impressed. "You seem to have the credentials to go far in the care business."

"Any ideas?"

"I know of a vessel that has been condemned, but it could be suitable for us, perhaps the start of a fleet. It's called *Privatisation*.

EXECUTION DOCK
"Gott strafe Engleland" snaps the sentry.
"Yah, Gott strafe Engleland" I say and clink my heels. I can be regimental too.

Out steps Portuguese Joe, his portly figure bulging out his white linen suit. He sees himself as a Vichy Sydney Greenstreet. I see him as Private Doberman.

"Ester wants to see you" he says, nodding to where she is walking suggestively away, swagger stick hitting her high boots.

When I come to, my head and hands are in a pillory. She backhands me across the kisser, an ugly smile on her glossy lips. She lights a cigarette, holds the burning match under my chin. This is when I know she means business.

"All ze names I vant."

I pass out again. Private enquiry agents who take the third degree or go to clink rather than talk are no better than idealists.

Next thing I know, Portuguese Joe's Pinkshirts are throwing ripe tomatoes at my mug.

THE DOCKS

I'm a very poor Catholic so it isn't dogma that inspires me to close down the scrape doctor. I park the Zodiac a street away, it starts to pour, my feet are soaking when I reach the bookshop. I'm cross. I'm thinking big sleep for Dr Junius.

She's well-stacked in a fussy sort of way. "Have you got *Pettigrew's Anglo Saxon Illuminations 9th and 10th Centuries*," I say.

"What?"

"*You* know, the one with the erratum on page 20."

She sighs, reaches under the desk. I hear a buzzer. I run up the stairs in my wet feet, put my shoulder to the door. Shock waves shimmer before my eyes as I look down on my own daughter. Jack the Ripper come up from Hell raises his bloody hand. I lunge forward, grab him. I shove my private detective badge in his face, drag him along the street, into the boot of my Zodiac. I give him to the Crusher for practising experimental tortures that involve Wagner's operas.

Was my daughter pleased about her rescue?

Not a bit of it. She says I'm in no position to judge her. But I've never been judgemental. For example, we're told Jehovah sees suicide as a mortal sin. But I feel sorry for those poor souls who in extreme despair or terminal pain end lives they never asked for in the first place. Does that make me more compassionate than God?

THE PLAYGROUND OF PERDITION

I've been listening to my new honey trap friend, Valerie, telling me how she went out for a perm and finished up in Vladivostok. Next thing, I hear a growling and I finish up as a prisoner of the Dobermen.

The Crusher says to me as he's crushing my fingers in a portable vice: "Barney, call me mercenary if you like but you can't live on thirty quid a week."

"Even if you live in a kennel?"

"You didn't have to say that."

As he resumes crushing my fingers I block out the pain using mental control. It's not difficult being mental if you know how.

He makes way for Valerie. "Ze gathering ov ze damned await you."

Four flunkies almost collapse as they carry a fat man sitting like a giant toad in a sedan chair.

"Fellow bolshies" he shouts, "dunces, running dogs, loonies and Slavonic low life. You are charged with judging this fearless secret agent. After we hang him you will be able to bid for his face."

I'm dragged to the scaffold. "England will be free" I shout, "from the Midlands to the sea."

After I'm hanged I go back to my office. Harriet is looking in my desk drawers.

"I want my money."

I lower myself gingerly into Singes old chair, the one he sat in by the fire when he wrote Playwright of the Western World.

I examine my swollen fingers. "After escaping from killer dogs and being the main attraction at a necktie party I don't wish to pursue trivial matters."

"You're a bloody Walter Mitty, that's what you are."

It's all rather frustrating. Here I am, trying to make a go of being a secret agent and I have this old bag of a wife hounding me for money.

EDDIE'S MASSAGE PARLOUR

Looking for a mink coat to give to Lushous Louise I discover an underground passage. I go along it, see a hooded figure and a man in a cage.

"You're not supposed to know about down here" Eddie tells me.

"Nothing slips past me, sister."

She gives me a withering look. I know I'm getting to her. Things are starting to warm up. And that's the way I like it.

"What's he done now?" I say, pointing to Bernard Holland, neck and crop in an iron container.

"I just don't like being called Wilma…keep going" she adds, shooing me along.

Minutes later I halt as a tall outline appears. Coming out of the darkness it looms before me.

Green blazer with boxing badge, a knife-edge crease in his flannel slacks, hands behind his back. Wellington Wheatly stands at ease.

"Take a look over there" he says.

The Crusher is sitting at a table with a look of horror on his pug ugly face. Above him is suspended a Sword of Damocles.

Wellington Wheatly smiles. "He was having big ideas so Eddie darted him with curare."

"I know his sort. He can give it but he can't take it. Harriet's a better torturer than he is."

I move on. I come to a door. On it is painted OLD BILLY.

"Not you again," says Billy Graveyard. "Mais ou sont les neiges d'antan?"

"I know, it seems only yesterday I was a juvenile delinquent. I think there's been a mistake."

Billy Graveyard picks up his pipe. "The first time I was in the land above seems only yesterday too. I came by brig from the Levant. A Hansom cab brought me here. Before I am laid in lavender I'd fain secure the future of my beloved tars."

"You want me to take them over?" I ask hopefully, relishing a new supply of fallguys."

"Assuredly not."

The Blonde appears mysteriously at his feet. "You rang. I'm sorry."

"What's become of Hermanicus?"

She points at me. "He had him last."

"Go away, Agnes" he orders "And tell Edwards to stop tormenting my creatures." He looks up at me as she scuttles away like a whipped hound. "These molls weary me."

"Agnes and Eddie are your creatures also?"

"Verily."

I dread the answer but I have to ask. "Am I one too?"

"No, your mind was probed and found to be too horrible."

"Pukka sahib, Hermanicus will be restored to you."

Bowing low, I make a sweep of the hand as they do in the Levant. He stares at me but I just smile, make a smart turn, march out. After a bit I find myself in the lair of the Ancient Mariners. Harriet is here. She's poking Umpa.

"How does this thing work?"

"He speaks only to the right sort," I explain.

She shakes her fist in my face. "Right sort indeed!...i'm handing you over to the New KGB."

"Now, now, Harriet, remember your vows."

I always said hypocrisy has its good points. Billie's here too. She produces a whistle from her bra. It brings out the New KGB. In an oubliette I see Herman, Sleepy Sid and Portuguese Joe up to their knees in rank water.

"All the rats in one trap" gloats Harriet.

"That's not nice" says Billie. "Just call them fruitcakes."

"Dead ducks" says the Blonde, arriving with Aztecs. She goes over to Umpa. "I want to know your mystery. Speak up."

"He's just a sacramental Pinocchio," I say.

"Let my people go!"

Umpa has spoken.

There's chaos. Pulling Harriet by the arm I lead her through tunnels out into the docks. It's a labyrinthine route alright but it's still an easy way out of a tight spot. Harriet and me stroll hand in hand.

I say to her "How many times have we made up in our zig-zag life together?"

"Who's counting?"

I suppose all those grievances, broken promises, unanswered prayers are lurking somewhere, ready to spring forward when the time comes for casting up.

"The Shadow may know what secrets lie in the hearts of men" I reflect. "but those of women must remain closed to him."

"You read too many comics."

HARRIET'S HOUSE

I founded the Marseilles Institute for Advance Intellectuals some time ago. I'm still not sure if it's a scam or not.

I say to Harriet, "Mr Morgue from the Ministry is coming here to see me about a grant. Take those curlers out and put your teeth in."

Harriet shows him in. I play him a burst of the Marseillaise on my mandolin-banjo. I tell him "It was a General Higgins who mustered the Highlanders and Irish at Culloden Field. I don't know what became of him."

One hour later

"Thank you, Mr Morgue, that derelict school will make a fine campus. I hope Harriet didn't distract you by winking and allowing glimpses of the tops of her stockings. You didn't have to look, you know."

The day of the opening
Billie takes charge of Mr Morgue. The Ancient Mariners are put down in the basement supping mountain dew. Mr Morgue calls for quiet:
"On this special occasion---"
"What d'youse mean by this occasion?"
Looks like Harriet has been at the licker too. Billie jumps up, kisses Mr Morgue on the ear. He, being well chuffed, paraphrases Leigh Hunt, "Billie kissed me when we met, jumping from the chair she sat in…"
"No fun without Punch" I say to our MP, who has just arrived. He's the fat man at the playground of perdition. I nod to my professors, who look more like the Krays than Mortimer Wheeler. They give him a verse of "For he's a jolly good fellow"
The first skirmishers come up from the basement, more follow with blazing brands. As I rescue Harriet once again I see a screaming Mr Morgue being dragged downstairs. Somehow I get her home. The Institute is glowing in the night as I put myself and the wife to bed.

THE SEVEN STARS
The Crusher has been sacked by the fat man and become a TV star. He stands in for Simon Templar when he has to fall down stairs or be defenestrated. He's also been allowed into the New KGB and there's a touch of the casting couch about that and Harriet too, don't you think?
I make my way to the pub, the lease of which was given to Billie by the cops and what has she done to deserve that?
Several strumpets sit around and what an ugly lot of baggage they are too. Apart from this scorcher. Red lips, black beauty spot, long legs and a figure

to beat the band. Alright if you like that sort of thing.

I certainly do. I sit up at the bar across from the Pirelli calendar. A wartime poster still hangs on the wall. Three officers are leaning over a seated blonde. Keep mum, she's not so dumb...careless talk costs lives.

The remains of a hangover are wandering about my head. Not a good time for the wife to find me. But then, what is.

"Ah my princess---"

"Don't talk soft. You don't want me any more."

"Oh but I do. I adore every one of the blotches on your dear face." I kiss her cheek. "Just joking, darling. Seriously, hand on heart, you are the bane of my life."

"That's nice of you but it's too little too late. I've come here to arrest you."

Captain Moonlight does not know the meaning of the word trepidation. He laughs at danger and though he sometimes feels like a time-traveller stranded in mediaeval eras he remains humble and proud but he is not above...

"I've got something for you."

"For me?" she cries, "Oh you should have."

...fobbing off his shrewish wife with a brooch he'd promised to Lushous Louise.

THE FORGOTTEN MONASTERY

I'm out of girlfriends so I'm back sucking around Lushous Louise, who says "I've a job for you. You will go undercover in Execution Dock."

Here I am as a toad in the hole. That's a sandwich man with four boards.

"I suppose it's better than being a scarecrow" I say.

"You fidget too much to be a scarecrow. Maybe you want to go back to Emma's Farm."

Since she took over that place there's been a higher turnover on account of the monks being fed on old bread and scrape.

Lushous Louise in unrepentant. "Is it not their Christian duty to eschew luxuries such as cheese sandwiches?"

"Correct, Miss Louise. I always said there's too greedy a monk in this country."

This is me agreeing with everything she says, hoping there is no mention of a certain piece of jewellery.

EXECUTION DOCK

And here I am, being interrogated by the New KGB after being exposed.

"Ve do not believe a word ov it."

"Harriet, why are you speaking in a Russian accent?"

"'Cause I'm the most unwanted wife in the country."

"I wouldn't go quite that far."

She's reaching for the knout when the shock-troop of my Ancient Mariners burst into the cell.

"This is a shakedown," shouts the Chief shock trooper.

He goes through my pockets as I try to explain he's on the wrong mission.

Lushous Louise is not pleased but I tell her I aint gonna work on Emma's Farm no more. So she gives me a few jobs tracking down pensioners who've escaped from their care homes. You need a social conscience to take on jobs like that because the money's poor.

I meet up again with Cousin Betsy. Who's she? you may ask.

"I am a right piece of work, a grubby mare who rooks horny old men as I sit on them in my black petticoat, letting them suck my fingers."

Comme il faut, I suppose. That's what Cousin Betsys do.

The scene of the crime is the Seven Stars. I slip into the snug where I'd left my hat. There are two empty glasses, a crushed cigarette packet, and Slippery Sam's dead body.

I won't deny me and him had differences, and yes, I did say "Bring him here till I thump him" but talk's cheap.

This is where Cousin Betsy holds court. They crowd into it to hear her views on current affairs and to look down her blouse. Portuguese Joe waddles in wearing a trenchcoat and a beret.

"What's up with him?"

"He's gone to sing with the French."

"Dirty bugger."

I hear singing. It's that time of night.

And there's Hariet. "I like coffee, I like tea, I like sitting on a boxer's knee"

"Don't blame me, Barney," says Wellington Wheatly. "She just plonked herself on me."

Harriet is irate. "Oh! You were telling me I was your sex goddess. Men are such liars---"

I cut her short. "That's enough of that salacious talk, and you a married woman too."

Trust Harriet to be carrying on when I have a dead body to take care of, and I'm not even sure it was me who bumped him off. The problem is Antichrist Atlas. She seduced me by showing off her big arse. Did she make me do it?

"No, you are not a hitman. You are only my familiar."

I couldn't walk among heavies disgraced as one of those.

And lo, a voice from above. "This is my familiar with whom I am not at all pleased."

Auntie stands on the bar in her fur coat. Only I can see there's nothing on underneath.

I'M between girlfriends again. Mrs O'Harnessey played with me for six months then traded me in for a younger model. So I have to fork out for Eddie. She's in her sexy policewoman's outfit. I'm taking down her details as she sits on my knee when Harriet barges in, stinking of 4711 and a-waving of her second best umbrella.

"Ah, Harriet, most beloved of strumpets."

I speak too soon. Her horrible sisters are behind her, carrying brollies too. The blows rain down, bodies blur and reform before my eyes. When you're in a forest of pain you can't make out individual trees but I could feel my specs flying off.

They march out and take Eddie with them. Here I am, aching and half blind, alone with my superior qualities like devotion, kindness and honour, the very ones women find so unappealing.

So I decide to go back to my old trade as a brothel bully.

A PRIVATE BROTHEL FOR CLERGYMEN
Rude old fashioned Mrs O thinks she's the inspiration for Modesty Blaise.

"Fancy that but is a knack for dislocating men's shoulders to be considered valuable outside of the SOE?" I wonder.

"You remember the Rev Whalebelly? He called me a grubby-maned mare and had both done."

"An unjust return for expressing righteous indignation at you dressing up as a sexy nun, don't you think?"

"I didn't realize I was an Anglican nun."

"He asked for high heels and didn't get them and him paying good money for it too."

"High heels is a matter of opinion," asserts Mrs O.

"We have to go with our pleasures, don't we?"

"Yes, but what about having some respect for the cloth?"

"The Book says better to be a believer than to be good."

Mrs O is not convinced. "Cousin Betsy would have warmed his ear for him, the hypocrite."

Cousin Betsy has her own principles and applies them in all Spanish honesty without warp or whimsicality to all she beguiles with her brass and blandishments. Her and Elsie the Suicide Blonde throw mattresses over the CofE contingent and trample until they stop squealing like cissies.

But there is no trampling back to happiness for Elsie.

THE former Duck of Denmark, Slim Jim, has developed a machine for making wives disappear.

"That'll larn 'em" he gloats as another one evaporates.

But he encounters opposition. "Where's our wives, where's our dinners?"

"Call in Scotland Yard" orders the mayor of Panhandle.

Scotland Yard, after looking at the wives' pictures, advises, "Let it be, husbands, and count yourselves lucky"

As certain men turn up at my Home for Unwanted Wives I tell them: "Take your pick but consider why these wives were unwanted in the first place."

Slim Jim has a confession to make.

"Be true to yourself" I tell him. "Do not neglect to wear your bowler at a sporty angle when you go among the bumboys. And yes, spats are making a comeback, though not suitable for those of a nervous inclination when worn without the accompaniment of a pair of trousers."

Slim Jim is reassured. "Thank you for your understanding. I'm sorry I could not get rid of Harriet for you."

"You can blame me" I say with Socratic irony. "I should have known, such are her powers of disruption, that she would break your machine."

I hear shouting from outside, banging on the door.

"Come out, you weasel. I'm gonna knock your block off."

Slim Jim goes ashen. "It's the wife, she's finally found me" and off he runs into the back garden and beyond.

Harriet finds out about my plot against her. She inserts a drug into my beer and I wake up in

ALIMONIA

We're lined up in chains. Amelia arrives on a horse. The prisoners, aided by cruel frauleins holding our Henry Halls, shout

"Hail, Mrs Grantly-Hogg, we who are about to be emasculated salute you."

We begin marching towards the mine. The rustics are singing "Oi be headed vor the last round-up" To her credit Amelia doesn't stint on style. We have drums, banners, wolf-masks and the cruel frauleins pretending to swoon as we cross the Bridge of Sighs.

The Squire advises "Find the one-armed man and preserve your Pavlovian privates."

"En avance, stubborn savants" urges Sir Giles.

"This is madness" exclaims Sleepy Sid.

This gets him a clip on the ear from one of the guards. "Now be a good loonie and keep quiet."

"O my underlings, do not stop" cries Amelia.

"Three cheers for her ladyship" shouts the guards.

Prisoners: " Hurrah, hurrah, hurrah."

"Three cheers for Miss Stark."

"Hurrah, hurrah, hurrah."

We come to the opening of the mine. "Miss Stark is here today," Amelia informs us" as a representative of North Korean Intelligence and requires philosophers for the court of the great leader. Hands up those who volunteer."

No takers. Amelia is unruffled. "Dr Ragamuffin, renowned for his ability to identify nutters at a glance and for writing sick notes without the need for an examination, will now go amongst you and point out philosophers"…an aside to Dr Ragamuffin. "Don't pick Higgins, he stole the money I left out for the milkman."

Funny the things I'm supposed to have done. Fu Manchu wouldn't be in it.

There's an explosion behind me. Then another one. Sound of screaming.

"Look, I'm not going to continue if you keep blowing yourselves up."

"Your ladyship!" a guard exclaims. "The nutters have got hold of the dynamite."

"Tell the white trash to get them down the mine."

The prisoners are put on a great slide and pushed down, some exclaim against it but being loonies they don't realize it's more humane than just chucking them down the shaft.

I zip down to a soft landing of struggling bodies, the Ogre is ripping left and right with those fishhooks of his. He knows me of course, he almost gives me a nod then continues with relish cutting out men's cojones.

You remember my act of kindness when I rescued the Ogre from the Blonde and Miss Stark. Well, he's now petted on me and when him and me go up from the mine there is general alarm with the cruel frauleins falling down with heart attacks shouting "Kamerad! Kamerad!"

Amelia rides up, slaps my face and makes me foreman.

"You are tough, unscrupulous and daft enough. There's a transport of awkward rustics coming in. Let's see what you can do with them."

"There's none more awkward than me, missus."

She reaches down, slaps my face again and rides off.

But I do know about rustics. Didn't I write *101ways to gull country folk*?

And as the chawbacons arrive I give them the Hathaway Man treatment. I put on a striped shirt and a patch over one eye. I walk up and down, fixing them individually with the other one.

Before long I have them listing to port. My next job is to round up the strays. I go on patrol, keeping an eye out for those large dogs with tusks that live in the trees. I soon come to a barn that has a sign RUSTICS COME IN, and sure enough I find a whole mess of them huddling together.

Another barn has a sign too. IRISH AND SCOTCH SWINE ENTER HERE. I'm too smart to go in there.

A third sign has STEP THIS WAY FOR PUSSY and like a bisto boy following the aroma of Venusian bosky (pubic hair to you) I enter into it.

Call me a euphemist if you know what the word means but those girls with their pre-Raphaelite figures under their cotton dresses can offer all the bareback tricks of the day but bad luck comes in boxes and I can still remember the last time I opened one.

I CALL into the thieves' kitchen. No, not the Stock Exchange, the caff on the corner. The waitress has bleached hair, a cigarette in the mouth, and an inch and half of ash hangs over me. "What ya want?"

"Tea and a chip sandwich."

She comes back with the order, plonks it down, says quietly, cigarette still in mouth "Billie's on the lam in Alabam" and off she goes, this nightingale on the wing, wiping her hands on her soiled uniform, leaving me open mouthed.

EDDIE'S MASSAGE PARLOUR
She's still giving hand jobs. Yes, it's tawdry but does it really matter, does anything really matter in this brief life, this blink of a cosmic eye?

I think getting paid does and Portuguese Joe owes me twenty quid. I track him down. I wait till he's in the buff. I put on the black cowl I'd taken from the Crusher for future use. That's me all over, always planning ahead. I put on a large dark mask with the eyes painted red. I light a smoke candle that spews black and heavy. I barge into the room.

"I am the carnation of Umpa, betrothed of Kali, do you dare defy me? Do you dare defy my servant, the wise and prayerful Barney Higgins?"

They climb under the birching bench and wail "Have pity on us, have pity."

Let's leave them there, coughing sorrowfully in the murky salon.

Barbary Coast
Sleepy Sid is five feet tall so just about fits in the eagle's cage.

"Stop your whining" I tell him.

"You could have taken the eagle out first."

"Just following orders."

"Who from?"

"Vera Vamp on the couch last night."

He shouldn't complain. I look after him. I feed him two apples a day. That keeps two doctors away but I can't protect him from the Ancient Mariners when they receive information that he's a "Coppers' nark! Coppers' nark!"

Let's leave Sleepy Sid there, shaking and crying as the Hill-Bills come down a-playing on their pipes, leading the Ancient Mariners over the cliff like Farmer Oak's sheep.

CAPTAIN Moonlight had enough of the Blonde so he dropped the dime on her. She's been let out of jail. I see her in a halfways house. She looks fragile in a blue costume. She has big eyes and smeared red lipstick. She's sitting on a bed, waiting for me.

"I'm sorry" she says, "for coming up against you and being a nuisance."

"Don't fret. You can't put a wise head on blonde shoulders."

She crying as she kisses the back of my hand. Let's leave her to her regrets.

FLAMING NORA'S HOTEL

Three dames in a stalled lift. Miss Stark's wondering how her North Koreans can get their hands on the nuclear secrets Reagan gifted the Pakistanis.

Ester is still on Berlin time but she knows at all times exactly what Mrs Grundy would say. You may not recognise Lushous Louise. She's got on her secret face that turns your dreams to stone. Let's leave them there.

One nutter instantly recognises another. Sir Giles and the Squire are sweating it out in the hot press. See Wellington Wheatly holding his hands above his head like the old timers do when mentioned by the M.C. He never was a real contender. Parrying punches with your face isn't the smartest of defences. There's no Bernard Holland, he's back serving a fistful at the granite jug.
    Poor Mr Morgue. He wasn't of good comfort and he didn't play the man. He's wrapped in bandages like a mummy but it's a small price to pay for being saved from Billie.
    Have a dekko at the fat MP rolled into a ball prodded by chambermaids as they come to change his trousers. You can almost see the shade of Billy Graveyard. He's just beyond our imagination, painting a mirage fit for a sultan.
    Let's leave them all there for the time being.
    Pythagoras is on my shoulder. He knows all good dinners must come to an end but still maintains that stockings are nice but minced beef is better.
    Oh, and there's Barney Higgins making a Queen Anne's Fan at you.

Wait till you hear this
Barney's office
This dame walks in. She has on a hat with a veil. I admire her effrontery as she steps up to my desk, she reaches over, places her nicotined hand on my cheek.

"I'm going to hang up my axe" she says.

But my heart is too cold. I've ventured far past Harriet's dreams and it's no use saying I haven't.

PART TWO

THE STRANGLERS ARMS

Mrs O is the last Leninist in Roachdale and I'm the last private eye. I call her thunder thighs but only in my mind when she's not around. One shouldn't mutter under your breath about her either because

"I will find you out"

Eddie's on a bar stool showing the room she has legs too. She's looking at two thespians kissing. The Crusher asks "Want another?"

"I'll wait. Mrs O wants me to look after two parties from the Sing Sing district of New York."

"My dad lived in California" Crusher inform her. "On this island."

"Alcatraz I expect."

Enter Bernard Holland.

"Sit over there with Higgins" Mrs O tells him.

Enter two gangsters.

Mrs O points at Holland and me. "This here is the Krays."

The gangsters shake our hands. "Say, fellas this is a real pleasure."

"These Krays" Mrs O says, "will get rid of that little irritation for you. But first, come and meet Eddie. She's what you might call arm candy."

Bernard Holland looks at me. "I do the job and you take the rap. Get it?"

What was I to do when Harriet betrayed me to the gangsters? Said I was a stool pigeon.

The Crusher isn't pleased either. "Don't fret, Barney, the wiles of wimmen are too much for an honest man."

"When you sup with Harriet you need a long spoon," says Duckie Baconbrains. (a fallguy I recruited from the rustics)

The Crusher muses, "I feel that way about Gerries. I have a nightmare about fat blond men and chilling displays of Lederhosen."

Harriet appears and takes Crusher to task. "Wiles of wimmen indeed! I knew you was barmy when you joined the Liberal Party."

Enter the Squire. "Don't talk like that to General Wade, you see he's blushing like a jade."

"News to me. Perhaps he's always been a General and I haven't noticed."

Harriet puts her hand on my arm. "Don't fret, Barney, even detectives don't notice everything. Like my birthday last week for instance."

So that's why she snitched on me.

EMMA'S FARM
I'm lying on the back seat of Mrs O'Harnessey's Daimler, hands tied under me, feet bound. I can't see much on account of Mrs O sitting on my chest and she's adding insult to injury by using my hat as an ashtray. We come to a stop. Crusher opens the door. Mrs O stands pointing at a pen.

"Drive the pig to market" she orders.

Crusher and the gangsters throw me in the pen where the sows gather round checking me out with their snouts.

After I've learnt my lesson at the farm I'm doused down with a hose, put in the boot and taken to the music hall where the stage sits on reinforced glass, I'm lying under it looking up at a table on which sits the head of Bughouse Cassidy, a moving memento of Harriet's Nobel Prize-winning accidental discovery in cryonics.

"Are you ready, Eddie?" asks Harriet.

Eddie is adjusting her suspenders. "Almost, give me two ticks."

"Lady Broomhilda, what will be your next astonishing invention?" Eddie wants to know.

"I'm working on a paralytic ray," she says, "that will transform law-enforcement. I've been testing it on Higgins when he's asleep but it needs more work. The Chief Woodentop has commissioned it. He said his big beefy sergeants are getting tired of dragging women by their hair across the floors of police stations and into cells. He wants a handy device that can render them spastic and would also be useful to control far-right marchers, elderly nuisances and mental cases."

Lushous Louise has had enough of this technical talk.

"Let's speak of getting rid of Higgins."

The Great Faultfinder stands up, points down at me. "Come up here and tell why you are so greedy."

I no sooner stand in front of them when I hear a loud crack and a trapdoor opens beneath me.

THE FOOTSTOOL

When Uncle Cecil founded the IOWH movement, the Institute of Whole-Hoggers. He called himself Uncle Moses but soon met his match in the plumptitudinous form of Mrs O'Harnessey who decreed it stood for Isle of Wight Halfwits and incorporated it into her Quean Anne's Footstool.

I had to admire how she extorted the *Stranglers Press* from me. It was a tour de force of confiscation. After she rescues me from the music hall she makes me sub-editor of the paper.

There had been a response to her advert "Domestics available in the comfort of your own home."

"This order we have for maids for C of E, do they want one each or two?" I ask.

"Devoted to simple living as they are" she replies, "one should be enough."

"And butlers for the bishops?"

"It's such a relief now those bishops have given up the pretence of believing in God. They can now put their faith in---"

"In real things like Santa Claus and the Santa Fe Trail."

Mrs O sighs. "I never know what you're going to say next."

"Neither do I."

But I must admit her editorials are a treat. She lets them have it straight from the shoulder. It is tortoises all the way. It made her cross when the Press Council sent her a warning about mixed metaphors.

The denizens of the Panhandle often have their pictures decorating police stations. One of them, Razor Ramsay Senior, even made it to the waxworks. But nobody could produce a likeness of the biggest nuisance of them all, the one known as the Monster.

It stalks the bustling Broad Street dressed in a hat and long velvet coat in which it conceals a stick that is used to strike women across the back of the legs. It targets the Council car park sending the chair-polishers into such a flutter of dents and scratches that it affects the whole system of paper passing.

Uncle Cecil is just back from weary Manchester. "Barney, old chap, you're looking more Neanderthal every day."

"I am not one of Miss Stark's failed experiments."

"I expect Mr Hyde thought he was handsome enough."

"Neanderthals were one of several branches of humans that went extinct. Did they have souls too? And if evolution is correct, at which point were we in possession of a soul?"

Uncle Cecil throws up his hands. "How in blazes should I know?"

"You put up a sign, didn't you. ASK THE SPHINX."

"I only charged ten bob to tell people what the planets had in store for them."

"I hope you don't mind" I say "but I've been meaning to ask you this. Why are you wearing a hat with feathers on it and a long coat. You're not the Monster, are you?"

"No, I used to be tormented by Aunt Cecilia, then one night in Jerusalem I was having drinks with Walt Whitman and he said to me, Now Voyager, sail out forth to seek and find."

HARRIET'S HOUSE

"I'll make you suffer" says the wife, waking me up. I take no notice. Typical wife talk.

"I heard you making noises" she says. "You were up to something."

"I was chasing half-naked blue stockings through the fertile crescents of their alma mater."

"Eh?" She fixes me with a stare. "You are a dirty bugger, no mistake."

"If you keep your knickers in the fridge, what do you expect?"

"I may as well, there's no food in it. And another thing, don't come to me when you can't get organisms elsewhere."

Chastity begins at home.

THE RUINS

All alone with only the stiffs for company I go down to see if they are still alive. And they are, a whole mess of them, in a ring, mumbling like bees in a belfry.

"What's this?" I shout, "the Cato Street conspiracy." Then I see him. "You scoundrels, what you doing with Umpa?"

An old duffer looks up. "Nay, nay, this here be the Great Shadrack our idol from long ago. And now he is restored to us."

This is getting spooky. I bought Umpa as a second hand dummy in Brighton. What if Umpa really is the Great Shadrack and I had used him profanely? I could be in big trouble. I kneel before him.

"O Great Shadrack, you are too mighty to be offended by a mere mortal.

Be merciful, enlightened one."

I'm not saying I believe all that but it doesn't hurt to cover yourself. I tap the old duffer on the shoulder. "What's your name?"

"Well, bor, me name be Spuddy."

"No, it's not. It's Uncle Cecil."

"Strike me down if I try to beguile you. You find me in a dodge. I heard a buzz these gaffers know what's hidden down here. But it's slow play. The coves are stalling me. Yet they are simple souls. I throw my voice and the dummy speaks."

SOME say the Blonde has special powers that lure men. But us Scorpios keep our feet on the ground even when we drive Zodiacs

Yet green-eyed blondes *are* special, evoking images of great trials, ghastly ends, besotted adventurers hung by the feet by pirates, despairing suitors playing Russian roulette, husbands breaking down doors with axes, and cops getting out of cars.

But not special enough to confound Captain Moonlight.

ALIMONIA
Amelia keeps her four husbands under the stairs and takes them for walks in her shrouded gardens like a quartet of whippets. She is greatly disliked by Lady Cadaver who has employed me to go undercover. She bade me wear

a leather cap which is fastened by a band under my chin and on top is an antenna and I stress that this is not my idea. I make contact with her factotum, Honest Harry, who tells me "I need help, Mrs Amelia says my cock has been weakened by excessive use."

"That's nothing" I say, "when I was her factotum she told me bow-ties are not allowed at my level, then she poured her coffee over my head."

"My goodness, I'd almost forgotten how corrupt you Britishers are." He pauses, remembering. "I know a little bird who tells me what to think, bids me promulgate the word and stay away from drink."

Harry hates England. He and his kind are given refuge, free housing and healthcare and still they bite the hand that feeds them. This is not complicated. Be decent with people of a primitive mind set and they think you're soft. I learnt that long ago. It would save you lots of money and trouble if you were to learn it too.

I'M hiding in the priests' hole at the Footstool, almost giggling in anticipation. Harriet and Mrs O are taking tea. I can see the surprise on their faces as the Aztecs burst in.

The first one prods Mrs O with his spear. "You belong me. You come now."

The second Aztec says "Chief Barney no speak with forked tongue. These squaws carry plenty blubber."

"This is an outrage" shouts Mrs O. "We are not fat and we are going nowhere—"

The first Aztec: "You must come. We buy you from Chief Barney."

"Can't be true" squarks Harriet. "Even Higgins can't be that horrible."

"Him heap horrible, you bet"

"What you want us for?" she cries.

"Montezuma, him want sacrifice."

I can hardly look as Harriet crawls and pleads. Mrs O pins Harriet's head to the floor with her boot. "Higgins is no chief. All he does is scrape along, his hoggish mind feeding off fools like you, taking them to the madhouse or the morgue."

News to me I'm that good.

"And who, except those in the nadir of their degeneration, would take to wife such a witch as lies below my boot?"

She has a point there.

"Shake yourselves of this spiv" she continues, "before he destroys you."

I never knew she had such Freudian insights. She lifts her boot. Harriet sits up in a daze. "I never knew I had such a wicked husband. Save me, dear Matron, and I will dedicate my humble existence to your order. Consider me dead to this sordid world."

So it is that Harriet becomes Quean Anne's Footstool's first anchoress. She means well and her vows are extravagant. It's a moving ceremony with the slow march and muffled drums as she is led to the cell where she is to spend the rest of her days.

I did offer to brick her in but Matron ruled that excessive.

Twenty four hours later

Harriet is propping up the bar at the Seven Stars. Matron has arrested the Aztecs, put them in the stocks at Cock Lane, and here's me taking the time to throw rotten tomatoes at those scoundrels.

PANHANDLE COURT

I'm not on trial here. I'm a witness. I don't know what the charge is yet but I can always improvise. I'm not talking big fees here but I think witnesses should have something for their trouble, don't you?

Judge Vera Vamp looks down on me. "Witness Higgins, how guilty is Hotspur Hardy?"

I can see the way the wind is blowing. "Ten years ago, your honey, while a member of the infamous Hampstead Set the accused touched knees under a table with the plaintiff who thought at the time it was the tablecloth but under hypnosis she now remembers it different on account of the new climate for witch hunting."

"Quite so," says the judge. "In England today a mere accusation is enough to ruin a man's life. White men have had their day. Bring in Lady Broomhilda, once renowned for her shapely and well-turned striking of the hockey ball and recently, at great inconvenience, rescued from Aztecs."

In trips Harriet in a short skirt, socks up to the knees, and carrying her hockey stick. Hotspur Hardy is made to stand, legs apart, and gets it six times where it hurts the most.

O you busy little woodentops. How the old-time coppers would be shaking their heads in disbelief.

HARRIET'S HOUSE

She says "I was a good little young conservative till I met you."

"Wrong" I tell her, "the first view I had of you was the top of your stockings as you went to collect fares on the upper deck."

"There's been changes on the buses since then" she says, "not enough conductresses to go round, I expect."

"On the other hand there's no shortage of plumpbottomed nurses."

"Or coach drivers."

"The first words you said to me were----"

"Bugger off."

"Expletives aint what they used to be."

"Oh, Barney, you think about things normal people don't."

"That's nice of you, I always say, a little philosophy forties the over-forties."

Harriet was never the type to be a young conservative. In fact, she's off to a Labour meeting now. The leader is an un-traditional non-binary gender-unspecific non-typical quasi-lesbian in an iron lung.

ON BOARD THE *SEWING BEE*

I have a new assignment.

There he lies with his head on the biggest book of prayers known to bishops. Captain Molehusband looks at me and says "Is this the best you could get?"

"So it appears, Captain dear" Miss O'Shea assures him.

"Master Barnacle" he growls, "you better be up to this." He gets up and goes to the door. "'Taint good enough."

Miss O'Shea calls after him. "Don't get in a pet, Captain dear." She turns to me. "Ten more minutes and the old fool would have told me."

"Told you what?"

"Never mind, just follow the plan."

"What plan?"

"I'll let you know."

There's more to this plan than meets the eye. I'm at the fete when Mary Jayne comes out of the fog like the woman in white. Pretty as a parsnip and prim and proper too.

I'm working as a waiter. I do a bit of pickpocketing as the Burlington Berties watch the antler dance. They go "Har, har, har."

BACK ON BOARD

I'm staring at Captain Molehusband and he doesn't like it. Have you ever noticed that pretentious people can be sensitive about their short legs?

"Another failed mission" he says. "And why must you go around with an antenna on your head?"

"Better than antlers."

"If you ask me he's a bit mental" says Miss O'Shea.

"More than a bit" the wife informs them.

Where did she come from? Out of a pit, I like to think.

Miss O'Shea nods. "You've done well. Harriet, finding out he works for the Big Boss, but who is the Big Boss?"

"Dunno."

"I don't suppose Higgins could actually be the Big Boss himself?" wonders Captain Molehusband.

Miss O'Shea is doubtful. "If he is, he's putting on a great act."

Here I am, standing on a stool with a noose round my neck and without a sixpence to bless myself with because Mary Jayne took my bounty from the fete and took a powder too.

A clock strikes 10. Be brave, Barney. I shall be but there's much left undone and much to learn. I still don't know what causes pip in poultry.

   Miss O'Shea lights a cigarette, puts it in my mouth.

   Lit end first.

   You're never alone with a Strand.

EDDIE'S PLACE

"The rope was too long" she says. "All you did was fall on the floor."

   "Harriet didn't know it was too long."

   "It's terrible," Eddie muses, "the way she treats you."

   "She's always nursing a grudge. All I did was brick her up in the cellar and forgot about her."

THE MUSIC HALL

Portuguese Joe is singing "Champagne Charlie is my name." Whoops! He's gone, disappearing down a trapdoor. That's the way Brutality Jones ends unpopular acts.

   Here's Cousin Betsy singing "The boy I shag is up in the gallery."

   "That's more like it" says Brutality Jones, "You have to hand it to her.

Her ability to transform classics and songs of praise into filth is remarkable."

He's made me stage manager because I have a mandolin-banjo and wear a suit and a green bow-tie. I prefer the term choreographer even if I can't spell it. Cousin Betsy is second fiddle. I'm third. Harriet is in charge of the sponging house in the cellar. Her and the Crusher are a folie a deux. She lets him kiss her down below. He can't be choosey. I think they're plotting. So are Eddie and me. We want the music hall back.

Brutality tells me to rescue Portuguese Joe. I tie a rope to Crusher's execution block and descend like Quatermass, Sleepy Sid made the block for him. Simple minded, yes. But was Tennyson far wrong when he wrote "Kind hearts are more than coronets, and simple faith than Norman blood."?
And what simple pleasure Crusher affords Harriet, posing like a ballet dancer in his black executioner's leotard.

Figures of men stand at attention. I'm on my knees before Miss Stark, after being captured. There's a helmet on my head. She tells me

"Our North Korean scientists are controlling magnetism. We shall be invincible. It is your privilege to test the prototype."

She presses a button. This wakes up the Higgins particles. I see the other specimens waking up too. With rigid faces, staring eyes and outstretched arms they charge at us.

Miss Stark looks at me admiringly. "I was aghast when the other exhibits came back to life. But you kept your nerve when others panicked."

"He is my champion" cries Harriet.

"Why don't you be mine too?" asks Miss Stark. "Join us down here as my Passepartout. We're thick as thieves."

"I have my position as stage manager to consider."

There's a tap on my shoulder. I look round to see an individual built like a sumo.

"This is Mr Kimono" Miss Stark tells me. "He says your name is well-known in Pyongyang. Many voices still chant your name." I feel the beginning of a warm glow. "Yes, we remember the rifles you sold us that had no firing pins. After we destroy what remains of your brain you will be taken back to Korea and paraded before our Great Leader. Nobody will dare say you are being operated by strings like a puppet. We call this political correctitude."

"This could never happen in Britain" I say. "A nation that stood alone with its empire against tyranny and reveres freedom of speech." (Although I must admit we are not so steadfast against female tyrants also known as wives.)

But Miss Stark and Mister Kimono don't stand a chance when I reactivate the exhibits and they overwhelm them with manic force.

I HAD it coming. Brutality and Billie knew I'd dropped the dime on them and Eddie and Harriet are still sore about something. The thing is, they don't tell you. That's the clever part.

Crusher is preparing his block. Eddie's in her body stocking and has put on a black coif for the occasion. Harriet's sitting on a beer crate, knitting away.

The Crusher waxes philosophical. "Back in the days of old Jack Ketch---"

Billie runs up. "Hold it right there. Our plans are foiled" she explains, looking daggers at me. "I better let Fugleman X tell you himself."

News to me I'm Fugleman X.

But I'm not. The man who strolls in to address this den of thieves is Brutality Jones.

"Don't plume yourself, Higgins" says Miss Stark. "A month in one of our prison hulks festering in the Sea of North Korea will have you spilling the beans."

"Why take him to this Korea place?" Harriet wants to know. "Can't we torture him here?"

"It's a great pity we got rid of our own hulks" says the Crusher.

Eddie nods. "They just sank. They were privatised and you couldn't see the barnacles building up."

"It was a dodge to hide Whitehall's liabilities---" I start to say.

"Enough!" shouts Billie. "Let Brutality speak."

"We need him alive" he says, "he knows where Room 40 is." He turns to me. "Barney, uh, sorry, Captain Moonlight, I appeal to you."

"A Tinkerton knows his duty" I tell them.

"Appeal to his attributes, greed and lust" Harriet suggests.

How well she knows me. But she's left out Revenge.

See now the wife undertaking her Sisyphean labour of pots and pans while Miss Stark and Billie attend me in stockings and suspenders. But too much Vim and Ajax must take its toll and on the third day Harriet is taken like a dying swan into Miss Wink's Asylum and I tell them where Room 40 is, having had enough revenge for one week.

IT'S long been my policy to seek personal advantage from the misfortunes of others so when a little bird tells me Brutality and Billie have been lifted by the Peelers I decide to take over the music hall.

I'm promoting Mr Memory who is an idiot-savant with total recall. I go out to round up some more stewards. I'm coming out of a low dive when a prehistoric dame steps up and holds me with her glittering eye.

"Beware the relics of the sea" she warns then fades back into the coastal fog.

And what do I find when I get back to the music hall? Only Captain Molehusband lying tied up by my Ancient Mariners. And what's more, Mr Memory is relating to him Bradshaw's Railway Guide then he recites every word from every episode he's seen of Crossroads.

I do like a captive audience so when six hours later I return from the bar I reel off for the captain a composition from my purple period "Ode to the war between the Corkmen and Culshie Mucks, Birkenhead 1950."

I finish off with my entry for the Bricklayer Poet of the Year award. Here's the last 3 verses:

You have left me but the sadness has not/ all my thoughts of you are stings/ my darling, I want to be tied once more/ to your marvellous choking apron strings.

Since you went away the heart's sad/ my days are blue blue blue one beside the other/ the cat's fallen in love, the dog's bitten off more/ than it can chew.

An army of rats have moved into the coalhouse/ and I can't get at the coal/ which is now slack/ why don't you come back?

How handsome is that?

As I pass one of the dressing rooms I see Sleepy Sid looking in a mirror, admiring his bewigged and made up face, saying to himself "Look at me, I'm Sandra Dee."

It's best I just move on.

UNCLE Cecil was booted out by his wife. He said it was on account of the seven year itch; he didn't say it was all over his privates.

I'm classed as a criminal too. That's why those turnip heads wouldn't let me into Stockholm when Harriet got her Nobel Prize.

The thing is, there's an unwritten contract between coppers and the public. They enforce the law and we don't take it into our own hands, as I have.

What a joke that is. Want to hear two more?

We are all equal before the law.

The BBC is impartial.

THE STRANGLERS PRESS

I'm almost sure I saw that tree move.

Next thing, Ginger Jones and his men burst in.

"Reason to believe" he shouts, "you're hiding Far Righters in here."

It's the CCCP (Capital's Camouflaged Community Police)

He takes off his light blue cap, wipes his brow, sees Mrs O'Harnessey.

"As for you, you fat cow, get into the scullery where you belong."

He notices Harriet. "You get this place cleaned up. My officer is coming for interrogation purposes."

I once put a broom into Harriet's hands and she dropped it like it was hot.

His officer arrives. It's Portuguese Joe wearing his helmet with the spike on top. He has with him three of the hottest tomatoes from the Seven Stars.

I'm beginning to think something's not right here. A general mellay breaks out. Joe sends his blonde squad into action. Mrs O and Harriet thump all round them and finally Ginger and his men march out like indisposed Spartans.

A VOICE SINGING
When Sultanas go stalking down the docks of night
Ding dong, down along, where's Dr Dee?
Above the garter, John Carter, plump lips where it's tight,
Wi' dishes and doxies, merry legs for a fee.
And old Uncle Cecil and all
And old Uncle Cecil and all.

"That's the ticket, Fruity" says the old codger. "I want one hundred posters of that."

He's getting his portrait painted. At the bottom of it in large letters is UNCLE CECIL WANTS YOU.

Whatever is he up to?

"Got any pickadillies, Barney?"

I'm fed up supplying him with fags which is why I'm back smoking pipes.

I'm missing my Camels though I wouldn't walk a mile for one.

I stare at him. "I'm not going to ask you why you're sitting in the lotus position."

"Didn't think I could do it, did you, eh?"

There's chanting. It comes from the Sultanas, his harem.

"You can talk of your mahatmas, Your festivals and fatwas, As a guru he's just dandy. He's higher up than Gandhi. We don't think of Muggletonians when Cecil's on the phone to us...."

I'm suddenly aware that Harriet is in the room. She's firing mental darts at me. At the Sultanas too. They're dancing about, rubbing their backsides.

"That's an unusual dance these girls are doing" I say.

There's a knock on the door. Miss Susie's husband enters.

"Miss Susie regrets that Higgins has not kept his promise."

"What's he talking about?" asks Harriet.

"In return for early release from Norfolk Island it was agreed that Harriet Higgins would take his place."

He goes over, takes her arm.

"That's not Harriet" I tell him. "That's her sister Kate, noted in her youth for her elegant and well-timed striking of the hockey ball."

Harriet goes through the motions. "What did I tell you?"

"You haven't heard the last of this" he mutters as he leaves.

"There were loads of boys came to see me play for the school" she says, all proud of herself.

"They were looking at knickers," I tell her.

I'M strolling down the Strand with Billie and the band begins to play. I take her arm in mine. "I'm being diplomatic this week."

"What's that?"

"Diplomatics is the science of deciphering old fogies."

"I don't relish the idea of any of my own ancient screws finishing up in Dr Ragamuffin's Pathway," she says.

"Is he even qualified?"

NHS Spokesperson: We take patient safety very seriously. His diplomas were not verified because such an action could imply that he is not being truthful which might hurt his feelings and therefore constitute a hate crime.

Chief Constable Woodentop: I don't know why committing a crime against an ethnic carries a heavier penalty than the same crime against a white British person. I'm not paid to think.

"I think England's going to the dogs," I say.

"Poodles not Alsations."

"We're just voices in the wilderness."

"Crying out from afar."

THE TITANIC

Follow me to Billie's pleasure palace, never mind the green dogs, Portuguese Joe is playing "Stars over Brooklyn" on the Joanna. There's a hint of sly danger.

Antichrist Atlas is protesting. "There is insufficient evidence to support the belief that I did moonlight flits and juked out of taxi cabs without paying."

Emily X confesses: "I *have* used my cleavage to get to the top and I have ruined several indifferently married men. This I do not deny. But the Archbishop, that leading practitioner of muttering Christianity, was already ruined."

I am looking at the Archbishop now. They've hung him from the rafters. Strumpets in their short skirts push him from one to the other. I hear a voice.

"Lady Broomhilda calling Higgins. Come in, Higgins, come in."

I begged Lady Cadaver not to lend her that broadcasting kit.

"I'm at the Titanic" I whisper, looking down from a hole in the attic floor.

"Get out while you can," she urges. "The council's given me back me door. I need you to put it on again."

"You should know I'm no good at things like that. I've always been a brain worker. Except of course when I was in the Army."

In any case it's not easy to get out of there because Billie is standing over me with the muzzle of one of Harriet's stun-guns in my ear.

Billie pushes me into the chamber. "I found him in the laundry room. He was a-sniffing of my knickers. So he was."

She must have pulled the trigger because the next thing I know I'm swinging from the rafters like the Archbishop.

Uncle Cecil points up at me. "There he is again, poking around where he has no business. One of the greatest nuisances the world has ever seen."

Such an example of the pot calling the kettle black, and no, I was nowhere near Billie's knickers.

"I quite agree" says the Antichrist. "He's very renowned for annoying women when they're in bed."

"And you can't leave anything down when he's about" adds Uncle Cecil.

Below me the proceedings continue:

Auntie and Emily X "Umpa Umpa"

The strumpets "Stick it up your jumpa"

Auntie and Emily X "Umbo, Umbo"

The strumpets "It's all mumbo-jumbo"

Auntie and Emily X "Forgive us our tribadism"

The strumpets "As we forgive them who trifle with our pudenda"

Enter the Monster.

Here she comes, dancing merrily in her velvet gown, her hat with feathers on, whirling an umbrella like she's herding wolves.

Harriet's back on the air. "Come in, Barney come in. the Monster's sent me a note demanding a ransom."

"Whatever you do, don't pay it."

"What with?"

The Monster points her brolly up at me like a mad astronomer challenging the moon. "Barney Higgins, come you down from there."

"You stay up there till I tell you different" commands Emily X.

The Antichrist vows: "He shall be spurned with disdain."

But they are not so sure of themselves when in come a small mob of Scotch trollops (not to be confused with the strumpets) who surround the scoundrels below me.

"Scots wha hae" I shout, "ye gaed doon an gang awa the noo."

Clever Captain Moonlight. He's arranged for thae Janets to lie in reserve.

That just leaves the Monster, who now knows the odds are against her. She tells them, "O you rainbow chasers, youse have come to this rendezvous like minor prophets but I for one and Barney also, know only too well your Spanish honesty. We have whitewashed your intent and laugh at you….Take them away, girls"

She comes over, looks up. "I told you before about trying to save England. You can't do it. The enemy is within."

She gives me a push and walks away. I bang heads with the Archbishop. He's a loser too.

The Monster's right. She know only too well about Catchpole. He comes from the Swamp. Orwell knew him as Big Brother. Hitler and his hun couldn't take the guts out of the British people. Percy Catchpole and his luvvies and traitors can. Watch out for him in Parliament, councils, schools, universities, courts and police stations. Watch what you say, what you write, what you think, and don't forget to bow to the foreigner.

THE MUSIC HALL
My recent downfall plays on my mind.

"You remind me of a selfish Don Quixote" remarks Slim Jim.

"Take him down to the sponging room" I tell the Crusher.

Slim Jim shouts as he's led away, "Shove your belles lettres up your bum."

I hear ringing. It's Miss Valerie. She's playing the part of a poor Russian widow wearing skin-tight leggings in my current production called *Berts Play*.

"Come to me now " she's telling me.

Well, if Whittington could hear bells talking to him, so can I.

"I'm on my way" Her fair words bemused me. I knew in my dreamy state that I had nothing better to do.

I park my Jaguar next to her battered car. This reminds me she's only a poor widow woman. She takes me to the hills. There are naked people dancing round a bonfire. It's almost more than my chaste pen can describe.

"Get your clothes off" she tells me.

Call me a puritan but I insist on keeping on my underpants.

"What's all this about?" I say.

"We're letting Umpa know he's not forgotten."

A band of men in black cassocks suddenly emerge from the bushes with the wife bringing up the rear.

"Barney Higgins" she shouts, "I thought I'd thrown out those shabby underpants. Oh, how you do show me up."

Father Finnegan looks triumphant. "Bless you, daughter. Once more you have helped foil the plans of this unholy backslider."

So, she'd followed me again. And was Harriet young enough to be his daughter? They'd an odd lot. They spend eight years learning about something that has only one text book and even that has no real provenance.

The Father says, rather colloquially, I think, "These innocents are no match for Old Bendy and you, Higgins, have led them into devil worship. Are there no limits to your vileness?"

"I was only dancing round a fire."

"Sure, Father" says Harriet in a tone of sad triumph, "he's a cross that's easier to bear when *you* know about it."

Next thing, she's screaming as a banshee arises out of the flames and the priests put their arms to their eyes.

"Be gone," the banshee wails, "ye murtherers of plausibility"

The priests scarper. Uncle Cecil comes out of nowhere.

"How'd you do that?" I ask.

"Just a simple illusion. It worked because they're gullible. Anyone who devotes their life to a myth has to be."

THE BLONDE'S PLACE

She slaps Sleepy's cheeks rat a tat tat when she finds him with her used panties in his mouth. She makes him swallow the evidence and he can't digest the elastic.

Sleepy was given charge of the special room she keeps for sulking in, and in her sullen moods she finds relief in pulling and twisting his nose, causing bone fatigue and then one day it comes away in her hand.

Sleepy looks in the mirror, he says to himself, "I'm a sight alright. One day I'll give her something to sulk about."

"I'll fix it" she says, "aren't I good to you?"

Dr Ragamuffin stitches on a brass nose. He's back in the NHS after his suspended sentence was suspended since hospitals don't talk to each other and he's making extra money as a physician at boxing venues.

HARRIET'S HOUSE

Bobby Barlow, another of my bete noires, had been living on the instalment plan for too long until I sent him to bed with his boots on.

"How could you do such a thing?" Harriet wants to know because he used to be one of her fancy men.

"Because I have an unconforming conscience; plus, any man who's been to Norfolk Island is never the same again."

Lady Cadaver reaches me on the antenna.

"Betty calling, come in Der Henker, come in."

That's my code name. it's Gerry for hangman.

"Der Henker receiving. A okay."

"Penzez de moi, che sara sara."

I think you know what she means and if you don't you need to get out more.

As for me I'm well on my way to becoming an Honourable. Even the queen calls Lady Cadaver "cousin" and sometimes even "Betty". As her agent I'm responsible for the sale of the right to be made an honourable consul in some mosquito infested country, not to mention her toe nail clippings. Her mansion is run at no cost by trannies. Ten pretty maids in a row. But they have to watch themselves. A look or a word out of place and they're sent to Coventry without a rail pass.

ALIMONIA

Poor Charles is in a cage with his coat out at the elbows.

"You'll get used to it," Amelia assures him, syphoning some of his blood out for washing her feet in. She sprays her hair with gold dust, admires herself in the mirror.

"Oh yes, my prettiness" she mouths, putting on her slap. Her hard eyes, which have seen deeply into the secret lives of Presbyterians, receive their warpaint and for one time only see in her reflection an image of her own lewdness.

ON THE ROAD
Uncle Cecil is on the run from Aunt Cecilia. It's on a crooked lane to Eastcheap that a hairy spinster lays spoony eyes on him riding along in the next caravan. "Dis Englander dats the man for me."

Talk about panic. His little legs take him into the hands of female Gypsologists analysing the stuff the travellers leave in their wake. One of them is quite tasty. She says, stroking his baldy head as he purrs like a tomcat, "What a find you are. I want to show you off."

So he's sent to the university where he is put in a cage as an example of primordial under development. He's fed on rabbit carcases and once a day he's exercised treading a big wheel like a hamster.

ALIMONIA
Miss Stark and Amelia are still in cahoots. I pass the cages of disgraced clergymen. Usual stuff. On the filch. This strange business of interfering with clothing. I hear Miss Stark singing "Ginger you're a nutter but you set my

heart a-flutter."

I've told you before about this nostalgie de la boue business, and if you still don't know what it means it's about time you looked it up.

I get my old job back as a cruel district attorney. I can browbeat with the best of them but I don't crush fingers in desk drawers and stuff like that.

I hope you are following this. If so, it's more than I'm doing. There's more to this case than meets the eye, especially as there's more than one dame sticking a finger into it.

That's not all. They're not paying me. So I meet up with Razor Ramsay the Second to plan a job. He says

"You done this sort of thing before? Not afraid to use a heater?"

I hold up a reassuring hand. "Try and stop me."

"You won't turn milky on me?"

"Not a chance" I tell him. "I need the lolly. You can't keep a high class doll on small time dough."

That's what Lushous Louise tells me.

Days later, after the robbery

Lushous Louise kisses my cheek. "You be Lamont Cranston and I'll be Margo Lane."

It's fun while the dosh lasts. I dress up in a cape, black hat and a scarf across my face. All you can see are my specs. I appear mysteriously, leave twenty quid in a chocolate box in her bedroom and depart unseen into the night.

Lushous Lousise says as an aside, "Men are such fools."

THE Big Boss sends me on a mission with the promise of forty quid.

Here's me treading softly through the graveyard over which no bird flies. Dieu sauve Higgins and Pancho the First too. He's one of the Squire's personalities. He's also one of the most unremembered kings in history though he was the first man to discover that a week has seven days and if he did hang, draw and quarter Slim Jim, the Duck of Denmark he says "I didn't mean to."

I tell the Duck, "He says he's sorry and won't do it again."

"Not good enough" the Duck's ghost says. "He even gave the peasants my head to make soup with."

Pancho the First sighs. "You see what I mean, Barney? You can't feed the hungry these days without being criticised."

I leave Pancho mumbling to himself in sorrowful Spanish and delve deeper into the graveyard. I see the back of a figure with an umbrella moving away. I decide to follow it. Curiosity may have it in for cats but not I hope for enquiry agents. I say

"Are you the Monster?"

"No, just a nightingale on the wing."

"What you got for me?"

"Percy Catchpole," she informs me, "has started a new wave of arrests."

"You didn't have to drag me all the way up here to tell me that. Not with my bad back."

"You're next."

"That's different. I suppose you want me out of the way."

"No, but I don't want to sell you any life insurance."

I don't know whether to believe her. You never know with these petit bourgeois operatives.

ALIMONIA

The Pope has been a busy man. In the last few months he has excommunicated Portuguese Joe's Pinkshirts for blowing kisses on church parade and now it's the Inland Revenue's turn for looting the monasteries. That makes for a tricky situation for us Catholics. From now on it may be more than global American companies who don't pay UK tax.

Every now and then Amelia loads up her Ships of Shame with unwanted customers and sinks them in the great lake of Alimonia or even Loch Ness.

A chief tax collector arrives unexpectantly at the next sinking. "All that stuff going down with the ship attracts Value Subtracted Tax."

Yes, they are so desperate after the pursuit of Net Zero destroyed the economy.

Amelia looks down from her sedan chair. "Can't you see what we're doing? We are improving the behaviour and artistic tastes of these lower classes."

"Call me picky" says the Collector, "but I don't see how you are doing that by drowning them, and I'm glad you told me that it's a work of art because there's an extra tax on that."

"You sir, are the epitome of bad taste, shagging your sister on the sly. Yes, word of this absurd romance has reached my ears and I will not hesitate to divulge it."

She'd just made that up but as in Stalin's Russia the accusation is enough and he finishes up cutting down healthy trees in Somerset.

THE FOOTSTOOL

Vera Vamp is standing at the trademen's entrance. I'm never surprised how many posh dames fancy a bit of nostalgie de la boue. As do I, as you know, but I never made time with his blonde beast on account of being too high class for her.

"Bricklayers are infra dig" she tells me, "but not if you were a foreman."

"That's what Stalin said when he got rid of the kulaks."

Harriet comes in with tea. "Am I one of those?"

But she's so nervous she knocks over the sugar cubes.

"I sent Harriet a solicitor's letter" explains Vera Vamp. She points at her and adds "Go and stand in the deep freeze for half an hour."

But it's too long. The ice crystals that form in her brain have her pointing up at the heavens. "Dear God" she croaks, "You have ruined my life. I didn't deserve Higgins."

To our great surprise the Almighty deigns to respond. "Nobody does. Only those with the strongest shoulders are given the hardest load. Look upon it as a blessing."

It makes me feel humble being a blessing and on the highest authority too. She goes off mumbling thanks and sucking her thumb. The blonde beast makes a whistle. Deformed creatures come crawling out of broom cupboards.

"They are from the mine" she informs me. "Your next mission is to put them in sacks, drag them to the quay, throw them in."

"I'm not sure my back would be up to all that dragging."

"Do you want a letter too?"

I wait till dark, throw in a bone to tempt the first creature into a sack and I'm nicked by two bobbies going home from the pub. Vera Vamp puts the case to Inspector Pompadour. "Come on sweet-lips, don't be harsh on him, he's just a loonie playing pirates. Would you like to see my lucky knickers?"

With typical copper perspicacity he works out what she's getting at and releases me into her captivity.

THE FOOTSTOOL'S PRISON
Scratched on the wall is RUDOLF HESS VAS HERE. I can imagine him sitting on his bunk singing the Horst Wessel song. Solzhenitsyn wrote that prison and camp were the making of him and cured his cancer. But he was always a strange character.

I'm ordered to attend a parole board. That's curious because I've been locked up for only three days.

Uncle Cecil tells me. "Be careful how you speak to Dame Looney. She is widely acknowledged to be in the front row of bits of stuff. Isn't that so?"

Dame Looney nods. "Yes it is, Lord Spuddy. I am truly no better than I should be."

"Jolly good" remarks Sir Giles, "but I would ask you to give lesbianism one more chance."

Dame Looney is taken back. "And forgo the plaudits of the multitude? I don't owe that to my public, do I?"

"Only history can judge her," says Lord Spuddy.

"Saving your worships' pardon" I interrupt, "but what about my parole?"

"What about sharing that sissy you've hidden away?" asks Sir Giles.

"I didn't know you were a shirtlifter, Lord Spuddy" says Dame Looney.

"Recreational use only, ma'am."
"Up against the chapel wall," I add to his further discomfort."
He waves me away. "Don't mind him, he's not the full shilling."
"You're not exactly a professor yourself" I say, backing towards the door.
Dame Looney asks, "Are you one of them too?"
"I think you're all nutcases" I say by way of Parthian shot as I slip out.

I'm sent to an open prison at Alimonia.

There's rumbling down the mine, the richest source of magnetism in England. It keeps the white trash busy pumping exhaust fumes down. Amelia's idea is the one the British ruling classes used for centuries on the workers: keep them debilitated so they can toil but too weak to rebel. But you had to feed them better if you wanted them to be able to advance into German machine guns and be cut down like corn on his lordship's estates.

Talk of the devil, here she comes a-riding on her pony.

"Higgins, take your horrible self to the soup kitchen."

"You may have once been Keeper of the Saucepans" Vera Vamp tells me "but that counts for nothing here. In fact," she adds, twisting my ear, "I will be holding court tomorrow for your new trial."

I'm not having this. "I have the right not to wash dishes under the Jennifer Convention."

"Don't heed him" says Harriet, "he's full of tricks.

"I don't feel full of tricks."

I'm handcuffed to the sink.

"You can forget about big tits and heiresses now" gloats Harriet. "Finally I have you where I want you."

And where's that? I'm back at the Footstool where Harriet has done a bunk because the Association of Black Police Officers are at the door. Or so they both think. Mrs O'Harnessey is repentant. "Oh, Barney, I am a lazy greedy woman and the tortures I have thought up for dopes like you have been horrible…."

"Nobody's perfect."

"But what can I do with the Barbadians at the gate?"

"It's Vera Vamp the blonde beast you should be worried about."

And right enough, we hear her in action, we hear thumping and battering and screaming.

O you judges at Nuremburg, you never knew anything like this. The sounds of the Lubyanka are a mere echo.

Mrs O is flustered. "Barney, this Quean Anne's Footstool I started, does it really exist?"

"Does the Holy Family exist? Have I really been a detective?"

"All these years as a former person, flinching in the face of ridicule and rolling in the gutter with B-girls must have taught you something."

"It has. Avoid women like you and devote your attentions to rich vulnerable widows and yes, even lying in the gutter one can look up at the moon and regret all those missed widows."

"Maybe I should become more Turkish" she says. "It may help salve my insecurity."

"You didn't have that before Vera Vamp came along. You was a good big girl till you met her."

"I just feel the need to eliminate everyone who knew I was a coppers' nark."

"All very Stalinist, I'm sure" I tell her. "But the judgment of fate may not allow it. If Marx and Engels had been alive at the time they would have finished up in one of his camps."

"History woud have demanded it. An historical necessity."

"And what would it have demanded of those fruits you had Crusher put to the question?"

"Nothing. In the days of chivalry and courtly love you wouldn't find knights and ecclesiastics lying with boyfriends or having a wank."

"Or doing both. Dear Mrs O I never knew you were a romantic."

"There's no heroes like the olden heroes."

She points behind me. "Who's this impudent saucebox strolling about with her hands on her hips?"

"Bad news, Barney" says Miss Stark. "Harriet's been kidnapped by the Roma."

"Poor Harriet" I cry, "my world is a smaller place without her."

Miss Stark has to laugh. "It's a long time since I heard such Spanish honesty."

"Thank you, Miss Stark, every path has its puzzle."

"Call me Veronika."

"You look a right corker in that petticoat, Veronika."

Mrs O is not pleased. "Come away from her, you Guildenstern."

"He's more a Rosencrantz."

Vera Vamp strides in, confronts Mrs O. "The game's up."

Miss Stark is smiling. "Never has a great Matron been so naked before her foes."

I hear bells. They are from the nearby church beckoning the humble and the hypocritical to their knees.

The bells of Seven Dials ring out for Sir Giles and the bells of Kuala Lumpur ring out for poor Umpa.

EXECUTION DOCK

The first prisoner, Cousin Betsy, upon being asked to take the oath, unbuttons the front of her blouse, places huge orbs of dangling temptation before the court, letting them settle on the Book of Amazement (not to be confused with scriptures of a similar name) and is acquitted on the spot.

You see all those philosophers – Theodoras, Euclid, Aristotle, Socrates, Epicurus – Betsy could have taught them about the nature of man.

My counsel, Vera Vamp, click-clacks over to me, a look of amorous contempt on her thin lips, in the grip once more, I fancy, of my nostalgie de la boue.

"Come with me" she says. She leads into the parole hall. "Higgins has been poking where he has no business," she tells Harriet and Father Finnegan sitting at a table.

The wife is smiling sadly. "Typical pagan."

"Sorry, Harriet, but I'm no better" the priest admits.

"You're a pardoner, aint you?" exclaims Harriet.

"Yes, I grant the odd indulgence but the reality is that I spent years training to be something I no longer believe in." He lights a cigarette, points it at me. "All these years when you thought I was thwarting your schemes, it was only for show. Secretly I envied you."

"Well I'll be damned" cries Harriet.

"But don't think I'm not grateful for your clumpish devotion" he says to her.

Then, before my very eyes, my loving devout wife starts to change. Her skirt rides slowly up her thigh, revealing ladders, her red lipstick begins to smear over a twisted vicious mouth, her blonde hair shows dark roots and her tits peep out of her blouse. I close my eyes, shake my head to clear it, but as usual Harriet is not to be disposed of that easily. When I look again I see her standing naked, with crazed eyes and blood dripping down her face.

I'm hit with a mighty slap across my face. My specs are hanging from one ear. Another cuff and off they fall.

"I'd seriously advise you not to step on those glasses" I tell Vera Vamp.

"Would you not give him a wee pardon, sir," asks the wife, softening her stance.

"Sure I'd only be wasting me time."

"Too far gone, you mean?"

"Irredeemable."

"That there's a very powerful word, Father."

"Isn't he worth it?"

Wait till you hear this

I've knocked off one or two punks but that doesn't make me a hitman though I'd still go down for a long stretch.
 Funny how governments think capital punishment cruel when they're complicit in the greatest holocaust ever known.
 It's called abortion.
 On demand.

PART THREE
Madam GeeGee's
Here I am being stroked by a doxie with dragon-lady eyes. Yes, it's Billie, just back from Higginsburg way down yonder in Arkansaw.

The hour is struck. At the tenth dong a baldy old coot steps out of a tall sideboard. "Freeze you heroes." Billie gives a pretendy scream. "Once more into the jaws of the honey trap, treads the fearless agent" says Uncle Cecil.

Billie shakes her lovely head. "Not tonight he doesn't."

"Ah, don't be pedantic. What about some small suggestic talk to begin with?"

"No."

"A dog must be bad indeed who is not worthy of a bone." he insists.

Sighing, Billie gets up, takes the dog collar from around my neck, puts it on him.

"You're an effing old cow" he tells her.

A red-tipped finger moves, presses a button and Harriet the Stepford wife emerges.

"And Higgins can't count neither. Unless he uses his fingers" the old sod informs us.

I feel like getting up and giving him one but my hands are tied. Tied to the leg of a sideboard.

"The order of the boot" orders Billie.

Harriet kicks Uncle Cecil in his whatsits.

"Now get back under the table."

Harriet does so in mechanical fashion. Billie strolls round the chamber.

"I'm beginning to think my agents have failed me."

"We wouldn't dare, Madam GeeGee," we cry in unison.

"No more will my riff and raff defy me. I shall skin my agents into deeper modes of devotion and cause stampedes in their hearts with one beckoning gesture.

"And as for you yellowbelly" she says to Portuguese Joe who is standing to attention wearing his Prushun helmet with a spike on top and holding a wooden rifle. "You are too fat and will henceforth live on char and wads – with margarine of course. Because giving butter to a wretch like you is as inconceivable as you being kissed and cuddled by a decent dominatrix." She turns towards us. "What say you, Uncle Cesspit?"

"Hi de hi," he says.

"Ho de ho," replies Harriet in automatic response.

"I spent years in a leper colony" he says, "I wasn't allowed butter neither. They wanted my nose but I made them settle for just two of my toes."

"I am not interested in your operations. Enough!"

Us exhibits freeze. She goes around, moving an arm here, a head there, until we are just as she wants us.

"The world really is an absurd place," she tells us.

MRS O'HARNESSEY'S DIGS AT THE FOOTSTOOL

I may not have mentioned that after the Ancient Mariners burnt down the Institute they went on a rampage. The coppers stayed put in their hidey holes, sent out their dogs but they cried to get back in, which was a mistake as the Mariners wrecked it too.

I was the only lodger who's not evicted to make room for the coppers and I'm not pleased when Little Lily Bullero gives them more fry at breakfast than I get.

"Don't be picky" warns Mrs O, "and don't rub them Peelers the wrong way."

She even lets them call her Sally which is forbidden to the likes of you and me.

Lord Spender of Grubstreet pushes his luck. He calls her that at…

MISS WINK'S SUPPER ROOMS AT THE ACADEMY
Harriet is giving a talk on matrimonial torment and I stand there as an example of what to avoid. Ester's there too. She sinks her teeth into my neck.

Harriet kicks me on the shin. "Barney Higgins, let go of that woman."

"Yes, you are eine terrible nuisance to us womens."

"He should be brought up before the Committee of Matrons of which I am of course the supreme matron with a lamp," Mrs O suggests.

Lord Spender bows. "And I am your stretcher bearer. Clad only in my robes and a laurel wreath, comme il faut."

Harriet is impressed. "We thankee, m'lud, but we know nothing of your Roman tongue."

Harriet always lets me down. "You're either classical or you're not" I snap at her. I turn to Mrs O. "I was before that committee last year. Talk about being literal. I had to jump through actual hoops."

"You must have got Mrs Merkel. She has refined schadenfreude to a new peak."

"Is that the same as strangling patients with their own bow-tie?" I ask.

"Now, now, Barney, I've told you before, a healthy fetish keeps a man virile in later life."

"I'm not that old."

"Ancient brains can be very imaginative" muses Mrs O, "because they have a large extent of experience to draw upon."

Uncle Cecil comes in. "If they are too ancient they go backwards. I'm on my second honeymoon."

Harriet has her say. "Used to be when old geezers was doting they sat in the corner drooling and giggling, smoking their clogged-up pipes, talking nonsense, looked after by their family. Now they call it big words, put them in smelly homes run by forriners."

Silence hangs. "Don't look at me" exclaims Mrs O. "I'm not a forriner. And I change the bath water at least once a week."

I'm not having this. "How comes it then that you confiscate their teeth?"

"Yes but to be fair" comments Uncle Cecil, "she does rent them back to us at dinner times."

"A mere service charge. At this Footstool we take patient safety very seriously and we don't want them choking on their teeth at night. Of course, one may moderate one's professional impulses with a natural self-interest."

Lord Spender raises his hand. "As a lowly stretcher bearer may I have the temerity to nominate you for another lamp?"

"It's only what I deserve." She steps forward, points dramatically. "Particularly having to put up with Uncle Cecil!"

But he's not bothered. He does a little jig then presents us with his backside'

"Them girls at my high-class convent" continues Mrs O, "come psalm singing twice a week to attend my patients and this old coot tells them he's bound up and needs a greasy finger up his ancient causeway."

"It's against natcher" exclaims Harriet.

I have to ask this. "Why is he wearing a nightgown and cap?"

Portuguese Joe, his chief features emerging from the end of a cardboard box that is assuming the shape of a parallelogram as Mrs O sits on it, has this to say, "I've noticed him like that before."

"I hope he's not the holy maid of Kent again" says Harriet.

"More like Wee Willie Winkle," I remark.

Next stop...

THE PUNISHMENT CHAMBER
Lord Spender is sulking in a cage of little ease. That's for being over familiar. Mrs O is cutting her initials in a dead slave.

"You should do that on live ones" I suggest, "so if they abscond the New KGB will know who they belong to."

"That is academic. None dare defy the power of my supremacy."

She's just sore because she didn't think of it first. She thinks making us wear antennae is enough but I know different. In fact, I know too much. That's why I'm hanging upside down. Harriet enters clapping her hands. She pulls my ears, biffs my nose.

"The bloody man's had it now."

"Not necessarily" replies Mrs O. "He only has to tell me where he parked that Egyptian machine."

INSIDE THE PYRAMID
"I said we would go places" I tell the wife after we make our getaway from the punishment chamber.
   "That was twenty years ago and where have I been?"
   "You've been to Wales and south London."
   "Only because you had me kidnapped."
   We soon land in Spanish Town, Jamaica, where the Grand Panjandrum is drinking blood and a-playing of his pianner.
   Now don't look askance at me. At the Marseilles Institute for Advanced Intellectuals we teach that there is no absolute reality. I never thought there was. Professors don't think so. Neither do I. I hope that's clear.
   The Grand Panjandrum finishes his sonata, looks up and says,
   "Behave yourselves or lose teeth."
   And now for the doggonest sight you ever saw. Portuguese Joe is naked, all rump and ribeye and he's between the shafts of a trap on which sits Ester the chemist from Cologne.
   "I'll never eat a cold frankfurter again" I say.
   Harriet is aghast. "If I'd known he was like this I'd never have let him live under my table."
   The Grand Panjandrum has to smile. "Hush, hush, sweet Harriet. When you was the Conductress you displayed yourself too."

"Stockings and suspenders is different" she asserts.

"Eh lass, I wasn't criticising you. Walking up and down those steps with your skirt caught in your panties was the pinnacle of your perfidious existence."

"Thank you, sir, but I have to go home now and make my husband's tea."

"Not so fast. There are those want that pyramid and those who know too much."

The woman who knows too much.

THE chair of the Committee of Matrons is occupied by the wobblised buttocks of Mrs Merkel. Here's Vera Vamp pulling me along by a rope round my Henry Halls.

"A year in the punishment chamber should be enough to reconstruct him" she says to Mrs Merkel.

"Your defence is eloquent but quite useless. He has no prospects."

"Yes, but you don't want to pre-judge the future. I mean, who ever would have thought of hooped petticoats making a comeback?"

"What was once will come again," I point out. "I expect it'll be bodices next."

Vera Vamp presses her point too. "There, you see. Barney will emerge from the dungeon depths as a fully-fledged suffragette."

"Yes, I see it now. And he shall be called Dopey Dora."

"I prefer Nancy Nutmeg" I say.

Mrs Merkel is outraged. "Really! I must protest."

You may be wondering how I've fallen so much. Or you may not. I'll tell you anyway. I'm working for The Way of the Arch, the English resistance movement.

Sounds important, don't it? But I know better. I know how I got here. By dint of double-crossing, greed, duplicity and disregard for the welfare of others I have transformed myself from a bricklayer into a shyster snooper who feeds off scraps for a bunch of losers.

I'M on patrol in the black museum. Pancho the First, one of the Squire's personalities, is right at home here. Harriet is waiting for him.

"Ah, Lady Broomhilda, most beloved of strumpets---"

"Where's the Squire? Where's my money?"

"Oh dear! Whatever will Mrs Grundy think?"

Harriet stops whacking him with her brollie. "You know Mrs Grundy? Oh, your majesty."

She kneels down in homage, unlaces his boots.

But he jumps out of them when the Quean of Spades makes an entrance. He rushes over, licks her hand.

"You may now beat Banagher" she says to her henchmen.

The said Banagher, another of the Squire's personalities, goes white and then, like a bolt from the blue, he bolts.

But he's hauled back by the henchmen who have forearms like Popeye. The Quean orders him to be thrown in the air. Then, looking down at the writhing

Banagher, she says, "The meat wagon will be here presently."

She sees Harriet. "And take her too. That overweight replica of...."

"Joan Crawford." I offer.

"That's right. She's like an overweight Joan Crawford...." She looks around. "Who said that?"

I keep schtum. She stamps her foot in anger. "I said, Who said that?"

CHECKPOINT CHARLIE

Leamas looks about him. "They tell me this is a safe house."

"Not quite," I tell him, "there's a loose floorboard in the kitchen."

"You can always tell a City & Guilds man," says Uncle Cecil.

I say in an aside to Leamas, "This old windbag may be useful as a fallguy."

"I won't say I'm unbalanced" states Uncle Cecil, "just a little unhinged."

Leamas looks at me intently. "The Russians are after the pyramid, a device of such vile intention that no honest man can experience it and stay sane."

There's an implication hanging in the air but I ignore it.

"I take my hat off to you, Barney," says Leamas, "as the pyramid's only known survivor....Tell me, why is Uncle Cecil wearing a kilt?"

Aunt Cecilia appears suddenly, grabs her husband by the ear, pulls him out.

"I am disgraced again," she mutters.

"It's her own fault," I say. "She only beats him once a month."

Leamas gets down on his knees and cries.

THE FOOTSTOOL
I tell Mrs O she's like a Rubenesque Joan Crawford and she turns on me.

"Down with faint praise, I should be lauded to the limit. I want young blood, not a boozer with a battered nose."

"Excuse me, I'm sure," I say, a bit put out.

"Don't talk like a fruit. By the way, talking of blood, the clinics don't want to buy mine anymore."

"Yours?" says Uncle Cecil.

"The old geezers. She has a cellar full of them," I put in.

"I know," he agrees. "I'm one of them."

Mrs O stamps her foot. "Lies! Another fascist fallacy..." She rounds on Uncle Cecil. "What you doing here anyway, I heard Barney shot you."

"It was Ginger Jones I shot."

"In the back?" she asks.

"No, in the chest. He was running at me in a cowardly fashion."

Harriet throws up her arms. "The man who shot Ginger Jones! I'm sorry I knocked you down this morning."

"That's okay," I tell her. "I was able to snap my jaw back into place."

"My hero" she cries, giving me a hug.

SOMEWHERE
I must say I take exception to swimming out to the middle of this lake where Leamas is treading water, in order to receive my orders. I can't see why the

Big Boss allows it.

"The Big Boss says to listen carefully," says Leamas. "Every week Mervyn Pratt gives a talk on Radio 4. When you hear him say, Common people don't know what's good for them, you spring into action. Got that?"

"Yes. a Tinkerton has the fortitude even for that and knows his duty."

"I want to make that clear."

No harm in wanting, I always say.

"Try to be more professional, Higgins, and accept that you may have to carry the can."

HARRIET'S HOUSE

She comes in. "I really don't mind being a widow. I expect there'll be a pension."

You won't believe what the fat cow does next. She brings in a wax phallus with a pair of specs drawn on it. She flicks her lighter and holds it to the dummy prick.

"Penises are not my cup of tea no more" she mutters.

"Well, you teased them often enough when you were the Conductress."

"I was a good little daddy's girl till I met you."

I can't believe this. "Your old da put Auntie Vi in the pudding club and was a black sheep to boot, they didn't call him the swinging postman for nothing."

"Higgins, I told you before, cut out the mixed metaphors." [ed]

This Jane arrives. She's wearing a man's suit. She says "Be careful, don't lose your leg in Winnipeg."

I catch on quick, it's Lovely Miss Nightingale who whispers in my ear, "Who do you think you were talking to?"

I find this whispering androgynously erotic. "Harriet of course."

"Don't you know a Big Boss when you see one?"

I hope you weren't assuming that the Big Boss was a man. That would never do. But Harriet?

Next thing, Nightingale puts on her locker-room face, whispers to Harriet, "You can be my big boss anytime."

Harriet stamps on the smouldering phallus, says, "Fugh you both. I'm off to marry Jesus."

"You don't even know what he looks like."

You have to wonder how Christianity would have progressed if its founder looked like Sleepy Sid.

It was only when I was prowling the corridors of the Footstool with night starvation that I discovered Lushous Louise and Sleepy having a rendezvous.

I confront them. "Come out from her skirts, you little rat."

(He's only one leg and one eye, you know. Not to mention a humpy back)

But it's the Squire who emerges.

Well, not quite, it's John Puddyfoot, one of his multiple personalities, with a propensity for ankle-biting. It looks like he's trying his luck with Lushous Louise (Mrs O being out of the question)

But wait, here's Harriet with her second-best umbrella who is still after the Squire's money. She gives poor John one across the mouth then she and Lushous Louise stamp upon his prone body with quasi-religious authority.

A PRISON HULK

I've been arrested by Mrs O'Harnessey on account of holding back on those jewels. The cement on her face cracks maliciously as he glares down at me.

"Captain Moonlight, you are improperly dressed. The wardresses are complaining about your hairy legs."

I throw my voice: "Wommanes conseil broghte us first to wo and made Adam fro paradys to go, ther as he was ful mury and wel at ese."

Mrs O rears up. "Who said that?"

"It was Chaucer, dear Matron."

"Well I'll settle his hash. Where is he?"

Dr Ragamuffin and Basher's Emergency Men arrive to take me on deck.

"No hard feelings?" says Dr Ragamuffin.

I shake my head. "That is very good," he adds, "I am seeing that you are a philosopher."

The Emergency Men throw me overboard. My hands are untied and though I can get bismonia I don't let the cold water get me down. I am after all a philosopher.

I trudge soakingly towards the music hall. Billie strips me in her changing room. I put on her pink dressing gown.

"I was abducted" I tell her.

"Poor dear, of course you were. Not those pesky Martians again."

I'm keeping a dignified silence when Miss Susie bursts in.

"You know you have a fugitive here," she says.

Billie and me look around

"It's Higgins we're after."

"I've paid my debt to Mrs O" I protest.

"Not here, you fool. Norfolk Island."

She calls for her butler-husband. "Jeeves, tell Basher we need his Emergency Men again."

He looks uncomfortable. "They might not arrest anyone in a pink dressing gown."

"Of course they will. They've all been bullies in homes for pensioners and mental cases." He moves towards the door. Miss Susie calls after him. "And don't question my orders again."

"I thought his name was Rupert" comments Billie.

"It used to be but after I spent all his money I just didn't feel the same about him. It was sad."

"You poor dear. At least you're over him now. No point in being maudlin."

Miss Susie sighs. "Thank you, Billie, I'm bearing up as well as I can."

"What's Higgins done to deserve Norfolk Island?"

"He tied up Harriet as a tethered goat in Alimonia so the Boers could have their way. Amelia saw him."

Eye witnesses! I've often thought of the poor criminals wrongly convicted on account of them. (Though I suppose it balances out the crimes they get away with.)

"Didn't you know" I ask them "that the sensible way to deal with Boers is to give them a sacrifice? And Amelia's not all there, is she?"

"And Queen Anne is dead" says Billie.

"Fancy the old dame kicking off like that" I remark.

"And don't be putting up any resistance when these men arrive" warns Miss Susie.

"Wound my heart with languorous languor" I reply.

Miss Susie shakes her head. "Just ignore him. They'll sort him out on the Island. There are two drill-sergeants there bordering on sadistic lunacy."

Are there any other type?

Here comes big Jack Brag with a face like unlaid ghosts.

"Emergency Men reporting for duty."

NORFOLK ISLAND
How to put his lights out
A course for impatient wives and would-be widows.

Uncle Cecil is downcast. "I knew when Susie stopped consummating with me I was going to be disposed of."

I didn't even get that far.

"Don't worry. Every clown has a silver lining but a bloke wearing plus fours and a deerstalker deserves all he gets."

"I suppose you think I should be back in the puzzle factory."

"Yes I do" shouts Harriet, coming in, her bonnet rouge proclaiming liberty, equality but not fraternity.

We hear a voice. "Nice dump you got here" smirks Bernard Holland, inviting himself in with a baseball bat. He bangs Harriet on the back of the legs and she jerks around like a puppet on a string. But that's as far as he gets. In comes the shock-troop of the Ancient Mariners and they give him a right good thumping. Give me the fools and I will finish the job.

THE FOOTSTOOL

"You have done well, Captain Moonlight, Norfolk Island is now almost in my power. Sometimes you even know what you're doing."

"Thank you, Matron. I do owe a little to my Ancient Mariners. I have three detachments: the shock-troop, the cannon fodder and the forlorn hope."

"I've heard of this Horace Himmler, the mastermind who's using stiffs to build another pyramid on the Island."

"Yes, my Mariners' lives were in my hands as I insinuated them through the mines and electric wire. But for you, my succulent siren, I laugh at danger."

"I'm glad to know that because you must go back. Getting rid of one rogue may release an even bigger one..." She eyes me keenly. "And another thing, my hero, you've been making time with that tart again. Against my orders."

"She needed someone to keep her warm."

"You leave that dog alone."

"Yes, Matron, her mushy thighs and overripe bum will no longer lead me into temptation."

"I think you are hard up. I never heard of you sleeping with your wife before."

OUT IN THE STREET
You too can have a body like Harriet's. If you're not careful.

That's not nice. Women get plumper every year. Though when I'm in the mood I admire their *embonpoints*. That's another of my favourite words.

Talk of the devil here she comes now with the new priest. He says

"Barney, we have a lot to talk about."

(Priests are like Japanese. You can be with them for years and never know what they're really thinking. I expect there are conflicts under the surface.)

I don't mind these two touching but I won't tolerate kissing on the lips.

Talking of which here come Noddy and Big Ears, Sleepy and the Crusher, holding hands.

"God will punish those who leap upon His altar" warns the priest.

The Crusher eyes him intently. "I've noticed you before, hanging around those school gates down there."

"And why shouldn't he?" retorts Harriet. "Isn't he selling the Big Issue?"

"Big tissue of lies" I say. "Those beggars have more money than me."

With that the wife and the priest move on. So do Noddy and Big Ears.

I was a grown man before I was told what those confirmed bachelors do to each other. If you really must know, they dance around each other with hands joined like couples in a country dance then they make bows and share a nosegay to sniff on. I don't know what the world is coming to.

THE MUSIC HALL
I go to Billie's dressing room, she's lying on her couch, a bored look on her cold creamed face. Herman is painting her toenails. Duckie Baconbrains is attending to her fingers. Herman receives a kick in the face.

"Out you dogs!" commands Billie. I turn to go. "Not you, Higgins. Go down and see what the Crusher's up to. I don't want that Bernard Holland croaked."

I go down to the sponging house. "Take it easy" I tell the Crusher. "All this screaming is disturbing her nibs."

He throws up his hands. "This is getting me down. When you put people to the question you're supposed to know what the question is."

There's a commotion above. "There's no show on" I say, "I'll go and see."

What a sight. The forlorn hope are storming the stage. Brutality Jones and his heavies are clubbing them back. The forlorn hope may be practising storming or they may be trying to get at the bare backsides of the scrubbers as they scour the stage.

I go back down. Eddie has taken over from the Crusher. She's wearing her full bodystocking.

"This is the devil's breath" she whispers into Bernard Holland's mouth. "It makes you putty in my hands."

His tumescence says otherwise. "When do we make our move?" she asks.

I pull her close. "Tonight. And tomorrow you will once again be Quean of the Barbary Coast."

We fly through the night in Eddie's Sunbeam with Bernard Holland tied to the roof rack.

THE BARBARY COAST

The armpit of the country where even Ancient Mariners fear to tread. We park near the great stone where in the old days Christians had their teeth kicked out.

We are greeted by Fugleman X. "Be obsequious to your new Quean" I say. "Tomorrow we coronate her."

So we do. Prisoners pull the gun carriage. Eddie, in her bodystocking, straddles the barrel of the great artillery piece.

"Keep it modest" I tell her. "Be serene and in your palace you will never have to wash another dish or dick."

"They wash their own. I have my standards."

The procession reaches the Alamo where we are greeted by old hags ululating and young blades making wolf whistles.

An aside to Fugleman X: "Arrest those blades. I need galley slaves for my longboat that will be set afire when it is time for Eddie's suttee."

Yes, I am getting carried away. Absolute power does that.

What a sea of deadheads await us. Thugs, robbers, bushrangers, beldames, drifters, tobymen. They come down from the trees, from the hills, out of holes in the ground. They are my people and I am proud to be their ringleader.

BARNEY'S OFFICE
Clothilda, the fattest woman to ever sail round the world, drops in to remind me I'm still working for her.

In theory that is, because I haven't had any time.

So I put on my false nose and tache and go to the door before she knocks it down.

"Oh hello" she says, "I don't think we've met. I'm looking for that idle bastard Higgins."

"As a matter of fact---"

This is all I get to say before my cheeks are being squeezed. "I have something for you" I just about manage to say. "Portuguese Joe is a spy."

"Who's he spying for?"

"For me."

"I always knew he was up to no good," she declares.

"I have my tentacles everywhere."

"You go back to keeping watch over my smugglers and strumpets and no slacking off this time."

As I've said, it takes a strong man to stand in a field all night with his arms out disguised as a scarecrow, and once was enough. But I don't tell her that, not as long as she's holding my gooseberries. I go to the Footstool.

"Higgins, did you know Monmouth has been taken?"

I love it when she's historical.

"Hey nonny no, hey nonny no," chants the Crusher.

It's difficult to feel sorry for him, even if he does have a ring through his nose. He's so dense he could easily turn into a black hole. He's in a large cardboard box. He starts to bark.

"Will no-one rid me of this turbulent hound?" asks Madame Mao.

"I shall call him Becket" decrees Mrs O.

"And I shall call you my prime suspect" cries Uncle Cecil, stepping in, lassoing Mrs O and deftly reeling her in. "Come on, duckie, I arrested you a year ago."

Becket catches his eye. "I'm taking him in too. Where's his lead?"

Madame Mao is not having this. "Leave him alone, you dogsnatcher."

Muttered agreement all round, and it's time for me to rescue poor Crusher. I attach a length of string to the ring through the nose and lead him out.

Mrs O takes advantage of Uncle Cecil's short attention span. "Why don't you and me" she suggests to him, "go for a stroll through the stubble?"

"Don't mind if I do" he agrees.

"I really don't know what to think" admits Mrs Grundy.

DRABTOWN RACES

Harriet has a job as a steward. Mrs O'Harnessey complains to her, "That Grantly-Hogg has two entries. It's against the rules."

"Rules are for fools" she informs her.

"We'll see about that." Mrs O strides off, bold as a bully, her short skirt showcasing the splendour of her tree-trunk thighs.

Harriet sighs, "I hope you know what we're doing."

"I'm in a tight spot alright."

"Be strong, Barney, and cut all sentimental ties with your horrible former life."

That would include her but I don't want to hurt her feelings.

The jockeys arrive. The whistle sounds. My sore back is killing me and my heart is chugging like a train. I make it to the finish. I lower myself to let my rider dismount. Breathless as I am, I still admire her bum-tight leggings and clinging sweat-soaked teeshirt.

BARNEY'S OFFICE

Harriet has brought the Squire here for me to thump. He hasn't let her fleece him and forgets to call her Baby Doll. She says to him:

"Your promises aint worth a scotch farthing. Like another blighter I know who ignores me, keeps me short and is a brawling bruiser."

"I'd like to meet this brute" I tell her. "I'd give him what for."

She gives me an old-fashioned look. Portuguese Joe walks in. "I'm on the lam again. Flying Squad this time."

"The Flies can have you." I say.

"At least I'm dealing with a higher class of detective" he remarks, looking at me

What a thing to say!

"Bugger off" I tell him. "I'm not having wanted men in this Tinkerton agency which I built up at the expense of sweat, toil and---"

"Deception" interrupts Joe.

I'm just about to clobber him when a group of men wearing donkey masks barge into the office spraying laughing gas over us.

THE FOOTSTOOL'S BASEMENT

Matron is sitting by the fire roasting Sleepy Sid's chestnuts. "That'll learn me not to trust little rats again."

I'm down here too. I'm in a bunker behind a bookcase beyond the boulders at the back of the basement. With Matron is a Sibyl wearing a hat with a veil who says "That's where noblesse oblige gets you."

I hear a cranking noise. I slip out of the bunker where I'm hiding. The pyramid appears out of nowhere. A small baldy man steps out. Many voices sigh as one. "Aaagh...Uncle Cecil." They start singing "Whenever I see the U.C. sign, the U.C. sign, always fine, whenever I see the U.C. sign, I want to make him mine."

Yes, it's the Sultanas stepping out of the machine.

"Hello stale servants" Uncle Cecil greets us.

I'm not at all pleased. "It's bad enough you taking the pyramid without permission but it wasn't built to carry around big girls like that."

"I couldn't rescue you without it. The coppers have closed all roads indefinitely because a car ran into a ditch."

"Why'd they do that?"

Chief Constable Woodentop: Because we can.

"Why is it a criminal offence to hurt the feelings of certain people?"

Chief Constable Woodentop: Don't ask questions of us. We do what we want.

I'm starting to have an idea. That usually spells trouble but it doesn't stop me. I'm thinking so hard my spectacles start to vibrate.

It's all about ditches. I used to push Culshie Mucks into them and many years ago a girl called Jane Shore was martyred in the one next to the Seven Stars. I put an ad in the *Stranglers Press*: Jane Shore may grant your wishes if she's prayed to at the Ditch.

However, candles go unsold and the collection boxes stay empty. But what can you do with heathens. We used to be at the forefront of idolatry and look at us now.

So I try a new tack. "Queue here for an audience with Umpa." No good neither. I'm listening to Ester talking to the Misses Marble. "Sie are now sausage meat."

"Oh deary me, we don't mean to be old," they say, becoming upset.

I'm not having this. "Calm down, you nebbing old biddies, she's only trying to sell you face cream with hormones in it."

A voice. "Whassa problem?" says Francis the talking mule who causes a sensation among the miserable lot who are ignoring Jane Shore and Umpa.

"Ester's trying to flog stuff to my pilgrims. No respect for religion, some people."

"Who's this tart on my back prodding me with an umbrella?" asks Francis.

"I'm Jean the Baptist," says the drab.

She's not, you know, she didn't wear a hat with feathers on it. And to cap it all here come some noodles singing the Monster Mash, and look there goes Master McGrath the butcher being chased by a pack of pigs.

Uncle Cecil's here too. He's stumbling towards me, so full he can't bite his finger. "I've news for you, Barney Bighead, you knave, you cur, you're gonna get thumped."

"Don't take it out on me 'cause Aunt Cecilia put Jeyes Fluid on your tomdoolies."

She caught him cruising for rough trade.

"Courtly love is not yet extinct" he says before I knock him over and he crawls away.

"Britisher sweinhund!" Ester calls after him.

We're both astonished when we see him, like a giant black bird, pick up his wings and fly away.

BARNEY'S OFFICE
I picked up a bit of dough from those jewels but I spent it. Or rather, Lushous Louise and me spent it.

"I wonder where it all went to" I say to her.

"Yes, I wondered about that too."

"I bet you did. I bet you stayed awake nights worrying about it."

"Why don't you rob the Blonde?"

EXECUTION DOCK
Where she keeps her Aztecs.
Whispering as I slip the lock and go in: "Jhesu Crist and Seiynte

Benedight, blesse this hous from every wikked wight."

If it was good enough for Chaucer...then I remember they didn't know about Aztecs in those days. But they knew about Blondes. They called them witches.

I crouch in the hallway, Bernard Holland has the drop on me, we go into a room where Aztecs are chanting. They have masks on. I feel a needle in my arm. When I come to I'm on a slab, hands tied behind me to a ring. I'm bare chested. There's more grease on it than Harriet's oven. The Blonde is rubbing it in.

"Higgins, you have failed the Grand Panjandrum." She beckons to the side. "Come my handmaiden and take your revenge."

And blow me down, who steps up but Harriet. I steel myself but the wife doesn't take her revenge. She biffs the Blonde, throws her to the floor and stands on her while she unties my laces.

"Come on, Harriet, my hands first. The Bride of Montezuma shall not have me."

So we leave that unholy place. I think we were the only Christians there.

THE SEVEN STARS
A glamour puss is left over from the weekend like a flat perfumed beer.

"I'm sorry" she mutters.

"Excuse me too" I say as I slug a sailor who has his hand in my pocket.

Somewhere in this fog of flab, faded mascara and tattooed hands is the Crusher.

Enter Moaning Minnie. "From les enfants perdus may the good Kaiser deliver us," she says, casting a withering eye over the company.

I have to tell you about the rise and fall of Moaning Minnie because she was my prototype to replace Plain Jane as the Conductress.

"You shall be my taliswoman" I say, feasting my eyes on her nyloned thighs bulging under the shortened skirt of her uniform. I follow her into the yard where Portuguese Joe has formed up his Pinkshirts.

"Quake before your new Conductress" I tell them.

She inspects the ragged file. "I've never seen anything like it in me life."

In comes the Crusher in tights and orange hood.

"Nothing here pleases me" she says to him. She points at me. "Arrest this nutter."

As I'm dragged down to the cellar by the Pinkshirts I have a feeling that I've unleashed a power that should have been left undisturbed.

The Crusher points to his furnace. "I'm making an iron mask for you. I hope you like it."

A voice says "Keep it for her" and I watch as Lushous Louise shoves Moaning Minnie and Portuguese Joe down the steps. The attempted coup has been crushed. The Crusher hastens to fit the mask on Moaning Minnie. Joe and me follow Lushous Louise back upstairs in disgrace, and for weeks afterwards I fancy I can hear sullen moans of indignation rising from that cellar.

IN darkest Pentonville there's a joint called the Star Chamber. Harriet's wearing a tight black number slit up the sides like the armchair she's filling. She's watching the Crusher take out his dick.

"Stop waving that thing at me," she says. "You know very well you're one of those. So stop it."

"Whatever are you at?" I ask.

"I'm making money, but not from the likes of him. He hasn't two sixpences to rub together."

She gets up, goes into the next room. A man is sitting in a chair. She plonks herself in his lap.

"You don't mind me sitting here, do you, darling?"

"Not in the least" says the man, looking at her daycollitay.

Harriet strokes his cheek. "You needn't be ashamed of being here, you know. We have our very own curate on the premises and we're all married women too. To keep it respectable. I do think young single girls should be more careful than they are. Don't you think so too?"

"Most considerate of you. But when does the show start?"

"Oh some time yet. If you come into the studio you can see the artistes. You'll find us quite avant garde. Almost dernier cri, I should say."

"But not pointless."

"Oh yes, pointless too, if that's what you like."

I look up to see a blonde beast coming towards us, thighs shimmering under nylons, heels detonating on the wooden floor.

"My client informs me you refused her a position here" she says in a steely voice. "It was because she has a wooden leg, wasn't it."

"She's just playing the discrimination card" the wife says to me.

"People play a lot of cards nowadays" I reply.

Harriet's heard enough. She goes over and clocks her one.

"Stop it," I tell her. "You shouldn't hit a woman."

They fall to the floor and start wrassling. After a bit the wife slaps the floor. "Napoo, napoo."

Vera Vamp gets up. "I'll be sending you a letter."

After she leaves a constable enters, says to Harriet, "Reason to believe you're keeping a disorderly house here."

"Ha! That's nothing, copper, you want to see my house after he's been there a few days."

I make an excuse and leave. I don't want people to think I consort with brothelkeepers.

I watch Harriet leave the court house with a wind-blown umbrella partly covering her face. She was expecting photographers but there aren't any. Not quite in the Cynthia Payne class.

THE FOOTSTOOL

Mrs O'Harnessey is at her most beguiling. "Barney, wouldn't it be better if you told me where the pyramid is? What if something should happen to you."

I'm not keen on this sharing concept but I do like the way she delicately hikes up her skirt when she crosses her legs.

To the secret acclaim of Tom, Dick and Harry. They're born again into the Footstool, begotten into priapism and defilement from which they can never escape.

Unless Mrs O decides otherwise.

"Alright boys, work Higgins over. He's only hisself to blame."

But there's a problem. She's made them sit with their cocks permanently rigid, fed only on soup maigre and Viagra, so it's not hard to smite them down.

"He's my hero" cries Harriet, who was avidly watching.

MISS WINK'S PRIVATE ASYLUM

I go in by the window.

"What's wrong with door?" asks Uncle Cecil.

"Because you've booby trapped it, that's why."

"Can't you take a joke?" giggles the old nuisance.

I ignore him. I have my dignity to consider.

Harriet has been appointed housekeeper. Here she comes. "Attention, attention, all youse untouchables face the wall now."

I hear Mozart. That's the violin quartet next door. Sometimes when I'm not facing or talking to the wall I take a peep. They wear masks but I recognise the legs.

All this means Quean Victoria is passing by. She affects the Alexandrian

Limp to tantalize the Squire but like the rest of us lower orders he's not allowed to look. But he has Harriet's permission to think about it as she passes.

"This here, your majesty," announces the housekeeper, "is where we keep the incomplete headcases. We call it the Lunatic Fringe."

The quean points at me. "This one here, why's he wearing short trousers?"

"Not my idea---"

"Shut it!" cries Harriet. She shoves a handkerchief in my mouth. "This one's going to public school where they starve and beat them and turn out deeply flawed men who become incompetent generals and timeservers in the House of Lords."

"I'm quite flawed enough alweady, dank you." I say.

"Tell him to pull his socks up."

"You heard, Higgins. Right up to the knee."

A glimpse of the goings-on at the Asylum and don't you hear echoes of Spenser's Fairie Queene in this saga of eloquence and sorrowful seclusion?

No, neither do I.

A ROAD SOMEWHERE IN THE PANHANDLE

"You won't catch me scrubbing parsnips in vicarages" states Harriet.

"That's not the point. You'll be looking for a lead," I tell her.
"What's a lead look like?"
"You won't know till you find one."
"I don't do vacuuming neither."
"So I've noticed."
"Why can't you leave those poor clergymen alone?" she asks.
"Because Vic is a fence and we need to know where the goods go to so we can cut him out, see?"
"I've always said there's too conceited a protestant in this country." She puts her hand on my shoulder. "And stop hopping about."
"I'm not hopping, I'm jumping."
After reading about Spring-heeled Jack I invented a pair of jumping boots.
"This is only a prototype" I add. "Once I power them with petrol I will be uncatchable."
"Oh Barney, I'll never doubt you again."
"How I think them up I don't know."
"You'll never have to worry about rozzers no more."
"That's right. I'll take over rackets here and start up rackets there where there's never been rackets before."
"You'll be unstoppable."
"I'll get a real gun. Stick 'em up, I'll say. Or, reach for the sky. I've always wanted to say that…"

There was no excuse for Harriet taking up with the vicar. Only last year I gave her a music-centre so she could stay at home more. She liked to dance to swing music and piano rock. Sometimes I'd even dance with her myself. How many husbands can say that?

BARNEY'S OFFICE
This poppet settles into the visitor's chair.
   "You're in radio, aren't you" I say, noticing the mike sticking out of her handbag before she places it on the floor.
   "You a mind reader or what? What's that in your pocket?"
   "It's only Pythagoras, my ferret."
   "You are funny."
   "Really, it is."
   "I believe you."
   This is Miss Susie and I'll have to watch myself if she's recording me. She doesn't know I know.
   "It must be wonderful being the detective who discovered the pyramid."
   "I have my moments."
   "My editor on the programme thinks highly of you."
   "Really? What's the name?"
   "Miss Stark."

"She's been betraying this country for years" I remark.

"Doesn't matter at the BBC. She fits in with our culture of bias, and nepotism and she is, like all of us, grossly overpaid."

Just one carriage of the Gravy Train.

"I suppose it figures" I say. "She always wanted to make a name for herself."

"What name was that?"

"I'm not au fait with her vocabulary."

"She does have a slight lisp but our sensitive young men adore her. But back to you, Barney. I take it you have parked the pyramid somewhere safe."

Entre nous, it's at a place called Eye of the Needle. There's a few wild ponies milling about but I never saw any camels go through it.

There's a bit of a cacophony as the phone rings and the door bell sounds at the same time. Pythagoras is disturbed. He runs for cover into her handbag.

I didn't know this at the time. But I find out after she leaves when I hear her screaming in the corridor.

IN MY JAGUAR

"Such a sluttish girl you are" I say to Lushous Louise as Harriet peers through the open window. "Taking advantage of me like this."

"Don't pander to her, Barney, she's no better than I am."

True enough. Harriet is not above using her body as a snare. She has little trouble finding suckers who will settle for the grog-blossomed blowzy type.

"All the same" I say, "it don't pay to rub her the wrong way."

Lushous Louise rubs my cheek. "You're so fair minded. You treat all us floozies the same."

"I don't change tarts in midstream if that's what you mean..." I turn to the wife. "Don't worry, I'll take you back. It's called noblesse oblige."

Harriet's face is a picture, tightening her lips till they hurt.

Tense silence.

"You know where you can shove your noblesse oblige" she snarls. "You'll pay for this."

As she scuttles off to the sound of Lushous Louise's jeers I have more dignity. I confine myself to calling after her: "It's a wonderful life if you don't have a wife."

"Tell me something I don't know" says Uncle Cecil strolling up to the car.

"Alright I will" I tell him, "word's got around you're a nark."

"This here general public what you are a-speaking of had a very high opinion of me when I drove the rent boys out of Palisades Park."

"Hypocrites of old used to burn and persecute those whom they lusted after the most."

"Oh get you" he lisps and prances off in the direction of Harriet.

And lo, the heavens opened up on him and I see great rain descending in a torrent and falling upon him.

THE DAY BEFORE NOVEMBER THE FIFTH

The door is open because I've just kicked it in. A voice says: "We're not opened yet."

I barge on through. I see this bird with a knight's cross at her neck.

I give it to her straight. "Turn an honest massage parlour into a clip joint, would you? Not in my manor, you don't. Who are you?"

"My name is Madam Von Tarantula. And the Sultan Clinic is not a clip joint."

"Sounds Turkish to me."

"Here we make philtres and potions used for men who can't get it up. You look as if you might need some."

Cheeky cow. But perhaps she's been talking to Lushous Louise. Best not to dwell on these things. That wasn't the shag that was. It's over, let it be.

Eddie said to leave the Alleymen alone. She got it from Miss Lovely who got it from the Big Boss. Orders can be mangled. What starts out as Send reinforcements we're going to advance, can finish up as Send three and fourpence we're going to a dance.

Eddie had warned me. "Don't you go trying to save England again. You know what happened before."

"The world's his asylum" chipped in Harriet.

Madam Von Tarantula gives me a love bite.

Next thing, I'm in a supermarket trolley. Boys are pushing me down the street. "Penny for the guy," they shout.

MISS WINK'S ACADEMY
Dr Ragamuffin strolls along the Strand, behind him are two of his hired

grief, street bullies who run his clapped-out baudie houses and cockroach hotels.

They can't save him. The Bogies run from their meat wagon. They make play with truncheons. Into their wagon he goes. Held for ransom.

I'm watching from the upstairs window of the Academy. Harriet is once again Miss Wink, she teaches Anti-American studies, Eddie lectures on Gent's tailoring and the right way to make rustics stand in corners. I'm the petty tyrant who enforces morale.

Miss Wink wants rid of the stiffs in the cellar. But their leader, Mr Pastry, a right Bedlamite lawyer, refuses to leave. Once we're out, he maintains, you won't let us back in.

"Isn't there a black market in guinea pigs?" asks Harriet.

"There should be" I reply. "If the Government is too sissy to hang those sex murderers they could at least use them to test new drugs and whatnot."

Harriet nods. "Better than using those poor Untouchables and loonies like Miss Stark did. Oh Barney, I hope they didn't experiment on you when you was sectioned."

"Your concern is touching. Seeing how you and Dr Ragamuffin signed me in."

HARRIET'S HOUSE
I'm watching Teatime with Tommy on the telly.

"What happened to my copy of the Dandy?" asks the wife.

"I can't bide people who read in the lav."

"Catch me doing that."

The Squire crawls in. "Can I help it if my heart is pierced by Lady Broomhilda's arrow?"

I say to Harriet: "There's been goings-on here, I just know it."

I get up, put on my hat. "A man can take it and take it, there comes a time when he can take it no more."

"Barney, Barney, please don't go!"

But I'm adamant. I brush aside her clinging hand, open the door. It's raining. I go back to my armchair by the fire. I say to her:

"You're on a warning." I take out a little black book from my jacket. I write down her name.

ON THE ISLE OF WIGHT

But it was the coppers who had my name. I can be quite stubborn so when Jane advised me to go on the lam I took no notice.

Who?

I never saw eyes so blue.

No, not her from Shoreditch or her of the fighting ships or her of the *Daily Mirror*. This Jane is a clever frail who visits me in jail. She's quite bonkers but she thinks prison is an exciting place to be where she can rub up against manly types like me who shower only once a week.

"Oh Barney, look at my nails, see how they flaunt"
"How'd you know about that?"
"The parole board knows all about you. Thanks to Little Lily Bullero."
"Her?"
"Yes, butter does melt in her mouth."
"Time's up" announces a warder. Jane gives me a wave.
"Don't fret, my love. I'll wait for you. I'll wait for you in Kalamazoo."
"Well, I'll be gormed.
This is an odd case when you come to think of it. Which I try not to do.

THE FOOTSTOOL
Here's Portuguese Joe (or PJ as he's known at the golf club where he plays a badger game with Eddie). "Heil, Barney, today my Pinkshirts are holding a witchcraft trial."
"Who's the guilty party?"
"Harriet. We found her rubbing a dead body."
"She *is* an embalmer" Eddie advises.
"Leave her to me" I tell him. "I'm the witchfinder around here."
Portuguese Joe shrugs. "Can't help you. Ester has claimed her first."
I know Ester is here. I looked at her this morning through a lattice screen putting on her stockings.
We hear a harsh voice. "Schnell! Schnell!"

It's her, marching the Crusher in at a fast pace. "Dis schweinhund, he is under mein bed found."

"He is very renowned as a peeping Tom. I shall have to sell him to WooWang" I say in a tone of sad resignation.

"WooWang sent back the last one on account of his wooden leg," Portuguese Joe informs us.

"Oh Barney, not Sleepy Sid!" cries Eddie.

Ester is dismissive. "Es okay, in das Reich ve dispose ov our handicapped too."

But Sleepy is forgotten when Harriet bursts in with a retinue of Bernard Holland and his puddlejumpers.

"There will be no witchcraft trial for Lady Broomhilda!"

There's me, bad back and all coming under attack again. I pull out my revolver. They soon freeze.

"Go on, it's only a fake" shouts Harriet.

I am surprised as anyone when Bernard Holland keels over holding his shoulder.

Harriet rushes up and throws her arms round me. "Oh Barney, I never knew you really were a gunman."

After this bit of bloodletting the other parties are told to clear off. I don't need company when I'm with a pretty girl. I take out my mandolin-banjo and sing to the wife, "If you were the only girl in the world."

HARRIET'S HOUSE

"I've heard enough of virgins and Aunt Marys for one day" I say to Harriet.

I'm in a bit of a bad twist. I catch her kneeling before the priest and she tells me she's praying.

"You're a skitter, Barney Higgins, and I hate you to bits. What do you think I was doing?"

EDDIE'S MASSAGE PARLOUR

She opens the door. "Oh Barney you're chasing me again." I hear a noise in the bedroom. "It's only Sleepy Sid" she says, "he's just adjusting his dress before leaving."

He comes out. It's a blue one with spots. He dances around the room, holding his dress above his knees.

"I'm not going out with Jane tonight, I'm not going out with Mary, I'm not going out with any girl, cos I'm a fairy."

Lady Betty tells me "You are to go to Alimonia. Find out what you can to discredit Grantly-Hogg. And remember, fortune favours the brave."

"A Tinkerton know his duty."

ALIMONIA

I'm in the woods keeping an eye out. I see this fella coming towards me with his head wrapped in cabbage leaves like a Roman. He points at this cage. I go in. I hear hissing. Then I smell it. I'm being gassed like badgers.

When you see me again I'm inside a giant clock and every quarter of an hour I'm propelled out and I shout, "Cuckoo, cuckoo, cuckoo."

Each time I come out Uncle Cecil takes a swing at me with his holy water sprinkler. Eventually he knocks me off.

I hear "Don't be a bore in Baltimore."

It's Miss Lovely come to save me.

But it's not. It's Amelia who, keeping her two faces under one hood, is not pleased. "What do I see? I see a spy. I think you more fool than knave but I must hand you over to Honest Harry and Bernard Holland who owes you one."

They take me to the woods where my old pal the Ogre lets rip and those two villains are flung into the trees.

Amelia is kneeling before me. "Dear Barney, show mercy to your dishy controller. Be a good boy and I'll make you foreman of my chain gang."

I'm considering this when she adds "And that monster of yours can have all the cojones he wants."

I hope you are reading between the lines here. It's not easy, I know, but this is a morality tale about the disaffection from Society of those we call outcasts.

But it all depends on what you call Society, doesn't it?

And whether you know it when you see it.

I'm in danger of being too philosophical here so I'll briefly mention Amelia's stocking tops and how her suspenders contrast with the white skin of her thighs.

I hid the jewels from that robbery I done with Slippery Sam in a deserted house in the country. I've suspected Razor Ramsay the Second knows too much and when I open the door to this house I have a good view of the pistol he's pointing at me.

With the jewels in his pocket he slides into my Jaguar and speeds off.

I have to make it back on foot. So I trundle on, wearing down my shoe leather till I continue barefooted, become blistered. My suit gets wet, I'm rummaging in woods, subsisting on roots….

Not quite, that's just me imagining I'm Robert Doughnut on the run in the 39 Steps.

I get back to the city. I'm not going into details. Some writers, even good ones, kick a scene or a joke to death.

Marlowe was doped, locked in a room. It was a great achievement to do simple things like standing up. Chandler gives us pages of it.

When I get back to my office the nurse from Miss Wink's Private Asylum is sitting there.

"You can call me Matron but it'll cost you"

I call her Keyhole Kate because she's always spying on me. She's quite bald, you know, under that wig and she's not particular about changing her linen (so rumour has it) and I'm not at all interested in her chunky thighs encased in fully fashioned stockings.

"The last time I called you Matron you tied a rope round my Henry Halls. Then you injected me and I could hardly walk."

"So I helped you, didn't I?"

"Yes you did. You pulled me behind you with the rope. And what a view I had."

(There was no linen under that thin white uniform, just as long as you know.)

"If I'd known that" she smiles, "I'd have tugged you harder...Miss Wink says you are ready for the first anomaly."

"What?"

Miss Wink, entering, says "Anomalies are idiosyncratic situations contrary to normal practice. For example, a mere slip of a girl like Nursey may control a big important man like Captain Moonlight."

"I'd hardly call her a mere slip," I whisper.

"I heard that! Oh Miss Wink, if it wasn't for my Christian fortitude I don't know what I'd do."

"It sustains us all, my dear. With notable exceptions" she says and I feel the force of her gaze even through the fabric of her veil. "If only he'd *believe*."

"He told me he was a hitman called the Slasher and you'd never know where he'd slash next."

Miss Wink shakes her head sorrowfully. "That's him all over. Last week he was a private eye and before that a district attorney."

"That's right, miss, with his mail-order detective kit and dummy gun. He thinks this isolation chamber is his office."

"Time for his injection."

Wait till you hear this
I'm back in my office now. Mrs O tracked me down. I always said landladies would make good detectives. I made up the money I owed her by becoming a pavement artist.

My eye catches the egg-timer that supposedly holds Harriet's ashes. It's in a pride of place on the window sill. I owe her that much.

I do miss her in a way. But I think a married can not be his true self. He compromises too much. Still, them were days.

PART FOUR

Miss Tweedie's emporium for menials

You may recall Miss Merrylegs. I hardly do myself. Something to do with cops. I follow her and Francis the talking mule to the office. She dismounts. She says

"Oh me, oh my, how can I stir you? Come to me, dick in one hand, fifty quid in the other."

Yes, I remember her now. But back to the present. Here's Mrs Clipper, a first class craft.

"Miss Tweedie, I want an undermaid with no followers. I also want Church of England so that she doesn't take time off on Sundays."

"All religions can be catered for" I assure her.

"Well, the Reverend Clipper does have strict morals and he likes to be familiar with the undergarments of our servants including our butler to see if they are decent of course."

I hold up my hand. "Greek is all the go, I hear, and fetish quite the fashion. Follow me, modom."

We go down to the cellar. Twelve green body bags hang from hooks. I give a shout:

"'Tis a cunning old rat that won't eat the cheese, right men?"

"Correct, sir!" respond the occupants in unison, as I taught them.

Portuguese Joe is sitting on a stool in the corner like little Jack Horner. He's wearing a one-piece combination of trousers and jacket.

"Buttons, take down this bag and let Mrs Clipper examine Daisy Dumpling."

Yes, it's Harriet's old ma. I've tried to get rid of her for years. Even Harriet wouldn't take her.

She seems her usual half-hearted self as she sits there smoking a Kensitas and watching Mrs Clipper poke her ma in the ear.

"My dear tulip" I say to her, "what did you do today?"

"I fell into a pit and broke my legs."

"Nothing special then. What did you see?" She shakes her head. "You should have an eye for the natural world."

"I saw some worms."

"I'll ask Dr Lovelock to see you. He knows about wives...I'll have to go now or I'll be late for choir practice." Mrs Clipper is shaking her head too.

"Buttons, put that old cow back in her bag...She's all I have till tomorrow, modom," I tell her and we go upstairs.

In my office there's an ancient mariner wearing a toggle-fastened duffle coat, a roll-neck jumper and wellington boots.

"Where you been?" I ask Grandpa Higgins.

"On the Atlantic convoy."

"Forty years overdue," I say to Mrs Clipper.

"It's quite alright. We have our lunatic fringe in the Church too."

Grandpa Higgins scratches his head. "War not over yet? Did I miss much?"

I think he's been in prison all this time.

"Where you gonna put me up?" he asks.

I have a spare body bag. "Go down to the cellar, I'll be with you shortly."

"Those bags are police property" Miss Merrylegs reminds me as she walks in.

"So Constable Cisco said when he poked his nose in last week."

"He's gone missing."

(Such a fuss he's making in that body bag.)

"Perhaps Clothilda had him for dinner."

"Is that why you have her in an iron cage in the cellar surrounded by barbed wire?" she asks.

"I was wondering who that horrible woman was, staring at me. Let's go and see." I notice another cage. "Who's that?"

"Before I put the choke pear in she said her name was Harriet" Buttons tells me.

"Didn't I put her in an egg timer?"

"You can't get rid of wives that easy."

"Wait till I get my hands on that Slim Jim."

"He sold you a pig in a poke."

"A cat in a bag, I call it."

"Call it what you like," advises Miss Merrylegs, "but it's still false pretences. I'd bring in Inspector Gorse but he's missing too."

Buttons has a question: "In the meantime what we going to do with...you know who?"

"Daisy Dumpling, you mean?" I ask.

"No, I mean---"

"I know, Clothilda, right?"

"No." He nods towards...

"She's only a trick of the light. I was talking to the real Harriet a few minutes ago."

Miss Merrylegs tells me, "Barney, you're going to have to stop pretending. Harriet is no longer with us."

"I have a sorrow in my heart" I sob.

"He needs to see a doctor" says Buttons.

"A classic case of refusing to face facts," declares the persona of Dr Lovelock. "I once had a patient whose son was feared drowned. Every night for years she walked the river bank calling his name."

"What happened to her?"

"She fell in and was drowned...All the while her son was living in a caravan in Bournemouth with her young sister."

Buttons is moved. "Makes you feel humble."

I consult Dr Lovelock.

"Thank you, doctor" I say. You have reminded me of the pointlessness of this existence."

"If you feel like that I shall book you into Cold Bath Manor, an establishment for the emotionally subnormal run remotely using a public address system by a bitter former headmistress not unknown to readers of the *News of the World*."

"It'll be like old times for you at Borstal" Miss Merrylegs suggests.

"I prefer the term Approved School."

"I suppose you're still missing her" says Grandpa Higgins.

"Who?"

"Harriet."

"Oh her, yes."

"I didn't like her neither. I met her before you and I thought from the start she was a bad 'un."

"And you waited till now to tell me, you prick," I say to Grandpa.

The Crusher has just come in. "She weren't all bad or I wouldn't have called her Baby Doll a year ago."

"Yes you're right. She deserved better" I say. "It's a state occasion when one of those royal birds kick the bucket but when my poor Harriet passed away nobody made a fuss over her."

"You certainly didn't," says Miss Merrylegs.

"I LOVE this time of year" Cousin Betsy says to me as I look at her paintings on the wall. Santa being crucified, the Virgin Mary on a broomstick.

"I see you have your own pre-Christian understanding of this traditional time."

"If you say so."

I see an array of handbags in the corner.

"You still nicking from the shops?"

"Only to supplement my benefits. I've got a racket going now with all these immigrants taking up the council houses and hostels from our own British scum. I'm able to get housing benefit and carers' allowance for over fifty hopeless cases."

"Where do you put them all?"

She goes over to a door. "In here. Go in if you can."

I force the door with difficulty and I see men jammed so close they can only stand up tight against each other. It's like Yeshov's hey-day at the Lubyanka.

"Keep your hands to yourselves" she shouts at them as I close the door.

ARSELICKERS ANONYMOUS
"My name is Miss Lickbottom," says Lushous Louise "and I'm in charge here.

"My name is the Crusher and I'm a fruit."

"My name is Dr Lovelock, noted for my manly figure and signature green bow-tie and I specialise in well-padded female bottoms."

"My names are many" says Percy Catchpole, "and I deal with face-crime."

A development of thought-crime in which people don't put on a happy face when thinking about homosexuals, transgenders and ethnics. I'll have to watch myself and stop moving my lips when I'm thinking.

"You're in the wrong room, mate" I tell him.

"No I'm not. I want to be everywhere, watching and listening.."

"Why don't you stay at home and mind your own business?"

Catchpole shakes his head. "I hate it there. My wife doesn't understand me."

That's because she's a recent immigrant from the Belgian Congo.

THE FOOTSTOOL
It's Sleepy Sid, considerably smaller after all that time bent over in a glass

cage.

"Look who it is. I still think about you taking those first steps, bumping into things cause you could only look down. How Mrs O and me used to laugh."

Here's Wally the Whale, singing and dancing as the floor vibrates. "Daddy wouldn't buy me a bow wow, Daddy wouldn't buy me a bow wow, I'm very fond of twat and there's nothing wrong with that, but I'd rather have a bow wow wow."

I think I could dislike Wally the Whale.

"He's not the same since his lobotomy" Sleepy Sid informs me. "He's dogs on the brain."

"Tell me, Sleepy," I say, "whose bitch are you?"

"He's my lap dog" Mrs O'Harnessey calls out, entering the room. Though he's not allowed on the sofa."

"I'm not even allowed in the bleeding house" he complains.

"Quite so. You have your burrow on the hill. Many a badger would be proud of that."

"So I've noticed. I've had to fight them off. And she makes me eat dirt."

"Who is *she*?" Mrs O asks. "Oh with what marvellous nicety does my surly hound invite more...."

"More dirt, madam?"

"Yes, Wally. Another mouthful."

CAMP CANDLESTICK

This is the ass with much to be borne that carried the maiden through the corn who milked the man with the crooked horn who told off the dog that chased the cat that killed the rat that ate the mouse that lived in the house that Jack built.

Cousin Jack that is. Of course he was never the same after meeting those soldiers in Southampton Fields near the British Museum.

"That's nothing" says Miss O'Shea, "my whippet once ate a consecrated wafer in York Minster."

Crusher has his say too. "What about me? I follow Miss Eddie about like a dog."

"Only when I let you" retorts Eddie. She turns to Miss O'Shea, "I hope God didn't mind being eaten by your dog."

Sound of thunder. "What makes you think I need to be worshipped and constantly praised? I'm not a bloody narcissist."

I think that was the Almighty. Anyway, there's the clatter of hooves on cobblestones. We look up and behold a pale horse and his name that sits on him is Death and Hell follows with him.

The company is wailing. Mrs Clipper is digging her spurs into Francis the talking mule who says, "This is the worst hymn I've ever heard."

"The day Delaney's donkey won the half mile race" sings Mrs Clipper who has had a drop taken.

Francis is not pleased. "I've told you before I'm not a friggin' donkey."

DOWN IN THE DUMPS

I'm singing to myself, missing my worst enemy:

"Underneath the table, sitting in a state..Harriet I remember the way you used to wait...my lily of the limelight---"

"Stop it, Barney!" Eddie interrupts. "You're like one of those husbands who cry crocodile tears at press conferences."

"I know a guilty husband when I see one."

Look out, here's the donkey express.

"Miss Tweedie when do I get my undermaid?" asks Mrs Clipper.

"Today, modom, she's in great shape, bubbling with excitement."

"He means she's got hot flushes and is menopausal" says Francis the talking mule.

"What do you know about women?" I ask, giving him a poke.

"You can tell a lot from arses."

"Watch it" I warn him, "or you'll be made into a stew and dished up before Dave King."

There's that name again. I shouldn't have said it, and there he is, smirking as usual.

"I come with a dispensation from Rome, me and Fibber McGee."

"What's Rome got to say for itself?"

"Permission to make dolls of the Mercy of St Agnes."

"You want to watch her" I warn. She'll take the shirt right off your back."

Enter the Blonde. I doff my hat to her bright red lipstick illuminating her face like a stigmatic wound. She strides over and pulls off my dicky,

No, not my bow-tie, my false shirt front.

"Typical male" scoffs the Blonde. "Can't even find himself a clean shirt."

"Oh St Agnes" pleads Dave King mockingly. "show mercy to this piece of trash who is at a low ebb."

I hear the voice of Harriet. "Poppycock. I left a drawer of clean ebbs. He never could find anything."

"Those happy days are over" I say sadly. "The Council evicted me. I'm now in a doss house bullied and starved by a one-eyed Mr Squeers and I've been attacked by a pack of angry terriers."

Be patient. This gets better. I think I'll tell you of the time I first met this cracker outside the Lido Lounge.

We're in the back seat of my Wolseley. She's pulled her skirt up and is sitting on my face. As you do. There's a tapping on the window.

"Barney Higgins!" shouts an irate voice. "What do you think you're doing? Who is that woman?"

The doll moves onto my chest. I think it over. I try to be fair. I put my specs back on, give my companion a quizzical look, I say: "She's got a right to know. What *is* your name?"

"It's Louise. Some call me Lushous. Though I can't say why."

You could cut the atmosphere around Harriet's face with one of the daggers she's looking at me.

"Really, Harriet, don't get into one of your states...And you, Lushous or whatever your name is, watch what you're sitting on in future."

I get out of the car. I don't notice the wife has a baseball bat. I get knocked into ...

The middle of next week
An ante-room of that part of the Footstool kept for the entertainment of the World Council of Churches.

"As gravity has its hold over men so does lust" Billie informs us.

Miss Susie says "There's no cooing and billing, just give me a shilling."

"It's difficult to grasp they're capable of higher feelings" says Edith of Nancy Town.

"Prepare to meet your exorcist" shouts Billie. "Are we all here? Are we omnipresent?"

The vicars on a row of crucifixes nod their heads and say "Let us pay."

A toady of Pickwickian build in a clerical gown sidles up. Eddie gives him an almighty shove. "Out of the way, old Dan Tucker...Make way for the exorcist. It's time" she calls "for you pulpit thumpers to get...."

The vicars in unison shout "Thumped!"

The four dames walk along the line of crucifixes. The vicars shout "Cleanse us dear sisters from our secret blights, for we are naught but shitheads in thy sight."

"My servants shall lick the dust" commands the exorcist.

"And we are the driest of that dust!"

We next meet the vicars at...

ALIMONIA
Prepare yourself, this is like a scene from Gustave Dore.

Several dames are lying exorbitantly on their backs smelling an odour of sanctity from the rotting vicars lying in a heap as the stripes on their backs disappear and doves fly out of their mouths, and cats scamper round destitute former members of the Lionel Blair Dancers.

"Has anyone here seen Kelly, Kelly from the emerald isle?" ask the Mike Sammes Singers.

And they don't enquire in vain. "I'm here, Madame, waiting for my carriage" cries an exultant Kelly.

Miss Stark ignores her. "A good curate is all very well" she says to Madame Mao, "notwithstanding their churchy smell, but they're really more trouble than they're worth."

"C'est ca, we can not live on hymns alone."

"Look at the state of them" observes Miss Stark. "I think Dr Lovelock should have given them some treatment."

I shake my head. "These creatures are what we call at the university last leggers or goners. You can expect them to expire between the Ascension and Whit Sunday."

(I enrolled in the university of life at an early age when Cousin Betsy took me upstairs. I still haven't graduated)

Madame Mao shrugs. "I do not 'ear much of the praying going on."

"Haven't got our money's worth, have we?" says Miss Stark.

I put up my hand. "Ladies, at this extreme junction they expect you to pray over them."

"I'd sooner piss over them" retorts Miss Stark.

"I don't blame you" I say. "Most of them don't even accept evolution ever took place 'cause it's not in the Bible…Take this specimen for example." I bring in Sleepy Sid. "Look at his small stature and rudimentary spinal cord, his long nails." I shove Sleepy out and in comes the Ogre slouching like a gorilla.

"See how he has evolved" I continue. "See how his nails, through the power of natural selection, are now like fish hooks on account of him having to fish for food.."

A bald head arises from the heap of vicars.

"He's having you on" cries Uncle Cecil. "Evolution doesn't happen that quick."

"Why not" I say. "You lot can talk about miracles but it seems us evolutionists are not allowed to."

Miss Stark agrees with me. "You're right. He thinks his lot have a monopoly."

We all sit upright when Amelia strides up. "So that's where that old croaker's got to….Uncle Cecil you have deserted your post…I left him standing guard over the explosives shed" she explains.

"He was hiding" I tell her. "He was seen snarling too."

"So would you if you'd spent 29 years in the Bastille" he exclaims.

"That's no excuse. We have to put a stop to these rustics blowing themselves up."

"It does waste the dynamite" I comment.

Oh God, not her again

"Miss Tweedie, my undermaid has scarpered." She spies Uncle Cecil. "There she is! Even without the wig and make-up I'd know that horrible face anywhere."

I knew it was a mistake to send the old fool in to rob the place.

"The Rev Clipper had his suspicions too. Though he has a place in his heart for Pan's People he tries not to control his exaltation when he saves the souls of ugly wretches in his cellar, when he sees angels and utters imprecations...So Miss Kelly the verger used to tell me before she disappeared."

I'm pleased to say, "I bring good tidings. She is here. She was driven mad and we took her in."

Mrs Clipper becomes agitated. "Not mad, I tell you, not mad. Bewitched!"

She falls in a swoon, beats the floor with her fists. "Such lies as she told."

"Hey you," I say to Francis the talking mule, "take your hoof off her neck."

BARNEY'S OFFICE
Dame Looney lowers herself into my creaky visitors chair. Widmerpool (my penis) isn't that interested so Captain Moonlight takes over the interview. He's not so easily manipulated.

"Let's cut out the lies" I tell her, "get to why you're really here."

That's the way to deal with them.

"Alright" she sighs, "WooWang wants Uncle Cecil to give up one of his nippons but he won't   do it."

"Why?"

"He was at Unit 731."

This was a place where the heroes of the rising sun carried out disgusting experiments on the Chinese. The Americans let them go free in exchange for the results of their "research".

THE RUINS

I wait till Uncle Cecil is playing with his Sultanas then me and my mumble-headed Manxmen sneak up on those Japs.

I hear a voice from behind. "Don't look back. You know what happened to Lot's wife."

But I do turn round. It's the Rev Clipper dressed as a Roman soldier. "I wield the spear that smote our Lord."

He runs amok and before I can stop him there are Manxmen and Japs lying dead on all sides.

DOWN WOOWANG'S ALLEY

I take an axe, chop off a nip's head, take it to the Chinaman.

"There by he hand of providence – with a little help from Captain Moonlight – is your revenge."

"You catchee trouble. It more better to bling him live."

You can't please some people. I make a dash for my Jaguar.

A bolt from WooWang's crossbow takes off my hat.

A PIT OF DESPOND
A voice. "Be warned of the yawning depths that are the loins of masked women."
 "Yes they might give you more than you desire. What's your name?"
 "Some call me Filomena."
 "Some call me Madame."
 "Look here, Madame Mao," I say "somebody's made a model of me in wax. What's it for?"
 "Do not ask me. I have other fish to fry. I shall ride a cock horse to Butterfly Cross."
 "You'll have spikes on your gloves and a switch in your hand."
 "As breaker of steeds I will be much in demand."
 "Who's this fish you want to fry?" I ask.
 "Not who but what. It's the Witch of Wookey."
 "Just call me Witchfinder Higgins."
 Filomena puts a hand on my shoulder. "I have warned you."
 "Tush!" I sing as I go out, "Oh do you know the muffin man, the muffin man, oh do you know the muffin man who lives in Drury Lane?"
 I notice the wax figure melting leaving only a pair of specs. Correct me if

I'm wrong but Auntie Atlas said I'd be immune to other witches if I ...to put it politely...lay down with her.

Of course I did burn up her book of mysteries by staring at it and she did fall down the hole I'd dug and covered over with leaves, and if I did do those things I didn't mean to.

I better go to Norfolk Island and ask her.

Amelia's not the only one who can have a mine. Miss Susie's there. She says, "I'll make Stakhanovites of them miners yet."

"You what?" asks Duckie Baconbrains.

"They're pillars hanging from a mine's roof" I explain. To Miss Susie I say,

"Don't expect him to know much. He was brung up in a rabbit hutch. Look at him twitching his ears."

A big blow across the back of my knees sends me reeling. I'm lying flat out when Miss Susie decides to put her foot down.

Right on my kisser.

You may be wondering how I got to the Island. Or you may not. I'll tell you anyway.

Clothilda, the fattest woman to ever sail round the world, brought me there like a commando on a mission along with Duckie Baconbrains as a fallguy.

I get to my feet. I say to the wall, "Little dost they know that I am a secret spy. My purpose that dame shall not suggest and never no more to call me fool."

I'm seeking out the mine owners, a cabal of Frenchmen. I'll recognise them by their sneering faces.

And that insolence soon disappears when I blow the entrance of the mine.

Not since the Suez scandal has there been such a row on account of me bumping off the entire French cabinet.

Clothilda is overjoyed. "Well done Captain Moonlight. You even got that prick De Gaulle. Were you nervous?"

"Nope. Cool as a cucumber."

"That reminds me," she smiles, hitching up her dress. "You have richly earned your reward."

I need help. Pythagoras is adept at causing panic in otherwise unflappable fat women. He jumps out of my pocket, runs up her leg, into her smock, hickory dickory dock.

Lo and behold Duckie has escaped the explosion and comes in riding on Frances the talking mule.

"Where'd you come from?" I ask.

"I come from Wookey" says Francis. "I was once a man until the witch turned nasty."

"I know the type."

"She used to ride about on me wearing slippers and spurs. I escaped once but the magistrates sent me back, why go somewhere else to be teased and taunted, they said, when you can have it at home."

"They had a point," I commented. "Other fields seem greener but you can't beat good old fashioned domestic disparagement."

"But she shouts, she screams, she dances on her hat."

"That's what they do after the honeymoon. Just shout back, Scold away, you disagreeable bitch."

"The baggage roars throughout the hall" cries Duckie. "Only loonies talk to the wall."

What a thing to say.

Think about this as a therapy. While the nutters talk to the wall for half an hour the trickcyclists could assume the lotus position (with whatever difficulty) and restore their own mental calm. Well, sanity is in the eye of the beholder.

Matron comes in followed by Sir Giles shaking a tambourine and singing,

"She has wings on her fingers and angels on her toes, she shall make mayhem wherever she goes."

"Here's Sally in our alley" observes Ducky Baconbrains.

Well, the music stops, time stalls. Sir Giles is the first to move. He strides over to me. "You sir are a party to this calumny." He takes off a glove, swipes it across my face. "Meet me in a field tomorrow for a duet."

Matron puts on her fiercest face, fixes Duckie with a stare and turns him to jelly, Sir Giles does a little dance. "She freezes her foes 'cause she knows her rights, this wise Medusa in her unconquered tights."

It's not like Matron to relinquish one of the elements of her sensual power but I expect she will find that stockings are better in the long run.

THE Titanic has become a private club as the sign on the door makes clear: MEMBERS AND NON-MEMBERS ONLY.

"But control your exultation" I say to the Crusher. You are far too horrible to be let in."

"Fibber McGee is allowed in."

"He has a dispensation from Rome."

(And I have a warning from Billie. I sing "I'll take you home again Kathleen" one more time and I'm barred too)

The Crusher's not giving up. "The Ogre's not banned and he's far more horrible than me."

"Use your loaf, the Ogre goes where he wants."

Billie has employed Ester as a greeter. "Velcome mein Herron. I insist zat you vill yourselfs enjoy."

Billie is not quite herself. She's had romantic trouble with a silver-tongued Sardine called Jim Dandy,

Here he comes now. "Viva Madame Zero!" he shouts. "Is she in?"

God knows why he calls her that.

"She's not here. She left a message: Get lost."

Jim Dandy is not fazed. "Viva Sleepy Sid!"

Sleepy has won a lottery, bought himself a peerage by making a large donation to the societies for the prosecution and persecution of British soldiers (the ministries of justice and defence) and now, being lame, boss-backed and one-eyed fits in nicely with the loonies, placemen, senileties, absentees, knife and forkmen and sore thumbs in the chumocracy known almost ironically as the House of Lords.

I stand aside and let in both Jim Dandy and the Crusher. I like now and then to show the kinder face of bouncerism. Besides, the drabs will skin them alive in there.

Let you and me go inside and see. The Ogre take my place at the door.

"Grin and bear it" says Growler Groves as he chokes me with hands like flower pots. I uphold the dignity of bouncers and the next you see of him is when he's crawling about on hands and knees.

One of the high-class sluts gets on his back. "Gee up Growler" He doesn't move. "Let's try Giddy up." Same result. So she dismounts, takes off her panties and attaches them to a cane like a fish held on a pole in front of a dog team. Even that doesn't work so she puts on a lead and pulls him along.

"I'm going to lock you up and throw away the keyhole" she says in a right fit of temper.

She opens a cubby-hole, pulls out Sleepy Sid and shoves Growler in his place.

"You're going to the warehouse, your lordship" she says menacingly. "He's going to give up the title" she tells me, "cos he's fearful about winning a lottery without buying a ticket."

Sleepy agrees. "There's a trick there somewhere."

"He needs a nurse to put him to bed in his cold room," the high-class slut advises, "where he will listen for one hour to tapes of Percy Catchpole instructing all Englanders on how to self-oppress."

I'm not so sure. "That could be a waste of time. He's only half-baked, you know."

"In which case we shall solder on an iron collar and put him head first in the water barrel."

"How far I have fallen in just one day!" laments Sleepy.

I'm touched by his anguish. "Can't we let him learn to self-suppress and do some self-guarding too?"

"Well alright, as long as he keeps on the collar."

Sleepy crawls over, hugs my legs. "How can I ever thank you?"

Lady Broomhilda appears and offers Sleepy some advice.

"Take no notice when those last-leggers, tired of life in a warehouse, begin to eat each other."

We feel an uprising of happiness at this unexpected comfort for the poor wretch. We sing: "Broomhilda is all my joy, Broomhilda is my delight, Broomhilda is my heart of gold, and who but Lady Broomhilda."

Later
It's a bad quarter of an hour when your three well-stacked female confidantes gang up agin you.

Eddie says: "Now Harriet is gone you can make of me an honest woman."

Lushous Louise: "Impossible. From now on I want all your favours and money too. You have made me promises."

Billie: "In bed, I'll wager. Such promises are never kept nor expected to be." She shows the ring I pinched. "Does this not signify our betrothal?"

"Ah my beauties" I say, "how can I choose one over the other?"

Eddie says she slighted.

Lushous Louise's life is blighted.

Billie says she's so ashamed.

"Let this rogue be blamed" says Lady Broomhilda. She walks around swirling her long Tudor gown, "All these years he's kept me short; so many times he's been in court; as his fancies, you're three of many; he needs not a wife, but wants a nanny."

THE FOOTSTOOL
Early one morning just as the sun was shining Mrs O opens her black eyes and reaches for a fag. Portuguese Joe winces softly as she pulls his ear.

"Let's face it" she taunts him, "You're no good for anything, are you?"

"I've been helpful in your fiddles---"

"That's enough of that. I want someone who can rob a bank and that's not you. So I've decided to stake you out on Norfolk Island. Medical students will descend on you to further their knowledge of anatomy, then the crows and magpies will take their share of you, feral dogs will then sniff you out, and finally, lawyers will pick through what remains."

Two hours later
Mrs O'Harnessey asks "Where is the man who has the courage and skill to rob Barclays? Can such a man exist?"
  "But he can!" exclaims Miss Stark. "And he is here, right in this hall."
  Mrs O looks around her. "I see no such plucky fellow."
  Miss Stark giggles at Mrs O's lack of perception. "Yes you do. It's Barney, Barney Higgins."
  I'm sitting here thinking about lashing Matron to a chariot and dragging her body in triumph thrice round the walls of Troy.
  "Barney! I've told you off before about that."
  "Sorry, Matron, I didn't know you were listening."
  "She can hear your hair grow" says Miss Stark.
  "And the beat of your heart."
  "She is the Helen of my Troy" I say.
  "I dwell in dark clouds." Matron tells us. "My dish is hunger and my bed is sickness. I have a job for you."

AT THE BANK
Here I stand, driven from Troy by the starkest of choices, much am I harassed, tossed in my mind, a prey to voices. Here I am, alone in a queue, staring at fragments that come into view, sirens and stars and faces in masks. And the girl with red hair looks up and asks "What can I do for you?"

"Twenty Players, please" is all I can say.

THE FOOTSTOOL
Matron is not pleased. "Go into the small kitchen" she tells me, "for now it is time for the Aunts to do unto you with reason and rhyme."

These Aunts are kept in unfurnished chambers till they are so cross they're ready with crochet needles and hooks.

I open the door and I see two fat Aunts who don't just dominate the room, they seem to be wearing it.

"Lay into him, Macduffs" orders Matron.

Here's Homer in a nutshell, says I to meself as the magnetism of the Aunts catches the steel plate in my head as they reach out for my tomdoolies with slow sad smiles on their pudgy faces.

"Now that I am in your grasp" I tell them, "consider bold Atlas, with whom you ran and sang and sinned. For I am her familiar too. You'll know my spells and voodoo when I whistle up the wind."

The Aunts shrink back in horror. I back out of the small kitchen and march away. Matron is impressed in spite of herself.

MRS Clipper is back. "Oh Miss Tweedie, there's a footman hiding in the bushes. May I have him?"

"He's a shy one, modom" I tell her, "but he does a very adequate Jack Benny impression."

"That's not the impression I'm trying to make."

"And what would that be, modom?"

"Last year Mrs O'Harnessey won the Turner Prize with a real life depiction of a bull in a china shop. This year her entry will be even more ambitious. So, for my entry I've decided to show twelve pretty maids in a row covered in flour."

"Naked of course?"

"Naturally."

Let's go over to

The Footstool
And see how ambitious Mrs O is.

"To avoir le chic I stop at nothing" she says, but it seems she didn't stop at copying Eddie's idea at the music hall. She has four shrivelled old timers on their backs gazing up through reinforced glass at several trollops from the Seven Stars. She also has a skeleton which she claims is a relic of Winston Churchill. She's missed the small label on it which says "Property of Southampton Medical School."

DON'T be vague, go back to the Hague. There's a bunch of them lying in a heap. Mynheer Closh lifts his head momentarily from the exorbitant backside of Meister Pickel Herringe.

"Dem strumpets, zey took all dat ve had."

"These netherman are out for the count. Get on the blower to WooWang and sell this lot by the pound."

"Hold on, Uncle Cecil" I say. "What about the Turner Prize?"

He ponders. "'Tis an idea. But they won't keep still."

"That's the beauty of it. A pile of wriggly sweaty naked Dutch maggots. It can't fail,"

But it does. Even WooWang won't take them. Says they smell. He thinks all Westerners smell.

However, Miss Stark takes them on approval.

THE RUINS

"Where'd you find him?" I say to the Crusher who is throttling Ducky Baconbrains.

"He was hiding in the donjon with an iron ring round his neck attached to the wall.

I give Ducky a poke. "You couldn't watch him. And I've noticed he's taken on airs lately."

"How glorious am I!" exclaims Ducky.

"Not here, you don't" I say as the wretch puts his hand up his petticoat and starts to J Arthur himself.

Peter Pieman comes in and says to Miss Stark, "Twenty sheep head pies as ordered."

"Who are they for?" I ask.

"The Bowibu, the North Korean secret police. They're in the cellar."

Ten minutes later Portuguese Joe rushes up, wearing his Prushun helmet with the spike on top. "There's trouble at pit. Ginger Jones is using sign language to make them revolt against you."

Ginger Jones!

"How he has turned against me" Miss Stark reflects. "Only last night he was licking my feet."

"Aren't they eating their pies?" I ask.

Portuguese Joe shakes his head. "No they only eat humans. That's all that's left in North Korea."

"Good job I had the foresight" smiles Miss Stark, "to obtain those fat Hollanders."

CRAVEN COTTAGE
The domicile of the dreadful Mrs Rouncival, a loutish lady unattractive enough to be virtuous but those high stiletto heels bring her no nearer to Heaven.

She is down to her Farthingale, which she will shortly take off, placing the petticoat over the head of Bobby Barlow, a naval rating gone AWOL. He's now her footman, prized for his splendid calves and maypole around which she likes to dance.

That's not to say he has it easy. He's ordered here, he's ordered there, poor Bobby is ordered everywhere, she even shouts at him to lift his feet. But they came for him one night, the shore patrol high-stepping along the cobbles, a bit twee but better than goosestepping.

"We can do that too" says the chief pretty officer.

Mrs Rouncival is not displeased. "Hello sailors!"

"We're working on double high-heeled time" adds the Chief.

"Now before you go" she says to Bobby, "you may pay homage to my regal figure."

When he hesitates she urges "Go on, this is your last chance."

So he kneels, she steps back, kicks off his head. "Oops a daisy." His bonce rolls in its shroud along the floor. "I said I'd never let them take you, and I sometimes keep my promises," she says virtuously.

Disgusted of Dulwich: "You're sick, sick, all of you."

You can't really trust coppers, can you? If you are ever on trial your defence (and the CPS) will receive only the evidence they care to give it. Disclosure? Your brief can't ask for something he doesn't know exists.

They have tunnel vision. Amelia has been abusing her husbands for years. That's okay because in their poor minds the female is always the victim.

What has Inspector Gorse got to say: "Look, don't expect us to think as the public does. It takes a special type of person who wants to join the police. It is a lot easier to persecute elderly men on the word of a fantasist than it is to   patrol the streets. Heaven forbid."

"One of the reasons shops go out of business" I say to him, "is the wave of shoplifting which you do nothing about."

The Inspector laughs. "You have an idealistic view of what policing is about."

Eddie says to him in a whisper, "Leave Barney's illusions alone. If it wasn't for them he'd see us girls as we really are."

I get glimpse of an angel singing "My old man said follow the band..."

"Who are you, celestial vision?"

"What's the score in Baltimore?"

"Look who it is" I say. "You've fooled me again."

(I usually know who it is but it pleases her to think she's surprised me)

"The Big Boss wants you to be an undercover bricklayer" says Miss Lovely.

"Foreman bricklayer."

"Alright, foreman bricklayer at Lady Cadaver's estate. She's building a folly."

"She'll recognise the artistry of my brickwork which taken in the abstract and sanctioned at a higher level---"

"Stop talking nonsense and take your hand off my leg."

"It'll be good to pick up the trowel again."

"So you'll know what you're doing?"

"I ask you, does anyone really know what they're doing?"

"Does it matter?" she asks.

"No, very little really matters."

LADY CADAVER'S ESTATE

Here comes my darling of Dutch dreams, Edith of Nancy Town. "This place is weird" she says, "I hear whisperings through keyholes and rustlings behind curtains."

"This is my muddled- headed Monkmen at work."

"Colonel Cadaver has soldiers standing to attention in full dress uniform outside doors."

"They for ornamental purposes. I expect they've seen my spies but they're not allowed to move."

"Crafty Barney" she laughs.

"I prefer brains to brawn" I say, springing up and grabbing two of Amelia's escaped husbands. "I wonder if there's a reward" I add, banging their heads together.

Edith looks puzzled. "Do you know these ruffians?"

"Yes, Sir Cuddy from the Tin Islands and Sir Childer from the Crystal Hills. She calls them her cross-legged knights."

(That's because she kept them under the stairs and let them out only once a day to have a slash)

"Are they dangerous?" Edith asks.

"My word, yes. They've turned into mutants."

I grab her arm, pull her to me until our lips almost meet. "Come with me. I'll save you." We walk away hand in hand and I'm not pleased to see Mrs Clipper.

"Miss Tweedie, you're fired."

"She's confused me with someone else" I say to a bewildered Edith.

"I think she's wise to you" says Francis the talking mule.

"You know where you can shove your undermaids" says Mrs Clipper.

"Really, modom, I'm sure this Miss Tweedie never shoves her dear domestics."

What she says next sends a chill down my legs. "When I passed your emporium I saw a line of body-bags walking by themselves."

Francis guffaws. "In equine terms, your Augean stables have been cleared."

"Asinine in your case" I retort.

"Come on Francis, let's giddy up" Mrs Clipper looks back and smiles. "By the way, you'll get no thanks in Fairbanks."

Well I never! She's done it proper this time. Have Mrs Clipper and Miss Lovely been one and the same all this time and I haven't noticed? Who is Mrs Clipper, what is she?

I don't know. Just kicking some ideas about.

I am not afraid to look upon Lady Cadaver's wrathful face. I am surrounded by enemies but I stand fast. I have to, seeing as I'm being crucified. I am agitated but not sad. I am wounded all over with wounds.

Come evening the Monkmen begin a wretched dirge. I don't blame them. They've all been rounded up and put in chains.

Lady Cadaver gives me a good prodding. "Look at the state of you,"

I bravely remain tight-lipped as she rubs Widmerpool the wrong way.

Even though she has her curlers in, stockings at half mast and has been padding about in old slippers, and those shimmering thighs with a hint of cellulite.

There's a sound of wailing as Portuguese Joe is brought before her in trembling and fear. Thrown at her feet. Then, in the greatest of misery, knowing he has to part with something very dear to him, turns his miserable face downwards and, fearful of the answer, asks "How much do I owe you?"

"Two ponies" replies Lady Cadaver. "Even though you spent your money before you got to the shop, you still have to pay me. What on earth were you playing at?"

"I was looking at the underwear section in a Littlewoods catalogue" he admits, "and it just happened."

The dirty devil!

Trouble when it comes next is in the shape of the Blonde. "Come on, Joe, render unto Caesar."

He pays Lady Cadaver the £50, slouches away, eyes downward from the steely gaze of the two dames.

The Blonde looks up at me with reluctant admiration. "So you've finally made it. You're now a real spy. And you know what happens to spies when they're captured, don't you?"

My ears are ringing as she lands slaps on them.

Lady Cadaver stops her. "Agnes, don't get the wrong idea. Look at the way I'm dressed. Higgins is paying for this. He calls it nostalgie de la boue."

A RESIDENTIAL NUTHOUSE

As you come in Marigold is on her knees crying as she strangles me.

Miss O'Shea tells me, "Don't blame her. Working here is very stressful.

That's why you are in a straitjacket."

"Ah, Higgins," says Dr Ragamuffin. "It is you I have been after for very long. None of your monkee business here. The people of the different sexes, for example, men and women, are kept separate."

"Widows in their knickers and honey in my horn," I croak, "I've never been so happy since the day that I was born."

"Raving again, doctor, shall she continue?"

"This is not a preferable treatment of practice."

"Ester goes to Berlin in a fine rig, home again home again, jiggety jig."

The doctor shrugs his shoulders. "It is a pity that his cookie has crumbled to this extent."

"Don't blind us with science" I remark.

"It all started, yes indeed, when he was banned from Morris dancing at an early age."

Miss O'Shea is impressed. "Amazing. You went to the heart of the matter in only five minutes."

He looks at his Rolex. "Now I must be going to check the dishing of grub. We must be careful not to overload their stomachs with heavy nosh."

"Quite right" agrees Miss O'Shea. "A bowl of skilly and some acorn bread. What more can loonies want?"

"Let us be calling them, patients."

"By the way," adds Miss O'Shea, "I had to take down that salt lick you put up for the patients. They were slobbering all over it."

"Like the cattle before them" I say.

Dr Ragamuffin goes out. I notice he's still wearing his bicycle clips. Marigold gives me a nod. Another day undercover and I didn't have to try very hard.

Wait till you hear this

Don't turn up your nose at my dirty washing. Most of us will have sad endings. Life is something we just have to get on with. Even when we can't.

There's always suicide of course. Which, when you come to think of it, if you ever do, is a pretty hostile review of the one-act play.

PART FIVE

In case you are wondering I'm still at the nuthouse, Dr Ragamuffin sold it to Miss Wink. Here she comes now. "I won't take off me coat. I'm not stopping."

"You know I haven't been fed" I complain.

She claps her hands. "Smiler! Bring some cheese and crackers."

He comes back with a tray. She pushes cream cheese up my nose.

"Even though you are the most insignificant operative of The Way of the Arch there must be something you can tell me about the Big Boss."

"What's in it for me?" I manage to say.

"I'm glad you asked that. The simple answer is...nothing. On the other hand stay schtum and Smiler will cut off your manhood and give it to the foxes."

"I don't approve of men doing women's work."

"I don't either. It's the role of modern women to do the emasculating."

"That's all very well" I say, "but they come running when the lights fuse or a mouse gets in the house."

"There's nothing wrong with wanting it both ways."

"Not at the same time, I hope" I remark as the Smiler holds out his hand.

"I think we have already been introduced" he says unsurely.

"It's the Ogre."

"You remember!"

"Detectives never forget" Miss Wink says looking at the damage his fish hooks have done to my hand. "Oh how symbolic. The red hand of O'Neil. Heraldry is such the latest fashion."

"Not so" I say. "The blood is being worn inside the skin this season."

"No matter." She claps her hands again. "Pansy put the kettle on and we'll have some tea."

"Stop it," Miss Wink cries, slapping my hand away. "You can't do that here."

The biscuit falls like sludge towards the bottom of my tea. "Which is only fit for a cat" I mumble.

"Take care or the cat will stroke your back, Turkish style" she warns. "You are being stubborn. I won't forget this."

"They say elephants never forget but it's not them who cast up at you about what you did to them five years ago."

Miss Wink gasps. "You dare to make innuendoes about poor innocent wives?"

Two portly figures barge in. Portuguese Joe is wearing his Prushun helmet with the spike on top and is carrying a wooden rifle. Mrs Merkel also has a German helmet, hers has no spike; more up to date, you see.

Portuguese Joe shouts "We have come to rescue you in the face of fearful odds."

"Well I never!" exclaims Miss Wink. "You never know what's round the corner, do you?"

"I do" I say, "where I used to live there was a bookie's and a pub."

Mrs Merkel spies a glass cabinet, runs over to it. "Ach mein Fuhrer! Vake up, ve need you back."

(Wishful thinking. It's Bernard Holland made up as Hitler as Miss Wink's entry for the Turner Prize)

"Kum now, see vat for you I have," she says throwing off her greatcoat. Bernard Holland's cock rises like Topsy.

"Frau Merkel, please excuse this harmless lunatic" I tell her, remembering that I still want to be rescued.

"He vas a lunatic, you say! But by Gott he vas not harmless."

Portuguese Joe is so excited by this replica of his hero lying in a coffin that he lets off an explosive Lionel Bart and the room clears in seconds.

SLEEPY SID'S DATE WITH DESTINY

He sits sizzling in his chair. He's only got one ear, you know. Lost one in the scrum. Boxing Day sales. Miss Shore is his therapist. She's her foot on a lever that's sending electric up his bum.

"When I'm cured I'll be free, I'll no longer walk like Sandra Dee."

"When you're finished" I tell her, "I'll put Miss Stark's magnetic monopoles on him."

"Don't torment him any more than I'm doing."

"I'm sorry but a wrong un is a wrong un in my book."

Miss Shore is struggling to accept the idea that this middle-aged man with a battered face and wearing an antenna on his cap can possibly be a consultant anthropologist. "Your book? You've never even read one. And what's that thing doing on your head?"

"It's a direction finder. It helps me locate the oddities of the human condition for my learned attention, all the way from Clothilda's wobbly buttocks to this relic of a man."

(It's actually a device that allows Lovely Miss Nightingale to make known to me the Big Boss's latest orders. I'm on a mission. Her parting words were Stay on rendezvous alert until I notify you of my amorous requirements.

Miss Shore shakes her head. "What I did say was, Keep away until it is my pleasure to recall you. And do remember that cowboys can be callous down in Dallas."

"But they don't go sleepwalking in their petticoats, do they?"

"Oh Barney, you promised not to tell."

"I only said it to you."

"Sleepy Sid's here. He heard you."

"Well then, we'll have to deal with him, won't we?"

Sleepy's very agitated. "You don't have to. I never heard anything about her sleepwalking in her petticoat."

She gives him the works. His head drops to his chest. She walks over to me, smiling with her fat red lips.

AT THE BLONDE SQUAD

The times are out of joint, what with Spanish practices in the factories and Ugandan business going on in the offices of Westminster resulting in cases of French pox.

This is all too geographical for my liking and it's nice to think some people know how to behave themselves.

I've never met any but then I wouldn't, would I? Being a detective, I mean. Portuguese Joe once said I was very useless and corrupt.

"Just the sort of man we need here at the Blonde Squad" says Commander

Stark.

BARNEY HIGGINS DISTRICT ATTORNEY is the sign on the door of my office. The Commander is all business. "I am the anvil and you, Barney, are the hammer."

"Hammer of the Scots?"

"Not necessarily though they do get on my tits a bit. Work hard and some day you can be the anvil."

"I never thought I could be one of them."

"What arrests have you made?"

I lead her downstairs. Uncle Cecil is pinned in Crusher's crushing machine and all you can see is his baldy head. A throwback to the Middle Ages perhaps but it is sheer pomposity to pour scorn on the tentative and well-intentioned methods of our forbears.

"I'll get you for this, Higgins."

I had arrested him for being Santa Claus without a licence. And he kneeled down and cried with a loud voice. "Look at my robes, look at the date, you can't arrest Santa at Fairyland's gate."

What a nerve and it didn't do my back any good dragging him to my Zodiac as the pack of kids ran after us shouting that I was stealing Father Christmas.

"We have our orders from the Big Boss" says Commander Stark.

"Is this the big boss in Pyongyang or the one who lives next door to Hancock in Railway Cuttings?" I say, wise to her tricks.

Uncle Cecil is like me, never knows when to shut up. "Three old ladies locked in the lavatory" he croaks, "they were there from Monday to Saturday, nobody knew they were there."

The Commander goes to the kitchen, brings in a leek, shoves it down his throat, Lucky Lucy come in, the Commander says to her:

"I thought Barney sold you to the pirates."
"He did, without a single blush."
"It was no way to treat a concubine" observes the Commander.
"But I managed to escape."
"I knew you could do it," I manage to say.

A ROOM IN REGENT STREET

I'm waiting for Mrs Clipper. Beggars can't be choosers. The door opens. It's the wife's identical twin.

"It's all very well, Henrietta, but you can't stop here."
"Oh sir, how can you serve me so?"
"Go fly a kite."
"What a hubristic uncouth overbearing fellow you are."
"You have the gift of the gob. Like your sister."
"How can you possibly go around with Mrs Clipper?"
"She's my latest flame, she's very sweet. I see her twice a week in Regent Street."

She plonks herself on a table, lights up a butt. "It's all or nothing" she whispers, a tear forming in her eye, "that's the way I am."

"Cut out the flim flam. I know who you are."

She makes a whistle. The door is flung open. In rushes Bernard Holland, his stick pounding on the floor and there's me with my bad back being attacked again.

Make no bones about her, the landlady is a tough old trout when she has an iron frying pan in her hand.

"I heard this racket" explains Brandy Nan. "I come up. I couldn't tell who was who, so I clouted you both. I think that's fair."

Henrietta is pulling Bernard Holland out by his feet.

"And don't come back" I call after them.

Listen. There's footsteps on the stairs. There's a choir in my ears. Brandy Nan hears it too. She throws her flabby arms round my neck. "'Tis the Cock Lane ghost returned" she exclaims.

We hear a voice. "'Tis not so, good mistress. I am the Lily of the Valley."

It's that tramp Little Lily Bullero.

"I am out of Limbo" she declares.

She means prison.

"In Christian times the lily doth stand for purity and chastity."

Not in her case.

I make bold as to say "Oh lioness from Limbo, we do you great reverence, how we praise our messenger from Gabriel."

Brandy Nan falls to her knees. "'Tis too much to bear."

"Let us receive the fruit of your lips. Pray, what is your solemn message?"

"I am with child."

"Ah 'tis the will of God" cries Brandy Nan, "'tis divine doings, 'tis---"

"No, 'tis the doings of Higgins when he shagged me in Flaming Nora's

Hotel"

The door is flung open once again. In rushes Bernard Holland. We take to wrassling till I subdue him. He lies very still. The old bat flares up at me,

"Are you aware it's against the law to put people into comas?"

"I suppose so. You can't do anything these days without the Government sticking its nose in."

I seem to hear the voice of Percy Catchpole. "Over the land and over the waves, I see in your tents and inside your graves."

Henrietta enters, grabs Bernard Holland by the feet, pulls him out again.

"Don't bang his head on the stairs" I advise.

Bump, bump, bump.

The door to the next room opens and in steps Clothilda, the fattest woman to ever sail round the world. She gives me a big Cornish hug.

"Hubris leads to Nemesis" I cry through the slobbers of her kiss. "Through many a twist and jape, I've finally met my match and for me there's no escape."

Brandy Nan: "No escape."

Clothilda: "No escape."

"I've finally met my match and for me there's no escape."

THE WAY OF THE ARCH
Miss Merrylegs has invited me to her place in Archway for some luncheon, after which she'll sit on my knee and provoke arousal in my truncheon.

"Oh oh!" she cries as she helpfully takes off my underpants. "There's enough semen here to starch your shirt. How often do you change these?"

When you're single again you can revert to being your dirty old self which Harriet would never have tolerated. Right?

Wrong. She was part and parcel of the grime.

"None of your business" I say in a huff, pick up my clothes, head for the door.

I hear Miss Merrylegs laughing. "Come back here you silly goose. I haven't seduced you yet into telling me where the bodies are buried. You don't really think I wanted you for yourself, do you?"

"You should have made that clear at the start" I say as I walk, still naked, into her bedroom."

Meanwhile back at the Footstool

Ester is saying "Ve do not haf our orders from Berlin."

"In which case" responds Lucky Lucy, "I shall return Sleepy Sid to his bathtub."

"Zat is right. He vill never find ze lost chord."

Bernard Holland is sputtering through his gag. He rolls off his bunk on to

the stone floor. "Whoops" laughs Lucky Lucy.
"Anyfink vor attention."

Let's give the screw another turn
I can see myself yet, lying on my back in an inhospitable guest house on The Way of the Arch. Miss Merrylegs looks down on me with contempt. "Men are such fools."
"Has he spilled all his beans?"
"He knows nothing. Put him in the bath, pour honey on him and feed him to the wasps."
That's her name for the mad women who hang about the office of the Liberal Party.
One does admire the stoicism of these people. They haven't been in power since the Great War in which they and their alcoholic prime minister needlessly embroiled Britain at terrible cost to our young men. But they're still plugging away. Inside their office a radio is playing "Somebody stole my Gal".

BARNEY'S OFFICE
Mrs O'Harnessey had said to me earlier, "I have to go to Norfolk Island to see how far Horace Himmler is progressing with the plan. Mr Big might even be there himself. I'll be away for about four weeks."

"That's a month" I say.

"So it is. There's no pulling the wool over your eyes."

"And don't you forget it," I say,

That night

The door is flung open. In comes the Gaffer. "This it, Bub". He grunts and a small automatic appears in his hand, it's a nice trick but I've seen it before. So has Herman. He's the little man I keep in the cellar. The gun is pointed at the place I keep my ulcers. Herman runs at him, the gun goes off. Plain Jane steps through the door. I see red. I'm looking at her lips as she says, lifting up the automatic with her handkerchief, "This gun's smoking."

"It's old enough."

"Well done Barney, it shows we're getting near when Mrs O sends out her hitman."

She sits on my knee. She strokes my face. She tells me, "Be strong. There's a lot of boodle out there waiting for us. And you are in for a fourth."

"Not likely" I protest. "I'm taking the risks. I want more. I want a fifth."

"There's no flies on you."

The Gaffer is stirring. "Look out Barney, he's got a hand grenade."

I go over and twist his neck. The Gaffer takes the long count. And the less said about that the better.

NORFOLK ISLAND

Mr Big is on the beach below Hanging Rock. He interrupts his picnic with Horace Himmler to march over to where Plain Jane and me are held captive. Ginger Jones guards us with a shotgun. I can't believe Mr Big is Alfred, Mrs O's husband, who we thought lived in her broom cupboard. He says to Plain Jane, "I have plans for you. You shall be the next...Mrs O'Harnessey."

But the present Mrs O is hiding behind a rock. She rises up and cries,

"How can you do this to me? I've slaved my hands to the bone running the Footstool for you and never a word of thanks. You never take me anywhere or talk to me or look at me..."

The old suffering wife routine.

"Enough!" shouts Alfred. "I'm sending you back to the Parlour House in Paris where you will join La Vielle Garde."

(They never die and always surrender)

Mrs O looks at the horizon. "I suppose deep in my heart I always knew I had to go back."

"Yes Sally, I only borrowed you."

She starts singing softly. "Over the line, hear the sweet refrain, angels are chanting the heavenly strain. Over the line – why should I remain, with a step between me and Paris."

I step forward. "Give Paris one more chance, that's what I say."

Alfred greets O'Rourke, one of his henchmen. "Taken care of Horace Himmler?"

The former hunger strike nods. "He thinks he's escaped. He's driving my car bomb towards the camp." He looks at me. "That oul pan looks familiar. Where did I see you before?"

You may remember he was one of the Culshie Mucks I pushed into the ditch.

I have a vision of St Jude, patron saint of hopeless cases. "Trust me to get the loonies and the losers. It's not easy being a second-class saint, what with His Nibs and Aunt Mary looking over your shoulder. However, I am entitled to some licence and just as His Nibs destroyed Sodom and Gomorrah...wait for it."

The ground begins to shake. "Sauve qui peut" shouts Alfred as the island sinks into the sea. I suppose this is the point where I renounce my freethinking and call to the Almighty to save me. But I don't.

I'm picked up by the Marie Celeste and I'm pleased to see that Mrs O'Harnessey has made it too.

THE CATACOMBS
Uncle Cecil starts to rise from his wheelchair. I give him a forearm smash on the kisser that has him choking on his shop teeth.

"I always knew you was a rat" I tell him.

I ring a bell. In comes Mrs Mortimer Wheeler. "You have a fossil for me?"

I point at Uncle Cecil. She shrugs her shoulders, wheels him out.

"He may be a nark and sponger" says Grandpa Higgins, "but he don't deserve that. It's only spilt milk."

"He can cry over it in the Catacombs."

"Not the Catacombs!" cries Grandpa.

"You've never had a great sense of direction, have you?"

I bring out a second wheelchair for him,

BARNEY'S OFFICE

Mrs Mortimer Wheeler is angry. "Them two old crocks are mouldy. I want my money back."

"And if she don't get it" threatens Mrs O "you'll be done over by Masher Malone."

"That sounds sore and I must say I agree with my mumbling Manxmen who want better ferries."

Mrs Wheeler looks at Mrs O. "What's that mean? Is it a code?"

"Sometimes he needs to be translated."

"I don't care if he speaks in Double Dutch---"

"He can do that too. He's just being surly."

"Did you say Girly?"

"Well he can be pretty in his ways."

"When he is this Miss Tweedie, does he dress up as a woman?"

"Oh yes, there's a girlish figure under that horrible hulk."

I think that's my business, don't you? Besides, Miss Tweedie has expanded her repertoire and she now hires out eye-witnesses and I do believe that sheeps clothing can be useful gear for wolves.

The door flies open and in comes Francis the talking mule with Mrs Clipper astride. "Come away, come away with William Tell, come away to the land he loves so well."

It seems Mrs Clipper has a drop or two taken. "Hee-haw, hee-haw."

Mrs Wheeler is astounded. "This is not natural."

"He could be a demon in disguise" I offer.

"What self-respecting demon would pretend to be a donkey?" laughs Mr O.

"That's the clever part" I reply, "you wouldn't expect it."

"I see what you mean."

"I can produce an eye-witness that saw the demon on his back galloping across Hampstead Heath."

Mrs O is agog. "You mean Mrs Clipper is the demon?"

"I mean nothing else," I say, pursing my lips judiciously.

Mrs O points at her. "Barney has found you out!"

And to our great surprise Mrs Clipper changes into an old dame in a velvet gown and a hat with feathers.

"Damn you, Higgins" cries the Monster. And smacking poor Francis on the backside with her umbrella she makes her escape by crashing through the window.

"What was wrong with the door?" I ask the two dolls sitting there with open mouths.

But the fun's not over. My two visitors have just left when Mrs Rouncival comes in with a hairy giant. I'm wondering what zoo he escaped from when he throws me against the wall.

"This is Masher Malone" she says. "He's just showing off. He thinks he's tough."

"You mean he doesn't know."

He smiles, he has tusks not teeth. I spring up. I hit him with a chair, a table, with Mrs Rouncival. I'm in the street when my bad back catches up with me. That tart weighs one ninety without her make-up.

IT'S the next day at my office. This broad steps over me on her way in.

"Hello you horrible brute of a pig" she greets me as I am lying face down near the door. "I guess you know what you're doing."

She's new. She's from Washington. Her figure blurs then re-forms. There's no amendment needed to her constitution. She parks herself on my desk. Her name is Horse Mistress Briggs.

"I was slugged as I came in" I manage to say.

"That was me."

"But I just saw you come in."

"I went out again to let down your tyres. I know you limeys. You need woken up."

"I'm still thinking about your proposition---"

She shakes her head. "What did I say."

She's figuring me for a fallguy but I have other ideas. What they are I still don't know.

"Aint you got the sand for it?"

I'm not sure where sand comes into her daring plan.

"C'mon, I knew you was a crook – it's written all over your face."

Crooked as a corkscrew, that's me. She hikes up her skirt, reaches over my desk for the office bottle, pours out two drams of Old Comber.

It seems she's calling the shots so I get up from the floor as she says "You're to go to Alimonia real soon. I know you can take care of the Inquisitor."

The Inquisitor!

"Who's he?"

"You'll find out. Pull yourself together."

Back in one piece I nod dumbly.

"That's better." She fires up a Lucky Strike. "Say, why don't you take this Captain Moonlight guy with you?"

AT THE GATES OF ALIMON

And so it is time for Barney Higgins to shed his identity and become Captain Moonlight. Watch him sneak into a dark alley to concentrate on the mysterious brain waves taught to him by Antichrist Atlas. Soon his mind is throbbing with power. A quick drag on his Camel then away, slinking softly down the street. He looms up suddenly before a man waiting for a bus, he fixes him with piercing eyes, urging him into a trance.

"You are now of the same thinking mind as me" he drones. "You will obey, you will destroy the Inquisitor and Horse Mistress Briggs."

But the man does not obey. He hits Captain Moonlight in the solar plexus and walks off.

Something in me laughs at that. The part of my mind that sniggers when people are telling me about their heart attacks---

"Get a grip" I hear the Captain say. So I get up, check my Chiefs Special and walk towards the gates. A weary unlaughing agent entering into further decline.

On the other hand I might be heading for the big time. I remember how me and the loonies from the mine tore into those cruel young frauleins, fearlessly giving Bucky Buchanan a kicking as he crawled away on his hands and half a leg.

He was a wrong un alright and he might have been pretending to be blown up by the dynamiters. So wasn't I right to make sure. Well, wasn't I?

I'm still walking towards those gates. But what if I don't come out again? Who'll take care of my well-stacked female confidantes?

"Don't kid yourself" says Captain Moonlight. "They've been stepping out on you for years."

I'm thinking of Billie taking off her kit. "Don't mind me" says this grey-haired duffer. "I'm old enough to be your rich father."

Never mind, I've got others to lose.

Lucky Lucy you're so juicy.

Are you ready, Eddie.

Miss O'Shea, come out and play.

And Matron walks on silver slippers while Alfred is waiting for his kippers.

Old Mother Bunce wasn't half a dunce and she didn't know what to do. So she cut off his cock with a carving knife and you never saw such a sight in your life. All that goo, goo, goo.

"Blood!" shouts the Inquisitor, "I'm talking about blood, sacrifice, devotion."

He flings up his arms. "And if your eyes offend you, cut them out. God wants you to do it."

I'm wearing a mask from my Lone Ranger kit. I'm looking for clues but I won't know what they are till I find them. But I know Miss Stark alright.

She points majestically "Look over there, look deep into the Cryptic Corner."

So I do. I see Traitor Blair riding a hobby horse and singing "In days of old when knights were bold, this story's told of Tony. Along with Brown he went to town with wars that were baloney."

Here's beefy Boris. "Pussy cat, pussy cat, where have you been? I've been to London to look at the Queen. Pussy cat, pussy cat, what did you there? I frightened a little mouse under a chair."

Bonny Prince Charlie says "Lavender's blue, Camiknickers, lavender's green; when I a m king, Camiknickers, you shall be Queen."

Airmiles Andy, striding and crowing like a bantam. "Seesaw, Margery Daw, Andy must have a new master; Andy must have but a penny a day because he can work no faster."

Miss Stark touches my arm. "O masked man, why are you so resolute in search of justice? Yield to the power of the Inquisitor and he will make you a sultan. And men shall call you Pasha."

"I prefer Kimosabi."

"Then there is nothing to be done. You are one of the sea-green Incorruptibles."

"What's sea-green about me?"

"It's what Carlyle called Robespierre."

"He met a sticky end, didn't he? I don't like the implication."

"Don't be angry, masked man, it was an innocent remark. Not everyone has your erudition."

"Well, make sure they don't."

The Inquisitor announces he's going to Constantinople, on his way out he pulls off my mask.

Miss Stark is aghast. "So it's you all along! An intruder. A viper in my breast."

I'm making secret acquaintance with the CIA who are in the guise of washerwomen. Boys will be girls when the need arises. Or when they just feel like it. I approach the first washerwoman who says in a girlish whisper "Meet me later, you big butch thing. I can take you to the cleaners."

It takes more than mops and moues to sway me. I move on. To Madame Mao. I recognise her button boots. Not CIA issue.

I feel a song coming on. "No wonder I feel this way, it's a bright and beautiful day. No other pleasures can I seek when we are dancing cheek to cheek."

And on that whimsical note let's take time out for a friendly word from our sponsor.

I'm Saint Columbus and I've been the patron saint of nailbiters for more years than I care to remember.

Nibbling at your nails is often a sign of anxiety and depression. That's how Barney (not his real name) felt until a few short weeks ago when he tried CHAMPION a scientific blend of heroin, cocaine and flour and just look at him now.

I come on tap-dancing in my spats, spinning my cane and singing

"Champion the wonder horse."

Back to Saint Columbus: You can take my word for it, CHAMPION may help to ease the symptoms of this modern scourge.

The chorus girls: It's Champion!

THE STABLES

A voice: "You thought you were the bees' knees, showing off with your fancy tap-dancing but I now know you to be a bungler, boozer and blackguard."

Thus spake Horse Mistress Briggs. She places a Return to Sender sticker on my forehead and I'm made by her three henchmen and Ester to walk on my knees into her horse box.

"Go and get me mine jackboots" commands the chemist from Cologne.

But it's not easy getting jackboots when your arms are tied behind your back and you're shuffling on your knees.

"Like un gut little doggie."

But I'm not going to be beaten. I bring them out one at a time in my mouth.

The Inquisitor, back from Constantinople and Washington, tells us "I persuaded the President that those old trouts in his Oval Office are barebreasted young women rollerskating around his desk."

Ester and her cronies cry out in admiration: "You can talk of ancient heroes like Caligulas and Neroes, but there's only one delusionist and that's the great illusionist."

"Illusionist!" I shout.

"And Hilary Clinton thinks I'm her sugar daddy" he resumes. "An improvement over that sleaze ball of a husband."

Ester and her cronies start up again. "The Inquisitor rules and that's a fact, his opponents will rue and then be whacked. Oh what fun and conspiration, confound them all in desperation."

"Desperation!" I agree.

The Inquisitor looks down at me. "What's this wretch doing here?"

"Woof woof!"

"His name is Appolonius" Ester informs him.

"But this cannot be " exclaims the Inquisitor. "Appolonius is the master of the Rosicrucians and I am his vassal."

Enter Aunt Cecilia. "No you're not, you old fool, you're mine."

And so, with the aid of digs in the back, the Inquisitor leaves the stage.

THROUGH THE MONOCLE

Ester tells me "Sie vill be a star. Ov ze travelling show. Ave eine drink to celebrate."

We wake up in a cage in a side-show. Punters stare at me and the monsters. It seems Mrs O told them they were in a hot desert, suggested they pour buckets of cooling water over their heads. Turned out to be acid.

Here she is, looking jaunty in her jodhpurs, with her is Molly Coddle, something in the BBC. I see the Waist's long arm reach out from his cage.

Molly Coddle slaps his wrist. "Put it back you rat" She says to Mrs O. "I saw him pick that woman's handbag."

"The scum we get here" bemoans Mrs O. She says to the Waist, "Stick to your trade. You are a forger, a forger. And this one here" she says, pointing at me, "has *notions*."

"You don't mean of his own?"

"Indeed I do."

"We don't' like notions at the Beeb. We like our viewers to think as we do. Because we know better."

"And you make Joe Public pay for it too."

"How totalitarian is that" I remark.

"That Higgins can be clever in his own way. In fact rumour has it he once read a book."

I hope she's not trying to make me out as a swot.

"Lookee here" Mrs O says, pointing at the next cage. "The two-headed man."

Two heads are better than one, so they say.

"Oooh what a sight" cries Molly Coddle. "Isn't that Jeremy Thorpe on the left, the head with the trilby hat?"

Mrs O stands with hands on hips, shouting at Thorpe's head: "Go back to your noisome sinks and stews and prepare for government."

She starts to laugh and before long all the creatures are joining in.

"Silence! All those laughing without permission will have their heads shaved."

Vera Vamp the blonde beast bursts into the tent. She comes over to me. She talks to me without speaking, calls me a fruitcake, still captivated, I'm pleased to see by the magnetism of my nostalgie de la boue. She says to Mrs O: "What's going on here?"

"This is a film set for the BBC."

"What's it about?"

"Sleepy Sid is playing Sherlock Holmes" says Molly Coddle. "He's delighted to get the part."

"Yes, he's walking on air" says Vera Vamp. "I just passed him hanging from a lamppost on the corner of the street."

"In case a certain little lady comes by," I remark.

"Didn't I tell you to cut him down once the scene was finished?" asks Mrs O.

"You certainly did not" avers Molly Coddle.

"I must have forgot. It matters not. I never quite liked this selling point of the world's humpiest detective."

"Anyway I have to get back. I'm working on Re-education through Labour."

"Is that a party political broadcast?"

"Unofficially."

We hear the Waist singing in his cage:

"Row, row, row your boat," [softly] gently down the stream.[louder] merrily merrily merrily, life is but a dream."

Wait till you hear this

The characters in this book are a species unknown to civilization. Most of the jokes come with a jag, a custard pie thrown in the sneering face of the Establishment.

You may not like them but it wouldn't do any harm to ponder on the issues behind them. Now would it?

PART SIX
She has legs up to her armpits, tiny tits and a big mouth.

"Is he gone?" says Flaming Nora, touching the empty pillow.

Hotspur Hardy lights up a Senior Service. "Yes, he's left... what's the tears for? I thought you was hardboiled."

"Nah, I have a little cry to meself every time I think of me cracking his skull with a hammer."

"Don't be tough on yourself. It's possible he had learning difficulties before he met you."

The door's open. I push on in. "It's a clear case of conjunction of the brain."

"You don't even know who we're talking about" snaps Flaming Nora.

"Yes I do. The barman at the Seven Stars keeps me informed."

"Ale sellers shouldn't be tale tellers. Who let you in, anyway?"

"You sent for me," I remind her.

"Oh you shouldn't have hurried."

"No trouble too much for you, Miss Nora."

"That was last bleeding week I sent for you" she retorts.

I nick one of Hotspur's fags. "Just give me the facts, ma'am."

"Tell him, Hotspur."

"She had a dawn visit from three tax inspectors, went through the papers."

"What they find?"

"Difficult to say since they were blind."

"But they must have found something" Flaming Nora adds, "cos they went out riding hobby horses and singing---"

"Diddly diddly de, what clever clogs are we."

"I'll look into it" I say, backing out and bumping into Brenda Bliss (former Bluebell Babe) who greets me with "Watch where you're going, you great lump."

She gives me the back of her hand. My specs hang from one ear. I'm hopping mad. You can't hit a woman so I pick up Hotspur and throw him out the window.

"You could've opened it first" cries Flaming Nora.

A head appears at the window. "Peppar's the name, treason's the game."

I go over and watch him drag poor Hotspur away by the heels.

"I hope you're satisfied with yourself" Nora comes up, twists my clip-on bow-tie. "We coulda got something for him."

"Saving your pardon" says Hotspur Hardy, climbing back in. "Major Peppar has released me on condition I spy for him."

"Struth, what a maggot!" exclaims Brenda Bliss, stepping back and giving him the boot.

I'm not having this. "That's no way to treat a former janitor at Miss Wink's Private Asylum," I tell her.

"And brothel" she responds.

What a thing to say.

"As a former Miss Wink meself..." starts Miss Nora.

"On account of your magnetic personality" I interrupt.

"Thank you, Barney. As a former Miss Wink meself I can confidently say that what went on in the shagging rooms and torturing cellar was kept completely separate from the Asylum part and was no concern of mine."

"That's telling her" I put in.

"And Barney as the resident brothel bully can verify what I say."

"I was only resident because the wife had thrown me out."

"But you kept to your duty both day and night" Miss Nora recounts.

"Yes that was my time in the lime and the light."

And now it grows dark

"What's that noise?" exclaims Brenda Bliss.

"Ah tis only the Cock Lane ghost returned" I say reassuringly.

"What you mean *only*?" she wants to know.

Flaming Nora is trembling. "He's come to murder us in our beds" she cries.

"I hear a horrible dragging along the corridor" says Brenda Bliss. "Oh, I am so frightened."

I stride over and fling open the door. Bernard Holland comes staggering in with a knife in his back. "He's done for me, he's done for me."

"Come on, man, get a grip. Who did it?" I ask.

But Bernard Holland is too far gone. He staggers some more, falls into the television. Flaming Nora is raging. "I haven't paid for that yet."

"It's not worth watching" Hotspur informs us, "not with all those repeats and petty political broadcasts."

Flaming Nora glares at him. "Who asked you, you snake in the grass."

"Bring him here till I thump him" I say as Mrs O'Harnessey comes in with two of her sweated labourers pulling a handcart, they throw Bernard Holland into it and pull him out. I take out my sheriff's badge and arrest Hotspur Hardy. I hear chanting outside. It's the Transitionals. "Down with men! Down with women!"

But they're up against the New Suffragettes who have placards saying "Give us back our identity. Don't degrade our femininity."

Wait. That's not all. Here come the Arch Eco-feminists protesting about petticoats because they're demeaning and what's more, oil is used in their manufacture.

Flaming Nora tells me to "sort em out. It's what you're paid for."

She's right. It's a job for Hardhearted Higgins who has battled the Beeb, the Blob---

"Hold on a sec, what you mean it's what I'm paid for?"

"Only in a manner of speaking."

"You seen the size of them dykes?" I say as she opens the door for me.

I come back through the window. "It's worse than I thought. The Bitches of Bretwalda are on the march too with a drum major in front"

"Heaven help us" cries Miss Nora. "Not a drum major."

"Yes" I confirm, "and it's Uncle Cecil."

"Uncle Cecil! What's an old git like him doing with them Bitches?"

(Yes it's him again. He's had the run of this tale long enough, but you try to get rid of him. I can't)

Brenda Bliss is at the window. "It's getting worser still. Look!"

It's Portuguese Joe and his Pinkshirts goosestepping through the mob.

"Barney, we're surrounded" she cries. "Do something."

I shall summon greater powers. "Call for Phillip Morris!" I shout. "Call for Phillip Morris!"

When that doesn't work I appeal to "Umpa Umpa stick it your jumpa."

Flaming Nora and Brenda Bliss support me by pulling up their skirts, showing their big arses. "Umpa Umpa stick it up your bum!"

Brenda screams as an ugly mug appears at the window. It's that man again who says "Phillip Morris regrets he has better things to do."

This visitation has a dire effect on Flaming Nora. "We're in for it now."

"We're in the soup alrigtht" opines Miss Bliss.

"With our backs against the wall" I add.

(Butcher Haig said that during the German offensive of 1918. You can imagine him with his back against the wall of his luxury chateau miles from the Front)

"What a smell!" cries Miss Nora.

Portuguese Joe in an aside tells us, "My Pinkshirts and me are pumping gas through the toilet bowl."

The fumes are so great we lie as if paralysed. I watch Bernard Holland get up with the dagger still in his back. He nicks my wallet then assaults the dignity of the two dames.

"Such as they have" he sighs then falls flat on his face. He certainly has taken his time to croak.

Mrs O returns and asks, "What's all this litter on the floor, and what's going on outside?"

"It's a revolution, my lady" replies her aide, Elsie the Suicide Blonde. Mrs O has other ideas. "They are calling for me. How wonderful am I."

Elsie eggs her on. "You are the sun in the midst of their night."

"Not to mention the morning" I add.

She sends out Hotspur and Elsie to sound trumpets. The mob goes quiet as she looks upon them from the window.

"Kneel down you lot before me who is your supreme leader" she commands.

There is silence for a few more minutes then the supreme leader scuttles back amidst a flurry of missiles, jeers, catcalls and whistles. She shouts, she screams, she tears off her blouse, her bra. She enquires of the ceiling: "How dare they not know my regality? Me, the Queen of the Pumpkin People."

Brenda Bliss reckons "We're up a gum tree."

"Without a paddle" agrees Flaming Nora.

"Come on Barney, think of something."

I ponder for a moment. "We could always send a message to the Pumpkin People."

"You're as bad as she is" remarks Miss Bliss.

"There's no such thing" says Flaming Nora. "Can't you see she's batty?"

"It's quite simple" I reply, "you either believe in the Pumpkin People or you don't."

"And you believe in me?" asks Mrs O.

"Yes, your nobody."

"I shall go now and sit upon my throne and reign down on my subjects" she says.

"Don't hurry back."

"Daft old trout."

"Stop it, youse two" I tell them. "Try to think outside the box."

"And finish up like you."

"Or like him" Brenda Bliss points at Bernard Holland.

"Ah poor Bernard" I say sadly. "Gone are the days of fond remembrance when we swopped lead together and grappled on cliff tops---"

"And robbed all around youse" sneers Flaming Nora.

And now I hear it.

"I hope you know how to panic" I say to the girls as Rasputnic the Siberian gorilla plods into the room.

"Slimey...oh blimey" he roars and is followed in by Alan Whicker holding a microphone. "Hotspur Hardy may be a spy but I'm absolutely certain Kim

Philby is not." He turns to Rasputnic. "How did you feel when your daughter was raped and murdered before your eyes?"

"Me no likee, oh crikey," responds the gorilla.

I go over and pull off his glasses and moustache.

"Look, it's not Alan Whicker, it's Mike Yarwood" cries Flaming Nora, pulling off her kit and striding stark naked towards the imposter.

An aside from her to the reader: "I don't do this very often, only when it's absolutely vital to the character and integrity of the script."

I'm amazed too. "No, it's not Mike Yarwood, it's Dave King."

"Crummy, oh lummy."

"How thin is the patina of civilization" I muse, "when dames can take off their knickers at the sight of Dave King impressionating an impressionist."

"Tawdy, oh lordy."

"I didn't write the blooming script." Dave King gives his signature giggle. "I don't blame her one bit."

"Nitty, oh gritty,"

"Why don't you give over, you big ape?"

"Be careful, Barney" warns Flaming Nora. "This is not just a gorilla, it's a Siberian one."

"They're the worst" Brenda Bliss reckons.

Fancy thinking a bloke in a gorilla suit can fool me. I give him a clout right in the mush. Next thing, I'm sailing through the window with severe bruised ribs. A Transitional looks down on me. "This 'ere is Dr Lovelock out of the telly."

"Well I never."

"Fancy that."

Oh, where is this leading to? I ask myself.

I'll tell you.

THE MUSIC HALL

I've fallen through the hatch they used to roll things down, just like Charles Laughton in *Hobson's Choice*. I'm lying under the transparent reinforced glass below the stage, looking up at Eddie and Billie in their stockings and bums.

"But hark to the crunch of gravel on the parade ground outside" declares Billie.

Door banging open.

Eddie is aghast. "We must sauve qui peut."

"Nein, nein, ve must vor ze submarine vait" says Von Schicklegruber.

"Vhy, I mean, why must we do that?" says Billie.

"Es ist fur das Reich."

"One hope only remains to us…."

"Yes, we must call for Hardhearted Higgins."

"Gott in Himmel, zis 'Ardhearted Higgins kannot kommen ze 'ere! Nein nein," he cries and rushes out, his arm in the Nazi salute.

I extricate myself and go to the back.

"Is there anybody there?" say the travellers knocking on the moonlit door.

I expect they've parked themselves on the nearest football pitch and good luck to them; if the coppers and councils are afraid of you why not take advantage of it.

But even they wouldn't take over the home of…

West Ham Intercity. "We've big boots and little brains, we put Millwall on the trains."

I'd heard the Gaffer was recovered and was holding court at the Seven Stars. Time to finally put paid to him. This is a bit like Ron Kray going to the Blind Beggar to take care of George Cornell.

Only it's not. There's a blue badge on the wall: BARNEY HIGGINS KNOCKED OFF SLIPPERY SAM HERE.

And if there isn't, there should be.

"Happy Halloween, Barney" the Gaffer calls out. He's dressed as a clown.

The bar girls are not glamour models but not nuns neither. "Who's that ringing our doorbell, who's that wanting our sweets?"

"Candy is dandy" smiles Lucky Lucy, "but brandy is better. Show him your pumpkins and he'll put on a letter,"

They're taking the Michael. I go out again. There's a crowd moving along the street chanting "Here we come, here we come."

But the most outlandish thing of all is that there is actually a bobby on the beat. "Move along, move along, nothing to see here."

Little does he know that I alone can hear the Echoing Voice who tells me: "Listen well, Higgins. Don't be foiled by the Old Bill, the Big Boss or even Mrs O'Harnessey, because they are always too little or too late or both."

"Such a jackdaw that dresses in peacock feathers" I say.

"Whom are we talking about?" the Echoing Voice wants to know.

..."Mrs O'Harnessey of course."

"An astute observation but not quite the point."

"And what in your educated opinion might the point be?" I ask

"Look here, you needn't get shirty with me."

"Excuse me for interrupting" says the bobby on the beat "but perhaps you should continue your conversation in the privacy and comfort of your own little cell down at the station."

It starts to rain. "Crikey it's cats and dogs" he cries. "The sergeant will be livid. She hates mud on the turn-ups of our trousers and wet helmets get her goat."

As the bobby pulls out his brolly I slip away.

I think this is where we came in. Time to jump into my Zodiac and head back to Clapham.

Look, I'm not one of your John Osbornes. None of that anger and chips on shoulders with me. Be thankful for what you are getting because we're entering into a dark age of wokery and repression where actors will be limited in what roles they may take and writers, what they may write.

So let us return to the thrilling days of yesteryear...

The pit and the pensioner

"How did he fall in" enquires Nurse Billie.

"Had a heart attack caused by improperly tested vaccines" explains Dr Lovelock. "That'll be five guineas."

"Is that the pit by the vegetable patch?"

"Yes the gardener didn't fill it in before he left to work for the BBC's Migrant Service."

The chorus girls: "Somewhere there's a place for us."

"It'll be handy enough" I remark. "Just have to fill it in."

That's what Mrs O's sweated labourers are doing right now. They'll be happy in their work. One can whistle, one can sing, and one can play on the violin.

That old spoilsport Mrs Grundy rushes in, pulls off Nurse Billie's wig, lies down in the pit.

"C'mon missus, get out of it," I tell her.

"Why?"
"Because the show must go on" I say.
"Why?"
"Well...because...because. Does anybody know?"
"Not me" says Nurse Billie. "I only had it on cos I was having a bad hair day."

How's it going so far? There's something almost transcendental about a story like this, something that provokes stress-relieving smiles from people who are easily pleased.

Come in, Mrs Clipper. She says "I've just been hugged by a big bear. Played havoc with my rigging."

"That was no bear" I tell her. "That was Rasputnic the gorilla from Siberia."

Mrs Grundy emerges from the pit, "And from such carry-on may the good Lord deliver us."

"How true those words are, even today."

Nurse Billie agrees. "I think there's a lesson for all of us there."

"So make peace with the Lord" persists Mrs Grundy.

"We never quarrelled" I say.

"I can't blame that poor gorilla" Mrs Clipper tells us. "My allure overwhelmed him. This last month I've received lots of proposals. One was even of marriage.

"And, Barney, remember how we used to meet in Regent Street. Time was out of joint as we defied the world with our passion." She starts to waltz with herself. "And as I listened to the car horns play, I removed my blouse, I was daycollitay."

Nurse Billie intervenes. "Mrs Clipper, don't deceive yourself. He can never be yours because he is subject to the unconscious orders of the Antichrist."

The Antichrist! That explains the deviations from my normal code of ethics. And they are nothing to write home about. Even if I had a home to write to.

"Make yourself scarce" says Auntie.

"Where to?"

"Over the hills."

"And far away?"

"Yes, I've ordered a Hansom cab" replies Auntie, "but it's stuck on the M25."

It's one disappointment too many. "I feel it coming on" I tell them.

"No Barney, no," cries Auntie Atlas. "Not your ivory tower!"

"Come back, come back" pleads Mrs Clipper.

Pythagoras decides to desert a sinking ship. He jumps out of my pocket, scampers up Mrs Clipper's skirt, Auntie shrugs her humpy shoulders in defeat and wanders off to vote in the referendum for an independent England.

Let's have a look at the Cow Shed where on Sunday nights you can hear the gospelgabs thumping the pulpit. A punter asks the Rev Brocklehurst why he's wearing a donkey mask. He replies, I wear this consecrated mask to signify to you the asinine character of your behaviour which leadeth you straight to Hell."

I say to the Crusher, "You sure you got enough mushy tomatoes and bananas?"

"Yes, I peeled the bananas too."

"And behold a ladder was set up on the earth and the top of it reached to Heaven and this angel ascending and descending upon it."

Two points here. Actually it's more like a set of steps that leads to the upstairs room where guns, drugs and overfed trollops in fishnet stockings are freely traded, and the angel in question is none other than the Conductress.

The Rev Brocklehurst, known for his impression of a candelabra at Amelia's mansion until he burnt the drapes, and is known to have visited Amsterdam, calls for a sacred ditty from Emily Flopbottom who obliges with "Knees up Mother Brown."

"Nah nah" cries a punter, throwing a tomato at her bonce, she ducks and it hits a big geezer called Charlie Brown who throttles the first punter, wanting to know what's wrong with Mother Browns.

This leads to a general mellay with much slipping and sliding. The Rev is in a flap, exhorting us to open our hearts and let the sun shine in. Unnoticed in a corner we see Mrs Clipper being interfered with. "Down, Scumbag, bad Scumbag," she says to Rasputnic. "Floozey, oh woozey."

But all is not lost for we have on watch that well-known memoirist, duellist and standard- bearer of chivalry...who pokes the gorilla, says, "If you want to talk dirty go outside. You'll find a trollop standing on the corner."

But Rasputnic doesn't want to go outside, he jerks me up by the feet, whirls me about him.

"But then again" I manage to say, "we do have freedom of speech."

"Not really, go sailey" and the brute flings me about, knocking over the rioters like bowling pins, he lets go and I fly into the pulpit thumper.

Mrs O'Harnessey appears on the scene as I get to my feet. "Well done, Barney, you have quelled this disorder single-handed. I wouldn't have believed it."

"He is my hero" asserts Harriet who has followed her in.

The Conductress (aka Miss O'Shea) tells me to go upstairs and collect my reward.

"One lump or two" enquires Lady Paramount, who often draws attention at the Lido Lounge with her version of the cha cha cha.

How was I to know she had booked the upstairs for her tea party? She stops stroking Uncle Cecil's head. "You've had your twenty quid's worth, go now and put on your Crown Topper at once."

I don't know what was in that tea but the next thing I know I'm in the kitchen.

The Duchess of Dolittle sips her tea. "You have sown merit, Lady P, in subduing the aggressive male pattern baldness of wretched little men."

"And what a scruffy horror this new maid is" observes Lady Tarantula. "Her skirt is so short I can almost her hairy quim. And those Minnie Mouse shoes!"

Lady Paramount laughs maliciously. "That's Nancy She used to be called Barney. I've taken photos to put him in my power."

"So clever of you to threaten him with public exposure of his deviant nature."

"Yes, Duchess, he wouldn't want his mates down the pub to know he's a lesbian."

"That's an idea" says Lady P, "but we need someone for him to be a lesbian with, don't we?"

"Not me, that's for sure."

"Me neither."

"Come on, Nancy," taunts Lady Tarantula, "tell us who you fancy."

"None of these bags" I mutter as an aside. They don't know I'm undercover here to dig up dirt on the Canal, it's called the Northern Poorhouse, a political project that costs big money and destroys the countryside in its path. All this to save twenty minutes at the most.

Lady P is at her Stalinist best. "Lady T, do we know how many plebs have croaked building the Canal?"

"Not enough, I fancy."

Such contempt for human life. Those politicians should be ashamed of themselves. We should round them up and gas them.

"Listen" says the Duchess, "I hear footsteps. The Big Boss has woken up."

The Big Boss!

Here he comes. I can't believe it's Stanley Unwin.

"Goodlerightio, ist the Canallewd mustly on timetidely notall fromly delaytiyo nus?"

"Yum, tut as spokely correctoid" Lady P responds,

"Diddleysquat unmeantibow?"

"Yum."

This is fiendish, they're talking Gobbledygook, a dialect found deep in the heart of Glasgow.

"Don't be daft" says Mrs Grundy to me. "This is an extract from *Finnegans Wake*. We may never know how dirty that book is."

I've had enough. I smooth down my skirt and pinny, stride out and announce "You are looking at Captain Moonlight and for you the game is up."

And where did Portuguese Joe come from?

"Some call *me* the Big Boss" he declares.

"So you're not Stanley Unwin?" I say.

"Indisposably nul."

Lady Paramoutn is radiant. "And only he knows what secrets lie at the heart of the Canal."

Blimey! Who would have thought Portuguese Joe would know big secrets like that?

"I'm leaving now and you better not try and stop me" I tell them gruffly.

I elbow Joe in his fat gub. That'll learn him not to know big secrets and not to be a Big Boss without telling me. I jerk open the door and as I barge down the steps I hear Lady P shouting "Close the bleeding door after you. Were you born in a field?"

I WAS in bed with Lucky Lucy when the Canal Gestapo burst in. I thought it was only the KGB who arrested people in their pyjamas.

I'm hanging upside down when in stomps Ginger Jones in uniform.

"Who sent you? What's your game?" he demands.

"Ask me another."

"When are you going to pay Mrs O her two years' rent money?"

"There are some things that even I can not reveal."

"So you won't talk, eh? Time to send in…"

"I am called Merciless Mary [aka Miss O'Shea]. Merciless to my friends. You are not one of those. Unless you really want to be."

"I do want to be."

"You have a choice. Slave labourer at the Canal, *or* you can join Ginger Jones and me in pulling off big jobs."

She slips the loop on the rope. I fall onto my head, which saves my glasses.

"Count me in."

Ginger helps me up, "This place has many spies but don't worry about being betrayed."

"That usually comes later" says Merciless Mary reassuringly.

"When we dish out the dough" says Ginger.

"Who else is in it?" I ask.

"South Africa Smith. I'll call him in. But one thing, don't mention his midriff support."

"Barney and me go back," he informs them, "I vividly remember him sucking his thumb when he dropped his ice cream."

"When was this?"

"Last Thursday."

MY IVORY TOWER

Ginger and South Africa Smith are out to get me because I called time on their big robbery.

Mrs Clipper comes to my aid. "I've brought along Scumbag as your minder. I've been teaching him pigeon English so he can talk to you on your level."

"Coo coo a-diddley do."

"I probably don't need a minder now that Harriet's gone. The times she crowned me with her brollie as I crawled politely up the stairs."

"Yes it makes all the difference" she muses, "when you have someone to greet you when you return home."

"What's this?" I murmur as I come across Portuguese Joe's collection of Eva Braun's underwear including the crotchless ones she wore when pissing into Hitler's mouth.

"What unholy filth is this?" exclaims the Mad Nun, snatching a copy of July's *Knickers World* out of my hand.

"It's just something Portuguese Joe left lying around" I tell her.

"What *do* you take me for?"

"You're the Mad Nun aint you?"

"I'm not as bonkers as people think" she smiles. "I've made a packet as a naughty saucygram nun."

That doll isn't just dressing up. She really was from a convent. She just didn't like the idea of spending the rest of her life with an imaginary bigamous husband. And they call her insane.

A dramatic freeze

We're all motionless as Bernard Holland crawls in, the dagger still in his back, moves under the Betty Grable.

I'm not pleased. "That table has sentimental value for me. The wife used to sit under it smoking her Guards or was it Cadets?"

"Kensitas" replies Merciless Mary,

"How quickly one forgets the endearing bric a brac of one's nupitals."

"The thing I remember most about her was her girlish sense of humour."

"Like when she planted false evidence to have me arrested as the Monster. I tell you, it wasn't funny being remanded with two Rippers and the Beast of West Bromwich."

"It's hard to believe but I heard you were once *on* a jury" says Merciless Mary.

"Yes, and I got three months for contempt of court, making a book on the sentence."

The door's flung open. Portuguese Joe runs in tied between the shafts of a cart upon which sits Mrs Clipper and they continue around the room to the strains of the "Blue Danube".

"I can't stand it!" cries Bernard Holland. "Why do I have to go around with a dagger in my back?"

"What about me?" exclaims Portuguese Joe.

Mrs Clipper lashes his back. "Don't you dare stop. Keep on going a-clippity clop."

But he doesn't, he collapses and it's time for medical assistance.

"I can see from here this could be a job for the shrinks, exposing his testicles in a public room. Bollock naked is what is technically the technical term."

"Oh Dr Lovelock don't deprive me of my donkey rides. He's plumper and smarter than---"

"I heard that" says Francis the talking mule plodding into the room.

"Go away. Sling your hook" shouts Mrs Clipper.

Head down, poor Francis shuffles away.

There's a banging on the door and two big blokes enter.

"We are from the Cruelty and have reason to believe there's a creature here that you're being cruel til."

Portuguese Joe staggers up. "I'm saved! You've come at last."

"Not you, fatso, it's the donkey we've come for."

Portuguese Joe breaks down crying. It's a shocking and sober reflection on how you can go from a Big Boss to a beast of burden in such a short time and let this be a lesson to us all.

NORFOLK ISLAND REGAINED

Mrs O has sent me on another mission. I come to this house which has a notice on the front door. "Sign of the times. Abandon all testosterone before ye enter here."

Not that they have much left, poor things, not as long as the PC cops, the woke brigade and Percy Catchpole rule OK.

I see the Antichrist walking towards me, but hold on, I also hear a voice:

"Psst, Barney, I'll say this only once….I'll wait for you in Kalamazoo."

"Saving your pardon, marm" says Miss Lovely, "your ten pretty maids are now laid out in a row."

"Neatly, I presume. You see, Barney, I do switch."

"Yes, Auntie, you are known for your sense of geometry."

She goes off to check her lobster pots. Miss Lovely brings out a bottle, starts to dance.

"Cha, cha, cha, cha, cha, cha, Auntie Atlas is wearing my bra." She sits down. "Barney, I take an almost astronomical view of you. You're in your own little world spinning through the solar system."

I can't reply to her celestial opinion of me because she's sitting on my face.

She gets up and I see Auntie standing with a parrot on her shoulder. She throws a bucket of water over my head. At least, I think it's water. I hear the ten pretty maids singing "Our day will come, then we'll have everything."

"We belong to the Cult of the Black Death" Auntie informs me. "You've heard of it of course."

I shake my head. "All I know is what I've read in the comics."

"The world is our lobster" says Miss Lovely.

"I like New York in June" I tell them, "how about you."

"Don't be facetious" cries Auntie and the ten pretty maids watch as Auntie and Miss Lovely give me a kicking.

"It's only French police who stand and watch as a British subject is being assaulted" I say to the maids.

"That's not quite correct" asserts Auntie, "those gendarmes only stand if they can't sit down with a glass of wine."

She leaves off as she hears...

The chorus girls "My boyfriend's back..."

Yes, it's Vlad the Impaler Putin. "Have I got a few missiles for you."

We go back to the house and there to greet us is the man turned his country from a breadbasket into a basketcase.

"I have been waiting for you, Comrade Putin" says Robert Mugabe. "For hours I have kept my eyes pinned on that door."

I bet that was sore. Putin seems a little disappointed.

"I was expecting your lovely wife too. Why is she not here?"

"She is at home. In bed with sciatica."

"I shall send my assassins to eliminate this Sciatica. He is well known to my secret police." He turns to Auntie. "I must say you smell nice for an

Antichrist."

"Yes this is my pricey perfume for romantic encounters."

She has a cheaper one for sordid affairs with people like me.

"I promised my wife as I dropped her off at the Moscow workhouse on the way to my airship that I would engage in no hanky panky."

"You are too kind to her" asserts Auntie. "Stalin destroyed his family yet you let her off with a workhouse. What's wrong with the Lubyanka or the Gulag?"

"Yes you are right. Things will change. No more Mr Nice Guy." A mad laugh. "And when she has gone I shall put me feet up on her precious antique furniture whenever I want and I shall have a wank without looking over my shoulder."

"Miss Lovely, bring us a pot of hot vodka" orders Auntie.

"And some arrowroot biscuits" adds Putin, "and pot of jam."

At this point I'm in her bedroom, under the bed.

"Come Vlad, lie with me on this here bed while we wait for our repast."

I know what goes on above me. If I had a pound for every time I shagged Auntie on that bed I'd have £1.50 by now.

Here's Miss Lovely returning. "Sorry, no jam left."

The Antichrist is aghast. "Here I am, entertaining one of the world's top megalomaniacs and I can't even provide him with a bit of fruity preserve to put on his biscuits."

"Sorry, no arrowroots neither."

"This is intolerable" shouts Putin. "I have lost face. I shall have to do something typically terrible to restore my reputation."

He rushes out. I follow the other two and we see Vlad the Impaler climbing the dangling rope ladder back into his air ship.

This beats the War of Jenkin's Ear. This is the story of how the fate of Ukraine hung in the balance over arrowroot biscuits and a pot of jam.

THE FOOTSTOOL

That's enough of that. Did you know Mrs O'Harnessey has opened a reformatory based on a book extolling murder, torture, ethnic cleansings, human sacrifices and what have you?

Yes, I mentioned the Old Testament before but it's worth pondering again how in the 21st century people believe in that stuff.

If I was caught talking to the walls there'd be questions asked yet Israelites can still talk to the Wailing Wall and not a word is said.

She has roped me in to her reformatory. When I'm not a professor in the faculty of Babylonian Numbers I'm also the janitor.

Mrs O confronts me, curling her thin cruel lips.

"Remember this, fine clothes cannot hide the clown. And before you attend to your janitorial duties you will remove your mortar board and gown. One of the Sisters has complained that you spoke to her in Babylonian when she asked you to mop up the evidence of the previous night's Celebration of the Smiting of Egypt."

"I did clean it up."

"Yes, but not up to the standard of this immaculate reformatory. From now on I want it tickety boo or we shall lose our contract to supply our graduates to the Canal and woe to you if I lose all that lovely lolly."

I no sooner pick up my mop when I am confronted by an apparition who says his name is Melchisedec who says, "There came before my face 36 creatures with faces of asses, faces of oxen and faces of birds.

I wondered and I asked them, Who are you?"

"It's only people self certifying. What are you up to?"

"I am the Messiah."

"I can tell you are pretty special by the way you just appeared."

"And I can tell you're pretty astute" he says "by the look in your big blue eyes."

"You're parking up the wrong tree."

"You should have expected me, my coming was predicted. I am a son of David. I was crucified and yet I am forgotten. It's all about this Joshua."

"What can I do about it?"

"You're an Old Testament scholar, aren't you?"

"Well yes but I'm more on the Babylonian side of things. Go and see Mrs O'Harnessey, she's upstairs taking a class."

After a while I hear screaming. I'd know that scream anywhere. It's been directed at me often enough.

I go up. Mrs O is running around with her arms in the air, her students are looking agog and aghast. Uncle Cecil is dancing up and down wearing his Davy Crockett hat.

But worse than that, Putin is back, rushing in with his rug to one side, revealing his bird's nest.

"Death to spies!"

An unseemly response to the entrance of the Dagenham Girl Pipers.

Ester is floundering too. "Oh weh is mir."

She can't talk, have you ever heard those beer hall brass bands or those old SS men and their marching songs? It's almost as pathetic as those other old fogies with their ukuleles singing along to a George Formby film.

But look who's in front of the girl pipers, twirling a baton and swirling his kilt.

"How come you're a girl piper?" I say to Portuguese Joe.

"I self certified twenty minutes ago and I'll soon be sharing a changing room with Julie Felix."

The first hint of real danger comes from somebody playing "Stars over Brooklyn" from an unseen pianner. Then comes mysterious chanting "Umpa Umpa stick it up your jumpa."

The company falls to our knees, "Umpa Umpa stick it up your bum."

We stare amazed as the shades of the living dead pass through us. Harriet, Bughouse Cassidy and Slippery Sam. And my soul swoons slowly as I hear the snow falling faintly through the universe. By your leave, james joyce.

Wait till you hear this

You've made it this far but tis no place for Christian folk or lefties, coppers and lawyers who build their houses on the heads of taxpayers.

"Doesn't apply to us, then?" says the Crusher.

"No, we're just common criminals."

The uncommon ones are politicians who talk up a crisis and award contracts for useless gear worth hundreds of millions to their cronies.

With the added irony that the stuff was made in China where the bug was manufactured.

PART SEVEN

Barney's office
I'm at the tomb of the unknown Harriet. That's the egg timer at the window.
   "Ye lady of Shalott used to look out her window too" I say to ..
   The shade of Harriet. "That's the least you could do seeing as you done me in. By the way, the cherubs up here have been keeping an eye on you and this biblical tours racket you've been running. Do you really expect people to believe that the very bush from which Jehovah spoke to Moses is in Milton Keynes?"
   "Holy relics don't have to be true to bring comfort."
   "You're right for once. For a scoundrel you have a wonderful innocence."
   "In a world containing Mrs O'Harnessey nobody is innocent."

Coming shortly:
She is brazen! She has secrets! She'll sell you for a dime. She is the flame haired denunciatrix of our time.
He was the man who lived and died! His boots were big, his brains were fried, and he took all crumpet in his stride.

Sorry about that. Let's return to the sanity of the Footstool
   I'm watching a middleweight bout on the old back and white. Both boxers are losing.
   Mrs O is warming her fat arse at the fire.
   "Rubenesque, Barney, Rubenesque"
   I can see her knickers.

"Lingerie, if you don't mind."
More like bloomers if you ask me.
"Nobody is."
Still, not to be sniffed at.
"You should be so lucky."
I wish she'd stop reading my thoughts.
"Then don't move your lips" There's knock on the door.
"What say you, Uncle Cecil, any more denunciations for me?"
"Who do you want denunciated this time?"
"You don't have to believe them, do you?" I ask.
"Of course not but they have a life of their own" says Mrs O. "Comrade Stalin got the whole Central Committee to shoot itself."
"I was under the table at the time" says Uncle Cecil.
Mrs O shakes her head. "It didn't happen all at once, you old fool."
Duckie Baconbrains hobbles towards us, using his severed leg as a crutch.
"What happened to you?" I ask.
"I was bitten by the crocodile."
"Can't be. Mr Tangle ate that crocodile. Are you sure you didn't imagine it?"
"You don't Imagine experiences like that. It was almost as bad as when Antichrist Atlas turned my pecker into a mouse."
"Is it a good mouse?" Mrs O asks.
"Not bad. Sleeps most of the time. It does like me lying on it though, like this."
"Dirty little sod" cries Mrs O who thrashes Duckie's backside which one has

to admit has not always been used as nature intended.

SOME people can't take a joke. I wasn't serious when I denounced Mrs O. I've been sent to her waxworks. Next to me is Portuguese Joe as Goering. He's the very model of a modern mas murderer, and there's Duckie Baconbrains straight from the Somme. A punter puts a coin in his mouth. He starts to sing in a croaky voice, "Mademoiselle from Armentieres parley vous. She'll do it for wine, she'll do it for rum, or sometimes for chocolate or chewing gum. Hinky dinky parlez vous."

"Thank you, Private Duckie" says Mrs O. "You have delighted us long enough."

We now witness the entrance of a doll-like creature giving us a polite version of the goosestep. "Eveninks und mornicks ich drink Varnicks."

Mrs O goes over and smoothes down Ester's party dress. "It' good to doll up your Judy."

"Your teutonic saucebox" I say.

Mrs O is indignant. "Who said that?" She barges around looking for any movement. "I said, Who said that?"

I keep very still. I did spend time inside a statue of Richard Burton but now I am a statue in my own right.

Mrs O continues with the tour.

"Observe how life-like this here Goering is. And this is the symbol of his terrible Death's Head units" (A candle on mop stick inside a turnip with eyes bored out) "And in accordance with the practice of Comrade Stalin (that's me) all his family must be exterminated too."

A voice is heard. "We do that in North Korea as well."

That's Miss Stark, she's from Pyongyang and in no hurry to go back.

Ester has her say too, telling us Germany is a superior nation and doesn't want the race to be polluted.

Isn't it bloody marvellous. On one hand you have all these master races, knights of bushidoes, chosen peoples and on the other hand you have the English who let anyone walk over them.

As Mrs O passes Portuguese Joe he raises his arm in the Nazi salute. Ester returns it.

Mrs O strides over. "You are very pretty in your ways, my dear, but we'll have none of that stuff here"

"He started it."

"That's what Goerings do. But you young Huns are supposed to be rehabilitated."

"You can't beat it out of them" Private Duckie informs us.

"I can jolly well try" and Mrs O lays into Duckie with gusto,

THE STAR CHAMBER
Slim Jim is the resident lounge lizard. I'm a superior brothel bully. Best mistake I ever made talking over this place. I'm sitting with Lushous Louise. I like this dame. Pert and saucy, a little horsey. She strokes my face goodbye, goes over to Masher Malone who is sipping whisky at a table near the band. You heard right. A band. I think it adds a touch of class, don't you.

They start to foxtrot. I watch the Masher back into another couple. Steamrollers don't have to look where they're going.

Miss O'Shea saunters over. (doesn't she get around). We go upstairs.

"Your cockerel is barely strutting" she tells me. "When will it crow? I haven't all day you know."

It's alright for women. They just have to lie there. Maybe I shouldn't have had all those shots.

"Sorry, your sixty seconds are up."

I follow her down. I see the snatch squad of my Ancient Mariners rush in and take away Slim Jim.

THE BLONDE'S STRONGHOLD

My autobiography *Case histories of a soldier detective* states that me and the Blonde tortured Slim Jim but don't read too much into that, it's quite unauthorised.

The Blonde is burning his arse with an extra long match. "Wait till you get my special enema."

"That'll be too good for this cowardy custard" I protest.

"I'm not a cowardy custard, more of a mummy's boy" he tells us.

"If you're one of them how come you got a wife?" I ask.

"None of your business and you can stuff your special enema."

"Isn't he getting brave" remarks the Blonde.

"You're forgetting that married men are more accustomed to pain."

"So how do we make him talk?" she asks.

"Talk about what?"

"I don't know, it's your plan."

"Beats me" I say. "I thought it was yours."

"Well, can't we just do things for their own sake? Does everything need to be planned?"

I hear notes of a familiar melody.

Slim Jim sits up. "You should remember this."

I join in. "A miss is just a miss."

"A guy is just a guy."

"And this I can't deny."

"That time goes by."

THE Star Chamber welcomes Billie the Conductress. Here she is, addressing the clientele: "At long last I am able to say a few words of my own…Until now it has not been contractionally possible for me to speak. I have found it impossible to carry the heavy burden of responsibility and to discharge my duties as Conductress as I would wish to do, without the help and support of the man I love."

The band begins to play "Can't help loving that man of mine." Billie gazes at me fondly. I should have known.

"And he is…" The crowd look in my direction. "The one and only…" I give myself a preen. "Masher Malone!"

I pick up my hat from the coat lady, a sneering Moaning Minnie and march smartly out.

"Barney has left the building" laughs Moaning Minnie.

MISS TWEEDIE'S
"I know this is hard to believe" I say to the Crusher, "but some blokes put their money in joint names."

"Doesn't apply to me. My Dobermen look after my savings for me. I keep my dosh at the back of their kennel."

He has savings?

"Yes, won a prize in a competition for painting."

He won a competition?

We go along to his new address, a development overlooking the canal, called The Kennels.

"These are from my brown period" he says proudly showing me paintings of triangles and squares. I don't like to ask him what he uses for paint.

"These I am calling Forty Shipyards."

I am speechless. He's been ignored for years because he's not all there and now he's on...

THE WEST BANK SHOW "We have for you tonight" says Mervyn Pratt to the studio audience "the sensational naïve artist who has amazed critics with his bucolic and, dare I say it, artless interpretation of cubic constructivism."

On comes the Crusher pushing a cart. He's wearing a smockfrock and breeches, puffing on a straw like it's a Craven A.

There's music. "The farmer in the dell, the farmer in the dell, heigho! the derry oh, the farmer in the dell."

"And in this cart" continues Mervyn Pratt, "are two shepherdesses. Auntie

Marge who can't tell her thighs from her buttocks and Fat Patricia who is slobbering with greed...ha, ha, ha, aren't our British noodles something? Let's have a supercilious round of applause for ...the Crusher."

I've seen enough. I emerge from the wings in a temper. "Happy April the First, ladies and gentlemen. I hope you agree that this big man here is a real sport. And it does take a big man to downplay his talent and be prepared to play the fool."

I take our bewildered artist back to his kennel.

"I was planning to move into a container next week now that I have all these savings."

I take a look at them. They're drawn on the Bank of Toyland and a...

Oh, come along, come along, enough of this nonsense.

MISS TWEEDIE'S

I hear a lone voice singing to the air of "Barbara Allen"

"So slowly, slowly raise she up and slowly she came nigh him..."

There's a naked man hanging by his feet, swaying. I go up to him. I look in his crazed eyes. I see blood dripping on to the floor. I say to him, "Explain yourself, Inspector Gorse."

But there is no response. I get into my Zodiac and drive straight to..

BARNEY'S OFFICE

I speak to Cousin Betsy. "Inspector Gorse" she says, "he went over to the seamy side ages ago. You're not much of a detective, didn't know that."

I almost lifted my hat and walked out, then I remembered I was sitting at my own desk.

"After he went on the pipe" she continues.

"So? I smoke one too, so did Stalin and Einstein."

"I'm talking about Chinese puff."

I glance up at my hatstand. You don't see them nowadays. I've tried to throw my hat on to mine but never quite got the hang of it.

Cousin Betsy has more. "Then he sleepwalked into the hands of a former torch singer called Imelda and it was an Irish mist he never came out of. So he got his brown envelopes and Imelda and her boys and girls got protection."

"Never heard of her."

"She got married, she now calls herself Mrs O'Harnessey."

She gives John Puddyfoot a kick. "He's biting my ankles again."

"I told him. Nibbling only."

"I don't know why you keep him under that desk."

"I have a reason for everything. Pythagoras is on his holidays so Puddyfoot lets people know when their time is up."

"That's slavery and bad manners too."

"He loves it. And it's a laugh when the Squire comes back to himself and wonders what he's doing under my desk."

"Alright, I'm going." She stops at the door. "What's the rush? You got a client coming?"

"Yes I have."

"Nobody would hire you. You couldn't get laid in a brothel."

I hope she hasn't been talking to Miss O'Shea.

The door is flung open from the other side. Cousin Betsy is lying tits up as Clothilda enters. I tell her to take a seat, which collapses under her weight, falling on to John Puddyfoot.

Mrs O'Harnessey enters with a shocked face. "I hope I'm not intruding" she says ironically looking at the three prone figures.

"I don't know what came over me" I say, "I really don't"

"I expect you're not well. Dr Ragamuffin was saying to me only yesterday that he didn't like the look of you."

"Yes he is an ugly bastard" mutters Betsy as she struggles to her knees.

Mrs O looks down at Puddyfoot. "Look who it is." She turns to me. "Who is it?"

"It's one of the Squire's personalities."

"We'll soon see about that" she growls, delivering three kicks to the fat head producing in turn the Squire, Pancho the First and back to John Puddyfoot.

"Now, Higgins, I know you're a bit of a brute and would be hitman..."

"Thank you, I try to live up to your high opinion of me."

"...but in future control yourself and no more mayhem like this. I almost feel responsible for creating such a monster" she sighs, walking wistfully to the door, knocking Betsy over on to her back

MISS WINK'S PRIVATE ASYLUM

I'll bring you up to date. I sent Basher and his Emergency Men to rescue the Ogre and they brought in Uncle Cecil instead.

"Dear Miss Wink, how is the patient today?"

"Bearing up. Today he is a suffragette. Threw himself under the tea trolly."

"But don't suffragettes know they have different genitals?"

"Some do."

"I expect Uncle Cecil is here for a good long stay" I say hopefully.

"Not at all."

"Why not?"

"He's not here."

She stands up to the sound of keys and handcuffs tinkling in her belt. "I know you're a loose cannon but I never thought you'd kidnap a judge."

I suppose everyone has a doppelganger and this is starting to taste of serious porridge.

"Why does the judge think he's a suffragette?"

"Dr Ragamuffin gave him electric shock treatment. Wired him to the mains."

"What we going to do with this fella?" I ask.

"I don't care. I hate judges. Most are pompous bastards who think they can make law as well as administer it."

"I have an idea. We have a revue at the Star Chamber called Jack in the Box. Cousin Jack is in this big box, see, and every now and again he jumps up."

"Is that it?"

"Not quite. We don't know when it's going to happen and when he does pop up we jump with surprise."

"You call that a revue?" asks Miss Wink.

"Well it might not impress you sophisticates but down at the Star Chamber we're just simple honest folk."

"You're simple alright but what's this got to do with the judge?"

"Don't you see? We put him in the box and give Cousin Jack a well earned rest so he can regain his dignity."

"It's crazy but it might just work and it's good of you to think of Jack."

"Yes, he's been a recluse for years."

"These recluses should be grateful people pay them any attention at all."

"I'm not too proud to reach out a helping hand as we make our way along life's stony path."

Miss Wink puts her hand consolingly on my arm. "I remember the trouble you took to arrange Harriet's memorial service."

"She deserved it."

"Perhaps I'm being picky but you might have waited till she was dead."

"Yes looking back I should have done but those were troubled times. Harriet locking herself in a room and ululating for hours on end."

"I don't know how you put up with her."

"For purposes of copulation only. Nothing more. I do have my standards."

"You may do but they're not sartorial."

"What you mean by that?"

"Why are you sitting there with a tea cosy on your head?"

"I'll stand up if you like."

"No, I'm not referring to your positioning. I'm asking you about your headgear."

"I'd forgotten about that... well, I had to rescue the Ogre who'd been drugged by Miss Stark. See, and when I took him to Alimonia, Amelia told me she was expecting the Retarded One."

"Meaning you?"

"No, King Pancho the First. Next thing we hear him knocking. Put on your hat, she says urgently, you can't be bare-headed in the presence of a royal retard, I'd left mine in the car so she improvises. In he comes, she curtseys and I bow. Then she pushes me out."

Miss Wink sighs, looks at her watch. "Somebody is coming about now to fix a lock which the nutters broke banging their heads against the door."

"Look who it is" I say as Doris Dorchester arrives. Three times winner of Britain's best looking locksmith and she's also a Kissogram girl, which is probably why she's dressed as a sexy Mrs Thatcher.

"Don't mind me. I've an engagement in an hour. No time to change."

"Barney, take off your tea cosy when a lady enters the room" Miss Wink whispers to me.

"Pardon me" I say.

She tells me to check on the judge.

He's tied to a chair for his own good.

"Cup of tea?"

He's shaking robustly, there's a tic twitching under one eye.

"Don't take on so, your eminence. I hope you behave better than this in the

Courtroom."

This gives me an idea. Put Uncle Cecil on the bench instead of him.

"Just finished out there" says Doris. She goes up to the captive. "Poor Uncle Cecil. What's the naughty boy been up to now?"

I smile knowingly. "That's not Uncle Cecil."

"It most certainly is" affirms Doris. "I can tell by the scars on his bonce. He's knelt before me often enough."

Dirty bugger!

I don't have time to contemplate this twist in the case. In barges six or seven rent boys. They drag me out to where Clothilda is standing like an angry obelisk.

THE STRANGLERS ARMS

They're a vicious lot alright and if I wasn't now standing on a stool with a rope around my neck...

You won't believe this but the ghost of Harriet Higgins, or is it Henrietta, is forming in front of me and she's telling me to jump. I should also have mentioned that my hands are tied behind my back and the stool is standing on top of a large block of ice.

And here's the Crusher prancing in wearing his torturer's outfit of a black leotard and orange hood.

"Nothing personal, Barney. I have to take on any wee job that comes along."

"You called me Baby Doll a year ago" I say, imitating Harriet's voice.

The Crusher looks around him. "Who said that?"

"Tis I, Harriet."

"Oh most beloved of strumpets, is it really you?"

"Yes it's me, the great love of your otherwise useless life."

"But sadly I can never be yours" he says.

On account perhaps of his preference for sodomy.

"But fear not, I shall offer myself unsparingly on the altar of your lust. Once a year on your birthday."

Mean old cow.

"Oh yes how I long to feel your thin lips on mine."

"And so you shall. But first you must put to flight Clothilda and her rent boys."

"And what is to be their fate?"

Oh who cares. Enough of this mush. It was Albert Camus who said that the absurd is the essential concept and the first truth. He was lisping a bit when he said it on account of shagging his secretary and receiving in return a dig in the gob from her 40 year old son.

"Captain Moonlight" says Lady Cadaver, "You are improperly dressed."

I would have expected some gratitude from her after I arranged her acquittal on a shoplifting charge.

"Tea cosies are optional this season." I reply.

"You dare cheek me after putting Uncle Cecil on the bench."

"He got you off, didn't he?"

"But at what price!" she exclaims. "I have to receive him each Wednesday in tight leggings and a clinging sweat soaked teeshirt."

"It don't bear thinking about."
"Not him, you fool. Me. And he calls me Betty to boot."

FLAMING NORA'S HOTEL

Barbara Carthorse, settling fussily into a scruffy bathchair, looking as if a butler wouldn't melt in her mouth.

"You can feel yourself privileged that I condescend to talk to you."

I point to my teeth. Realization dawns. She puts her hand to her mouth, hobbles out. She's back in a minute. Inspector Pompadour strides in.

"I've come about a murder."

Barbara Carthorse swoons. Flaming Nora puts a phial of ammonia under her hooter. There are two uniformed bobbies looking at us from around a corner. I can just see their faces. One of them blows his whistle.

Flaming Nora is furious. "Hey, where's your warrant for blowing whistles?"

She rushes over, tries to take it from him, he turns away, she smacks his backside.

"Be careful, madam" the Inspector warns, "that's the law you're assaulting."

"I don't care. This is a respectable hotel."

"I need to know who you got staying here."

Nora counts on her fingers five or six residents including a worn out priest.

"I forgot we have a priest hole" I say. "Tell him the Roundheads have gone."

The Inspector puts up his hand. "You'll tell him nothing of the sort, not without my permission."

"What about the murder?" I ask.

"It hasn't happened yet" he mutters. "I'm the one who asks the questions."

"What's he on about?" asks Barbara.

"He wants to have a feel of your arse" I tell her.

"Outrageous. I shall insist on proper foreplay."

"Who else you got staying here?" he asks Flaming Nora.

"We're coming to the dregs now. Him over there, that's the Crusher."

"I hear him some nights biting the pillow" remarks Mrs Carthorse. "He has visitors too."

"Is he allowed pillows?" I ask.

"Only at weekends."

I shake my head. "I call that coddling."

"Why's he got a cardboard box over his head" asks the Inspector. "He can not be interviewed in that state unless he can claim religious justification."

"That's his new room" Nora tells us.

"I invented it" boasts the Crusher. "It's the answer to the homeless problem."

The Inspector turns in exasperation to Flaming Nora. "And what about you. Have you a husband?"

"I used to have one."

"And where is he now?"

"Behind the wallpaper" I say.

He beckons to one of his coppers. "Find out if Reginald Christie has done a bunk from the slammer."

I see Ginger Jones sneaking down the stairs. The coppers see him too, tackle him as he runs for the door.

"Put him in the evidence bag" orders the Inspector.

I point out to Barbara that she has cream on her nose.

She wipes it off, says to me. "If I were you...No, I can't imagine it. I would kill myself."

"I don't want you to take this the wrong way" I tell her, "but you're a right ugly cow."

She rises up, tries to reach me with her handbag. The Inspector stops her advance. "I'm glad you're mobile again, madam. I may have to take you down later to the station."

"Will I have to take my clothes off again?"

There's the sound of struggling outside, whistles being blown.

"I think I may be losing my mind" sighs the Inspector.

A copper comes in. "Don't be alarmed, sir, just a mopping up operation. Jack Spot hasn't paid us for months."

Flaming Nora has an announcement to make. "Welcome to the Jacobite and most genuine claimant to the throne."

It's Henry Stuart, Cardinal of York.

"Yes, I'm the great pretender---"

The Inspector steps forward with a shotgun and splatters the Cardinal against the wall.

Wait till you hear this
I'm glad that's over. I expect you've worked out Flaming Nora and Mrs O'Harnessey are one and the same.

"What, over so soon" complains Uncle Cecil, "it was only starting to wake up."

"Yes, my bra was wired," admits Barbara Carthorse.

"Mrs O'Harnessey wants to know, "Am I still one of the top impostors in England?"

PART EIGHT
Trumpeter House

Mrs Caroline Crockett, suave, sophisticated and only slightly mad, tells us that "I feel so sorry for Lady Muck. My Reginald is so true and faithful."

He has been since she kicked him between the legs as he was leaving Flaming Nora's Hotel with Miss O'Shea.

Take no notice of the three fat tax inspectors – triplets by the look of them -standing in a line dressed in academic gowns and mortarboards with holes where their eyes had been.

"Higgins, you're late" Lady Clitheroe tells me as I enter the great hall.

"Sorry milady, I was in the library."

"Not studying the latest Finance Acts, I hope."

"No milady, they're in the Index Librorum Prohibitorum."

"He sounds intelligent" remarks Mrs Crockett. "Where did you find him?"

"Wandering in the woods with a tea cosy on his head."

"He's quite a hunk."

"That's why I kept him."

"Do you know where he's been?"

"No, but I put him in a tin bath."

"Give him a good scrubbing?"

"Until his back was red. He was such a sissy. Said he didn't like water on account of having escaped from the galleys."

"He probably meant the gallows. Has he any conversation?"

"He has some" replies Lady Clitheroe, "and I must say it's a relief to get away from quibbling old tarts like you and converse with ingenuous philistines like him."

She snaps her fingers. The tax inspectors trudge gropingly towards Mrs Crockett. "What the fu—". They pulverize her with their sausage fingers.

Lady Clitheroe lets me loose on the grounds but there's been no grub since lunch and being a hunk I need lots of it.

Here's a serving wench at last.

She's brought a bowl of gravy and onions. "I need this," I say, "I'm all tuckered out being put into a bath and made to read books."

"Don't worry" she says, "nothing will harm you here. You'll be okay providing you obey orders and you'll not meet your fate in New York State."

Look who it is.

"Once Lady Clitheroe tires of you" continues Lovely Miss Nightingale, "You will be tied to a machine like Victorians in her factory. Blind and in chains, at the mill with slaves."

"I may wear specs but I'm not blind."

"I was paraphrasing the Bible."

"Only heretics do that" I tell her.

I hear a voice behind me. "Whit are yesuns deein' here?"

It's a small kilted figure striding purposely towards us. It's Tommy Tiptoe.

"I could ask the same about you" I say with a clever reposte.

"This wee hoose is mah ancestral heim."

I'll have to humour him. "Ach Jo, nae greet this wee hen will gee ye a cuddle ach aye le noo---"

"Awa an shite" growls Tommy Tiptoe, "yer nae Scots."

"Watch your language. And don't be pointing that dirk at her."

But the nightingale is already on the wing. Tommy is nimble on his toes too. I watch him run after her. Say what you like, she may be bossy and short with her operatives but she's well worth chasing after.

I wooed her in the summertime, I wooed her in the spring, and the only thing that I did wrong... was just about everything.

I didn't expect to find the Rev Clipper here. "We may continue in sin that grace may abound" he intones.

Here's that Grace again. "I hope you are not turning religious on me" I tell him.

"I would not be averse to a little gratification---"

"Oh no, we're not like that here" says Lady Clitheroe from her window.

"Oh yes, we are" shouts Uncle Cecil, just back from the raincoat over the knees festival in Great Yarmouth.

"Oh no, we're not" I call out.

"Don't you think you're a bit old for this type of thing?" asks the Rev Clipper.

We're down below searching the cellar.

"Uncle Cesspit" calls Miss Lovely, "come out of there this minute."

But what comes out is one of Amelia's husbands. I take a close look at him.

"Didn't you used to be Lawyer Longboat?"

"Yes I was till Auntie Atlas landed on my belly and knocked the stuffing out of me. Then I was taken to Alimonia on a prisoner exchange."

"That's nothing" I tell him, "compared to Emma's Farm."

"Same difference, this *is* Emma's Farm."

"Can't be. I see no bamboo here."

"He's right, Barney. What we see is shaped by what we are. The bamboo is over the hill."

"It seems that what I want is always over the hill" I reflect sadly.

"Was Amelia cruel til you?" Miss Lovely asks Lawyer Longboat.

"The things she made me do were out of this world. I can't wait until I get to confession."

"Best not mention it," she tells him. "The Church doesn't like the supernatural."

"Only its own version" I say.

I help Miss Lovely to her feet. "Before I send you over, angel, I want you to know that it'll hurt me too, on cold solitary winter evenings I'll think of you.."

"Stop it, Barney, you're not Sam Spade."

"And he's not Lawyer Longboat any more. Listen to him."

"I'm a slipkin, a slopkin, a pipkin, a popkin...Cock a doodle do, cock a doodle do."

To hell with this. I march up to the front door of Trumpeter House. The tax inspectors let me straight in once I've banged their heads together.

King Pancho the First is circling the throne on his own hobby horse. "Oh my underling, do not stop" urges Lady Clitheroe "and make the noise of clippity clop. Come on, no slacking. I'll teach you to look up my skirt."

Her ladyship rings a bell and I watch awestruck as the lid of a chest creeks open and a creature slowly emerges.

"Hey you, bring me the head of John the Baptist."

Strike me barmy if it's not...the Alderman. "Yes milady at once."

How far he has fallen. A man who used to hobnob with Papa Doc and Richard Nixon. And now before our very eyes he beings out on a platter the head of...Lord Lucan. He leaves it at the feet of the throne, goes back into his chest.

"Oh John, forgive me for I am the mother of harlots and the abomination of the earth."

It amuses me the way some people blow themselves up.

She calls to Pancho the First. "Who told you to stop?" She returns to the head. "You can help an old pal, can't you? Remember when we roamed the wilderness brushing aside locusts and girding our loins?"

I'm not sure her ladyship is quite at her best today. I stride forward as if directed by the hand of providence, pick up the head and run out of the room.

"After him, quick!"

I run across the lawn pursued by Pancho on his hobby horse, behind him stagger the three tax inspectors bumping into each other.

I run into an annexe and who do I see there but Mrs Simpson.

The chorus girls: "Hark the herald angels sing, Mrs Simpson stole our king."

"You can have him" I tell her.

"What are you doing here. Back in the States we keep our white trash in trailer parks."

There's the sound of steel toe caps, a boot dragging menacingly across the floor. She gets it up the arse. She rises up , she falls down like a dying swan.

"What a drama queen" I remark.

"I don't know why he doesn't just keep mistresses like the rest of that lot," says Bernard Holland.

"Don't you have to have a wife before you have a mistress?" I ask.

"That's one for the constitutionalists, that is."

Bernard Holland drags her out by the feet. "One husband not enough for you?" he snarls.

"Two tits good, no tits bad."

Watch out here's Sally in our alley.

"They seek me here?" asks Mrs O'Harnessey.

"Yes dear Matron" I say, "we were anxiously awaiting your arrival."

"Feel free to crawl." She looks about. "Where's Mrs Simpson?"

"She's away getting divorced."

I don't know how it happened but this dame came from a tree on to my shoulders, her thighs tight around my neck. I'm used to being strangled by Harriet but I don't like having my ears pulled.

"I am your onus" says the Old Woman of the Sea, "and I will know the magnitude of your sins and your open secrets."

"Not my open secrets!"

"Yes, and you shall be regenerated by the power of baptism. Take me to the head of John the Baptist."

What she doesn't know is that there's only ever been one severed head in this epic and that belongs to Bughouse Cassidy.

Miss Lovely cries out: "Don't let her take you away. I'm sorry I was rude to you."

"My beloved can be very unforgiving when dames are rude to him" snarls the Old Woman of the Sea. "Apart from wives, that is. And I, Ophelia the Oracle will be his next one."

"Barney, take off her shoe. Do it now. What do you see?"

Blow me down, if it's not a cloven foot.

Miss Lovely pulls her off me by her hair, stomps her into the ground till there's nothing left but dust and face powder.

"Oracles are rare" I tell her, "so we shouldn't have wasted one. We could have chained her to a tripod and charged people to Ask the Oracle."

"I know you don't like to miss a chance to gull people but it had to be done. If I had left even a single bone she could've regenerated next time it rains."

"There's more to this baptising lark than meets the eye."

"No it's just a meaningless ritual like the rest of the devotional drivel."

"But what about---"

"That was only a succubus by the name of Antichrist Atlas."

"Hello again, Barney" says Auntie, "Time to gather orange blossoms in the spring again."

"No I say no I will not, no."

"Ach you will, you will."

"Not on your---"

"But I've been on the shelf too long."

"Don't be coming down on my account."

"Behold!" cries Auntie and she turns herself into a flame-haired temptress. "Come and try me out."

Miss Lovely cries "Leave it alone."

But Bernard Holland sniffs her out and sparks fly as us two heroes grapple on the edge of a cliff. Who will win the fair princess and get to drink from her poisoned chalice. Find out next Saturday morning. And don't be letting your mates in by the emergency exit. And don't be jumping down from the balcony at the end of the show. We know who you are.

IT'S all go at the *Stranglers Press*. Sleepy Sid is scurrying about with one mad eye. I say to Portuguese Joe, "Don't draw your umbrella if you're not going to use it."

Dave King is the acting editor. He tells me, "Barney, this is getting us nowhere. You say you're our lead writer and in two days you've come up with one line."

"I know but it's a good one."

"Yes, THE BLONDE STILL AT LARGE! is no doubt a riveting start but it needs filling out. Give me ten or more paragraphs."

I'm shocked. "Ten or more! That's a whole page full. What *do* you take me for?"

Dave King resigns himself. "Perhaps it's just as well. When you do write it's nothing but lies. We've been sued more times than *Private Eye*."

"Not quite. I used to send Muldoon and Bucky Buchanan round to make them see sense."

"Whatever happened to those two?"

"They were working for Major Peppar too. They were in this safe house when the roof caved in...And besides it's the stuff we don't publish that makes more dosh. Portuguese makes up stories about businesses being on their last legs and I send the boys round with a copy."

Here's trouble in the voluptuous form of Mrs O'Harnessey. She pulls Dave King's jumper over his head, pushes him down the stairs.

"That's the way I deal with editors who are too frugal in their praise of my wonderful self." She turns to me. "Apply your sick brain to the business of getting rid of Lady Clitheroe."

"Is there any need" I say, "she has no designs on you."

(At least that's what she told me in bed last night)

"What nonsense, she's too expensive for you."

"I'm not rubbish, you know. Only last year I was in Vienna to meet Sigmund Freud. Old Bean, says he, damp down your thoughts, leave some thinking for the rest of us."

"Really, your anachronisms are most marvellous." She turns to Dr Ragamuffin. "He dares to have fun with me. Certify him now."

"Come now," I say to him, "think of your hypocritical oath. You must make your own opinion."

"Dr Ragamuffin is quite entitled to his own opinions" Mrs O states reasonably, "providing he keeps them to himself."

THE DONJON

Elsie the Suicide Blonde gives me a reassuring smile. "You'll probably enjoy it, really you will."

"Disembowelling yourself is not my idea of fun" I tell her.

"Well at least you can bite off your tongue, and now we must await the arrival of Emily X."

"I am your jailor" says Emily X. "Play fair with me and I might be fair to you. Now you will bend the knee for me" quoth she as she gives me the elbow on the jaw which it appears is more solid that her elbow.

"Look what you've done, you brute" she grumbles, rubbing her arm.

"It didn't take him long to get into trouble" remarks Elsie.

"Serves her right, I'm not down here blowing kisses to all and sundry."

"Hark at him, getting tough" says Emily X.

"And he's calling us *all and sundry.*" Elsie then changes the subject. "Here, guess who I spied last night...Lovely Miss Nightingale sleepwalking in her petticoat."

An idea reaches her semi-dormant brain. "I wonder what Higgins knows about her nocturnal activities."

"She's only pretending" I tell them. "Basher picks her up in his meat wagon and you can guess the rest."

"Does he have to pay her?"

"They insist on it, these tarts" I reply.

"Before or after?" asks Elsie.

"She wouldn't as much as unbutton her blouse without it" I tell them.

In her slip, in her nightie, every night and all, Miss Lovely is both high and mighty and God forgive her gall.

I hear a voice in my head. "You rat, Higgins, I don't deserve this."

"The Star Chamber awaits her" I say, "where morals and propriety take no solid form."

Just like me.

"Just like Eddie"

"What's she got to do with it?" Elsie wants to know.

"She's Lady Clitheroe" Emily X informs her.

"By the way" says Elsie the Suicide Blonde "why was Higgins assigned to me?"

"They wanted rid of him."

At this point I'm almost expostulating. I decide to turn the tables.

"Yes they were scared of me, of all the pain and suffering I dish out, most fitting for a man of steel."

Emily X is unsure. "I never knew he's a man of steel."

"Yes and I'm marching halfway through my five year plan."

"You got early parole?"

"I know you jest and I may even make you one of my well-stacked female confidantes."

"Such forbearance as I never heard."

"His forgiving nature" remarks Emily X "is the other side of the steely coin."

"Coin? In his case it's a shield."

"Quite right" I tell them "I still have the historical shield of Sir Higgins the Horrible."

Elsie says sotto voce to Emily X: "I've seen it. It's a dustbin lid."

TRUMPETER HOUSE

"Who was it said I was the most useless and corrupt private eye in Britain?" I ask Portuguese Joe.

We take to wrassling and I put him in a coma like I did with Bernard Holland.

Lady Clitheroe walks in. "What's that fat lump doing lying on my floor?"

"He's doing nothing milady"

"Take care, Higgins."

"He was dumped there by Amelia being surplus to requirements."

"She has a nerve."

"Quite so, milady and it's not the first time. Old Pennyworth who was reported missing on Laker Airways was actually seen digging in her mine."

"I wish she'd take Colonel Beauregard over there." She points at Uncle Cecil who is singing "Oh I wish I was in the land of cotton, old times there are not forgotten—"

"Shut up you feeble old fart" she cries, kicking him between the legs.

Uncle Cecil is groping along the floor. "I'll be quiet now, no need for any more of that."

"Crawl over and lie down next to Portuguese Joe" she commands.

"Yes milady" he sighs "Is it all right if I rot in chains later?"

"Maybe tomorrow."

"Why shouldn't I, why couldn't I, rot in chains with you?"

"Barney, is Miss Tweedie's still on the go?"

"Yes I've put Grandpa Higgins in charge."

"Good, my daft friend Lord Spender has a job on. He wants his own place robbed."

He wants two artistes who will provide post-prandial entertainment while the Gentleman Caller opens the safe."

A voice from without: "Come into the garden, Eddie, for the black bat of night is flown. Come into the garden, Eddie, I'm here at the gate alone."

AT LORD SPENDER'S MANSION

There's quite a shindig in play. "Welcome stranger" says Mrs Clipper, noticeable in her skin tight leggings. I think she may be in on it.

But not Ginger Jones. "I'm wanking with tears in my eyes cos the girl in the picture aint you."

That's not the sort of talk I like to hear in mixed company.

And what about Horace the Horse cantering by. "Ring a ding ding, ring a ding ding, hear the girls sing, some they do laugh, others do sigh, to see big Horace go cantering by."

Enough said about him the better. I'm glad to see the presence of a clergyman.

"Temptation's got a hold on you, preacher?" asks Mrs Clipper.

"Not so" asserts her husband. "I don't even sleep with my wife."

Work that one out. I suppose it's because she's a married woman.

I bump into Lucky Lucy.

"Watch where you're going, four eyes" she snaps.

"What a childish thing to say" I reply putting my thumb on my nose and waving my fingers in a Queen Anne's Fan.

She picks up wireless set, throws it at me.

"That'll teach you to make gestures at me."

Joe Muggins is aghast. "Who'll pay for that? Eh? Me, that's who. I'm only a working man you know."

"There's a motor bike leaving tonight for Tangier. Be on it" is Lucy's cryptic response. "I'm a woman I am and I can throw radios if I want."

"It's only travellers and grooming gangs who are above the law" I remind her.

Old Mother Bun is fifty and ten but she does lie down for gentlemen.

"Help me, Mother, help me"

She feels Grandpa's forehead. "I hear bells ringing. Put him in bed with a warm nurse."

Mrs Clipper pulls him along by the ear. "Who let you in?" she demands then realizes she has the ear in her hand.

"Came off in 1940" he explains. "What *I* don't understand is that we was encouraged to kill the Boche yet when I eventually got round to doing that they put me in the clink."

"I hazard a guess it was after 1945" I say.

"Yes it was axially, over in Hampstead Heath."

Attention is drawn to a creature crawling under the Betty Grable.

It chokes me up. "My poor Harriet spent time under a table too" I say sternly to Lawyer Longboat. "And she went to you in good faith, and what did you do? You got her charge of shoplifting reduced to Assault and Battery."

He just barks at me. I see Lord Spender skipping across the room in a petticoat. "I'm a little teapot, short and stout---"

Mrs Clipper raises her hand. "Lord Spender *please*."

"I can be a little teapot in my own mansion if I please. What say you, Dr Lovelock?"

"He may proceed at his own pace once he has shaved his legs and does not start Lawyer Longboat growling again."

Lord Spender gives Mrs Clipper the finger. "So there!"

The lady is enraged. "Barney, go over there and thump him."

"As a brothel bully I'm a bit out of practice."

"Now!"

So I do. Thump him, I mean. But she's got a cheek objecting to his lordship when she's sashaying about showing off her bits and pieces.

A door crashes open. Watch out here comes Dangerous Dan. "Fi fey fo fum I smell the blood of an English mum---"

"Barney, do your duty" says Mrs Clipper who crosses to the intruder. "Dangerous Dan, you should know Hardhearted Higgins is over there and he's not in a good mood."

"Be she alive or be she dead, I'll grind her bones to make my bread;"

"That does it."

"Two thumpings in one night" I muse reflectively, "that's…"

"Asking a lot" she admits.

"But he started it so I'll finish it."

She puts her hand on my shoulder. "I can only admire your platitude."

"It's just the way I am."

"Come back safely."

But Dangerous Dan (aka the Crusher) doesn't want to be thumped. He joins Lawyer Longboat under the table and they both growl defiance at Hardhearted Higgins.

That was easy, say you, but you can only beat what's in front of you. Anyway it's put me in the mood. The door bell rings. Somebody says it's the Mormons. "Bring them here till I thump them" I call out.

Talk about misshapen identity, who I thought was Lucky Lucy is actually

Antichrist Atlas. Le lit de ma tante. She's conquered many men from that bed and I was one of them. Grandpa sees her too. "What's she a-doing of?" he cries. We're standing still but the room is moving.

"This'll learn youse alright" taunts the Antichrist.

Mrs Clipper is frantic. "Don't let Higgins cause your displeasure."

"It's not just him" booms Auntie. "Find me ten righteous women and I will cease your destruction."

But the mayhem continues. I'm lying on the floor. Bernard Holland and his henchmen run over me. Auntie grabs Bernard Holland. She pulls him by the ear to look down at me.

"That's Hardhearted Higgins…" she says with only a modicum of irony "…and he can be very ruthless with people who run over him."

I make a big snarl. Bernard Holland scarpers. Auntie kneels, puts her fag in my mouth.

MISS TWEEDIE'S
Miss Merrylegs is pushing me in front of her. "Put him back in his body-bag."

I like this drab. Beneath that harsh exterior beats a heart of stone. "Get on with it."

Merrylegs commands and I obey, over the hills and far away.

But Uncle Cecil doesn't want to go back into his nice quilted body-bag. He's saved by the entrance of Miss Valerie.

"You're two months behind with my wages" she says to me.

Bowing low, I make a sweep of my hand as they do in the Levant.

Merrylegs is disgruntled. "You don't greet me like that."

"Ah but you weren't one of the Sultanas" I explain.

"Neither was I" states Miss Valerie. "Higgins is potty and I want my money."

Uncle Cecil pipes up, "Wasn't you one of the Beverly Sisters?"

"Shut up you old fool" says Merrylegs. She turns to Miss Valerie. "Higgins never pays anybody."

"That's not fair" I protest.

"Alright, let me qualify that. Unless you're of ample female proportions and you offer a sexual service."

"I wouldn't want her to think I'm stingy" I say, slightly mollified.

Enter Dame Looney, affecting a Grecian Bend, Alexandran Limp and sporting a Hapsburg lip. "You'd need a thumbscrew to get money out of him."

"That can be arranged" suggests Merrylegs.

I say to Dame Looney: "Don't you think you're overdoing the aristocratic bit?"

"You have no conception of high class erotica, that's your trouble" she replies.

"You can't turn your back for a minute" I declare as I go over to Miss Valerie who is throttling Uncle Cecil. "That's overdoing it too."

"He deserves it" she retorts. "Dropped his trousers in front of me."

"And he don't have any knickers on" adds Dame Looney, suitably affronted.

"I dint mean it" he protests. "Me braces broke. I think I should go back in me body-bag, if you don't mind."

MISS WINK'S ACADEMY
The Rev Brocklehurst had a vision telling him to reject God and worship Gud instead. But it's not all jam and Jerusalem with this convert to Gud.

It's down to his manly responses when he performs hands-on healing for some of the wives.

"It is a mercy that your parishioners don't know their collection money paid my rent, my holidays and other nice things" observes Lushous Louise.

"They are a bunch of fools. It 's all I can do to keep a straight face when I'm droning out my sermon."

"If were you I wouldn't preach the same one every week" I advise. "That's what make them sleepy"

The door opens. It's Ginger Jones, buttoning his fly. Dame Looney is being blackmailed by him so she tries to placate him.

"Did you have a nice wank, Ginger?"

"Yes thank you."

She nods approvingly as if he had a nice one just to please her.

Uncle Cecil is back, "It's no way to treat your god-given piece of meat."

He's such a hypocrite.

"Be careful, Ginger, this old geezer's off his rocker" warns Dame Looney.

"You're not the full shilling yourself" he responds.

"You wouldn't be neither" I say, "if you'd spent twenty years trying to translate *Finnegans Wake*."

"Oh the thought of it" she sighs, falling down in a swoon.

Uncle Cecil says to her statue of Joyce's head: "Now look what you've done."

"He only wrote one good book" I remark judiciously. "It's called *Dubliners*. Don't blame him for the rest being took serious."

"If only you had told me twenty years ago" sighs Dame Looney.

It's suddenly all go. A burly figure in a trenchcoat bursts in, he brings in a

smell too.
"Peppar's the name, treason's the game.
Take that"
He gives Ginger a bloody nose.
I soon have Peppar on his knees.
"And you either like Brut or you don't" I say. "I don't."
Clothilda has followed him in.
"I love your hourglass figure" I say to her. The size of the hourglass being neither here nor there.

I go with Clothilda to her pub, the Stranglers Arms. In the attic she keeps her old fogies who couldn't pay their slates.
"Don't they mind being held hostage?" I ask.
"They love it. They play cards and gossip all they want."
Well, you can't say Clothilda doesn't look after these old dames, can you?
Alright, you can if you want. As St Augustine says, We're all entitled to our opinion.
At least we used to be.
Lumme, such dials as I never saw, I think to myself as I look at their bright-eyed drooling faces, chanting "Gobble gobble Gertie, gobble gobble Gertie..."
"How they do enjoy a sing-song." Clothilda smiles compassionately.
"Gobble gobble---"
She blows her whistle. The chant peters out.

"No point in them tiring themselves too much. Bless 'em" she says. "By the way, I've heard tell you're a hitman."

"Our hero" call out the old trouts and fogies.

"I heard you got rid of Otto the Terrible Turk."

"It wasn't difficult."

"Our hero!"

"Shut it you old croakers. And stop dribbling. You are only allowed to do that before your porridge." She says to me, "It means you'll have no trouble disposing of the Antichrist."

"Won't I?"

"Come here, intrepid adventurer" I hear her say but I'm looking at one of the old dolls sitting there like Whistler's mother in a poke bonnet, finger to her lips.

By gum, it's the Antichrist herself.

I go back to my office. The Antichrist is waiting for me wielding an iron rod.

"Dance beefy Barney and Auntie will sing, I'll whistle and crow and go ding a ling."

And thrown in for bad measure is Uncle Cecil who was took to hospital last week when he drank weedkiller. I was praying hard. But he still survived.

Auntie has made him suicidal because he was cheeky to her. She points at the open window. He flings himself out of it, lands on top of a bus going to Millwall. Ever been there? Don't bother.

As for me, I'm going round my office like one of those mediaevals with dancing mania. After about an hour the Antichrist says she's sending me to a rest home under the charge of Lucky Lucy.

THE BARBARY COAST
I knock on the door of a mansion.
 "Who's there?"
 "A weary traveller seeking respite" replies Lucky Lucy.
 "You won't find any of that here."
 "The Antichrist sent us."
 "Wait a minute, I'll fetch the Grand Panjandrum."
 The door creaks open and blow me down if the Grand Panjandrum isn't Portuguese Joe in a black cassock.
 "Fork over the dough" he says. He turns to his monks. "Higgins must be baptised before he enters our realm."
 They take me to a river, throw me in, put me in the trunk of a hollow tree, give me fish heads because it's Friday.
 I never knew Joe was a chief monk unless he's been one all these years and I haven't noticed.
 "What about all the jobs you've pulled?" I ask him.
 "Gud works in mysterious ways" intones the Grand Panjandrum.
 I hear a voice. "I'll say he does" observes Lucky Lucy striding up. "I don't mind Higgins put in a tree but Auntie paid for full board."
 "By the bones of St Filbert" he vows, "he'll get his tommy and shelter from the storm. What more can an honest man want?"
 "Higgins isn't honest" says the Antichrist suddenly appearing out of Lucky Lucy.
 She pulls the ear of the Grand Panjandrum. "Can't you do anything right?"

I DON'T know about you but I find all this confusing. It was Sam Butler who said Life is one long process of getting tired. I think it's one damned thing after another. So did Uncle Cecil when he found out that his membership of the Mickey Mouse Club had been rescinded on account of his age.

And the future aint what it used to be either. The past was bad enough.

"Jairmany calling, Jairmany calling."

"You guys won't be laughing when the Fuhrer rises up from the deep freeze" Mrs Simpson informs us.

"I hope he's learnt his lessons from the first time."

"Yah" says Ester "ve must der Engleland virst conquer."

"We've now got at least four submarines" I say.

"Und spineless politicians."

Little do they know we've got scarecrows all along the coast and we can mobilize the Boys Brigade on their school holidays.

As I've said before, it takes a strong man to stand in a field all night with his arms out. I know, I've done it. Well perhaps not all night, I did get cramp after ten minutes or so.

I make no apologies for having an interest in the private fabrics of lady skaters as they burl round and round. Eddie says I'm not all there. At least I don't wear stick-on nipples.

"What say you, Dr Ragamuffin?"

"London belong to me."

You see, he's not right neither.

I'm not sure what mistake Portuguese Joe made in his time as the Grand Panjandrum but she's making him pay for it. She's made him believe he's pulling an oar in a Roman galley. Take a look: we see him sweating and puffing and blowing as he pulls in and out on an imaginary oar. And there's me beating time on a make believe drum.

I don't blame Eddie for putting on airs. She was Lady Clitheroe after all. She might feel uncomfortable sitting on my chest in her bra and panties.

I like people to have their pride. She doesn't accept any dough now unless it's put in an envelope. That's class.

She's got determination too. She vowed not to change her knickers until Lord Clitheroe promised a divorce. Pity he turned out to be bankrupt. Still, you have to admire her effrontery.

SET THE SCENE
A middle aged professional swindler and his companions known correctly thereabouts as tarts.

"All those invoices I sent out" I complain "and not one bite. I need a debt collector."

"But you *are* a debt collector, stupid" Merciless Mary reminds me.

"Those were the days" I recall. "How I relished the threats and strong-arm batterings."

Mary nods. "You were the best."

"As brothel bullies go" says Miss Valerie.

Here's me singing and dancing. "It's not what you do, it's the way that you do it."

"And that's what it's all about!" cries Mary.

"What are you doing here?" I say to Duckie Baconbrains who is sitting with his hands nailed to a wheel chair.

"I caught him knitting" explains Miss Valerie.

For cissies only

I feel sorry for Duckie because he's got on a lemon smock. I pull out the nails, giving Valerie a dirty look. They're about nine inches long. The nails, that is, not the looks.

This reminds me of crucifying Herman in Eddie's establishment. Ah, well, when all else has gone I've still got my memories.

"And wouldn't you know it" I say. "He's back to his knitting."

A real man doesn't like to sewn or knitted at.

"It's the way we look at life" explains Duckie. "A man is a cissie as long as he chooses to be a cissie and no-one can stop him."

"He's expostulating again" I say.

Merciless Mary agrees "I was afraid this would happen."

"How many times did my mother abandon me as a child?" says Duckie.

"Here come the excuses" I sigh.

"Fourteen. And that was before I was five."

"I don't believe it" I tell him, "I was a big lad before I could count up to fourteen."

"See how Barney catches you out" exclaims Miss Valerie.

"I don't care, I will take a dare."

"That's how he finished up in this wheel chair " explains Merciless. "A doctor was called. He took an overdose."

"Is the doc okay" I enquire.

"No, Barney, it wasn't the doctor."

"That may well be so but I still think there's a petticoat at the root of all this."

"There was once but I used it to bind his feet...Come my fettered friend," she adds as she sends the wheel chair hurtling down the stairs.

"What's the shortest distance between two nipples? she says to Portuguese Joe, caught with his knickers down.

"Oh I'm in Havana" he cries. I think he means Nirvana but you never know with Portuguese Joe.

"Come on you big butch thing, eat up your cucumber."

"Another of your pyrrific victories out there?" says Ginger Jones, pushing open the door.

"Give him one, Barney, talking to you like that."

"Not so fast. I've come as an emissary from Mrs O'Harnessey. Come to collect two years' digs money. Or else."

I give a little jig. "Let's face the music and dance."

It's odd that Ginger would beard the lion in his den. It's even odder because I remember shooting him, cutting off his head and putting it down the toilet. Or am I thinking of Herman.

"Has anyone seen Herman lately?"

But there's no reply as Merciless Mary, Miss Valerie and Portuguese Joe roll theatrically on the floor. Miss Valerie, her face grey with incipient terror as she smells the sulphurous vapours, cries "The Beast has come!"

Ginger Jones is less than happy. "Look, you bitches, don't make a federal case out of it."

THE FOOTSTOOL

I'm looking at two of the hardest eyes that ever glared over a briar pipe. Bernard Holland is ripping it.

"Did you put Ginger Jones in one of your body-bags?"

I remain tight lipped. Bernard Holland bites in two the stem of his pipe.

"He was no great shakes but he was our creature."

"He wasn't even a shake" I say as I watch my adversary put his finger on a button and in comes Mrs O'Harnessey.

"Look, Matron, Higgins won't say where Ginger Jones is."

Mrs O raises a painted eyebrow. "I expect more from a former gangmaster on Emma's Farm."

"Oh take a running jump."

The spine tingles, the heavens rumble.

"What a childish thing to say" she remarks, leaning over and pulling off his scalp. She hands it to me.

"What are you going to do with him?" I ask.

"He's only a wretch You can take his place."

I wouldn't mind pressing that button now and again, summoning Mrs O, but I'll have to watch myself as she has now one of those thought-reading meters that are so small they fit inside the auditor's ear.

In comes Inspector Pompadour.

"Barney" she says, "open the window and let that bluebottle out."

"Mrs O'Harnessey, I have received a complaint from Uncle Cecil that you shrunk his head using Ju-Ju."

Gasps all around. Snitching to the rozzers is almost unheard of.

"Where's the rest of it?"

"Barney, give him the scalp."

The Inspector studies it using his magnifying glass. "The problem as I see it is that there is hair here whereas Uncle Cecil is bald."

"Of course he's bald if you've got his hair" I reply.

"Stands to sense, don't it" she says, stroking herself as she pulls up the hem of her skirt.

"Dear Mrs O'Harnessey, why don't we forget all about Uncle Cecil's malicious allegations…"

"I'm not sure I can."

"But I insist."

"I don't like coppers coming in here, insisting."

"It's insulting, that's what it is" I add.

"Forgive me, all I want to do is---"

"Is what? Take me shopping?" she says, adjusting her garter belt.

AS I was saying, these big league blondes don't blush very often and some of them like St Agnes are well in with priests. She rules her Aztecs with an iron fist and can inflict on them Montezuma's Revenge.

Her most recent disciples are Dopey Dora, Dopey Dolly Daydream and Nervous Nelly.

"When I'm painting her nails" declares Nervous Nelly, "I am not just applying Cutex I am serving her in my own little way."

St Agnes is not impressed. "And it is vey little. Look what you've done. I'm sending you out tarting for me. Go on, you trollop, get made up and use the Max Factor not my good stuff."

"As much as I dislike talking about my self---"

"Shut up, Higgins. Unless you want to be our next martyr."

"He's nobody's martyr but mine."

"Madame Guillymot! cries Nervous Nelly,

"This is scary" I say, "she came through the wall."

St Agnes stamps her foot. "You fools! She just stepped out of that built-in wardrobe."

"That's right" I say. "Leave the miracles to St Agnes"

"Look, the two Dopeys have fainted" Madam Guillymot informs us.

"Pull down their knickers" orders St Agnes. "That'll revive them."

I'm not so sure. "An unseemly procedure for two apostles, don't you think?"

"No."

"Alright, I'll do it."

Madam Guillymot has heard enough. "Right, everybody strip. I want to see all arses in an orderly line."

So we do. Madam strolls along the line like a drill corporal. "No, St Agnes, not you of all people."

"Yes, I am humble too. I share the pain of my people."

News to me.

"You can at least put your knickers back on."

"No, the least among us is the most before the God of the Aztecs."

"I find that very odd" says Madam Guillymot. "What say you, Barney Higgins?"

"We can't understand them but these martyrs are denying themselves to satisfy their own needs. It amounts to selfishness."

"We have at least one cool head amongst us. I shall employ you to keep order at my Molly House."

AT THE MOLLY HOUSE
Madam Guillymot addresses her clientele.
 "Listen up you seething mass of deviants. This here is Hardhearted Higgins, former district attorney, brothel bully and Korean War veteran, dishonourably discharged I may add, and if any of youse even so much as think of scratching anybody's eye out or using their lipstick, Hardhearted will take the slipper to youse. What say you, Hardhearted?"
 "That's right, it's a matter of extolling thee who were born askew, notwithstanding a date with destiny under the pale moonlight---"
 "Thank you, Hardhearted---"
 But I can't stop now. I strike up a few jigs and reels on my mandolin-banjo. The sluts (even by my standards) take to wild leaping and dancing. The cork is out of the bottle. The tyranny of repression is dispersed as they fling themselves about and break up the furniture.
 Later as Madam evaluates my first (and last) day in charge I suck on a few Camels and gauge whether my reputation is still where I left it.

FLAMING NORA'S HOTEL
Growler Groves has come down with cupboard fever. He was found with genital engorgement under Nora's bed. What was worse, he was lying flagrantly on his back singing "South of the border down Mexico way."
 She says, "The country's come to a proper state when you can't kneel down to say your prayers without hearing "South of the Border" when you are asking the Lord for rightful retribution."
 "Against who?" I ask.
 "You of course."
 "But why, dearest, you light up my life."

But it is difficult to adopt a romantic posture when you are stuck in stocks. I give it a go, "Straight from my heart I cry to thee, oh Flaming Nora hear my plea---"

"Shut it, you're off key."

"Is that why I'm in the stocks?"

"Yes when I go for a guy I go all the way. You're going nowhere."

Take a look at this temptress. Built like a piano, laced corset, tree trunk legs. Alright if you like this sort of thing. John Puddyfoot certainly does. He's busy nibbling at her ankles until he gets her boot in the face. This brings into play another of the Squire's personalities.

"I hope, madam" says Pancho the First that John Puddyfoot has not discommoded you."

But Flaming Nora is as tough as her old boots and demands of Pancho her fifty quid fee. When he refuses she releases me and says "Give him a good pummelling."

So I do. I like a good pummel now and again. I drag him up the stairs like Hamlet. Where she keeps Mr Punch. Long nose, goggle eyes, hunched back.

"La mort is quick, la mort is slow, it's always there wherever I go" he chants, laying into Pancho with a rubber rod.

Is it Death itself he tries to kill so that the world will honour this misshapen dwarf who Nora keeps all to herself in an atelier under the roof. It's a rum job, this, bringing up the dregs so that Mr Punch can assuage her guilt for her, but I prefer it to the stocks.

"Us Greeks can take it" cries Pancho, "we can take it."

"I bet you can" I say, "but that ole trout downstairs don't want any more stiffs than can be avoided."

Hearing chunky heels on the stairs I say louder, "And our honeyed patroness who we treasure and can not do without."

"Spoken like a true devotee of my magnificence" she says in an ironic tone.

We hear a motor. "Look Barney, there's a furniture van running over the roses in my graveyard."

Horace the Horse tramps up to the front. "Is Growler Groves still in there?"

"He might be" replies Nora. "What's it to you?"

I grab her arm. "Watch yourself. That furniture van belongs to the Secret Police."

"Well perhaps he's already been here and I haven't noticed," she shouts down.

My advice is to throw him out the window, which Mr Punch does.

In the meantime Horace the Horse has found her door marked "Step inside for sex, free grub and fags". That's where I came in. That's the spider's main web and poor Horace, he finishes up in the stocks too. I take no delight in that. Ever since I brained him with a poker I've felt a certain friendship for him.

HERE comes Sleepy Sid, hop hop hop. And there he goes. He only takes a moment to croak. He does a spastic pirouette as a form of death rattle then down he flops. Miss O'Shea is back too. Not by popular demand but because Inspector Pompadour is pushing her into the room.

"Your knickers may be taken down and used in evidence against you" he tells her as part of his investigation into the venereal spread of cupboard fever.

"Hello hello, what's all this then" he says, poking poor Sleepy with his foot and looking accusatively at yours truly.

"Don't look at me, gaffer. Another case of the fever, that's all."

"That's all!. That's all! The workings of society have been disrupted and that's all you can say."

He turns furiously to Miss O'Shea.

"Honest, guv" she exclaims, "it aint me that's doing this."

"It's Miss Valerie" I chime in.

"Who?"

"You know, the tart you visit every Friday night."

"Oh no no, not at all...that's outrageous. Not *every* Friday night."

"Barney, the Basher's downstairs" Miss O'Shea informs me.

"Bring him here till I thump him."

"He's come from WooWang. That last liver's no good."

"Wasn't Richard Burton's, was it?"

The Basher comes in, says to the copper: "You're not the Peeler as is coming to arrest Barney Higgins, are you?"

"I have thought about it."

Basher turns to Miss O'Shea. "Uncle Cecil wants a date with you."

"I wouldn't take that old shite on a shovel" she exclaims.

"I know how you feel" agrees the Inspector. "One time I had to caution him for peeing against the wall."

"Though to be fair to him, he never does it on he carpet" she says.

"Breeding tells," I say.

A shadow falls over us. It's Horace the Horse, who demands "Where's Growler Groves?"

Growler's been standing in Flaming Nora's wardrobe for the past two weeks after he escaped from the Secret Police. He's in quarantine but I'm not going to tell Horace that. A chap's medical history is his own affair.

Wait till you hear this
I wanted this to be slapstick but it's more slapdash.

I also wanted Ester to release those Russian prisoners. They must be over 100 by now.

I sent word to the Big Boss telling him I quit. The last straw was being an undercover Santa at the Witches Wonderland. I won't tell you what the little bastards did to me. Though it could have been worse: I could have been an elf.

Have to go now. I'm expecting several Artic blondes who have been intensely attracted by my graceful dancing at the Lido Lounge.

PART NINE
At the lair of the Blonde Beast
Take a look at the Voice. Fat baldy head, bulging cheeks, Himmler spectacles.

At least that's how I picture him. I've never seen the Voice. Very few have. He gives his instructions on the radio. Anyone can start their own station, it's just a question of being on the right wavelength and having the right antennae.

"It's as well Otto the Terrible Turk heard you sneaking about. Fancy trying to burgle me."

Vera Vamp has it wrong. "It was cold" I tell her "and I was stamping around a bit to get warm."

"Another humiliation for the master criminal."

(I expect she's referring to Miss Stark leading me out of the wardrobe by a rope round my neck and a bag over my head. But we don't talk about that.)

"Excuse me, guv" says Otto, "but is it okay for me and the boys to step out for an hour or two? We're having a rumble with Razor Ramsay the Second and his gang."

"What say you, Captain Moonlight?" smiles the blonde beast.

"Bring plenty of TCP" I gurgle as Otto the Terrible Turk strides over and starts to throttle me.

"Did I tell you to strangle him?"

My assailant jumps as she presses a device that sends electric to the harness binding his privates.

"So that's what Captain Moonlight looks like. I've waiting ages to get my hands on him."

"Don't worry, Barney, he just got out of bed on the wrong side."

"I have only one side, my bed's against the wall."

"Now off you go. And if you bring me back a really nice present...well, you never know, I might be wearing my Sunday knickers...if you're lucky."

Otto's perplexed. "But today is Friday."-

"Out!" she cries.

"Thick as a plank" I say.

"Why's Captain Moonlight burgling people?"

"Well you see, I was minding my own business when these rozzers came running after me---"

"Coppers running?"

"Not quite, sauntering more like. So they give up the ghost and I proceed on my way."

"Where to?"

"To where I was going."

"I see."

"I hear this singing. Ow much ees dat doggy in de window?"

"The one with the waggly tail?"

"Woof woof."

"Sounds surreal."

"No, French."

"Not that Madame Mao again?"

"Such a girlish figure."

"I suppose she has. Somewhere under all that fat."

"Chubbiness is in the eye of the beholder."

"Two chins are better than one."

There's the sound of screaming.

"Who told you to do this?" Vera Vamp demands of Otto the Terrible Turk as we rush into the room to a big jade tied to a chair and Otto pouring petrol over her.

"Didn't I send you to settle with Razor Ramsay?"

"He phoned for a postponement. His granny's poorly."

"That's too sad" I say, "but what has Mrs O'Harnessey done to deserve this?"

I do admit to the thought that if she goes up in smoke I'd hear no more about that digs money, though it has to be said this dame has teased, tyrannised, tormented and taunted me for years, and if she went to all that trouble the least I can do is call for my musical Manxmen.

"Hey, hey baby! We wanna know know know, will you be our girl?"

Mrs O may be choking on petrol fumes but her spirit is undaunted.

"Certainly not! The idea of it. Go fugh yourselves."

"Sorry, Mrs O," I tell her. "My men don't do that for anyone…you don't, do you?" I ask my uneasy looking henchmen.

A dramatic freeze. Otto stands motionless in the act of lighting a match. He is now free of all worries, twinges, longings, lust and tiredness. In other words he is dead.

Vera Vamp comes to life. She marches out, returning with an eager Uncle Cecil who is about to realize a long-held dream. Or so he thinks.

"You've waiting ages for this" she says, brandishing her electric device. "Get down and start licking."

Mrs O'Harnessey holds out a leg.

I'M getting better reception on the roof.

A voice on the radio: "This is me, the Voice. You can't see me shaking my fist but I am mad, plenty mad."

Crackle crackle

Another voice breaking in. "This is Pompadour of the Yard. Last night a warehouse in Limehouse was broken into, the nightwatchman tied up and two tons of Union Jacks recently imported from China for the Jubilee taken. We believe this to be the work of thieves."

The Voice, breaking back in: "All that gear was lost because Otto the Terrible Turk failed me. Captain Moonlight, take him out."

That'll be easy since he's already popped his cork.

Inspector Pompadour comes back on: "Don't rest easy, Captain Moonlight, because we're hot on your trail. Once we find out who you are and where you're hiding and what you look like."

"Hah!" I scoff. "I'd like to see the scuffers finding me out."

"So would I" says Mrs O, entering with Jim Dandy and her sweated labourers. "Take Higgins to the Ivory Tower."

Jim Dandy jumps into action. "Viva Madame Zero!"

"I wish you'd stop saying that." She calls to her sweated labourers: "Stop….Higgins, when you are in the Ivory Tower, contemplate and be honest with yourself."

My Ivory Tower is more a point of view with a dome that wasn't built in a day. It has bagheads, draggletails, distorting mirrors and billy goat crossing but not I hope…

Nobby Nobs. "Oh Barney, you bring a lump to my throat."

"It's called an Adam's apple. Who let you in?"

"Gobble Gobble Gertie."

"It's her genes, she tells me, can't help getting fat."

Sound of singing. "I wish I was in Dixie, hurrah hurrah, in Dixieland I split my bra....Oh Barney, there you are. Hey ding a ling, what shall I sing? I can't get any thinner, don't tease and tempt me, Oh, Barney, do give me some dinner."

"You're already bursting out all over" I say as a young man strolls in.

Gertie is excited. "Oh look, it's my boy Petticoat." Who dramatically lifts up his petticoat but his moment is short lived as Horse Mistress Briggs barges in and pulls him out by the ear.

"Women are women and men are men" she cries.

We hear a noise from under the desk. The Alderman appears.

"Look" says Nobby Nobs "He's got staples all over his face."

"One of those punks" I say.

Horse Mistress Briggs knows him. "He did that to spite me."

One of those rebels" I say.

"Take them out, Barney" she asks.

"I'll give him a local anaesthetic first."

The Alderman is alarmed. "No, take me to London."

"You are in London, you dozy twat" Nobby informs him.

"Where am I?"

He staggers out. Horse Mistress Briggs makes an announcement. "I'm expecting Buffer Beane. How many cannibals are there left in Scotland?" she asks me.

"Ask Auntie Atlas."

"You don't know. All those encyclopaedias you've dusted and you don't know."

"When I was a medium I knew these things."

"Did you go one step beyond?" asks Nobby Nobs.
"One? I must have covered a hundred yards."
"Was it difficult coming back?"
"If you ask me, he's still out there."
"Lost on some astral plane?"
"Wandering the Himalayas."
"That's only in books."
"You can't believe books" I say.
Nobby stops laughing. "I hope I'm not here when Buffer Beane arrives."
"I have news for you mugs, he's already here."

She opens the bathroom door. A head rises from the toilet. Buffer Beane creeps in, gives Gertie an electric handshake, strangles her a bit, then bites off one of her fingers as a snack. He takes out a tin of Brasso, sipping it politely to wash down the finger.

"You shouldn't drink that straight" I advise. "Even my Ancient Mariners put it in their tea."

The door opens. Portuguese Joe sees Buffer, enters no further. He's just a waiter now, having been sacked by St Agnes for sending poison pen letters to the Corinthians.

"I like the look of him" says Buffer.

Joe visibly pales. "Have to go now. I'm waiting at Lady Paramount's Tea Party up in the dome."

But Buffer Beane is not to be deprived of an upcoming outrage. He zaps Joe with a paralytic ray and drags him away, giving us a relevant verse:
"Hokey, pokey, whisky, thum. How'd you like your tatties done? Boiled in whisky, boiled in rum, says the King of the Cannibal Islands."

I'm not tolerating this nonsense. "This is my Ivory Tower and I wear the trousers here." I tell them.

Nobby has to laugh. "I wouldn't call those ballet tights trousers."

It might here be remarked that having had my trousers confiscated by Horse Mistress Briggs to stop me going out I was forced to put on Mrs O's leggings.

"You did what!" cries Mrs O entering in a rage. "Have you lost your marbles?"

I'm singing and dancing. "I put my right foot in, I put my right foot out, I give my foot as shake and I turn it all about---"

"Stop it immediately!"

It was worth a try.

"As Dr Lovelock I recommend a warm bath regime for nervous disorders. Plastic ducks may be required for severe cases."

"Oh do you now? I suppose you want me in with you."

"Yes, with lots of bubbles."

"Not of your making. And I am already perfumed and perfidious. Open your sealed orders."

"I don't have any."

"Yes you do."

Blow me down, I do. In my back pocket.

"It says Give Matron one more chance and your money too. Sounds important."

"Sealed orders are always important."

"Take a look out the winder" advises Nobby.

So I do. And blow me down again if it's not the Waist being hauled up to Lady Paramount's Tea Party by means of a crane.

"He'll bring the roof down" I remark.

"And he's not alone, there's also Clothilda. She came by helicopter."

I feel unease in my pocket. Pythagoras my ferret has good instincts. I put him on my shoulder.

Billie comes in, she says "You look ridiculous."

"I know" says Pythagoras. "But he does feed me."

"Keep mum, Pythagoras, she's not so dumb."

"He could stroke me a bit more."

"You are as bad as Uncle Cecil."

Billie is adamant. "No way. He only plays with himself."

Uncle Cecil!

"I was only having a good scratch" explains the old coot."

Tension is bristling as Auntie Atlas makes a sudden arrival. She intones "Billie Billie play your part, here comes Cupid with a dart."

The spell works and we see Billie kissing Uncle Cecil on his baldy bonce.

"Dear Auntie" I say, "when did you find it in your iceberg of a heart to help that old nuisance find romance?"

"Be careful of what you lust for" she replies.

"Poor Uncle Cecil."

"After Billie has finished with him I'll sell him for a scarecrow."

"He hasn't far to go."

"I have a dream" she tells me, "I have a vision. I see him crying, crawling, begging for forgiveness, trying desperately to kiss my hand."

"The dead hand of doom."

"Barney! Don't refer to any part of my anatomy like that."

"Sorry, I just got carried away by your invective."

I want to test the spell. I say to Billie, "We can go places, you and me babe."

"No, we won't because….[singing] my heart belongs to Cecil."

"Don't be upset," says Auntie, "these sweater girls are not good for you."

"And you are, I suppose" exclaims Billie.

"At least I didn't put him in a sack and throw him overboard in the Solent."

"I never did. Bernard Holland drugged him."

"It seems I wasn't wanted on the voyage" I say.

"See how philosophical he is."

"That's right, Auntie, you have to be when you're dealing with women."

Billie looks lovingly at her new beau. "Uncle Cecil doesn't have to be philosophical. He knows all the moves and is dreamy like Perry Como."

"I'm her diddle diddle dumpling."

But their moment of endearment is transitory as the Waist, Horace the Horse and the Crusher crash through the ceiling.

There's a call for Dr Lovelock.

"You been practising long?" asks Billie.

"I don't need to practise. Take a long at this."

"What is it?"

"It's a stamp of approval from the Board of Doctors."

Billie examines it. "No it's not. It's a Green Shield stamp."

"Come on, Crusher, let's get out of here. If I wanted to be insulted I could have stayed at home."

"Where's home?" he asks.

"Good point. I no longer have a place of love and refuge now my poor dear Harriet bides with the angels."

"Hypocrite" Billie calls me. "Good riddance to the old bag – that's what you said to me."

"Language is often just an expression of emotion, not to be taken literally."

"If you say so."

Moaning Minnie enters in full blush of her bloated and bosomy authority: "Blast you Higgins, why'd you blow up our Tea Party?"

"If I did, I didn't mean to."

"I'd even set up a maypole so us stout and strapping spinsters could dance round it."

"It's not like you to enjoy yourself" I say.

"Who said anything about enjoying ourslelves? We had maypoles before the coming of Jesus and you'd never know what we might conjure up."

"You'll need some bells for that. Small tinkly ones" I inform her.

Billie shakes her head. "She's talking about Wikka, not Morris dancing."

Moaning Minnie says:"We go round and round until we enter a frenetic condition devoid of earthly pleasure and on the brink of melancholia."

"I still say you need bells."

Moaning Minnie walks up and down, pondering. "Maybe he's right. Maybe that's why it never worked before."

"That's it!" exclaims the Antichrist. "That's the key I've been searching for all these centuries."

Moaning Minnie puts her lemon-sucking face up against mine and sings apropos de rien: "Early one morning just as the sun was rising---"

Auntie strides over, pushes her away. "It's an incantation that'll muddle your senses and make you a slave of the Wikkas."

"Or may be the Cargo Cult" says the Crusher. "I was in that once on the Isle of Man. I didn't like all that waiting for stuff that never came."

"That's because the Isle of Wight has hogged all the ferries" I reveal.

"I have the power" Moaning Mary mutters, "I knows about men like you." She cracks me on the skull. "Knock knock on wood."

"Come in."

"There's one in every nuthouse" she adds.

"More than one, surely" I say.

A new arrival. "My name is Sir Giles. I met you at the bus stop. I'm collecting to relieve the distress of impoverished fortune tellers."

Some chance he has of getting any of my hard-fiddled dosh.

"They should have seen it coming" I tell him.

He's on the point of replying when Mrs O'Harnessey barges in and reclaims him. "This one here has escaped from my asylum. He says he used to be King Zog of Albania and they got rid of him because he was cruel and corrupt."

"He must have been really bad" I say, "if he was too much for Albanians."

"No Barney, that was his delusion."

I say to Sir Giles, "Go back to your bus stop or you'll miss the bus."

"Yes come along with me" says Mrs O, "Missus Megrim is waiting. She has on her most exciting stockings and suspenders. Just for you."

"I don't mind if I do" I say.

Mrs O sighs. "I'm tempting Sir Giles, not you."

THE SEVEN STARS
The radio springs into life. "This is an important message for Captain Moonlight. Climb Mount Niitka, climb Mount Niitka."

Drat! I thought I'd get a bit of peace once I got rid of Harriet and the Big Boss.

Cousin Betsy is tipsy. "Why would I want his used johnnie" she slurs, opening the toggles of her duffle coat.

"Not in here, darling" I tell her.

"What are yousuns looking at?" she shouts at the men standing at the bar. One of them, a weedy man with specs, lights his pipe, has his Condor moment, smiles at me.

Blimey, it's Hirohito's double. So that's what Mount Niitka is about.

"You nips don't give up so easy, do you?"

"We remain undefeated."

"You don't look much like a god."

"I don't feel like one. Particularly when I have piles and heartburn."

But that's the least of his troubles as a parachutist crashes through the window and hits him on his imperial dome.

"I'm D B Cooper" he says before Uncle Cecil throws a bucket of water over him.

"Hey what's that for?"

"Bird droppings."

"That's not a nice way to treat a modern hero on his return to earth," I tell him.

"Say, guys, can I have a towel?"

"Where's the dough?" I ask.

He looks around him. "I know, I was passing Nelson's Column and I set it there."

"It's lucky we have Uncle Cecil here, he used to be a pillar saint."

"Only in a way. I did spend a morning on top of a phone box."

"We'll just have to catapult you up."

"Hey, what is this? I've just pulled off the most daring robbery of all time and I'm welcomed by a pair of nuts."

"That's lovely, that is" I say indignantly. "Look at poor Uncle Cecil's downcast face that once held an expression of valour as he steeled himself to be catapulted into the unknown."

"Gee, I'm sorry, fellas. I guess you mean well but Nelson's Column is what you people call a pub. Anyway, my priority is finding a place to crash."

You just have. "Couldn't he have your body-bag?" I ask Uncle Cecil.

…"Not a chance. Put him in the cellar."

"Can't. Rented it out to Auntie, she has seven vampires asleep in their coffins."

"Put him in the beer garden shed."

"That's where I keep my hermit."

"Say, fella, I don't want to disturb no real life hermit. Mama wouldn't like it. I'm from the Midwest and---"

"And I'm from the Florida Highway Patrol" drawls a trooper in mirror-finished sunglasses. "C'mon Uncle Cecil, you bin takin' broads over state lines agin."

The old reprobate shakes his head. "It's a fair cop and in a way I'm glad it's over."

After he's led away D B Cooper and me set out to find his loot but we come up with nothing. But is does solve one of the enduring mysteries of American aviation: what happened to D B Cooper? Answer: He went back to his Mama.

WHILE the old nuisance in his Panglossian splendour makes the best of it in Tampon Bay I consider why so many androgynous sauceboxes are invading Dame Looney's Dancing School (for stout and strapping spinsters) and I wonder why the Income Tax won't let you start a dancing school and call it a charity. After all, it does the old bags a power of good.

"Doesn't it?" I say to Miss Beltone.

"Making them pay to dance with each other is one thing but telling them the soft shoe shuffle is the latest craze is quite another."

"You're missing the point. You can't have them jiving and falling down with heart attacks, now can you?"

"And where does Dame Looney come into it?" she asks.

"She doesn't. After her breakdown I found her work as a maid in Eddie's gent's tailoring place."

"You're so horrible."

Portuguese Joe comes in. "You bet he is. Tell her how you let Buffer Beane bite off my cock."

Shock and horror.

MCC Male Voice Choir: It's not cricket!

"Belt up you lot. He's in charge of his own cock, not me."

It gets worse.

An uncanny voice: "Hink minx the good witch winks, the fat begins to fry, nobody home but Jumping Joan, the cat lies down to cry."

"Why, it's Auntie come to startle us with her pulchritude."

"Thank you, Barney, and I am quite famous for my bawdy quips, you know."

I burl her around singing "You're nobody's darling but mine..."

Miss Beltone, returning from the lav: "I see you're getting the dancing school off to a good start."

I return to Miss Beltone and tell her, "We'll start the old boots with the Lambeth Walk and work up to the Hokey Cokey."

But the old bats rise from the dance floor with fierce faces, tight as ticks, mad as monkeys. "We want our money. Give us back our pension money."

"Back you brutes, back" I cry, "wasn't Ginger Rogers here showing youse what future felicitation the ballroom can hold for you."

But there's no reasoning with them. I look behind for support but the rest have scarpered.

Yet salvation is at hand.

"A moi, mon braves!"

I call to my Ancient Mariners and it's a close run thing but they finally have the biddies under control and they go off together hand in hand to drink stout and rum and blackcurrant.

WHERE some horrible hunters have bear and elk heads Mrs O'Harnessey has Lawyer Longboat's on her shelf.

"And such a liar he was too" she remarks.

And considering the longstanding gulf between the legal profession and the truth, he most have been exceptional.

"But I thought he was working for you."

"So did I, but behind all that piss and wind there lurked a conniving brain." She turns to the Crusher. "I hope you enjoyed torturing him."

"The Torturers' Union has rules about that."

"What are they?"

"I don't know,"

"What say you, Barney?"

"Nothing in the comics though I must say they're a bit gory for simple minds."

"You are not really a totally sensible person are you?" she says to me.

She don't like me answering her rhetorical questions so I say nothing. She don't like being taken literally either. One time she told me to kiss her arse and got annoyed when I did so.

"Cat got your tongue?" she demands.

You see, I can't win. These days I can't win with anybody. Specially dames. If it was raining virgins I'd end up with a poofter.

"I want you and the Crusher to go down to Kings Cross and pick up some losers."

"What for?"

"As a keen amateur surgeon I had a small success emasculating the Waist. Now I'm testing myself to go further."

I'm all for people bettering themselves so we go down to the tracks and bring in a no-hoper called Old Tosser.

"Welcome elderly gent" she says, "I'm here to relieve you of your scratch."

"I'm pleased to hear that. It's been bugging me for ages."

"Come along with me and please stop fidgeting."

Half an hour later she's back. "That old stager had his head screwed on alright."

Old Tosser stumbles out of the surgery, his head back to front.

"What have I done to deserve this?"

"Only your probation officer knows for sure. But don't be downhearted. Wombells Menagerie is always looking for oddities. I'll be your agent."

"That's kind of you but I will miss not seeing where I'm going. I got used to it."

All the sentimental fool has to do is walk backwards. "You took your chance going with her into the surgery."

"I just followed her tits."

"Yes, she does have a good set. If she really wants to be a surgeon they might get in the way a bit."

"I want her to put me head to rights, where is she?"

I seem to have summoned up Auntie Atlas. "Make up a brew of thistles and thorns, throw in some gore and old cows' horns."

"What have you done with Mrs O?"

"My ways are myriad, mysterious and unknown to coppers."

"What am I to do with this old screw, he needs a hoperation."

"Don't touch him. He's part of the Blob."

I have notions of a giant jellyfish from outer space slithering after helpless maidens."

"You're a right vagabond, you are." I tell him. "You'll find no helpless maidens here."

"We'll see about that!" he declares.

And off he goes walkings around the room.

"It's no use, it's too late," Auntie informs me. "Mrs O has released the might of the Blob."

"If I can stop him walking so fast..."

"No good, once set free the kinetic energy of the Blob is infinite."

"Blimey! There must be a way."

"There is but you won't like it."

"Oh no, you're not sacrificing me."

"Come on, don't let the side down. Think of all the Higginses at Culloden,

Singapore and the Charge of the Light Brigade."

Something needs to be done urgently because there are now two of them! I watch them go round and round with winks and knowing smiles on their ugly mugs. I remember my valiant ancestors and march boldly forward through a tremor of pain as I penetrate the veneer of illusion.

I am not prepared for this. Lying naked wrapped in each others arms are not one blob but two.

"Love and let love" lisps Clothilda, caressing the backside of Moaning Minnie.

SOMEWHERE NORTH OF LONDON

I'm on the run from Auntie. Old Tosser's in the back of the caravan ironing the bacon. Yes, he still with me. Old soldiers never die, just their privates.

He's lucky to be my valet since I don't have fussy standards. Well you wouldn't would you, living with Harriet all those years. Having a valet gives me more time to work on this play I'm writing.

"I shall be the doyen of the West End." I tell him.

"I prefer the Portobella Road meself."

"It'll be money for jam."

"I like lemon curd too."

"I shall have a mansion with a bridge for you to sleep under. But you must keep up your duties."

After all, poverty has its responsibilities as well as rights.

But what's this? He's turned green. He says, "I must work the works of those who sent me."

I stand back. I say "Who are you that I brought in from the cold and gave to you bread and bacon?"

"In my masters' house there are many caravans, if it was not so I'd have told you."

A crowd has gathered outside, I say to them, "Those of you who are helpless maidens depart for you know not what waits within."

Old Tosser pulls me back. "It's not my fault. I haven't slept for days. Every time I drop off a horrible face appears at the window and talks to me. He calls himself the Lord Chancellor. He represents the House of Lords and the big cheeses of the Civil Service."

So that's what the Blob is.

"Is that why you turned yourself green and said Take me to your leader? And you called me a wanker. Which makes you a hypocrite."

"I've left that behind me."

"Don't be ashamed of it. Priests do it, sophisticated beasts do it, even the recently deceased do it, let's do it, let's have a wank."

And on that melodic note I shall return you to the studio.

BBC ANNOUNCER Fifty Met police have been charged with loitering and voyeurism as they stood and watched scantily dressed looters empty a number of stores and burn down a warehouse.

A preop spokesperson states that interference with the human rights of looters, shoplifters and burglars will not be tolerated.

In further news hundreds of civil servants working from home in Swansea are going on strike in order to have their pyjama jackets printed with the DVLA logo. Their spokesperson stated, It's a matter of identity.

The current prime minister has been made to resign after he misled Parliament by stating, My old man's a dustman, when in fact he is a refuge disposal operative.

He was this morning filmed outside number ten chanting, Let's all go down the Strand. To which the crowd responded, Have a banana!

The Russian armed forces which subdued France in three hours are coming across the Channel in dinghies.

I'm on the phone to Miss Beltone when St Agnes enters in a temper.

"Traffic jam. Inconsiderate drivers rubbernecking at my human sacrifices being thrown over the cliff."

"No respect for religion, some people." I remark.

A sorry figure trudges in. "What's this?" exclaims St Agnes. "Back from the dead."

Duckie Baconbrains explains apologetically: "I landed in a bush and managed to climb out."

"The cheek of it" I say.

"What'll my other Aztecs think" St Agnes murmurs.

I try to reassure her. "Look on the bright side. You can get two sacrifices out of him instead of one."

"No, give him credit. He's the only ever survivor."

"The llama god decreed it" I suggest.

"I shall make him into a zombie so he can serve me better without hesitation."

"I've noticed him hesitating before."

"Nothing escapes you."

LOCH NESS

Auntie Atlas lives in a rented cave after the Cranky Wee Brat snuck out from under her bed and declared it independent.

We find her walking along musing to herself: "What I need is a champion to restore my estate and magic powers....But wait, who is this hulking fellow appearing from the fog? Why, tis Hardhearted Higgins. And he's got a sack over his shoulder and he's singing merrily"

"Over the water and over the lea, and over the water to char, char, Charley."

"A fine Jacobin sentiment but aren't you a little late in the historical scheme of things?"

"We Higginses have our own timetable."

"What's in the sack?"

"A Stuart prince no less."

"Where you putting him?"

"In the tower."

"Of London?"

"No, the tower in the swamp."

"Won't you get your feet wet?"

"No fears" I tell her. "Portuguese Joe takes over."

We go in the cave and blow me down there are three creatures putting their fingers in jars of treacle and sucking them.

Sometimes Miss Beltone lets me suck her fingers. It's never the same when lady dentists do it.

"They're not mine. I'm taking care of them for WooWang" she explains.

"That's kind of you" I tell her. "I've often said how magnanimous you are, haven't I, Joe?"

"Not that I can recall."

"It's alright" I say, "he doesn't know what the word means."

Auntie nods. "I quite understand. Once when I woke up from hibernation I struggled with the word *deleterious*."

The Crusher comes in strutting and bellowing, "The cat's in the plum tree, stuck there with glue and Hardhearted Higgins knows long words too."

"If you and Joe are both here, who's looking after the princes?" I ask.

"Don't look at me" mutters Joe, "my feet are wringing."

The Crusher is suddenly downcast. "This big bloke chased me with a stick."

"You acted like a coward" I tell him.

"I wasn't acting."

Let's move on. I'm not waiting any longer for that monster.

We've only one prince left and my mission is to get him to France. But what I thought was the *Sewing Bee* turns out to be the Ship of Shame and I'm tied by pirates to the mast.

"Aye we meet again" snarls Captain Molehusband. "Ye'll be setting out on another of your perfidious adventures, I'll be bound."

He walks away and I hear Joe but I can't see him. He says, "The gig's up for you, nobody makes me walk into a swamp and gets away with it."

"Where are you now?"

"I got the dope from the Antichrist. Now I can be invisible at two places at the same time."

"I bet old Molehusband can see you."

"That's because I'm visible to him but invisible at the cave and the tower."

The Captain comes back. "Afore long you'll be flotsam and jetsam. Aye, it's in the brine ye'll be."

"I'll be flotsam" I say.

"No, you be jetsam" Joe replies.

"Come on, lads, take this serious."

The Blonde comes over. "Don't let them rile you, Captain."

"Thankee, missus, when do she go down?"

"She'll be scuttled at half past five."

"Aye we'll be long gone be then."

"I shall but you'll be on your bridge. Tell him, Barney."

"Captains go down with their ships. Didn't you know that?"

"And it'll be so atmospheric" says the Blonde, "with all the loonies in the hold singing We be headed for the last roundup."

The Captain collapses. "Ah look," she adds, "he's all tuckered out."

"It couldn't have been easy" I say, "cramming all those bogtrotters, nutters and old folk into the hold."

"It wasn't and believe it or not some of them didn't want to go. I don't know what St Agnes would think."

"But you're St Agnes."

"Only on feast days."

"I suppose that explains it" I say.

"I'm not sure that it does because during the racing season I'm a highly strung horsewoman."

"You do get about."

"Yes but I have to maintain my mystique so at Ascot I wear a hat with a veil."

"Ingenious."

"What about me?" asks Portuguese Joe

"Don't listen to him" I say, "he's taken the Antichrist's silver rupee which makes him invisible."

"I can see him."

"I can't."

"That's because he's behind you." She makes a show of mock outrage. "You'll never guess what he's doing now. He's waving his dick at me."

"He stops at nothing."

"I think I'll cut it off."

"It'll only grow again."

"What manner of beast is this?" she cries and runs off, hands to her ears.

The Ship of Shame went down without me and Joe. The bogtrotters, nutcases and old folk were nearly rescued by Border Control but when it was seen they were not illegal migrants they were left to their fate.

ROOM 40

A bucket is put over my head by Billie who says "Aunt Cecilia and me are members of The Way of the Arch. You are going to be briefed by the Big Boss. He says "I have no choice. My best agents are in foreign prisons."

"This one is expendable" says Aunt Cecilia.

Billie taps me on the shoulder. "He has the heart of a lion and only 16 previous convictions."

"But he does fall for the honey trap" warns Aunt Cecilia.

"Not necessarily" I say, slightly miffed.

"What's he say?" asks the Big Boss.

"It's a question of nectar" Billie informs him.

"Such an odd thing to say. He's not a nutter is he?"

Aunt Cecilia whispers to him, "Borderline, but you don't want him too much on the button, do you?"

"Quite. Higgins, you have come to my attention more than once."

"That's when I was selling secrets to Bernard Holland who was selling them to M fifteen who was selling them to the Russians. I got them from the previous years Eagle annual that told you how to split the atom."

The Big Boss sounds impressed. "Talk about clever."

Aunt Cecilia agrees. "It's almost diabolical."

"We want you" says Billie, to go down the forbidden mine under the North Korean Embassy."

"I've been down the Catacombs before. I was almost made Chief Troglodyte."

"But beware" warns the Big Boss, "there are elderly outcasts in the tunnels. They hunt in packs in dark passages."

Aunt Cecilia adds "Try not to bash them too much. It's not their fault society has deemed them not economically useful."

"They might be better tolerated" I object, "if they tarted themselves up. The dames, I mean. Wigs, eyelashes girdles etc."

"That's very superficial of you" says Cecilia. "Senior citizens should have dignity, not going around in stockings and suspenders."

"Why not. Most women in the Fifties did."

"That's enough of talk like that" declares the Big Boss. "You know, I do believe the omens are against us. Our design is doomed…At least that's what it says in these tea leaves."

"I wouldn't know" I say. "I didn't get a cup of tea."

"You can take that bucket off now" I hear and when I do the room is empty apart from Billie and me.

FRIDAY NIGHT AT THE SHARECROPPERS BALL
Madam GeeGee has gathered her swell mob. I'm being praised for once. I'm standing there with a tarboosh (fez to you) on my noggin.

"Only last year" she announces, "Barney Higgins was sitting on the Stool of Shame on this very platform wearing a very different headgear."

(A dunce's cap if you must know)

"Who's blowing that bloody bugle?"

A voice: "Ahoy there, traitors!" cries Uncle Cecil, arriving with his host of nippons. The delegates flee in the face of a bayonet charge.

Madam GeeGee is furious. "You idiot, Higgins. I only wanted to get rid of the clique who are plotting against me. Some chief of security you are."

She takes a whistle out of her bra. Basher and his Emergency Men run in and try to take back my tarboosh. I swipe them away and call to Uncle Cecil to control his troops.

"Mitsabishi, kamasaki, ikebana ha!" he shouts.

"What's that mean?"

"It means they smile and nod their heads. You may as well talk to the wall."

I hope he hasn't heard me talking to the walls. He can be quite subtle in his digs.

Later

"Why on earth did you employ that old coot?" says Madam GeeGee, tapping my dick with her crop.

"He told me he had mongooses trained to sniff out plotters. Then they turned on him and it was like Animal Farm. So he had to use his nippons instead."

The chorus girls: "Oh it's my delight on a Friday night in the season of the year."

But Madam GeeGee (aka Billie) doesn't forgive and forget. Here she is indulging her indignation by stretching me on the rack.

I'm only glad Welington Wheatly isn't here to see it. Him and me boxed 15 rounds for the Empire eliminator and he never fought again.

But Nursey is here.

So is the Crusher, but he don't count. He's sitting on his potty chair in the corner.

Nursey pushes the Waist forward. "Come in, Mr Waist" exhorts Nursey, "time for your little treat."

She takes off her clothes. The Waist puts on her knickers and he's no longer naked.

Madam GeeGee comes in. "Nursey, you're fired."

"Oh you wouldn't do that to a poor orphan girl."

"Stop gurning." She turns to me. "She wants more for wearing less."

"It's called sexploitation" I tell her.

"She's already cleaned out Bernard Holland. She won't sexploit me."

"It's a good job you're tightfisted" I assure her.

"There's no gap in my fences." She gives her girdle a shake just to make sure. She trips out, comes back with a shovel of ashes, makes the sign of the cross, tips it over my head.

"Well it is Ash Wednesday" she says.

She goes out again, returns with a chamber pot, pours the contents over my head. "There you are nice and clean again....do you still think I'm tightfisted?"

MATRON has decided she wants for her Footstool a learned academy to overshadow the one at the Garden of Oblivion so she has confiscated my Marseilles Institute for Advanced Intellectuals.

"But that exists only in my head."

"All the more cerebral" she replies. We hear screaming.

"Must be those failed experiments Commander Stark sold me," she explains.

Come with me and we'll shut them up." I say.

Down we go. When she's not looking I handcuff her and put Commander Stark's headphones on her. I look on with interest as the magnetic monopolies control her brainwaves.

"I am Captain Moonlight."

"You are?"

It's difficult to keep a straight face.

"I've come to rescue you."

"You have?"

"Yes, I'll take you to my castle."

She is now submissive enough to be led to her own flowery dells. I blow the horn to rally the Last of the Caledonians and the birdcage stiffs marinating in captivity.

It is after midnight as I walk on footpath and on road, singing to the moon, the short journey back. The tall trees standing sentry through the night salute me.

CELLAR OF THE BLONDE SQUAD

It's my turn to put on the headphones. Uncle Cecil too.

"You are now a puppet in my hands" Commander Stark informs me. "Now, what is your greatest wish?"

"I'd like coppers to go back on the beat."

(Don't be surprised. The streets have been surrendered to knife crime, shoplifters, drug dealers and other scum who make life difficult for us private eyes and the more respectable criminal)

"Ha! An impossible dream...and you?" she says to Uncle Cecil.

"I want to be chief panty sniffer at the Blonde Squad."

"We have no vacancies in our forensics department. But I'll keep my old drawers for you if you become one of our informers."

"Unwashed?"

"Ah that's another matter."

She says to Constable Cisco. "Turn up the intensity."

"Are you sure?" he asks. "Their protoplasm is already showing. What if they have strokes? What will the Press say if it gets out?"

"Parliament has already muzzled the Press."

"They've set up secret courts too."

"I've been in one" Uncle Cecil manages to say. "Under the toilets at the Old Bailey."

"Who asked you? Go jump in the lake."

Later at her house

Uncle Cecil knocks on her door, dripping wet, shaking himself.

"Come here, cretin" the Commander orders. "Take off those clothes and dry yourself with the dirty washing in the laundry basket."

He comes back naked. She has her feet in a footbath.

"Pick up those nail clippings from the floor. Over there! With your teeth...Lie down, open your mouth" she tells him, lighting up a Silk Cut. "Like the good little ashtray you are."

Poor old croaker that he is. But not to be over pitied. We may be under the heel in life but we're all cremated equal.

HIGGINS the Hammer recalls:
The Hill-Bills of Albion used to be hairy Keltic wood dwellers before they were driven upwards by the Angular Sextons. The former, no longer prey to wolves, multiplied and were fruitful.

The Sextons, coarse grained and cross, went at it ding dong with each other and the poor wolves, and it is believed by anthropologisers that their clumpish manners were due to the absence of schoolmistresses.

What the Book of Emma 22 tells us is that some of the Hill-Bills came down from the high lands and took their blondes for spins in chariots. This turned the heads of the Angular Sextons who did not want their own blondes to realize they didn't get taken out anymore.

That's what came to pass and there was great agitation. So, the Hill-Bills, who eat their babies without salt, come down to raid the caravans of Sleepy Sid's fellow-travellers and WooWang wanted more nips for his Remember Unit 731 ceremony, details to be announced and in the Valley of the Queans Portuguese Joe in his best Howard Carter voice says "Come with me to the pyramid, don't be afraid."

I know a trap when I hear one and talking of which there's Harriet who used to say "Come with me to the stores, the fridge is empty and I need new clothes."

Any man who goes shopping with his wife deserves all he gets.

IT'S getting dark when I get back to my office. But you don't need good eyesight to see Eddie lying in her underwear on my casting couch.

"You're not giving me much of a part" she complains.

Isn't there a song about not putting your well-stacked female confidantes on the stage Mrs Worthington.

Harriet enters with a face like thunder.

"Eddie is now Lady Broomhilda" I inform her.

She weeps, swoons, begs for forgiveness. So I give her one more chance.

STEP forward Hopping Herbert. We're in the Ruins. Hear his wooden leg tapping as he leads us into the chamber where Blair and his minions hang like drycleaned badgers glaring at us.

"These be the traitors who furthered the cultural destruction of this England."

We follow him into another chamber.

"These be the corrupt cops." He points at Inspector Gorse. "Tell us how you solve crimes."

"When they can be bothered" I say.

"We target a suspect, deprive him of sleep, shout at him till he's ready to confess. Some of them even come to believe it. That's how psychological modern policing can be."

"I'm no angel" says Matron "but knowingly sending an innocent man to prison is beyond contempt."

One thing I've noticed about rozzers is their Them and Us attitude. Who do they think pays their salaries and pensions.

Not so much me, I must admit. But even villains pay VAT.

I hear plodding and puffing. In comes Clothilda. She's with a small man in a black uniform. She says, "This here is Horace Himmler. And this here..." She points at me, "..is Barnaby Huggins."

"I vill him to ze vipers nest take. For ze questioning!"

"These Englanders have nothing to do with me" I assure him.

"Come now, Herr Horace," Clothilda intervenes," he has come of his own will to give you the plans of the wonder weapon."

"These here drawings" I say, pulling some papers from my pocket are based..."

My mind goes back through the cobweb of time and space to Uncle Cecil Junior sitting in his attic a lit candle on his head as he focuses hard on his pilgrimage to cosmic Rome, his thoughts ransacking each other into logjams and I can only wonder what wayward inventions his red eyes behold.

"Achtung, vot ave ve here gotten?" he exclaims eagerly perusing the plans of the warehouse Razor and me intend to rob.

PLAIN JANE RIDES AGAIN

We await the present incarnation of the Conductress. Here she comes, and to her credit gives us due warning.

"I can't force people to be my sex-slave. You have to be daft enough to want to do it."

She goes over to Duckie Baconbrains. "Have you tried consciousness raising?" she asks and biffs him on the ear. "Try that for size."

She turns back to us. "I'm particularly interested in late developers and former debutants. I also want those who understand the vanity of worldly goods so they may unburden themselves to me. Moreover, I want anybody with a knowledge of spells or Ju Ju to assist me in shrinking heads."

With that she starts her ascent and as we wait for that tantalizing moment I wonder does anyone know Plain Jane, can she be really understood outside the realm of dark suspicion.

Take a shufty at this

Come into my kitchen says the housemaid to the guy who's come to read the meter though he doesn't know why she locks the door behind him and takes away the key, the man is inconsolable when he knows he can't get free. Eddie's in a maid's cap and apron, high heels, that's all and Dangerous Dan stares manfully as her fat breasts rise and fall.

Come in Mother Shipton: "The elusive butterfly will once more flutter over the head of dockland's nutter."

I go over and hold a paper butterfly on a stick over Dangerous Dan's head.

Mother Shipton has more words of wisdom for us.

"Take this not as fiction or fable, just make the cry Mabel, Black Label"

Well what more can I say. Either you're a playwright or you're not.

Let's see what's happening in Alimonia. I'm game if you are.

Amelia's in top form. "But he that shall wait upon me shall forfeit all his pride, he shall put up with things like seagulls, he shall not run away and he shall walk in sticky fear and damp underpants."

No chance of me running anywhere seeing as I'm lying flat on my back under Crusher's crushing machine. I'm only glad Wellington Wheatly is not here to see it.

But Matron is. She says. "I want what I want when I want it."

She wants jam on it.

Amelia's not having it. "Now now, Mrs O, you're not at the Footstool now. This here Crushing Machine (mark2) is far more scary than anything in your Palace of Punishment"

It really is. It blows Matron right out of the water. And that doesn't bear thinking about. Or maybe it does.

Amelia turns her ire onto the Crusher himself. "Why are some of my husbands going about with their arms in plaster of Paris?"

"I only put them in my machine cos they called me a big lug."

"I had planned to have them walking the plank at my next Ship of Shame and now that's off because they'd sink to the bottom."

Matron offers words of consolation. "How disappointing that must be but sometimes in this life you have to shrug your shoulders and carry on."

Amelia is not pleased with Matron's smirking irony. "I don't need your commiserations when I have at my disposal one the most classical philosophers of his era."

No, not Pythagoras. Up steps Archie Medes who says, "Come with me to the Casbar."

Amelia is now seriously irritated. "Crusher! Take Higgins offa your machine. I have a new customer for you."

But Crusher is not out of the woods yet. He may successfully squash Archie Medes flat as a pancake but he's sent out on his knees to cut the lawn with a tiny pair of scissors.

She summons Honest Harry. "Where did you put Higgins?"

"He's in the slag heap."

And so I am. I was expecting my own stall but I'm here in this hovel hewn out of the heap. I'm with the Untouchables born into poverty and shame.

The Chief Untouchable tells me, "With no hope in this life we seek another in Mrs Grundy."

I suppose that comfort from illusory notions is not illusory comfort.

Hang on a bit here's Emily Flopbottom to recite for you in her best classroom voice. "Lloyd George knew my mother, my mother knew Lloyd George—"

"That's enough of that filth" I tell her and stop sniggering at the back. It's time for another melodramatic episode brought to you by Bummalo and their world famous hemorrhoid crème.

The chorus girls "Early one morning just as the sun was rising.."

In comes weary Harriet after another night burning charcoal in the Forest of Nottingham, a drudge of drudges, clad only in a threadbare shawl, unnoticed even by the randy outlaws riding through the glen.

But Barney has tidings that she is the long-lost child of the well-heeled Baron Broomhilda. So he guides her over to a tub of scummy water, makes her wash for the first time in living memory. He stands back, lifts up his arms in salutation. "But miss, you're beautiful!"

She seems almost grateful when I help her to her feet and I feel almost sorry for her. "No longer will you have to make your weary way in of a night to piss on the fire to put it out. You were lost, now you're found."

And with that I return you to the studio. There's more where that came from.

"Oh I hope not" says Miss Bit of all right.

Come in Uncle Arthur (struck off doctor). "This is my long-lost niece. We met in a professional capacity."

Yours or hers?

The chorus girls "What are we going to do with Uncle Arthur?"

"I don't care who you sleep with as long as it's not my teddy."

Riveting, isn't it?

No.

Just a tiny bit enthralling?

No.

Perhaps that last scene was not a good idea but I did promise Uncle Arthur a walk-on part, and it's just as well I did because days later he was in hospital and had what they called a negative patient care experience. He passed away.

THE SEVEN STARS
Lushous Louise turns to me, "I now find that blackmailing small timers like you is below my dignity."

I can see her point. She's built for better things.

But much to her chagrin, the Blonde enters and says "Come along, Barney, I'll let you pay my rent."

She crooks her little finger, walks slowly away, pulling me behind her with the aid of Widmerpool.

Lushous Louise doesn't like competition. "I hope he's more use to you than he was last night."

What a thing to say!

The Blonde tells her she can make mountains out of molehills.

"Hey you," I call to the Crusher who is arguing with Harriet.

"Leave that woman alone, she's bad enough with her nerves as it is."

"She called me the Milky Bar Kid."

"What do you expect, decked out in those chaps and boots?"

"I was going line dancing."

"He has the mentality for it" I say to the Blonde. "Never grew up proper. His old ma still has to half-chew his grub for him."

"Mouth to mouth?"

"Best not to think about it."

Let's go over like Asmodeus to see what's happening in Alimonia.

Amelia's pinched face comes into view and there's Uncle Cecil dressed as a monk and he's holding her holy water sprinkler (a club set with spikes).

She smiles down at him. "You're not far off the mediaeval mark."

Looking on are her three husbands, holding up their trousers. The old coot dances over and threatens them with his sprinkler.

Amelia, just out of the Shires, strides over in her tight black jodhpurs.

"Am I not one of the top equestriennes in England?"

The gagged husbands can only nod vigorously due to her reasonable desire for them to be seen and not heard.

"Only flesh and blood can stand it" she says, her blue-tipped fingers exploring their stigmata.

She regards Uncle Cecil, points to the floor. "Comme ci, comme ca."

He lies down. She puts one foot on the staff of his penis.

He looks up. "How well you place yourself, Missus. I can only imagine how much practice was involved."

"Yes, it's a top technique I developed allowing my husbands their monthly relief."

And as she stands on him, shifting her weight she induces a forceful ejaculation.

That's enough of that, thank you. I'm down at the docks and I've been made Special Agent by Major Peppar and I have the badge to prove it.

I creep up the stairs. Her door is open. That makes me think but not enough, there's an aura of perfume and stockinged thighs. A small voice says, Watch yourself, but I'm not listening.

There's a table with books on it. I put my finger against the spine of *The Man from Laramie*, crouch down...I whisper "This is it, bub, spill your guts or fade."

A voice, making me jump. "That's telling him."

It's Miss Stark with a hard face and a pistol. I make a great spring for the door and I would have made it too if my back hadn't given out, making me stumble and stagger bent over till I trip on the shaggy rug by the door and fall awkwardly with the handle nearly taking my ear off.

"You'll pay for this" I warn her, getting to my feet. I feel a spasm of deep regret as I lift my hat, push back the spectacles on my bloody ear and walk out.

Miss Lovely has told me to follow Cousin Betsy. She's appearing at the music hall. I catch her act.

"The dame makes a curtsey, the dog makes a bow, the dame says Your servant, the dog says Bow wow."

How provocative she is. That Bow wow is too much for the rabble. They roar and stamp and try to storm the stage. A shot rings out.

The Stranglers Arms

Clothilda is strangling me with my own tie. I'm not terribly fussed as Harriet often throttled me as I was sleeping.

"Hey you" she shouts, "get over here."

Razor Ramsay the Second jumps up, the bubble gum he was blowing bursts onto his ugly mug.

"Higgins says," she continues, "he was only at the music hall to watch Puss in Boots."

"I don't like coincidences" he says. "Let me finish him off."

"Too dangerous, besides if he knew anything he'd have told us by now."

"Perhaps. He don't like cops and he don't drop dimes."

Actually I do now and again but only for the purpose of revenge or personal gain.

"Alright Higgins. Scram."

I get up painfully from the chair, lift my hat and hobble out. It's teeming down, I put my collar up, pull down the brim of my hat and the rain runs down into my mouth.

THE BADLANDS

A voice: "Peppar's the name and treason's the game."

This is Major Peppar greeting O'Rourke, the carrot-topped bruiser who responds with: "It's proud I am to be of service to a patriot such as yourself."

"Not quite right, old son. I'm more of a traitor if you follow me. I'll teach them to accuse me of borrowing mess funds."

"Ach a fine gentleman such as yourself always has creditors at his heels."

"I'm tortured by them too" I admit.

"Well, we're in the right place, Navigator- General" says Peppar, "to gather up your navvies."

O'Rourke looks upwards. "Aye it seems only yesterday dat the Hill-Bills came down from dose hills, ravaging and taking prisoners."

"Them were days" I recall.

"They don't make Irish like dem no more."

"Point of order, old chap, they were English."

"How'd you know dat?"

"Tacitus in his chronicle makes it quite clear. They were carrying umbrellas."

O'Rourke's face is becoming red. "They were not, twas the pipes they were playing."

Shoves come to blows. The navvies gather round ominously.

Major Peppar calls for assistance. "Barney, help me out here."

I suppose I have to. He's paying me. And besides, O'Rourke is far too guttural for my liking.

Just then, Harriet rides up on her bike, throws me my mail-order revolver, the navvies freeze and to my surprise one of them keels over and just for fun I shoot two more in their legs.

"Get out of it the lot of youse...And you too Peppar, I don't need company when I'm with a pretty girl."

I take Harriet in my arms and sing to her, "If you were the only girl in the world..."

OFFICE OF A SHYSTER LAWYER

When you think of Fat Patricia you think of Mrs Thompson's dowdy brothel down at the Markets.

Well, don't you?

She's dowdy too. Fat Patricia. £ signs in her eyes but money can't buy taste nor moderate her broad Ulster accent.

Here she is, growing dishonestly old with a straight face. "Put away your brass rubbings. I've taken an abnormal attachment to you."

She talking to Michael Meddler. He's as greedy as she is. How else could he have paid big money for his nose hairs to be transplanted on his blind alley of a dome. He says to her: "You said no strings attached."

"I said nothing about chains."

Her nameless husband gives a small cough, "I've, er, a good mind to---"

"Get back to work, you runt" orders Fat Patricia, holding his nose to the grindstone.

Enter Mrs O'Harnessey. "Forgive my girlish giggling but you don't have to be so literal."

"I'm a country gab and proud of it" asserts Fat Patricia, buttoning up her coat over her bloomers.

"Gabardine is so yesterday" says Mrs O.

And what is this that we hear?

"Forasmuch as it pleases the Grand Panjandrum of his great mercy to take unto hisself the goods of our dear sister soon to be departed, we therefore commend her pot belly to the depths of Hell, already turned into corruption, looking for the resurrection of her husband's organ when the sea shall give up its dead."

The chorus girls: "O hear us when we cry to thee, for those in peril on the sea."

A curtain falls.

Enter a well-dressed man in a suit, snap-brim hat and a green bow-tie.

"Au nom du people authentique justice est faite."
"

THE FOOTSTOOL

Mrs O'Harnessey in her pranks gave poor Duckie forty wanks, when she saw what she had done she told him it was all in fun.

Duckie goes off to change his prostate past Mrs Upper Crust, curling her lip and feeling frightfully irritable.

"I say, though thou exalt yourself as Matron and set your saddle among the stars, who could ever bring thee down?"

"No-one" declares Mrs O, "and as a former schoolmistress---"

"You were one of those too?"

"Yes, I used to be a hairdresser as well until the day Teasy Weasy stole my scissors. I never got over it and to maintain my peace of mind I became an apologist for perpetual punishment."

"A cri de coeur, if I ever heard one."

"Back in the old regime" continues Mrs Upper Crust, "when Lady Muck and I dined with Pappy Doc we used up all the partridges he shot---"

"Perdrix, toujours perdrix."

"Quite, we had a page boy called Parker who was tasked with looking after the snakes. We gave him injections to build up his immunity but he over-reacted. Before long he had a head like a Mekon."

"Typical male. I've seen them swell up at the slightest instigation. My latest example of which is called...."

Flourish of trumpets

"...Barney Higgins, caught in flaggers with one of my charladies. Sixty five if she's a day."

"If you ask me it's a question of ageism" I say.

"Hark at him!" exclaims Mrs O. "We don't need lessons from a former bricklayer like you."

I'm suddenly contrite. "Yes, I did brick the wife up in the cellar."

"I wouldn't have minded so much" declares Harriet, entering unannounced, "but it was on our honeymoon."

I take her hand. "I was only putting you in purdah. So full of eastern promise you were and you still have that schoolgirl complexion."

The chorus girls, "You'll be a little lovelier each day with fabulous pink Camay."

"Yes, Lady Broomhilda, what is your secret?" asks Mrs Upper Crust.

"Well since you ask, I use a face-mask of maggots."
"Top breeders recommend it," I say.
"They eat hard skin, you see," explains Harriet.
"You have such weird knowledge" states Mrs Upper Crust.
"Yes, I had a book of spells but it went up in flames."

I was just looking at it, frowning, trying to puzzle out what it meant when it began to smoulder. Couldn't take it, see. Direct exposure to the mind of a deranged detective.

The priest himself got hot when I told him to stop making mysteries out of molehills.

Back thunders

The Vatican. "You watch it, Barney Higgins, or you'll get it across the back of the legs."

"Get lost. I'm not in one of your orphanages anymore."

Remember Tommy Tiptoe?

"Ah'm as crabbed as thae come, country dishes leave me cold but ma strange heart goes pit a pat for a city lass known as…"

Miss Frosty Pants. "I am a scowling secret lovelady who arouses clumpish devotion. I give men nary a glance as I ride proudly past on…"

Francis the talking mule. "She's a frivolous tart. I mean, what good is a straw hat and a necklace made of treacle when you need four new shoes? Answer me that"

"Give over" I tell him, "there's plenty would like to be in your position."

Here's a new face. He didn't like the old one. "Call me Hermanicus, and I have the stigmata to prove it."

Would you believe it. I nail the wretch to Eddie's cross and he's all proud of it.

"I know that face!" exclaims Miss Frosty Pants. "It looks in my windows."

"Sorry, Hermanicus" I tell him "I'm sending you back to Santy's Grotto"

Tommy Tiptoe says, "Ah've a sofa you can rent."

"Don't go there" I warn him. "You can see the herpes jumping off the cushions."

Next time I see that face it's looking at me from the TV screen and it's not even turned on.

THE FOOTSTOOL

Mrs O wags her finger at me. "You're a fool to yourself, taking up with that Madame Mao. It's terrible the way she exploits people."

"What's this about?"

"It's about the Garden of Oblivion which she and Elsie the Suicide Blonde has set up again. They've even got their own song."

"Which is why got me to write you one?"

"Correct, let's have it."

I bring in Crusher's Awkward Squad for a rendition of the "Matron Song."

"A fairer matron there never was seen than Mrs O'Harnessey – the Footstool's queen. There's wild coyotes and strawberries too and she won't wash dishes nor mop out the loo."

"Not bad, not bad at all. The next thing we need is a hermit of our own."

"Didn't know they had one."

"They don't. That's the point. Try to keep up."

"What about Harriet?" I ask.

"No, I'm still grooming her as a nun. We'll give Crusher a try. By the way, why's he dressed as a soldier?"

"Don't ask. But Guardsmen do it."

"It don't bear thinking about."

"Not even for experienced landladies."

She goes over to the Crusher, clouts him several times on the chops.

"What's that for?" he stutters.

"You know."

All this dreaming of army camps has done him no good. He once joined the Household Cavalry and spent a year peeling vegetables.

But being saved from being a hermit didn't do Harriet much good. Mrs O was intent on her followers paying their way.

Harriet is inflamed. "It's so unfair! I can't be a nun and walk the streets too."

Mrs O tells her "You can multi-task can't you? Besides, there's a market for that type of thing."

She changes the subject. "The Crusher's no good as a hermit. He has no odour of sanctity. And he keeps escaping when he hears the chimes of an icecream van."

"Don't they have any other tune but Greensleeves?" I ask.

"Good point, but not strictly relevant."

"When you get one, what will he do all day?"

"Contemplate on me of course. And - I have just decided on a whim- he shall wear an iron mask."

"Steady on, Matron, these men in the iron masks are always causing trouble."

"Not if they're shackled."
"That's one way to stop them running after icecream vans."

EDDIE'S not as stupid as she looks. She keeps her brains hidden behind a low neckline.

I give her a snatch. "Oh Eddie you have tossed and turned, and for Barney you have yearned, so come with me this very day, over the hills and far away."

"Kiss me, Barney, kiss me" she pleads, taking off her topless bra.

She's not well, you know. Been under the doctor for weeks. Never mind what for. Even Eddie deserves some privacy.

A hooter sounds. Time for chow.

Ester the chemist from Cologne enters pushing a trough on wheels. Her Russian POWs hurry behind her on their knees. They are dismayed to see what's in it. Nothing. German humour.

Duckie Baconbrains is serving time as a POW. "She has us in stitches" he says, holding out his bandaged arm then looking up as Harriet enters affecting the Grecian Bend with the aid of a big stone round her neck.

"Whatever are you at?" I ask.

"I had an illumination on the way to Dame Ascot."

"Who's she?" demands Mrs O gruffly, entering behind her.

"She said I have to marry Jesus" explains Harriet.

"What's the stone for?" I ask.

"Jesus was stoned, wasn't he?"

"Look here my girl" snaps Mrs O, "don't you go listening to no Dame Ascots putting stuff in your head. Jesus was crucified, see."

Duckie Baconbrains goes off to play Russian Roulette with an automatic. I'm almost at that stage too as Harriet goes on about spreading the Gospel in Roachdale and its environs.

Mr O is annoyed too. "And don't you have nothing to do with them missionaries taking up positions on poor natives and such like."

In comes Rev Brocklehurst. "I was one of them as well, with a special vocation for the lost lovelies of London. I think I'll take a wee peep in this here Mirror of Diana," he says, going over to an old mirror on the wall that has seen much cellulite (and the odd varicose vein) and, according to him, is rewarded by a vision of the Conductress, cig in mouth, cane swishing at her side, herding along the great lump of Portuguese Joe, a mooing Harriet and a chittering Herman on all fours.

But you can't believe a man still in his pyjamas with a mortarboard on his head.

Then the Rev who lost his faith down the back of the sofa in Eddie's massage parlour, goes over, gives her a hug and gets a knee in his Henry Halls.

"Hugs by appointment only," she says.

See, I told you she was classy. I bounce the Rev down to the cellar where I come across the Antichrist. I've never seen her before fading in and out, sitting on a washing machine.

"What's up?"

"I'm in no-mans land" she cries, "help me and I'll make you real."

"Complete with a soul?"

"Yes yes."

"Not a second-hand one?"

"No no. I'll bring down an Irish mist and you chase the Devil in Dublin City."

"What's Old Bendy got to do with it?"

"Come now, be reasonable. You need to get one that'll fit."

"I'm not sure about this" I tell her. "Compromise myself with Old Bendy and it'll be all round the spirit world the next day."

That's it as far as I'm concerned and I'm not going to rescue anyone in the middle of one of John Bloom's spin cycles.

"I may only be a rescuer of maidens" says the Rev "but I could tell you a thing or two about witches…..I was arrested in my pyjamas by the Antichrist. You have the face of a disreputable milliner, she told me, and apart from supervised outings to the local Yates Wine Lodge I was imprisoned in a hat box until she stopped menstruating."

A likely story. There are no Yates Wine Lodges in London.

THE BADLANDS

I'm having a short one with a game publican called Clothilda. Miss Adair my new well-stacked secretary is with me.

Clothilda nudges me. "You been in the Badlands before?"

"Been there? I used to terrorize the place."

"Him and the Lone Ranger" smiles Miss Adair.

"Don't confuse me with the Cisco Kid."

"So you are not afraid of the Wikka Woman?" says Clothilda.

"I say Bah to the old trout."

"You really got the balls for it, to take her out?"

"I've dated worse."

"Alright, take down this message for her."

Miss Adair licks the stub of her pencil, looks up expectantly. Clothilda begins…

"Hold on" interrupts Miss Adair, "this is blunt."

"Try the sharp end" advises Clothilda and she then puts the message in an envelope, seals it with a sloppy red kiss.

"At the heart of her cult" she adds, is a fanatical coterie of Ancient Mariners."

"Miss Adair has a way with sailors."

"I call them stooges" she agrees.

"That's not all" Clothilda says. "She keeps Uncle Cecil in her cellar and slaps him silly."

"Might improve his looks" I say.

Clothilda smiles at Miss Adair. "Barney's no oil painting neither."

"Look who's talking" is my witty response.

This is where I get clouted with an Irish screwdriver. I'm lying on the floor listening to these two jades running me down.

"He's as good a fallguy as ever fell over his own feet" laughs Miss Adair. "Just joking. But we better be careful. He can be very merciless when he's annoyed or laughed at."

Yes I'm mad at Miss Adair. In fact, I'm mad at both of them. Or maybe I'm just mad.

"I don't do this very often" Miss Adair says through the jumper she's pulling over her head.

I can't believe it. She's letting Clothilda have a good grope at her while they think I'm still out of it.

Alright, I can believe it. I'm just keeping the pot simmering while we await the arrival of...

The Rev Brocklehurst, peppery as a Welshman. "How can you do such a thing? How can you cause such pain in the heart of Jesus?"

"It's all this watching telly on Sunday" I put in. "It is ruining Chrisianity."

"Oh you are so right. I don't have a Devil's box in my vicarage but I urge all those who succumb to the lure of Rediffusion to put a sheet over it on the Sabbath."

Clothilda is not impressed. "Give over, you old hypocrite."

Miss Adair is already half undressed. "Come on, big boy. Come and rescue me."

"I'm not really that big" he whispers to her. "The doctor diagnosed Failure to Thrive when I was little…And I'm not really a hypocrite, you know, I'm only C of E."

We come to the main gate. Miss Adair announces us.

"Pay attention, alien creatures, this here is Captain Moonlight, scourge of the Panhandle, nemesis of wayward schoolmistresses and duellist extraordinaire."

"You missed out the part I played in running through Wat Tyler."

"Yes, and here's the sword" she cries. A sword suddenly appears in my hand. I make a few practice thrusts as she shouts "Let us in to see your witch. Or suffer the wrath of Captain Moonlight."

"You can't come in today" says the gimp sentry. "It's a bank holiday."

"Correct me if I'm wrong but I wasn't aware that this is a bank" observes Miss Adair.

"Could be for all you know" is the response from the stubborn sentry.

Miss Adair walks up to him, pokes him in the chest and is not fazed by how far her finger goes in.

"Listen here, George---"

"Don't call me that. My name is Rodney."

"What's wrong with George?" she enquires. "It's a perfectly good name, there's been kings and saints named that. But it's not good enough for you, oh no, you prefer a puffy name like *Rodney*."

"Go away, Wikka Woman's not at home today."

We hear a voice. "We have interlopers?"

It's a frow being carried in a sedan chair.

"The Wikka Woman I presume," asks Miss Adair.

"Heavens no, I'm Edith of Nancy Town on my way to a photo opportunity in a dreary Dutch studio." She says to Rodney. "The usual stuff."

"High jump for both?"

"Just him."

I have the sword. I fence my way into this tunnel. I hide in a rail car. It starts to move. It's being pulled along by men in rags. We come to a halt, the men move aside to reveal a figure with white hair, red lips and red eyes. She's wearing a short skirt slit up the side.

It's Calypso. "Not too Susie Wongish?" she asks.

"Don't tell me you are the Wikka Woman."

"Alright, I won't." I give her the note. "This is a code" she says. "It tells me to execute the bearer of this missive" She starts to laugh. "Who does she think she is, telling me what to do." She steps closer, taps me on the nose.

Higgins, I'm going to give you the opportunity to save yourself. Are you willing to take it?"

"I'm always ready to do that."

"Live here in the Garden of Oblivion as my consort and find the freedom of eternal peace. I do regret not being able to venture outside. This underground railway brings the pilgrims down to me."

"Using beggars as pit ponies."

"I always suspected you were sentimental."
"I've nothing against eternal peace but I'd rather not enter it just at the moment, maybe later, thanks all the same."

FLAMING Nora's Hotel was a home for the migrates until such time as their council houses were refurbished. Claim you're a Christian and a homosexual and you're taken by the hand. Guaranteed. I don't know how they kept from sniggering when they passed each other in the corridors. Maybe they didn't.

Say what you like about Calypso but it's due to her generosity that I'm able to speak to you now in an unsacrificed state. She accepted Miss Adair in my place.

I humbly walk to the appointed room. I am expecting company.

Billie is icumen in, llude sing Barney, knickerwet and soft white flesh from bum down to her knee, sing sing Barney.

Billie turns Darwin on his head, she makes monkeys out of men.

Here's Billie now. I hear her knocking and she can come in.

"I don't normally do this, you know" she says.

"Of course not but it doesn't make you a bad woman if you do."

She makes a lengthy and senuous display of taking off her black silken gloves, building up to a climax of long red nails.

MISS WINK'S ACADEMY
Harriet's just leaving. "This is a sorry place. I'm glad I'm not Miss Wink anymore now that Jesus wants me for his rainbow."

Tommy Tiptoe is eyeing the talent. "They come as a boon and a blessing tae men, the lushous, the lassies ain thae Panhandle hen."

Lushous Louise is having none of it. "Not on your Nellie, you scotch git."

"Lushous Louise came tae toon a-riding on a pony, she put her knickers on me heed---"

"You'll be so lucky."

"---and said she wouldnae phone me."

I'm watching Billie refresh her face with a compact and powder puff. Sex goddesses come and go but

The chorus girls "Little things mean a lot."

However that's not to distance myself from the skill shown by dimpled skaters as they burl round and round divulging their knickers.

Here's Dickless Tracy: "I'm just back from Brussels."

"They never learn" says Plain Jane "They keep going over there and getting their pockets picked....Also, our guest chef, Monsewer Mackerel reports that he has had his ears boxed by Barney Higgins."

"Like most bouncers" opines Lusous Louise, "he thinks he can clobber people whenever he feels like it."

Plain Jane agrees. "Yes, he should know better at his age."

"No need to make a federal case out of it," I tell them and go off in a huff but I soon snap out of it when I come to the Showcase of Splendour with Mrs O displaying her thunderous thighs and at her feet in classical pose is the new hermit in his iron mask.

"Shoo him away" she tells me pointing at her former failed hermit who is down on one knee pointing a broomstick at her.

"It's alright" asserts the Crusher. "It's not loaded."

Look out, here's Miss Stark. "So you're the bouncer. Come with me."

We go down to where she keeps her experiments to see if the surplus population can hibernate to solve the food crisis, and if that's not being philanthropic I don't know what is, and where would knowledge be without intrepid experimenters?

"This one here won't go into suspended animation."

I'm not surprised to see that it's that troublemaker Mr Pastry, who is lying on his back. She sits astride him, starts to throttle him.

"You are adept at artificial respiration, I see."

"Have to be, in my line of work."

The old coot opens an eye. "Please missee don't send me back to Van Dieman's Land."

"He gets confused" Miss Stark informs me. "I used to hire them out as pallbearers at Von Dietrich's funeral home. If travellers can work them so can I."

"I agree, there should be equal opportunities for all in this green and pleasant land."

Mr Pastry sits up. "It's not the oul work I mind. It's better than driveways. It's singing those wretched dirges."

"It's a question of attitude" I say. "You should try and get into the spirt of things."

ALIMONIA

Amelia is talking to Uncle Cecil. "I want Fat Patricia brought here in a sack. I want her dragged down to the lake and thrown in."

And where am I while the old codger is getting his orders? I'm in her wardrobe, the next to go in the lake. I make a noise like blowing into a beer bottle or the call of an owl.

"Hark!" exclaims Uncle Cecil. "Tis the ghost of Barney Higgins."

Amelia cowers down. "Stay away spirit, you are too early, we haven't drowned him yet." To Uncle Cecil she adds: "That's Higgins all over. He always comes too soon."

What a thing to say.

"Oh this is dire" cries Uncle Cecil "we must invoke the mercy of St Agnes."

(Who is represented in antiquity as kneeling on a pile of faggots)

"You'll do no such thing" says Amelia.

The phone rings. She puts on her telephone voice. "Haylow aim afraid yew must hev the roeing nember."

She slams down the receiver, shouts at Uncle Cecil, "That was the bloody Blonde. Why'd you bring her into it?"

A booming voice resonates.

"Ye have learnt nothing from Adam's original sins, ye have joined with Harriet in tormenting the blameless and prayerful Barney Higgins, but mark ye this, he like Dreyfus will be vindicated at your displeasure and downfall."

"Spare me, O spirit and I will take a revolver into a quiet room and be a gentleman to the end."

"Rather defeats the purpose, doesn't it?" she says.

"I'm not a gentleman."

"You're not much good as a sex-slave neither."

"Matron has no complaints."

The chorus girls: "All the nice boys love a sailor."

Mrs O in her sailor suit barges in, picks up Uncle Cecil by the scruff of his neck and carries him out.

I don't think she is being very polite, rushing in like that and taking attention away from the Ghost of Barney Higgins.

"Don't think you've seen the last of me" says the voice of Uncle Cecil. "I'm just lingering under the surface in a realm of shallow profundity."

FLAMING NORA'S HOTEL

Under the covers, on the bed, where love is done but never said; put down the notes, nothing's free; that's the way with Billie and me.

"You think the bills pay themselves?" she snaps, just as Portuguese Joe enters the room.

"Look who it is" I say. "I wonder what he's snivelling about today."

"At least I'm not Billie's booby."

"And his face bearing the shape of the last whore who sat on it."

Several Bitches of Bretwalda: "Don't call us that."

"You called me Duckie" I reply.

Chief Bitch of Bretwalda: "Come on girls, don't dilly dally with the likes of him. West Ham Intercity are here."

"I bet they wreck the place again."

"That was the Neighbourhood Watch" Billie informs me. "Just because they didn't get a group rate."

Portuguese Joe smirks at me. "When the wife's away..."

"She's gone on a retreat, if you don't mind, something like that."

"Don't be vague about your wandering taig."

"That's no way to talk about...whatshername..."

"Harriet" Billie reminds me.

"That's right, Harriet, my very own bugbear."

"Who goes bump in the night" says Portuguese Joe.

"How'd you know that?" I ask.

Joe taps his nose. Billie kicks off one of her high-heels, it flies through the air with the greatest of ease and hits him on the mouth. Stark has made me District Attorney of the Blonde Squad because she needs all the help she can get.

COMMANDER STARK has made me District Attorney because she needs all the help she can get. I've put a notice on the wall. "I'm the DA and don't you forget it."

Harriet is wielding her bucket and mop. "Why have I to clean your office, you never were that fussy about cleanliness."

I point up at the notice. She goes out shaking her head.

Lushous Louise says "I'm not used to getting up in the morning. Haven't had time for anything."

"It is half eleven but don't worry" I tell her. Women with shaggy hair-do's don't look all that different in the morning especially when they sleep with their make-up on..."Now where's that book in which I put down all my arrests and kidnappings?"

"How the devil should I know?"

"Cause you're my secretary."

(Pity about Miss Adair)

"That's not what you told me on the couch last night, you said my job was to---"

"Alright, I'll get Miss Beltone to do your filing for you."

I call her in. She says "It' remarkable how many departed spirits haunt the Himalayas."

She's alluding to our recent séance.

"It is the earnest desire of the departed souls that you come here and do filing."

"I cannot ignore the orders of Fate so deftly conveyed my you, you big butch thing, but as a lady who lunches I cannot do any actual work and I'd like to remind you of what you promised me when you took away my private fabrics to help with your enquiries---"

"Okay I'll get Dame Looney to be your p.a."

"Good gracious" the Dame says as she comes in. "What is going on here?"

She over to where Sleepy Sid is on his haunches in a glass cage.

"What is the reason for this?"

Brushing aside a crocodile tear I say "I had to do it. Poor Sleepy has gone prematurely senile. I found him in the donjon below, brought him up here so he can at least see what's going on."

"You poor poor man" sobs the Dame, tapping the glass, smiling sadly. "Cut down before your prime."

(Sleepy was never destined to have a prime)

"But look over there, look at DA Barney, your protector and friend and I hope you know even in your befuddled state that you are not alone."

So I give orders to Lushous Louise who gives them to Miss Beltone who passes them on to Dame Looney, by which time I've forgotten what I wanted in the first place. That's what's known as the chain of command. I got the idea when I was in the Army.

WOOWANG'S ALLEY

Poor Crusher lying face down, wiping his nose on the ground.

When you're a derelict in today's harsh society nobody wants to know you. I certainly wouldn't.

Look at this brazen hussy lifting his head with her boot. Look at her short shabby skirt and the ladders in her stockings over plump legs. Alright if you like that sort of thing. I certainly do.

"You've a nerve lying down on the job" Billie tells him.

"I was told to keep a low profile."

I step out of the shadows. "Don't worry, it's going to plan."

"Is that part of your plan?" says Billie looking up at the sky.

"It's only Uncle Cecil trying to levitate."

"What's he looking at?" Billie wants to know.

A Dantesque underworld of shebeens, bagheads, draggletails, distaff battle-cruisers, abram men, staggering hopheads and wide eyed scullery maids at area gates. The Panhandle according to Uncle Cecil.

"Barney!" cries Billie "there's somebody down there holding a crossbow."

I look into Billie's eyes, as big and round as pennies. I see no fear there. All I see is resignation, despondency, confusion and a tendency to eat wine gums in bed.

Uncle Cecil comes crashing down, an arrow in his breast.

"Stop this hovering about. You nearly fell on Billie there."

The Crusher says "If I was hovering I wouldn't wear heavy boots".

"He was shot, wasn't he" Billie reminds him.

"That's only WooWang, he don't like people flying over his airspace but we'd better scarper."

CELLAR OF THE BLONDE SQUAD

Billie comes in, stands abashed in front of my desk.

"Before I send you over, angel, I want you to know I could have fallen for you big time but I won't play the sap for you."

"You're kidding me, aren't you?" Billie says, laughing nervously. "Tell me you're kidding."

Long pause.

"But you're human, Barney, tell me you're human."

"I suppose I am."

"Give me a cigarette."

"I don't smoke" I say, taking a long pull on my Camel.

She starts gubbing. I'm not a D.A. who worries about dames who gub. I go into the small room where I keep my instruments, close the door. I peer into the periscope I've installed to look into Commander Stark's changing room, I hear my prisoner crying: "How can you do such a thing?"

IN THE STREET

I'm talking to the wall again. I tell it about strapping games mistresses, highly strung horsewomen, short skirted skaters, jumping volleyball players. Add blondes according to taste and you have a dish fit for...

Dave King. "About time you brought me into it again."

"I didn't think you cared."

"You've never liked me, have you? I can sing, dance, crack jokes. And what are you? No wonder Commander Stark gave you the boot."

(Some unpleasantness over a periscope)

Dave King takes it on his toes and I hear the footfall of a witch.

"Woe is me" wails Auntie Atlas.

"What are you whining about now?"

"I let the Cranky Wee Brat live under my bed and now, lo and behold, I find a whole mess of them squealing and moaning. So I fly out and I see a giant penis---"

"Stop it there. You know what you saw was a missile. If you want a shag you should ask for one."

"Now that you mention it I am on the pill."
(You'd have to boil her first)
"Watch out" I say, "here comes a patrol."
We merge into the shadows as a troop of Girl Guides march by singing "We love to go a-wandering"
"Phew, that was close."
"Come on, Barney, cut out the cant and tell me how much you pine for me."
And there before my very eyes, Auntie transforms herself into a pair of black tights, the mound of her pudendum looks me straight in the face and says "L'etat c'est moi."

THE massage parlour inspectorate has asked me to do an investigation. I'm here at Eddie's. She has a customer. He's only one arm. He says, "I'm n-n-not paying no w-w-wanking tax when I do it at home."
"Who is that one-armed man?" I ask her.
"Can't you tell O'Rourke from his stutter?"
"I remember him now but he didn't have a stutter and he had two arms."
"He told Auntie he'd give his right arm for a night of bliss."
"Careless talk costs arms."
"That was a false one anyway."
What a cheat! Fancy complaining he lost his arm. In my life there have been many women, strange and wonderful and grasping and I could say they've cost me an arm and a leg but I begrudge them nothing.
I've never liked O'Rourke. Red headed, a southpaw and a face like a smacked arse...What more is there to dislike?

There's plenty. But nobody's blameless and we'd better let him pass for what he's worth.

Which isn't much. I remember when he and his navvies ran amok in the Tabord Inn in Torquay. They were lucky the Plod stayed away.

As usual. Which is why more landlords are keeping Alsatians behind the bar. But I'm moving away from the point. When I enter a massage parlour I look at whether there's too much hygiene, whether the masseuse's manner is sufficiently shameless and whether there are available, for those customers fixated in the Fifties or on their mothers, a supply of stockings and face powder. I'm pleased to say I gave Eddie a five rating which she can post on her door.

THE FOOTSTOOL

It's been a sore point with Matron (bless her jealous heart) that Amelia has a chain-gang and she hasn't. So we rounded up some of my Ancient Mariners and Muddle-headed Monkmen.

Matron addresses them: "…And you will pay proper respect to your foreman Barney Higgins."

It's only what I deserve.

My turn now: "Listen up you rag tags and bobtails, yes you are the rabbits and I am the weasel. Matron has put you in this inaugural chain-gang because of your history of sex scandals. You think you're all Tory MPs now, is that it?"

A voice. "And we're not district attorneys neither."

What a thing to say!

And blow me down if it's not Mr Pastry.

"What are you doing here when you should be hibernating?"

"Miss Stark hired us out to clean this massive pile, it was damp and it had its own asylum where they kept the inbreds and poor girls who were inconvenient and knew too much. And fat fruits waddling about the halls in tight trousers. We called it the Petrified City."

"News to me" I say.

"Also known as Buckingham Palace."

"You insolent pup. Do you want to go out of the frying pan into the fire?"

"I say phooey to your fire."

Matron's heard enough. "Don't bandy words with Foreman Barney" she shouts at him.

"It would help" I tell her "if I could have a horse, a shotgun and dark glasses."

"Don't be presumptuous. You may be foreman but you're still a member of the chain-gang."

And so Matron strides away with her breasts high and her lips pursed.

HARRIET won her case for desertion and I get put back on the Cruel Husbands Register and in case you haven't heard, I'm also the world's greatest liar.

But is it any wonder I'm never there. Dishes stacked, stuff all over the floors and sore points laid throughout like mines.

Just imagine if I did clean and housekeep.

Harriet talking to her kitchen cabinet. "It's only Betty doing women's work."

Mrs O says "My chambermaids and laundresses would like their own skivvy. I shall call her Abigail."

Billie, standing close, the butt in her mouth singeing my nose. "I shall call you Molly."

I may find her hot smoky breath abnormally erotic but I steady myself, hold my head up and try to be proud.

Once you start helping around the house you could finish up like Sleepy Sid, dancing, wearing a tutu with spangles and sequins; "Lavender's blue dilly dilly, lavender's green, when you are king, dilly dilly, I'll be your queen."

There's no way back from there.

THE AGONY OF ST AGNES

"In my religion" the Blonde tells us, "we don't find womanly forms offensive. We don't cover them up like lepers."

Big Jack Brag, having lost his pillion pussy: "Has anyone here seen Harriet, Harriet from the Emerald Isle?"

You remember the time Father Finnegan roared up on his Norton with Harriet's arms around him?

No, neither do I, but it must have happened because she still talks about it in her sleep.

So big Jack Brag tells us.

He heard it from Portuguese Joe.

The Blonde is not pleased. "You should address me as the Loved One."

"Take a ride with me, babe."

"Barney" she says "someone somewhere wants a dig in the beak from you."

"The Loved One likes people to be polite and obsequious to her" I tell him.

"Yer what?"

That's the last straw. I sock him on the ear, he flies back against the wall, then with his back against it, his mouth open, he slides down it until he's resting on his knees, trying to suck in air. I help him up by his tie, I pull out my revolver, shove the muzzle in his mouth. Three clicks can be heard above the sound of him wetting himself.

I put that in just in case you were having any doubts about my manly prowess seeing as I've been honest about my little embarrassments.

THE SEVEN STARS
The Rev Brocklehurst, hand on heart: "Blessed are the pacemakers and the big-bottomed nurses. Give me a gin and orange."

A more experienced degenerate would have seen through those over priced legs and greedy hands. He'll find out when he tries to pay for the drink. Maybe just as well seeing how the gin could be methanol from China.

Uncle Cecil orders a pint of the best bilge water, says to me: "It was clever of you get me off, make em think I'm a halfwit."

(Inspector Gorse had come to arrest him for paying bribes to Inspector Pompadour. Instead of him)

Lushous Louise tells the Rev to get his spondulics out.

"Alas my dear lady, my nocky boy is sleeping."

"Watch it" I warn him, "this is Miss Wink you're talking to."

"Yes news of her appointment did reach me at my vicarage when the Gentleman Caller was leaving off some stuff."

The Gentleman Caller is a burglar and conman. He even had a go at being the Tichborne Claimant and his project failed only because he was about 100 years out of date.

Lushous Louise call it a night?

Not on your Nellie. "Uncle Cecil will you walk into my parlour..."

"Said the spider to the fly. I should be honoured" he says, bowing with a gravity that does him proud and after she puts her hand in his pocket they stroll off arm in arm, displaying the chic appropriate to a decomposing nabob and his paid companion.

THE THREE LAYERS OF LIMBO
The first was founded in the 14c by Higgins the Hateful who had borrowed money to be repaid in the afterlife so he was quite happy to stay where he was having a few jars with one G Chaucer. "Thou shalt make castels than in Spayne and dream of joye al but in vayne."
  "Such a cheery chappie you are."
  But we're forgetting about Baal's fire. Chaucer is not only snivelling, he's melting. All that's left is a pair of teeth.
  The chorus girls: "You'll wonder where the yellow went when you brush your teeth with Pepsident."
  This is bizarre but freedom of expression and liberty go together.
  The chorus girls: "You can't have one without the other."

In the second there are in the region of thirty to forty well-upholstered doxies which Higgins the Handful reckons is a good region to be in.
  But look, it's Josef Stalin whispering through the keyhole of his darkness.
  "Of all the treasures a state can possess, the human lives of its citizens are for us the most precious."
  The ghoul of ghouls would never say that.
  But he did.
  The ides of Martha, poor woman's Mandy Rice Davies, says "Who let in

these cuckoos? Not one can be trusted to say their prayers at night."

"That's old school" asserts the Rev Brocklehurst. "Nobody's listening."

Mrs Rouncival says she'd listen.

"Well she would, wouldn't she."

And it's a great comfort to Mrs Grundy to see Higgins the Handful chained to the mast of the celestial Ship of Shame.

The third came into place in the realm of Queen Betty and we see Tom Tug going at it ding dong with the Alderman but it's more ding than dong and Tom Tug claims the Portsmouth defence while Mrs Grundy looks into the future and sees murderers let out after six years to kill again and people having holidays in Turkey.

Peter Pieman says "Stay away from turkey, doesn't mix with pastry."

Jack Pudding wants to know "What's wrong with black pudding?"

"Never on a Sunday" says Mrs Grundy.

Billy Shakes asks "To durst or not to durst"

Madame Mao instructs us to "Revenons a nos moutons."

Higgins the Hurtful has the last word. "Sheep or turkeys, you can't have it both ways."

NORFOLK ISLAND

I think Harriet still fancies me. I call it the dark side of love.

"I'd rather roll in a bed of nettles" she declares. "No make that thorns."

I hear puffing and plodding. I look up to see Clothilda, the fattest woman to ever sail round the world. She says she brings tidings of great moment.

"Horace Himmler and me now control this island and all its slave workers – including you --and so we can start to build our wonder weapons."

I may have been a slave on Emma's Farm but I'm not having this. I quickly disable Clothilda by pulling off her wig.

"Come Harriet dear, we must be going. I have a raft waiting."

"No, I must stay" she cries. "Clothilda needs me. I am her bit of fluff."

"Well I'll be gormed. You never really know people, do you? Even after all these years."

She agrees. "We don't even know ourselves."

MRS O was cross when I got back from the Island. She gave me this drink, when I woke up I was in a coffin. I hear this voice

"O God from whom all holy decisions and good counsels and all just works do proceed, give unto thy servant that peach which the world cannot give. We are here to celebrate the life of Barney Higgins who will ever be forgotten as a man, a husband and as a father."

"Stop talking nonsense and take your hand off my leg."

"O Lord lead me not into temptation and deliver me from manual stimulation nor make me suggestible to widows in tight leggings."

"This isn't about you. He used to get on my tits good and proper he did, but he deserves a bit of a homily, don't he?"

"I just forgot myself for a minute. Who are we talking about?"

"Barney Higgins, you dope."

"Ah yes, dear Barney never knew how doomed he was but he valiantly carried on with his---"

"Scams, fraud and various assaults and batteries."

"I remember him now and such empathy as he had. But there was a lighter side to...."

"Barney."

"Yes, good old Barney was a great man for a risky joke and who could forget him patrolling the streets in his Hopalong Cassidy outfit."

"Lone Ranger."

"He was a nutter."

"Oh do be kind to your loved one's memory, he was no more mad than I am. Let us cheer him on his way to the heavenly Concierge who lurks like Cerberus in his celestial cubbyhole at the Hotel California, let us go and free the Mad Nun from her corset while we join together in a chorus of "How much is that doggy in the window."

"The one with the waggly tail?"

There's a bang on the lid.

"Come in."

Crikey, they're shovelling dirt on me already.

"And do you dearly departed take this woman Antichrist Atlas to hold and behold..."

Sound of the Wedding March.

Wait till you hear this

This frail comes in. Her eyes hint at a bargain her soft lips might keep. Yet she looks hesitant, shy and only slightly sinful like kisses in a cathedral.

A jingle comes on the wireless. "Cyril Lord, Cyril Lord, this is luxury you can afford."

"I'm expecting a little parcel from Paris" whispers the frail. She goes to my bookshelf, looks at the sign: Please do not ask for the lend of books as a poke in the eye often offends. Her shoulders start to shake slightly. I can't tell if she's laughing or crying.

The cast
Barney Higgins.. aka Captain Moonlight, breathing the smoky air of freedom.
Harriet Higgins.. aka Lady Broomhilda who snuck back from the dead when I wasn't looking.
Mrs O'Harnessey.. Landlady of a curious organization called Quean Anne's Footstool.
Uncle Cecil.. One of the sweepings of the world.
Portuguese Joe.. Sleeps on both sides of the pillow.
Sleepy Sid.. Quasimodo in lipstick.
Billie, Eddie, Lushous Louise.. Barney's well-stacked female confidantes.
Amelia Grantly-Hogg.. Collector of husbands and consort of a prince.
The Crusher.. Inventor of a crushing machine and a right Herbert.
Ester.. A Teutonic trampler.
The Squire.. Man of multiple personalities.
Miss Stark.. Agent of North Korean Intelligence.
Herman.. Hermanicus Homunculus.
The Blonde.. Two times winner of Blonde of the Year award.
Antichrist Atlas.. Archfiend of Celtic Scotland.
Lovely Miss Nightingale.. Barney's dishy controller.
The Waist.. Emasculated drag artist.
Duckie Baconbrains.. Man with the unfinished face.
The Ancient Mariners.. Barney's odd men out.
Bernard Holland.. Barney's bete noir and author of "Guide to prison etiquette."
Miss O'Shea.. She never gave me an inch but I once gave her nine.

Inspector Gorse   back in uniform, now one of those new-fangled traffic wardens.
Ginger.Jones.. Space cadet.
The Ogre.. Once he saw a little bird come hop, hop, hop and he cried, little bird, will you stop, stop, stop.

Printed in Dunstable, United Kingdom